NO GOING BACK . . .

"How long have you been standing there?" Anna asked.

"Just since the last verse. You have a beautiful voice." Her nearness made Storme's senses spin. The desire to pull her into his arms tugged at his resolve to keep his distance. "You're a sweet, lovely woman," he dared to say.

"Thank you," she whispered.

Storme's heart jolted. He knew he should back away, but he wanted only to step forward, wanted to press his mouth to the slender column of her neck. He took a deep breath. "I better be going," he said. But his feet stayed rooted to the spot.

Before he could talk himself out of it, he reached around, cupping his hand to the back of her head, and leaned down. Her warm palms flattened against his chest. She closed her eyes as he pressed his mouth to her full, warm lips. He wrapped his other arm around her back and pulled her closer, kissing her more deeply, rocked with a powerful sensation as her mouth parted, her tongue eagerly meeting his in an urgent exploration. . . .

BOOK YOUR PLACE ON OUR WEBSITE AND MAKE THE READING CONNECTION!

We've created a customized website just for our very special readers, where you can get the inside scoop on everything that's going on with Zebra, Pinnacle and Kensington books.

When you come online, you'll have the exciting opportunity to:

- View covers of upcoming books

- Read sample chapters

- Learn about our future publishing schedule (listed by publication month *and author*)

- Find out when your favorite authors will be visiting a city near you

- Search for and order backlist books from our online catalog

- Check out author bios and background information

- Send e-mail to your favorite authors

- Meet the Kensington staff online

- Join us in weekly chats with authors, readers and other guests

- Get writing guidelines

- AND MUCH MORE!

**Visit our website at
http://www.zebrabooks.com**

APACHE ANGEL

Jackie Stephens

ZEBRA BOOKS
KENSINGTON PUBLISHING CORP.
http://www.zebrabooks.com

ZEBRA BOOKS are published by

Kensington Publishing Corp.
850 Third Avenue
New York, NY 10022

All Kensington titles, imprints and distributed lines are available at special quantity discounts for bulk purchases for sales
promotion, premiums, fund raising, educational or institutional
use.

Special book excerpts or customized printings can also be created to fit specific needs. For details, write or phone the office of
the Kensington Special Sales Manager: Kensington Publishing
Corp., 850 Third Avenue, New York, NY, 10022. Attn. Special
Sales Department. Phone: 1-800-221-2647.

First Printing: January, 2001
10 9 8 7 6 5 4 3 2 1

Printed in the United States of America

*To my wonderful husband, Clay,
for all your love, support, and patience.*

*To my editor, my family, and all my
dear friends who never gave up on me, no
matter how many times they heard me
say . . . "I'm almost done."*

Chapter One

'*Out West a man learns to fight for what's his, and take care of his own.*'

New Mexico Territory, June 1885

He never expected to travel this road again, but he could think of no other place he would rather be headed. Home . . . and he was damned anxious to get there.

Storme Warwick knelt in the center of the dirt road and grabbed his gelding's front hoof, cursing this delay that would prevent him from reaching the ranch before nightfall. He dug the tip of his knife under the inch-size pebble that had caused the mount to go lame and pried the stone free. Standing, he tugged his hat brim down against the glare of twilight's golden streamers snaking through the firs and cottonwoods, the last vestiges of day fighting a losing battle against the night as dark shadows slowly worked their way upward along the grassy forest bed of the Sangre de Cristo Mountains. With aggravated resignation, he slid his knife in the leather sheath attached to his gun belt and prepared for the ten-mile walk ahead.

"Watch your back, mister!"

Storme tensed for only a split second at the woman's unexpected shout, then reached for his Colt, clearing the holster as he spun around. A shot rang out from the dense woods. The bullet plowed into the ground between his feet, scattering dust in a small cloud. His horse bolted down the road. In the distance, Storme caught a glimpse of a man on horseback before a ray of sunlight bounced off the nickel-plated barrel of the rifle and tarnished his view in a blinding white ball.

The attacker fired again. Storme darted to the side of the road, emptying all six rounds from his pistol before slipping behind the nearest tree.

Who the hell was shooting at him?

He didn't question why. He knew being a bounty hunter earned him more enemies than friends, and the Apache blood running through his veins only added to his lack of popularity. Pressing back against the thick sheltering trunk of the cottonwood, he tossed his hat to the ground and quickly reloaded.

What bothered him just as much was the fact that he had been so occupied with thoughts of returning home, he hadn't even sensed he was being followed—and not just by one person, but two!

Storme didn't recognize the woman's voice, but he definitely owed her for calling out when she did, and he hoped she had enough sense to stay hidden until this was over. Caution on high alert and his heart pounding, Storme peered around the edge of the rough bark. Through narrowed eyes, he stared into the shadows that quietly slipped between the dense columns of trees, searching for a movement or sound that didn't belong among the stirrings of nature.

Nothing.

Wait!

Storme squinted harder, barely making out the shape of a lone rider weaving his horse in retreat through the distant reaches of the forest. Surprised, but grateful the man had given up so easily, he holstered his gun. His heartbeat slowed. There wasn't any need to go after the attacker. If the man's determination to gun him down was strong enough, Storme knew he would try again. They always did.

The light breeze brushed against his face, cooling the moisture that beaded on his brow. Retrieving his hat, Storme settled the black Stetson in place, wondering if word had spread in Pleasant Grove about his return to the ranch. He glanced again where the rider had disappeared higher into the mountains, unable to discount the possibility. He hadn't been liked by most of the townsfolk when he had lived here, and nothing in the letters he received from his half brother over the last seven years indicated that anything had changed.

Yet the woman had called out to him . . . and saved his life by doing so.

Storme stared across the road, frowning at the hard knot that suddenly tightened his gut. There was no sign of her, but his body hummed with the feel of her presence. His blood raced with an apprehension more acute than he had ever known. He told himself it was only because he owed this woman a life-debt now, and honor demanded he repay her in kind. Nothing more.

So why did he sense he was about to walk off a great precipice and must quickly learn to fly?

Storme swallowed the dryness that hovered unwelcome in his throat and shook off the odd feeling. "It's safe to come out now, ma'am."

Anna Alexander tensed at the slow, powerful command in his voice, wincing as the rigid bark of her tenuous shelter poked into her back.

Safe? Did he think she was crazy, or just plain stupid?

Watching him handle himself and that six-shooter with the

speed of a seasoned gunfighter, she could tell the man was no stranger to trouble, and Anna didn't need his problems. She had plenty of her own.

She glanced at the light fading fast all around the mountain and stifled her groan. Now, she could add missing curfew at the boardinghouse to her list of trials, and knew Mrs. Harrington might dismiss her for this tardiness.

Four weeks ago when Anna garnered the position of maid, the housemother had firmly gone over all the rules. She was amazed at how many there were, but being responsible for the virtue and well-being of the single girls working at the train depot restaurant, Anna really couldn't fault Mrs. Harrington's strictness. Especially since the older woman was kind enough to offer free room and board in addition to the job.

And Anna needed the job if she hoped to save enough money to reach San Francisco soon.

"Ma'am?"

Her heart pounded at the tightened intensity in the stranger's tone. *Good heavens!* She didn't want to be out here alone with him. The last time she was alone with a man, she had landed herself in serious trouble with the law.

"You have no reason to fear me." His voice drew nearer with each word.

She had no reason to trust him, either. Anna's hands shook. She tightened her grip around the smooth, wooden handle of her derringer, chastising herself because she wanted to believe the soothing sincerity in his tone.

A twig snapped, echoing in the stillness and rattling her nerves harder. Anna swallowed the knot of panic as the man's footsteps rustled through the grass, coming ever closer. *Blast it!* She shouldn't have given her presence away. But she couldn't just let him get shot in the back. It wasn't right, no matter what his troubles. Releasing a tense sigh, Anna realized that she would have to deal with the consequences of her generosity, whether she wanted to or not.

She raised the pistol and stepped out from behind the tree. "That's far enough, mister." She aimed the gun at the center of his broad chest.

He stopped, standing tall and proud with just a few short feet between them—still much too close for Anna's comfort. Straight black eyebrows arched high on his prominent forehead, disappearing in the concealing shade of his hat.

"You can put that away." He nodded down at her weapon. "I intend you no harm."

"The gun's fine right where it is," she insisted. Sweat dampened her palms as she stared at him. A red bandanna partially hid the leather strip tied around the corded column of his neck. His long hair hung loose beneath his hat and gleamed like polished onyx in the sunset. The hard planes of his face, the high cheekbones and smooth bronze skin strongly hinted at Indian blood, and every chiseled line in his long, square jaw and firmly rounded chin spoke of his strength and dominance. To her chagrin, she found him handsome as well as intimidating.

"I just wish to offer my gratitude for your warning, ma'am, and declare my indebtedness." The warmth of his smile echoed in his dark brown eyes. He crossed his arms, the rolled-back white sleeves revealing strong, defined muscles that reinforced her vulnerability, in spite of the derringer.

"You're welcome. And the only thing I want is for you to leave."

He glanced down at her gun, then back, his smile fading. "Are you out here alone?"

"That's none of your business," she snapped, irritated that he didn't appear the least bit threatened by her weapon.

"It'll be dark soon. Let me see you home."

Anna glared her dislike of his stubborn insistence. "I don't need your escort."

His gaze narrowed to thin slits. "Why, do you have one? Are you acquainted with that gunman?"

"No." Anna jerked back, affronted at the accusation. *Maybe*

I should've just let you get shot after all! "I was only taking a walk, and lucky for you I was, mister."

He hesitated, then nodded. "And I'm grateful. I won't return the favor by leaving you out here alone." He lowered his arms to his sides and stepped forward.

Anna's blood raced in waves; nausea rolled in her stomach. "One more step, and I swear I'll shoot." She forced herself to remain calm. If this man tried to lay one finger on her, she wouldn't hesitate to pull the trigger . . . and she knew she could do it.

She'd done it before.

He raised both hands in surrender. "You have my word that I won't hurt you, ma'am."

Anna detected no deceit in his voice, but she had been around enough men to know that their promises were easily broken, or only given when they wanted something in return. "And you have my promise that I'll pull this trigger if you come any closer."

The warning in her velvety voice fell far short, overshadowed by panic. A strong protective instinct Storme didn't feel all too comfortable with kicked in and dug its claws deep. He assured himself it was only because he was indebted to the pretty lady.

"There's nothing to be afraid of."

She firmed her mouth in doubt. Her full, round breasts rose and fell with every quickened breath. Through hooded eyes, Storme followed the voluptuous line of her waist and slender hips outlined beneath her rose-flowered dress, then retraced the shapely path back up to her thick knot of reddish gold hair that shimmered like fire in the evening light. Her green eyes reminded him of the color of new spring grass, with golden flames blazing on the horizon. Twin spots of pink tinged her cheeks, enhancing the paleness of her smooth, creamy face.

"But I do understand your concern. You should consider a larger gun, ma'am, or aim lower and shoot fast if you hope to stop a man with that thing."

"I appreciate the advice." She squared her shoulders. "Good-bye, mister."

Storme stood his ground and saw her jaw tighten with displeasure at his action. They eyed each other with challenge as the minutes ticked on, until a prairie dog barked in the distance and broke the heavy silence. Storme cut his stare to the side, noting the deep purple sky of night slowly surrounding the mountain. "Do you live out here?" he questioned, searching his memory for any families who used to live in this area north of town. None came to mind, but then he'd been gone a long time.

She lowered her arm, shifting her aim to just below his belt. He arched one eyebrow, hoping he hadn't been too quick offering advice where to shoot.

"I . . . I'm leaving, since you won't." She stepped back. "Don't try to follow me. I *will* shoot you."

He admired her courage, but he didn't believe she had the guts to follow through with her threat. "You do not wear the look of a killer, ma'am."

She lifted her chin defiantly. "Perhaps you should look again."

The confident turn in her voice, and the sure anger that lit her eyes, gave him pause to question his judgment. When she backed away this time, he did nothing to stop her.

Anna shivered as darkness settled like pitch over the valley where Pleasant Grove nestled sat two miles south of the mountains. Scurrying sounds of various desert crawlers whispered in the hazy moonlight, and an occasional howl of a lone wolf filled the night and sent chills through her veins. She hurried along the uneven rock and grassy terrain, careful to watch for snakes as she dodged the squatty piñon trees and oval pods of sharp-needled prickly pears with their pale blooms bursting at the tips.

Not for the first time since her encounter with the handsome stranger, Anna scolded herself for walking alone tonight, instead of with Elise and Caroline as she usually did. But after being cooped up cleaning all day, she had been desperate for some fresh air and didn't want to wait for the girls to finish their work at the restaurant. Slipping away from the boarding-house while Mrs. Harrington visited with a couple of lady friends from town, Anna hadn't meant to be gone so long. She hadn't intended to get distracted with musings of her future, or to walk so far, either.

She picked up her pace, praying she wouldn't lose her job over this.

The single light from the third-story window of the boarding-house glowed like a welcome beacon. Mrs. Harrington's rule that lamps couldn't be lit unless the room was occupied told Anna her roommate must be inside. She wondered if Samantha Crowley would be willing to keep silent about the missed curfew, and also help her sneak in.

In the week since Samantha's arrival they had gotten along well. Anna still didn't know much about her, though—except she came from New York and, at nineteen, was a year younger. But Anna knew she would have to ask for help, if she hoped to keep Mrs. Harrington from learning about this tardiness.

She approached the white-clapboard house from behind. Muted sounds of loud music and raucous enjoyment drifted down from the saloons at the far edge of town. It still amazed her that the small community boasted four drinking establish-ments, but with the traffic she had seen pass through daily on the Atchison, Topeka, and Santa Fe Railroad, she supposed there were a number of travelers in need of a drink to quench their thirst from the desert dust.

If only her father had opened his saloon out West, instead of in Missouri.

She shook aside the introspection. Nothing would have been different. Her father still would have gambled them into debt.

Her mother still would have died. It was time to forget the past. She had to concentrate on her future now.

Pale moonbeams played havoc with the shadows, dancing in ghostly appearance over the fenced yard. Anna slowly lifted the latch on the back gate so as not to agitate the grinding squeak of the hinge, then slipped inside. Hiking up her skirt, she ran across the expanse of cropped grass to the right side of the house and stopped beneath the widespread oak that stood as the lone sentry of shade against the hot afternoons. Blackness graced the kitchen window on the ground floor and the second-story room where Mrs. Harrington slept. But Anna knew the housemother never retired early and would still be downstairs in the parlor, indulging in her nightly ritual of tea with the girls.

She released a grateful sigh. *Thank goodness the parlor is on the other side of the house.*

Anna glanced up to the half-opened window on the third story, glad Samantha had decided to skip tea tonight. Squatting, she searched the ground for something to throw, grabbed a two-bit-sized pebble, then straightened and took aim, tossing the rock into the air. It hit the house below the window with a soft thunk. Huffing her irritation, Anna bent to search out another pebble, discovering one slightly larger than the first. She scooped it in her hand and aimed higher. The rock sailed through the opening.

"Ouch!"

Oops! Anna covered her mouth, stifling the chuckle that bubbled in her throat.

Samantha came to stand in front of the window, knotting the chenille robe around her waist, then pushed the framed glass all the way up. "Ben? Is that you?" she called out in a resonant whisper.

"Ben?"

"Anna?"

Anna frowned, stepping into the moonlight that filtered

through the thick, leafy limbs stretching outside her room. "Ben who?"

"Never mind that." Samantha braced her hands against the broad ledge and leaned farther out the window. "Where have you been?" she whispered louder. "Mrs. Harrington was up a few minutes ago to see if you wanted to take tea with them."

Anna gasped. "What did you tell her?"

"That you went to the necessary, and were going to bed when you came back." Samantha smiled.

Anna's relief came swift . . . and fleeting. She wasn't inside yet.

"Where *have* you been?" Samantha asked, her grin slipping.

"Out for a walk." Anna dismissed the vague explanation with a quick wave of her hand. "Will you come down and unlock the back door, so I can get in?"

"I can't. I broke the rule about being late to work. I have to stay in the room tonight."

Anna's shoulders slumped. She planted a fist on her hip and tapped one foot. Samantha couldn't come downstairs without passing by the parlor, and Mrs. Harrington. *Now what?* She rubbed one hand over her chin, pondering her next move.

"You could climb up, ma'am."

Anna's heart slammed against her ribs at the deep, confident voice that sounded at her back. She whirled around on one heel and saw the handsome stranger she had met on the mountain, now leaning casually against the trunk of the oak tree.

"What are you doing here?" she demanded in a harsh whisper.

His wide, engaging smile softened the hard lines of his moon-lit face and fairly stole her breath away. "Making sure you arrived home safe."

"Who's out there with you?"

Anna looked up, warily shifting her gaze between Samantha and this man she still wasn't sure she should trust. "Someone who owes me a favor." And may have just offered her the only solution to her current dilemma. She stared at the stranger. "Will you help me climb up?"

"It would be my pleasure . . . Anna."

The sound of her name rolled like warm honey from his lips. Anna swallowed, wondering why he had the power to make her tingle with more than just caution, when no man ever had before.

"What's going on down there?"

Anna tore her gaze from the stranger and glanced to her roommate. "I'm going to climb up."

Samantha's eyes widened. "What? Are you crazy?"

"It'll be fine, " Anna assured, praying she was right. She had never climbed a tree before, and still wasn't convinced she should trust this man. "I have . . . someone to help me."

"Who?"

"I'll explain later." Though Anna had no idea what she would say. She really didn't understand any of this herself, except that she had to think about her job right now.

Anna approached the tree where he stood, and to her utter surprise the man walked away. Stopping, she stared at his back in baffled silence.

Is he going to help me, or not?

She heard the slight squeak of the gate latch opening, then less than a minute later he returned, leading his limping horse. Without a word, the stranger tossed his hat to the ground, then jumped to the stout limb hanging high above and latched on with his large hands. Pulling up, he swung one long, denim-clad leg over, then smoothly shifted his body upward to sit on the broad branch.

"Put your foot in the stirrup, and when you lift up, place your other foot on the saddle."

Anna took a deep breath and shoved her hesitation aside. Walking over to the horse, she mounted as the stranger had instructed.

"Now, reach your left hand up and take hold of mine. I'll help you stand."

She did as he said, sliding her fingers along the callused strength of his warm palm. He tightened his hold around her hand and gently tugged. Placing both feet on the saddle seat, she used his support to stand, but nothing prepared her for his swift shift of hands. In a single fluid motion, he grabbed her under her arms, swept her up, and planted her bottom firmly on the limb between his straddled legs.

Sweet Jesus, but he was strong . . . and fast!

Anna rapidly sucked in air, trying to catch her breath. His thigh pressed intimately against her backside. He lowered his hands to her waist and lightly dug his fingers into her flesh. Panic welled in her stomach. Anna closed her eyes, reminding herself she wasn't at the saloon anymore, and this stranger had given his word not to hurt her. She had to trust him.

"Are you all right?" he whispered.

His warm breath brushed against her ear. The calm concern in his voice eased her rioting nerves. His masculine scent drifted on the air, a pleasing array of woods and spice that stirred her senses. Anna nodded, then opened her eyes.

Storme hadn't missed her fear when he placed his hands on her waist. He thought about her threat to shoot him, the panic that had flashed in her eyes, and not for the first time sensed that something troubled her deeply—more than just witnessing a gunfight, then finding herself alone with a stranger. He wondered if some of her wariness had to do with his being a half-breed.

Or had the Spirits sent her to him for a reason? Was that why he felt this strong pull to her?

"Whenever you're ready." He stared into the creamy glow of her soft, moonlit face, all the while telling himself to forget how pretty she was and stay focused on earning her trust for this climb. "Turn sideways a little, then put your left foot on the branch."

She nodded, biting at her lower lip.

"I won't let go of you," he assured her.

She nodded again and reached one hand to her skirt, then paused, frowning. "Don't look."

Storme suppressed his chuckle. Of course, he was going to look. What sane man would pass up this opportunity? "I would not dream of dishonoring you," he answered honestly. *Looking caused no harm. But getting caught in the act was a different matter.*

She shifted so her back faced him and hiked her skirt. When she placed one booted foot on the branch, Storme's breath caught at the view of her shapely black-stocking-clad calf and rounded knee.

It took every bit of his restraint to rein in his lustful thoughts and remember the task at hand. "Now stand up, and grab the branch above."

She did, giving him an up-close view of her nicely rounded bottom. Storme swallowed and shook his head. Bracing back against the hard bark, he pushed himself up to stand behind her, never releasing his hold on her narrow waist. Lifting, guiding, he helped her climb up two more branches until they were even with the window, ever mindful to keep his hands, and his thoughts, from wandering.

Storme kept the solid trunk against his back, and now that they were much higher up, his hands a little firmer on Anna's waist. He could feel her shaking beneath his touch and wondered if her fear stemmed from his increased hold, or the height. He hoped the latter.

She glanced over her shoulder at him, worry in her gaze, but the moonlight also revealed a small sparkle of trust in the green depths of her eyes. Storme's heart pounded triumphantly at the sight. He removed his left hand from her waist. The trust instantly fled her widened stare.

"You're safe, Anna," he promised as he reached up to grab

the branch above, his fingers brushing against hers. "Now, I want you to make your way to the window."

Her bottom lip trembled until she captured it between her teeth.

"I'll be right beside you." He watched her throat ripple as she swallowed, admiring her courage when she stared skeptically toward the house, then adjusted her hands tighter around the branch above and took that first step.

"Be careful, Anna. Oh, my stars, I can't believe you're doing this," the brown-haired girl at the window cried out in a shocked whisper.

Anna cautiously slid her feet along the thick limb.

"You're doing fine," Storme encouraged as they came to within several feet of the window ledge. The branch groaned, then cracked. The sound split the quiet night, stopping Storme's heartbeat and shattering his confidence. Wrapping both hands around the limb above, he pulled himself up, freeing the branch of his weight. "Anna, move! Get to the window."

Heeding his urgent command, she slid her sweaty, shaking hands along the rough bark and moved one step, then two. The branch groaned out another warning.

Samantha gasped. "Hurry, Anna!" She leaned forward, reaching out one hand.

Anna lifted her right foot, frantically searching the empty air until she found purchase on the solid support of the wooden sill. She released one hand and grabbed hold of the framed edge of the window, then, with Samantha tugging hard at her skirt, climbed into the room.

"My goodness, are you all right?" Samantha gripped her shoulders.

Anna took several deep breaths, grateful to have the support of the pine floor firmly beneath her feet. "I'm . . . fine." Her heart pounded with leftover fear at her daring accomplishment, then swiftly changed to concern.

Shrugging off Samantha's hold, Anna turned toward the

window. She couldn't stop her smile at the sight of the stranger standing safe on the branch, leaning casually back against the broad trunk as though he helped women climb trees every day, and never for a second doubted their success. Moonbeams shone through the leaves, brushing his handsome, bronze face in a warm glow. Her pulse beat faster.

She leaned out, pressing her palms flat against the windowsill. "Thank you, Mr . . ."

"Storme Warwick." He nodded once.

"Thank you, Mr. Warwick. I'd say we're even now."

His confident grin heated her already racing blood. "Not yet . . . Anna."

Chapter Two

What did he mean, 'not yet'?

Anna stared at Storme's retreating back as he sauntered across the yard. She didn't want him in her debt, and she certainly didn't want him coming back. She leaned a little farther out the window to catch a final glimpse of his tall form before he disappeared into the darkness. A warm sensation tingled in the pit of her stomach. He *was* rather handsome, though. *Maybe it wouldn't be so bad if he came back to see me.*

Anna frowned. What was wrong with her? She had come to Pleasant Grove to hide out until she could earn enough money to be on her way again. Nothing more.

"Well, I must say your taste in strays has improved." Samantha turned away from the window, a pleased grin on her face. "I like this one much better than that blasted Sebastian you brought home last night."

Anna arched her brow in surprise. "What's wrong with Sebastian?"

"He's a mangy cat." Bitterness spilled into her roommate's voice.

"He's a kitten," Anna defended, recalling her walk the night before with Elise, and the gray kitten mewing its orphaned distress beside its dead mama.

- Samantha shrugged. "So, that just makes him a small cat."

"What do have against cats?"

Samantha narrowed her pale blue eyes, then glanced toward the window. She crossed her arms. "All right. I suppose if we're going to share this secret about you being late and climbing in the window, it's only fair you know something about me. But you have to promise not to say anything."

Anna quickly nodded her agreement.

Samantha released a deep sigh. "Well, it was just me and Mama when I was growing up, and she worked real hard to take care of us. But when she died, I—" She hesitated, a wounded look flashing in her stare. She reached up and tucked several loose strands of straight brown hair behind one ear, then lifted her chin slightly. "I didn't have any other family, and nowhere to live for a while, except in the alleyways. I survived by digging for food behind the restaurants, but sometimes . . . well, the cats refused to be chased off, and I had to fight for those scraps."

Anna's eyes widened. "How old were you?"

"Eleven," Samantha whispered.

Good heavens! No wonder the girl didn't like cats. Anna knew what it was to be without a home, not knowing where she would find her next meal or bed for the night. Until she came to Pleasant Grove, she had been living that way for a little more than two months. She hadn't been forced to fight animals to survive, though, and she was a grown woman who had gotten herself into a big mess, not a child left all alone. "If you didn't have any relatives to take you in, why weren't you sent to an orphanage?"

"Because I ran away from the authorities." Samantha's thin

eyebrows pulled together above her nose. "My mama grew up in an orphanage, and she used to tell me some horrible things about those places. I didn't want to go."

Anna stared, admiring Samantha's courage and perseverance, even as her heart reached out with sadness for the girl's ordeal. She didn't know anything about orphanages, but she understood all too well not wanting to be forced to live somewhere. She had never wanted her father to give up their medicine show and buy the saloon in the small Missouri town. But when her mother took ill with consumption, that's exactly what he did, and, at fourteen, Anna was too young to have any choice in the matter. For the next two years, she divided her time between caring for her mother in the living quarters above the saloon and helping her father serve drinks and clean up once the doors were locked for the night. After her mother's death, her father's grief had augmented his drinking and his gambling debts, both severely draining their money supply. Anna took over running the saloon, managing to stave off the creditors and turn a small profit. Then her father died, and she suddenly found herself being held responsible for his IOUs, and forced to take drastic measures to clear the large poker debts he had left behind.

"Things turned out fine, though," Samantha continued in a steady voice, a gleam of fondness rising to sparkle in her eyes. "I met a real nice widow woman who gave me a home and schooling."

Anna sighed, shoving aside the painful reflections of her past, and smiled her relief for Samantha's good fortune. "I'm glad she found you, and helped."

"You might say we found each other. We became good friends. The last thing she said to me before she died two years ago was, 'Samantha Sue, you stay out of trouble.' "

Anna arched her brow. "Have you done that?"

"Up until this morning." Samantha chuckled. "And now getting tangled up in your little secret," she quipped, winking. "Tell me about your new friend."

Blood rose hot in Anna's cheeks. "He's not my friend. I don't even know the man." She gazed out the window as unwanted memories rushed in—the feel of his strong, secure hands on her waist, his warm breath brushing across her cheek.

"Then why did you stay out with him and miss curfew?"

Anna forced aside the vision of Storme's handsome bronze face. "I wasn't with him." She crossed the room and sat down on the edge of the feather mattress.

Samantha followed, her bare footsteps muffled on the braided rug that covered the planking between their single, rod-iron beds. She plopped down on the patchwork quilt, then pulled her knees up to her chest and shoved the cotton gown and robe down over her legs. "Where did you meet him?"

Anna stared across the narrow aisle at her roommate and pondered how much to say. The girl had done her a huge service by lying to the housemother, and compounded this new trust by sharing a painful part of her past. Anna at least owed her the truth after all that. Quickly, she recounted her walk to the mountains and her encounter with Storme. She could only shake her head at Samantha's query why someone had tried to shoot him, but she wondered the same thing herself. She omitted the part about pulling her gun on him, not sure just yet how far Samantha's trust would go. Anna didn't want Mrs. Harrington to find out about the derringer. The housemother had stressed that she ran a respectable house, and Anna knew that respectable girls didn't carry guns. Respectable girls didn't have a reason to hide out from the law, either.

"Well, now I understand all that talk about a favor," Samantha said, "and you two being even."

Anna nodded, then bit at her bottom lip as Storme's parting comment rang in her ears again. *'Not yet . . . Anna.'* Just what exactly did he have in mind for clearing up this indebtedness he claimed?

"Thanks for not telling Mrs. Harrington I wasn't home,"

she said, as much to express her gratitude as to chase her thoughts, and the topic of conversation, away from Storme.

"Oh, you're welcome." Samantha waved one hand in a dismissive gesture. "I figured you had a good reason for being late, and I didn't see any need for both of us being in trouble."

Anna cocked her head. "Why were you late to work, anyway?"

"Oh." Samantha rolled her eyes and blew out a small breath. "Elise introduced me to Ben Warwick this morning, and we stood outside talking. I tell you, that man's a real charmer. Before I knew it, I'd lost all track of time." She straightened out her legs and swung her feet over the side of the bed. "I wonder if he's related to Storme?"

Anna shrugged. "I've only met Ben Warwick once. I've heard Elise mention that the two of them are friends, and he's giving her away at her wedding. But that's all I know." She pictured Ben's square, tanned face and light brown hair and eyes. She had to admit both men were tall, and there was a similarity in the line of their jaws, but she couldn't say they bore much physical resemblance beyond that. She could say, however, that Storme was also quite charming. The depth of honesty in his gaze, his concern about her safety returning home, and his efforts to help her sneak inside had enchanted her.

Anna recalled the earlier confusion at the window when she had gotten Samantha's attention. "I take it you and Ben got along fairly well if you were expecting him to be outside tossing rocks, instead of me."

"I thought we had." Frustration tightened Samantha's jaw. "He promised to come see me this evening, and Mrs. Harrington said I could come down if he did. But he never showed up during visiting time. Charming or not, I've got no hankering to latch myself to a man who can't keep his word."

Anna knew from talks during the nightly teas that the girls had all come West to work at the restaurant in hopes of finding husbands. "And no reason to. He isn't the only available man in Pleasant Grove."

Storme's handsome image popped into her mind. Was he available? Anna frowned at the curiosity that sharply nipped her heart, then chided herself for her interest. What did it matter? She had dreams of leaving, of singing with a theater troupe, not getting involved with a man or settling down.

"You're right." Samantha nodded. "And maybe I'll just remind Ben Warwick of that the next time I see him."

"Just be careful you don't get yourself in more trouble," Anna cautioned, then pushed herself up off the bed. "And speaking of trouble, I better get changed into my nightclothes, in case Mrs. Harrington comes up to check on me again."

Anna started across the room, reaching up to the back of her neck. Her heartbeat slowed when she didn't feel the thin chain and tiny clasp she expected to find. A sickening dread clenched her stomach and slowly curled her searching fingers. She stopped and glanced down at the bare spot where the heart-shaped pendant should have been resting against her bodice. She frantically scanned the floor, retracing her steps to the bed, then over to the window.

"Something wrong?" Samantha asked, concern heavy in her voice.

Anna blinked back the tears that rose in her eyes. "I've lost the necklace my mother gave me."

From the center of the mantel, the cherry wood captain's clock chimed the midnight hour, each beat ringing harder in Storme's ear.

Where the hell is my brother?

He had been waiting almost an hour, his concern mounting when he discovered that the wranglers' quarters were as deserted as the house. He downed the whiskey, welcoming the warm liquid that seared his throat, though it did nothing to ease the apprehension churning in his gut.

Storme recalled his brother's urgent message asking him to come home because of rustlers who had stolen close to a thousand head of Lazy W stock over the last few weeks, and couldn't help but wonder if the thieves had struck again. Despite the lateness, he considered riding out to check, and would have if he had any idea where to start looking on the hundred-thousand-acre spread.

He filled the glass again, then set the whiskey bottle back on the liquor cart and crossed the room. Several ornate brass sconces lined the wood-paneled office, but he had lit only one in his quest for a drink. Gray shadows weaved eerily along the walls in dancing cadence with the single flame. The silence loomed like a heavy mist. Storme's heart raced.

He shouldn't have come here . . . into this room. Haunting memories battled with the growing unease over his brother's whereabouts.

Brown-velvet drapes were drawn closed over the bank of windows he knew gave view to the southern portion of the Lazy W ranch. Storme's gaze fell to the wide mahogany desk occupying the space in front. The polished wood glowed in the light's reflection, the dark surface cleared of all but a few neat stacks of paper, a lantern, glass paperweight, and writing instruments. It was all too easy to recall the sight of his father sitting in the worn, black-leather chair. Storme clearly pictured a stack of open ledgers shoved to one side, papers scattered about, his father's favorite quill within easy reach. From behind that desk, Randolph Warwick had handled the numerous affairs involved in running a prosperous ranch.

Storme's father had always believed the only thing more important than land and cattle was family and justice. He had instilled those same qualities in his sons, as well. Storme's heart ached with the remembrance of their many discussions about the ranch, their shared opinions of life's values, their heated arguments over the varied beliefs between the Apache ways and the white man's world that Storme didn't always want to accept. He sighed and let his shoulders slump forward. It amazed him how much he still missed the man. In the last seven years, rarely a day passed that he didn't replay in his mind that moment his father was killed. A sharp pain ripped at his gut.

It never should have happened. He was the one who had gotten into a fight with that army private. The half-breed that soldier had vowed to see dead. The day Storme had been rounding up strays with his father near the base of the mountains north of their ranch, he knew that bullet had been meant for him, not the elder Warwick.

Storme shook away the disturbing memory and downed the whiskey, then set the glass on a table near the unlit fireplace.

The groaning creak of strained wood sounded from the hallway outside the office, and jerked Storme's attention. He listened, hearing the faint, stealthy footsteps approach, and reached for his Colt, sliding the gun free of its holster as he pressed back into the darker shadows beside the fireplace. Through narrowed eyes, he stared at the office door that stood slightly ajar, his alert on high as it eased open wider and the long barrel of a rifle peeked from behind the wooden barrier.

"Drop it," Storme ordered, cocking his own pistol into ready. Whoever held the rifle didn't move. "I said drop the gun," he commanded again.

"Storme?" The brim of a brown hat came into view around the edge of the door, followed by a face masked in surprise.

Relief, quick and peaceful, washed over Storme at the sight of his brother. He smiled, holstering his gun. "I didn't hear you come in, little brother."

"That's the way I intended it when I saw the strange horse in the barn." Ben Warwick stepped inside, a grin spreading across his face. He propped the rifle against the wall beside the door. "I half thought it might be you, but I wasn't sure since I didn't expect you this soon. You made good time." He crossed the room in hurried strides, tossing his hat on the cowhide sofa. "Damn, it's good to see you again." Ben wrapped him in a bear hug, taking Storme unaware at first with the air-crushing strength. "How are you?"

"I am well." Storme blinked away the moisture he couldn't keep from his eyes, and hugged Ben back just as tight. "And you, my brother?"

They stepped apart.

"Fine." Ben's smile widened. "God, I can't believe you're finally home. It's been too damn long." Ben raked him with his stare. "You look real good, Storme. Not much different than I remember." He cocked his head from one side to the other, eyeing him closely. "Except maybe a little rougher around the edges."

Storme recalled the tall, gangly boy Ben had been at eighteen. Tough, strong, but not yet grown into his full potential . . . until now. The reminder of how much he had missed over the last seven years slammed hard into his conscience. "I can't say the same for you, little brother." Storme swept an assessing gaze over the broadened shoulders that reached level in height and width with his own now, at the firm lines that graced Ben's jaw and chin and replaced the boyish roundness he remembered. His short, sandy brown hair ran in waves, brushed back off his forehead. His eyes, the color of weathered acorns, stared out from an all-too-familiar face. The strong likeness to their father sent a renewed sadness of loss arcing through Storme.

Ben shrugged, chuckling. "Yeah, I finally grew out of that skinny kid you used to know."

And journeyed straight into manhood. Storme wished he had been here to help guide him on that path, then shook aside the melancholy, refusing to let anything tamp his happiness at being home. "Our father would be proud of these changes in you, little brother. As I am."

Ben squared his shoulders at the compliment and lifted his

chin. Pride beamed on his face, then seriousness pulled his cheeks taut. "He'd be just as glad to see you finally back home, too."

Storme frowned, strongly suspecting his brother might be right. Their father had loved the ranch as much as he loved his sons, and had made it known many times that he wanted them both to run the place after he was gone. Most days, Storme was able to convince himself that his father would understand he'd left in order to keep Ben from suffering the same fate that had befallen the elder Warwick. Other days, the feeling that his father would be disappointed with his choice haunted him in waves.

"It's good to be here." Even if he could only stay a short while. Storme choked back the emotion that jammed his throat.

An infectious grin curved Ben's mouth. "C'mon, let's celebrate your return."

Smiling, Storme nodded, grabbed his empty glass off the table and followed his brother across the room.

Ben pulled the cork from the whiskey bottle and filled a clean glass, then the one Storme held out. "To homecomings." Ben raised his tumbler.

"To brothers." Storme paused, letting a moment of silence fill the spot that once would have been their father's voice completing the Warwicks' celebratory ritual. He could see the same remembrance of days gone by shimmering in Ben's eyes, as well.

Storme lifted his glass until it clinked against his brother's. They downed the whiskies at the same time, then smiled at each other. A wealth of love circled Storme's heart. *Damn.* He was glad to be home. He'd missed his brother fiercely.

Though he and Ben had lived in separate worlds for a time, they hadn't grown up strangers. Storme was five when Randolph Warwick learned about the son he had sired with a young Apache girl during his days of silver mining in Arizona. By then, the elder Warwick had built the Lazy W and was a recent

widower with a two-year-old son. He had wanted to bring
Storme home to the ranch, wanted him to know his little brother
and live in the white man's world. Storme's mother wanted
her son raised with the Apache, and had garnered the protection
of Chief Cochise to keep him there. Threatened with death if
he tried to take Storme, Randolph Warwick's only recourse
was to bargain. For the next several years, he drove fifty head
of cattle to Cochise's village every fall, and was granted the
right to stay as long as he wanted to see his son. Ben always
came along on those visits, and the brothers had grown even
closer when Storme was thirteen and came to live at the ranch
for good.

Or he had thought it was for good, anyway.

Ben refilled his glass. Storme declined any more and set his
tumbler on the cart's marble top.

"Sal's gonna be real glad to see you," Ben said. "Course,
it'll be a few days. He's up in Santa Fe with his daughter. Her
husband is down with some ailment, and he's helping out on
their farm."

Storme fondly recalled their father's longtime friend and
foreman. If not for Salvador Sanchez's devotion to the ranch
and the Warwicks, Storme wasn't sure he could have found
the strength to leave his brother and the home he loved. Sal
had been foreman on the Lazy W for the last twenty years, and
his wife their housekeeper until her death eight years ago. The
couple had raised their only child here, and Storme knew the
foreman doted on his daughter.

"How is Sal?"

"Doing all right. You know he's getting on up in years,
though. Hell, he's pushing sixty." Ben slipped behind the desk
and sat in the tall, leather chair.

Storme straightened, a little disconcerted at the sight. Ben's
strong likeness to their father was almost like seeing the man
himself sitting there again. Storme swallowed the grief over

his father's death, along with the reminders of the changes in his brother that he had missed over the years.

"Like I wrote you, his rheumatism acts up something fierce in the winters now." Ben took a sip of the whiskey, then set the glass down. "But that assistant foreman I hired last year, Winston Goff, he's working out real good. Damn smart man."

Storme knew about the new foreman. Ben was insistent that as half owner, he be kept apprised of the ranch's business. There had been bittersweet enjoyment in the informative letters from his brother over the years. Storme always felt closer to home on the days they had arrived . . . and also a little more lonely.

"I look forward to meeting him." Storme pulled out one of the pair of leather-padded chairs angled in front of the desk, and sat down. He leaned back and propped his right ankle over his left knee. "Now, little brother, tell me why I came home to find no one here."

Ben raked one hand through his hair. "I was at a town council meeting, and Winston has all the hands riding guard tonight." A grim look crossed his face, and a stiff edge deepened his tone. "The rustlers hit again last night. Third time this week. Best I can tell from the count today, they got another hundred head. That makes a little over two hundred total for this run."

"Any idea who's behind this?"

Ben shook his head, his shoulders drooping as though a heavy weight suddenly settled on them. He blew out a harsh sigh. "I'm not so sure I should have sent for you, Storme."

"Why?" He jerked back in the chair, not bothering to hide his surprise at the comment.

"Because I may have just had you walk into some sort of trap." Ben reached over and pulled opened the top side draw. "The rustlers left a note this time. Tacked it with an arrow to the fence post near where they cut the wire."

A chilling spider-crawl sensation winged its way up Storme's spine. His gut told him with all certainty that the connection to his Indian blood was no coincidence. He took the note Ben handed across the desk. Steel bands of wariness tightened his chest as he read:

Tell your Injun brother he will watch
you die, then it's his turn.

Anger pulsed swift and hot in Storme's veins. He didn't care about the threat to himself—he was used to people wanting him dead—but no one was going to hurt his brother. "Who knew you sent for me?"

Ben leaned forward and placed his arms on the desk. "I told Sal, of course. He sent the wire for me from Santa Fe when he went up there. Told Winston and the hands, too."

Storme knew that over the years a good number of the wranglers who used to work for their father had moved on, and Ben had hired others to replace them. "How well do you trust the hands?"

"They've all worked here long enough to prove their mettle and earn my trust. Why?"

Quickly, Storme related the shooting incident on the mountain, including the glare from the rifle, and being warned just in time.

Ben frowned. "Any guesses who it might have been?"

Storme shook his head. "Is it possible the hands mentioned my return to some of the townsfolk?"

"No. I asked them not to say anything. Figured folks would find out soon enough once you got back. What about the woman? Who was she?"

"Her name is Anna." Storme recounted how he had talked with her afterward, chuckling slightly as he told about being held at gunpoint with her small pistol, then how he made sure of her safe return to the house behind the train station. But through the recounting, his thoughts unwillingly wandered, heating his blood with memories of her pretty face, her slender waist that fit so nicely in the span of his hands . . . her long, shapely legs when she had hiked her skirt. He said nothing about helping her climb the tree, or his heart-stopping alarm for her safety when that limb had cracked.

Ben explained that the boardinghouse was where the waitresses who worked at the depot restaurant lived, then he sat back in the chair and rubbed one hand along his chin. "From your description, though, that sounds like Anna Alexander, the new housemaid that hired on not too long ago."

"You know her?" The stab of jealousy caught Storme unaware. He quickly reminded himself that he had no interest in Anna beyond his debt, and certainly had no reason to feel any claim toward her.

"Met her at the restaurant a couple weeks back. Haven't seen her since. Rather glad about that, too, now that I know she carries a gun." Ben chuckled, but his humor was fleeting. "You think she might know something about the shooter?"

"She claimed not to, and I believe her."

Ben arched his brow. "What makes you so sure she isn't lying?"

Through the wary alarm that had prevalently burned in her eyes, Storme had seen the truth in her angered stare when she denied his accusation to knowing the shooter. "She had no reason to call out if she was involved."

Ben paused, then nodded his acceptance of the reasoning. He lifted his glass and downed the rest of the whiskey in one gulp. "You going to report the shooting to Sheriff Hadley?"

Storme took a deep breath and pushed his thoughts of Anna aside with more reluctance than he wanted to admit. "Not right now. I'll do some checking around first, see if I can find out who it was." Storme had nothing against the older lawman who had served as the town's sheriff for more than ten years now. He knew Sheriff Hadley was a fair-minded man, and had always appreciated the fact that the lawman never questioned his word about anything. But Storme was used to working alone, and he preferred it that way. Besides, if the shooter *was* one of the townsfolk, he would just as soon let it lie. He wasn't home to stir up trouble, just catch the rustlers and move on.

"How much have you told him about the rustlers?"

"Everything, including the theft last night. But I'm the one who found the note, and I didn't say anything about it to anyone." His mouth thinned in a grim line of displeasure. "There's obviously more behind the rustlers' intent than just stealing cattle, and I thought you should see it first."

Storme agreed. This reeked of revenge, but who was behind it . . . and why? He curled his fingers around the note, the creased edges nipping into his palm. He had any number of enemies. Pinning it down to just one wouldn't be easy. "Does the sheriff have any leads?"

Ben shook his head in disgust. "These rustlers are good at covering their tracks. And the sheriff's been too busy lately keeping Lloyd in line to give it much attention."

Storme tensed at the mention of their neighboring rancher, and his longtime enemy. The bite of past anger clouded his mind. He shook his head, refusing to travel back to that memory. "What's Dodding up to now?"

Ben grunted, shrugging with a resignation that said he understood even if he didn't agree. "Fighting to keep the land he's always freely grazed his cattle on. He's got a veritable war going with several of the farmers and sheepherders who've moved in and staked claims."

Storme wasn't overly surprised. Free-range boundaries were fast becoming a past way of life as more people came west and strung barbed wire around their property. He had seen enough range wars over grass and water rights to make him doubly grateful their father had the foresight to acquire clear deeds years ago and spare the Lazy W the same battle.

"Lloyd went too far this time, though," Ben continued in a more aggravated tone. "He strung a fence across a section of Caney Trail. Now, he's planning to charge folks a fee to pass through.''

Storme sat up straight, shocked at Dodding's audacity in trying to make folks pay to use the main road from town. ''How does he claim it as his land?''

''He says he's working a deal to buy the section it runs through from the railroad. But he hasn't produced any deeds to that effect yet, and the town council's fighting his claim to the road. Until it's settled, the fence has to come down. Which is exactly what we told him at the emergency council meeting tonight.''

Storme knew from past experience that Lloyd Dodding wouldn't relinquish anything he considered his property—not without a fight. ''How did he take the news?''

''With a lot of bellyaching.'' Ben grimaced. ''Sheriff Hadley asked me to represent the council tomorrow. I'm suppose to meet him out at Caney Trail midmorning to make sure Lloyd follows through.''

Storme's mind raced with a connection between Dodding and the trouble at the Lazy W, unable to find a solid lead. But that didn't discount his enemy as a suspect. Dodding had sworn long ago that he would see Storme dead someday.

He couldn't overlook the possibility that day had come. ''I'll ride out with you.''

Ben's jaw fell open, then slowly closed. He narrowed his brown stare. ''Why? You looking to open up an old war?''

Adrenaline pumped through Storme's veins at the thought of facing his enemy again. ''No, but perhaps Dodding is.''

Pale shades of pink and blue tainted the skies, winking above the mountain peaks in a slow prelude of dawn's quest to chase away the night. A crisp chill nipped at Anna's cheeks as she hurried along the path, scanning the ground for her lost necklace—the only tangible memory she had left from her childhood

. . . from her mama. Her stomach contracted into a tight ball. She had to find it.

Earlier, she and Samantha had sneaked outside and searched the yard and underneath the oak for the missing necklace, Anna's spirits sinking when the pendant was nowhere to be found. She knew she would have to broaden her search, and pondered how best to explain to Mrs. Harrington why she needed to go to the mountains, without revealing that she had slipped out for a walk the night before. To her relief, Samantha had graciously offered to hide her absence from the house-mother again. But Anna didn't have much time.

She quickened her pace as she trudged through the forest, using the toe of her kid boot to knock aside twigs and pine needles. She hadn't spotted so much as a glimmer of hope as yet, and her last shred of faith rested with her prayer that the necklace had snagged on the tree when she hid from Storme. She made her way over to the tall cottonwood, dread clawing at her insides when she didn't immediately spot the pendant. She squatted, and ran her fingers through the tall grass in a searching sweep. Something suddenly stung the back of her left hand.

"Ouch!" Her cry echoed across the mountain. A severe burning instantly seeped under her skin, and intense pain shot through her wrist. Anna stood, spotting the scorpion in the grass, its segmented yellow-brown tail weaving from side to side in its hurried escape.

"Anna, what's wrong?"

She jumped at Storme's shouted inquiry, and spun around. Her pulse blazed with heated excitement as she watched his hurried, long-legged strides carry him down the slope, his thigh muscles bunching in a powerful display against his denims.

Good heavens! What's he doing here?

He rested one hand to the gun strapped around his lean hips. White cotton strained across the expanse of his wide chest and shoulders. A narrow strip of leather hugged his neck, and as he came closer she could see small, colored beads woven in the shape of an arrow. Beneath the shade of his hat brim, his dark eyes scanned the forest with intent caution, his jaw set in hard lines of concern. She took several deep breaths, finding him every bit as handsome and intimidating as she remembered from the night before . . . and more thrilled by his unexpected presence than she knew she should be.

"Are you hurt?"

Her heart pounded faster at the worry in his voice. "It's nothing really, just a scorpion sting." She lifted her hand, wincing slightly as the burning sensation seeped deeper into her skin. "What are you doing here?"

"Right now, I'm looking after you." His smile robbed the breath from her lungs, and chased away any thought of protesting his attention as he gently took hold of her hand.

She could feel his strength in the callused palm pressed against hers. His searing warmth sent shivers racing up her arm. He raised his other hand, and lightly ran one long, bronze finger around the burning redness that stained her flesh. Anna watched as he leaned over to inspect the wound, mesmerized at the tenderness in his touch that contrasted with the hardness that honed his tall frame. He brushed the tip of his finger across the wound, grazing the stinger and sending needle-sharp pains slicing through her skin. Anna issued a low groan.

Storme looked up. "Sorry," he whispered. Then he pulled a knife from the sheath attached to his gun belt.

Anna's eyes widened at the sight of the long silver blade, and a spasm of uncertainty leapt through her chest. She swallowed, telling herself it would be fine. Storme had promised last night he wouldn't hurt her. He had been only kind and helpful to her so far, and oddly, she did feel a certain sense of ease in his presence.

He placed the blade flat between her skin and the stinger, then pressed his thumb down and pulled the knife slowly back. The scorpion's small splinterlike defense came out, a tiny dark sliver against the shiny steel. He released her hand and slid his knife back into the case. The fiery pain still throbbed in her hand and darted past her wrist, but the heat that reached in and seared her heart had nothing to do with her injury . . . and everything to do with this gentle, handsome man.

"Cool water will ease the burning."

Anna nodded, knowing he was right. She had been stung before when she was a child, singing with her parents' medicine show as they traveled from town to town hawking wares and elixirs. She remembered her mama making her soak her leg in the icy stream, and how quickly the heated pain had fled. But she really didn't have time for that indulgence now. Mrs. Harrington would be expecting everyone to breakfast soon.

She opened her mouth to form a polite denial to his suggestion, but before she could utter a sound, Storme scooped her up into his arms and headed off through the trees.

Chapter Three

"What are you doing?" She squirmed against his hold.

Storme tightened his grip beneath her legs and around her slender back, sucking in his breath as her soft breast pressed against his chest. "Taking you to soak your hand. There's a stream not far from here."

She drew her thin, auburn eyebrows together, and curled her small nose. "I can walk just fine."

Storme smiled. He wouldn't argue that, he thought, recalling the sassy sway of her hips as he had followed her home last night. "Movement will only make the venom seep into your blood faster, and hurt worse." He couldn't argue the fact that he liked having her in his arms, either . . . more than he knew he should. His pulse raced, roused by the faint smell of lavender that drifted from her hair. "And you're no burden. You weigh little more than a dove in flight."

She stilled, a blush rising in her cheeks. "Well, thank you for the compliment, and for your help. But I'm fine, really. Besides, I need to leave."

Storme kept walking. "Where do you need to be?"

"Back at the boardinghouse. I have work to do. Please, put me down."

The slight panic in her insistence this time, and the gun in her pocket that jabbed against his stomach, made Storme stop. The last thing he wanted was for her to fear him, or feel a need to pull her derringer on him again. He lowered her to her feet. "The stream's not much farther, Anna." He pointed ahead where the narrow creek snaked through the tall pines and blue spruce rising up with the sloped ground. "Just take a few minutes. It'll help with the pain. And I'll make sure you get home."

She glanced over her shoulder, then down at her reddened hand she held pressed against her white blouse. A small smile formed on her full, shapely lips as she peered up at him through long, thick lashes. "All right, I suppose I could spare a few minutes."

Storme's blood hammered through his veins at her acquiescence. He was pleased to see the hesitancy toward him gone from her eyes and a sparkle of trust once again gleaming bright. She headed off through the trees, and he fell into step beside her, resisting the urge to take hold of her arm, to slide his hand along her slender limb. Storme shook his head. *Damn!* What was wrong with him? He had never had so much trouble keeping his hands off a woman before.

Dampness grew thicker on the air as they neared a group of willow trees shading one side of the stream where it widened to form a small pool before continuing on its downhill flow. Birds chirped their revelry from the tops of the sagging tree limbs. Sunlight streaked down the mountain, hitting one edge of the liquid surface and reflecting back the blue-flowered columbine that sparsely lined the banks. The grassy ground turned softer, more spongelike near the water's edge. Anna pulled the folds of her brown skirt to one side and knelt, then immersed her hand into the pool. She closed her eyes and released a heavy sigh.

Her hair was wound in a loose knot at the nape of her neck, the morning light shimmering like fire and spun gold in the thick mass. Several short, wavy strands hung loose and brushed against the sides of her face in a tantalizing display that beckoned for his touch. Storme squatted in front of her, knotting his hands into fists to keep from reaching across the narrow distance between them and wrapping her hair around his fingers, from pulling her into his arms. Her pale skin glistened as smooth as pearls. The soft flush in her cheeks reminded him of a newly blossomed rose. Storme swallowed, wishing he didn't find her so alluring.

"What brought you up here this morning?"

Her shoulders tensed. She slowly opened her eyes, a wary glint hovering in her green orbs. "What are you doing here?"

Storme wondered at the evasiveness that prompted her countered inquiry. Granted, they were barely more than strangers still, but he knew from years of tracking outlaws and questioning leads that more often than not people evaded answering because they had something to hide, and again his instincts hummed with a strong certainty that something deeply troubled Anna. What was she hiding? "I was searching for some evidence that might tell me that shooter's identity."

She arched her brow high, her face beaming with interest. "Did you find anything?"

His heart pummeled a rapid beat. He'd found something, all right. Something lovely and unexpected. Something soft and tempting. Something Storme knew this half-breed bounty hunter had no right to desire with the surprising depth that he did.

He shook his head, as much in answer to her inquiry as to clear his wayward wanderings. To his frustration, the shooter's trail had played out less than a quarter mile up the mountain, and outside of a few drops of blood, he hadn't found a single clue.

Her hopeful expression faded. "That's too bad. I wish I'd seen something that would be of help. But I only saw the glare from that rifle, and just enough to tell the man was wearing a dark hat." Sincere regret dominated her velvety voice. "I hope you find him."

He appreciated her wish to help, as much as the honesty in her voice. He rarely received support of any sort from people. He liked that it was coming from her this time. "I will." He smiled. "Now, it's your turn. What brings you out here again?"

A look of despair instantly dimmed the glow in her eyes and on her cheeks. "I lost my necklace last night." Tears swam in her eyes, pulling hard at his heart. "I was hoping to find it, but . . ." She shifted her stare briefly toward the sky. "I don't have time to look any more right now." She pulled her hand from the water and stood.

Storme straightened and stared down into her sad face, unable to stop himself from reaching out and wiping away the single tear that slid along her cheek. To his surprised delight, she didn't flinch or attempt to move back. Gently, he took hold of her hand, his blood racing at the sight of her small, slender fingers lying so delicate against his darker flesh, her skin as soft as satin beneath his touch. He rubbed one finger around the puffy skin next to her thumb, glad to see that the redness from the sting had already started to fade.

"Thanks for your assistance, Mr. Warwick." There was a faint shyness in her tone, and in her soft smile, that drew him like a moth to the firelight.

The desire to kiss her rose fast and fervent in his chest . . . and scared the hell out of him. Storme took a deep breath, and straightened, releasing her hand. He owed this woman a life-debt. Kissing her did not fall under that obligation.

"Anytime, Miss Alexander."

She stiffened and took a step back. "How did you know my last name?"

Storme puzzled at the alarm that flashed in her eyes. "From my brother, Ben."

"You talked to him about me?"

He shrugged. "I explained what happened last night."

She cocked her head, the apprehension in her gaze easing only slightly. "I hope your brother stays quiet. I'll lose my job if Mrs. Harrington finds out I wasn't home."

"Even for such a cause as saving my life?"

"Perhaps she would make an exception." She hesitated, furrowing her brow. "But I was already late before I called out to you."

Storme nodded, understanding her dilemma. She shouldn't have been here last night. He was damn glad that she had been. And he would still like to know why she got so bothered over him knowing her name. "You have my word I won't say anything. As for my brother, I didn't tell him about you sneaking inside."

Her smile of relief shot across like a radiant beam and speared the center of his heart. "Thank you for that. Now, I really must be going before I'm late again."

"I'll take you back. Just let me fetch my horse."

She bit at her bottom lip and looked up at the sky. Storme fully expected her to decline his offer, but to his amazement she nodded. "Just to the edge of the grove behind the depot will be fine, if you don't mind."

A warm gladness spread through his chest. "I don't mind at all, Anna." He nodded toward the pool. "You keep soaking your hand. I'll be back in just a minute."

Sunlight gleamed bright, burning the morning dew from the grassy range as the temperature steadily rose in a sweltering promise of the hot, humid day ahead. Storme stared at the ranch spread out in the lush valley, smiling at the contentment that settled over his soul.

He thought about the times he had ridden this same road home from town with his father and had listened to the man talk about the hard years of building the Lazy W. He could still hear the ring of pride in his father's voice:

'My pockets may have been lined with silver when I came here, son, but a fistful of money didn't keep the rustlers away, or bring the rain when we needed it. A man's got to fight to hang on to what's his, and it's damn nice when he can sit back and see the fruits of his efforts.'

Storme sat back in his saddle, slowing his horse to a walk as he rode under the scrolled, iron arch that spelled out *Lazy W.* He bypassed the road that veered off to the right, but glanced up the hill where the ranch house stood among a sparse group of oaks. A steeply pitched roof shingled with hand-split cypress covered the two-story, square clapboard. Storme remembered how his father had always taken time every morning to stand on the wide verandah and sip his coffee while he stared out at the ranch and the land that had meant so much to him.

Storme shifted an appreciative gaze over the distant hills that rose to encase the valley, at the various clusters of small longhorns—calves old enough to be weaned and fattened off the grass, but still young enough to bawl their distress at being separated from their mamas—that dotted the surrounding range. He passed by the familiar bunkhouses and outbuildings scattered about the ranch yard, and rode ahead, watching as two wranglers herded a small remuda of horses into one of several fenced corrals that sat opposite the large, two-story barn with its red doors thrown open wide.

On the outside, nothing much had changed over the last seven years, but Storme knew appearances could be deceiving. A lot had changed. His father was gone; his brother grown. Most of the wranglers were men he didn't know. But this was still his home, his land, and it always would be, no matter where he roamed.

Storme never regretted his years living the Apache ways. He loved his mother, and his people. But when the army raided their village, killing her and many others in his tribe, and his father had come to the reservation to claim his son, the love and admiration he carried for the man had easily swayed his desire to live the white man's ways on the ranch. Randolph Warwick had tried to make the townsfolk accept his half-breed son, but opinions ran strong against Storme, and too often were backed with fists and guns. Storme had quickly learned that no matter what the heart desired, some things just couldn't be forced.

He reined his horse to a halt outside the barn just as Ben strode from the shadowed confines, leading a saddled sorrel. Three men followed. Storme didn't recognize the tall wrangler with the tanned, freckled face and a wad of chew in his cheek, or the short, Mexican vaquero, but the other young man with them looked slightly familiar.

Ben looked up, then tipped his hat down against the sunlight. "Did you find anything?"

Storme knew his brother was asking about the shooter, but his pulse kicked up as Anna's pretty face floated through his thoughts. It wasn't every day he found a beautiful woman alone in the woods, or had his heart ripped in two by tears over a lost necklace, and the ride down from the mountain had strained his senses even further. She had sat behind him on the horse, posture stiffened, her hands gripped on the back of his saddle. It wasn't hard to guess she was trying to avoid any physical contact with him, but he had felt every move of her body anyway, and more than once he had thought about pulling her around in front and kissing her—and still wished liked hell that he had. He sat up, sharply reminding himself again that his interest in Anna concerned his owed debt. Nothing more.

"There was some blood splattered on the tree. I must have

hit him, but not bad enough to keep him from coming back to cover his tracks." And probably not bad enough to keep the man from trying again.

Annoyance darkened Ben's narrowed stare. He shook his head. "Damn, I was hoping you'd get a lead."

"You talkin' 'bout a lead on the rustlers?" the tall wrangler inquired in a deep-throated voice. He spit a stream of tobacco juice into the dirt.

"Not sure yet, but it could be. Someone took a shot at my brother last night," Ben replied.

Over breakfast, Storme and Ben had discussed how much to tell the wranglers, and agreed the men needed to know everything in order to protect themselves and the herd. But Storme didn't want to mention the threatening note yet, not until he had some time to try to figure out who was behind this revenge.

The vaquero and the young wrangler exchanged concerned glances.

The tall, lanky cowboy arched his red eyebrows as he glanced over. "Glad he missed ya, Mr. Warwick."

Storme nodded, chuckling under his breath. "Me too. And call me Storme."

"This is our new foreman, Winston Goff." Ben made the introduction.

Winston sauntered over and stuck his hand up. "Nice to meet ya, Storme." Shocks of red hair stuck out from beneath his black hat.

Storme shook the foreman's hand, impressed by the clear, honest look in his blue stare. "Likewise."

"And this is Hector Garcia." Ben pointed toward the middle-aged vaquero.

Storme greeted the man as he walked up and offered his short, beefy hand.

"*Señor* Ben is *mucho* happy you come home. He talks good things about you."

Storme shifted his stare to Ben, seeing his smile and offered one of his own. "It's good to be back." He looked down at the vaquero. "I met your wife this morning." He recalled the short, black-haired woman he had discovered cooking breakfast in the kitchen well before dawn. Ben had written about hiring Maria as his housekeeper when she and Hector had come to the ranch looking for work a couple years ago. "Nice woman. She's a good cook, too."

Garcia grinned, deepening the weathered lines in his round, brown face. *"Sí."* He patted one hand over the slight bulge of his stomach.

"And you remember Cale Parker, don't you, Storme?" Ben waved a hand toward the young cowhand Storme had thought looked familiar. "Jim Parker's son."

Storme nodded, recalling the older wrangler that had worked at the ranch when he was still here, and the man's young son that had always tagged along. Cale couldn't have been more than eleven when Storme left, and had grown quite a bit since then, but he still recognized the blue eyes beneath the wide brim of his hat, and the sharp cleft in his chin. Storme also remembered that Ben had written about Jim getting kicked in the head by a steer and dying not too long ago. "It's good to see you again, Cale."

"You too, sir." Cale grinned, revealing a row of crooked white teeth.

"I was sorry to hear about your father."

Cale nodded, his mouth firming to a straight line that reflected the faint signs of continued grief. "It's real good to have you back, sir. We're glad for the help to catch these rustlers."

Winston spit a stream of black juice into the dirt, then glanced up with a steady stare. "He's right 'bout that, Storme. Ya can count on us. Me and the boys are ready to be rid of these thievin' bastards, and we welcome any suggestions you have on makin' that happen."

Storme nodded his appreciation of their support and his

gratitude at the men's obvious devotion to the ranch. "We'll catch them, don't worry."

The wranglers smiled, offering nods and muttered assurances of their agreement to that fact.

Storme glanced over at his brother. "You ready to go meet the sheriff and Dodding?"

Ben grimaced. "I'm never ready to meet with Dodding."

"Don't blame ya." Winston shook his head and hitched his thumbs into the waistband of his denims. "That man's 'bout as sociable as a live rattlesnake in a hot skillet."

A spotted cactus wren flew low across Caney Trail and landed in a small nest amid the prickly *cholla* spines, seemingly unaware of the blacksnake crawling up the spindly plant in search of its next meal.

Storme shifted in his saddle and tugged his hat brim lower against the sun's midmorning glare flooding down from the azure sky. Unlike the little bird, he knew right where that predator Dodding would be, and Storme was ready . . . for anything. He was also curious to see if his enemy carried a nickel-plated rifle these days and might be wounded.

"Hope Dodding doesn't shoot you on sight." Ben's grim concern cut through the silence.

Storme glanced over where his brother rode beside him along the rutted road. "He won't, not with the sheriff there."

"I don't know." Ben shook his head, discomfort clouding his brown stare. "He's never liked you. And I remember how violent things got between you two over Miss Lewis."

Storme frowned. A dull ache spread through his chest at the memory of the schoolteacher he had been in love with several years ago. Linette Lewis had been concerned about her reputation and insisted they keep their courtship a secret. But Dodding had been interested in courting her, as well, and when he found out she was seeing Storme, the hotheaded rancher had set out to ruin her standing with the townsfolk. Forced to choose between the young half-breed she wanted and her reputation and job, she fled Pleasant Grove, leaving Storme a note that had simply said: *'I'm sorry. Good-bye.'*

Ben's face tightened with contrition. "Sorry. I know you don't like to talk about her."

Storme shrugged. "It's all right, little brother. I've learned to live with the past," he answered honestly. His heart had healed a long time ago, and he rarely thought of Linette anymore. But his vow never to fall in love again, or subject another woman to the prejudice that followed him, still sat strong in his resolve—along with his simmering anger at Dodding.

"I'm just afraid Lloyd's hatred for you might make him lose control, and do something stupid."

Storme knew the concern was valid. Past experience had taught him that the rancher was a dishonorable fighter and a coward. "Or seek revenge by stealing our cattle and trying to shoot me in the back."

"Why would he wait all these years to get even?"

"It's hard to judge a man's mind, or his intentions," Storme cautioned.

"Maybe so. Dodding's all the time carrying around one grudge or another." Ben's brown eyes glowed with a savage inner fire. "But if he tries anything against you this time, he's going to have to deal with me."

Pride swelled, mingling with the love that overflowed in Storme's heart. He raked his stare over Ben's muscled frame. "Dodding would do well to be afraid. You've grown into a formidable opponent."

"Damn right." Ben squared his shoulders. "I'd also like to see Chasing Wolf try to cut me up now," he grated through clenched teeth.

"He would think twice, little brother." Storme recalled his own fight with the brave after finding him using a knife to taunt and inflict wounds on the little white boy. Storme had

given no thought to being only nine and Chasing Wolf a young
warrior of fourteen winters when he attacked the brave. He
also remembered the pride on his father's face for his defense,
and that had meant far more to Storme than his victory or the
honor he had gained among his people.

Storme faced forward as the path curved around a small
stand of oaks, his adrenaline pumping when he spotted three
wranglers working to tear down a section of wire stretched
across the road ahead. Off to one side, Dodding leaned forward
in his saddle, arms crossed over the leather horn as he puffed
on a cheroot and talked with the sheriff.

Storme's fists hardened like granite around the reins as he
stared at the rancher. He couldn't see much change in Dodding's
stocky build, except for the paunch that had thickened his waist
and hung slightly over his belt. Storme spared a glance at
Sheriff Hadley, noting the shot of silver that now streaked the
dark hair visible beneath his hat.

"Good. Looks like Lloyd is abiding by the council's decision." Ben's tone reflected his relief.

Storme's tempered pulse roared louder in his ears as they
approached to within a few yards. The wranglers stopped work
and turned to stare.

The rancher sat up straight. His gaze narrowed. He puffed
several more times on the lit cheroot, then tossed it into the
dirt. "I thought this town was rid of you for good, half-breed,"
he stated with hot contempt.

Storme reined his horse to a halt. "Think again," he sneered.

Dodding's long, angular jaw hardened. Steel fire blazed in
his gray eyes. "You won't be staying long."

"Long enough to make your life miserable," Storme taunted.

"Why you sonofab—"

"Don't start anything, Lloyd," Sheriff Hadley warned, shifting his stare. "You either." The man's tanned, leathered face
broke into a smile. "But it's good to see you again, Storme.
Ben."

"And you, Sheriff." Storme nodded. Ben offered a brief word of greeting.

"Ain't nothing good about it," Lloyd snapped, shoving the brim of his hat up and revealing the front edge of his short-cropped black hair. Anger reddened his face. "I thought I told you never to set foot on my property again, Injun?"

Loathing welled like bile in Storme's gut. He gritted his teeth as the threatening words rose in his thoughts. *Tell your Injun brother . . .*

"Dammit Lloyd, this isn't your property," Ben snapped. "The town council told you that last night."

From the corner of his eye, Storme saw his brother visibly bristle. He let a smile lift one corner of his mouth, impressed at Ben's fortitude. "Seems I'm not on your land, after all."

Dodding tensed, drawing his blue shirt taut across broad shoulders. "It'll be mine soon enough, half-breed," he retorted. "Just a matter of paperwork. Ain't that right, Sheriff?"

Sheriff Hadley rolled his eyes. "Paperwork you gotta have." Impatience tinged his voice.

"Let's don't forget that little bit of paperwork," Ben forcefully interjected, "includes a stipulation that says you can't buy the main road to town, Lloyd."

"We'll see about that. If I'm gonna own both sides, I want the whole damn thing," the rancher ground out harshly. "But the fence is coming down. For now. You have enough for that blasted report to the council. You two can leave." He settled his hands high on his denim-clad thighs, within easy reach of the pair of Colts strapped around his thick waist.

Ben sat back in his saddle. "What do you think, Storme? You ready to go?"

Storme nodded, glancing from Ben's knowing stare to the empty sides of Dodding's saddle. No rifle. No wound. Nothing to connect him to the shooter or the rustlers, and no reason to bring up either, except to start trouble. He stared at the rancher's face, at the hard glare in his eyes. But there was no doubt that

Dodding's hatred was as strong as ever. Storme knew that the fact the man didn't carry a rifle and wasn't wounded only meant his wealth afforded him the means to own several weapons or choose to hire the job done if the coward didn't want to dirty his hands himself.

"Good day, Sheriff." Storme laid the reins against the gelding's neck, reeling the horse around.

"Don't come back, Injun," Dodding bit out.

He froze and glanced back over his shoulder. "Don't cross my path and force me to," Storme warned with just as much venom, then kicked the gelding into a hard run.

"I should just forget about Ben Warwick." Irritation heavily laced Samantha's voice.

Anna paused from dusting the stools lined in front of the mahogany counter and glanced across the dining room. It was on the tip of her tongue to agree, but she didn't. After damping down the girl's emotional pendulum between ranting over his broken promise and pining over his charm all day, she knew Samantha didn't want agreement. She wanted answers.

"When you see him next, maybe you should just ask him why he didn't come by last night," Anna suggested.

"Why should I ask?" Samantha huffed, her blue stare burning icy hot. "He's had all day to come around and explain *that* himself." She slammed the polished knife down with enough force to rattle the silverware and crystal glasses already placed on the linen-covered table.

Anna arched her brow and darted her gaze toward the swinging door on the far wall, expecting the strict restaurant manager to poke his head out to inquire about the noise. Mr. Chesterfield didn't, and Anna breathed a sigh of relief. She didn't want Samantha to get in any more trouble.

"Not only am I going to forget about him, I don't plan to

ever speak to him again.'' She stormed across the room and disappeared through the swinging door into the kitchen.

Anna shook her head, strongly suspecting ten seconds from now Samantha would change her mind about that . . . again. But she did sympathize with the girl. Much as Anna hated to admit it, she had spent a good portion of the day herself waffling between despair over her lost necklace and wayward thoughts of Storme Warwick. Even now the memories of his warm, gentle touch as he had tended her sting, his strong arms as he carried her to the stream, sent tingling heat racing through her.

She stared down at the tiny red dot, remembering the concern in his dark gaze, the trusting tone in his deep voice. She had also seen the fleeting spark that had revealed his thought to kiss her. Working in her father's saloon, Anna had fended off enough unwanted advances from half-drunken patrons and arrogant gentlemen to know the look of desirous intent in a man's eyes. But she hadn't seen anything lustful in Storme's stare this morning, just a low blaze of serious interest . . . and, heaven help her, she had wanted him to kiss her.

Warmth rose in her cheeks. *Goodness, why does he kindle such stirrings in me?*

She had accepted his offer of a ride to ensure she wasn't late returning, but all the way down the mountain, Anna had forced herself to keep some distance between them, fearing she just might give in to the unexpected desire he stirred and *ask* him to kiss her.

She blinked, then took several deep breaths. What on earth was wrong with her? She had no business being attracted to the man. She didn't want to be attracted to him. She needed to forget about Storme Warwick, and stay focused on hiding out, on keeping her freedom. Once she had enough money, she was heading to California and pursuing her plan to join a theater troupe—one sailing straight away for anywhere in Europe.

She glanced toward the front window where the late-afternoon sunlight beamed its brilliance, sparkling like clear diamonds against the crystal and silver that graced the elegance of the dining room. Right now, though, her immediate concern was finishing here at the restaurant so she could search for her necklace again.

Quickly, she dusted the last few stools at the counter and straightened, flattening her hand against her lower back, which ached fiercely after scrubbing floors at the house all day, then being pressed into service here when Caroline had suddenly taken ill. But she was free to go now, grateful the fussy manager didn't trust her ability to wait on the crowds that would soon arrive on the train, and the locals who sometimes came to dine, as well.

"Goodness, what is Samantha in such a snit about?" Elise Weatherford held the kitchen door open long enough to shoot a last curious glance over her shoulder, then released it to swing shut.

Anna untied the apron at her waist and draped the white cotton over one arm. "Ben Warwick."

Elise arched her blond eyebrows. "Still?" She crossed over to the counter and sat on the end bar chair. "She's going to have to find some patience and subtle persistence where that man's concerned. She wanted to meet him because she thinks he's handsome, but I told her he's not in any hurry to get tied down to one woman."

"And how do you know?" Anna arched her brow teasingly. "Did you try to latch on to him yourself?"

"Goodness, no." Elise waved a dismissive hand. "We're just friends. He's a good man, though." Her hazel eyes sparkled. "Not my Wallace, of course."

"Of course." Anna sighed, almost envying the love that beamed on Elise's face. What would it be like to find a man that could spark such a glow? Storme's handsome image sprang into her mind, and her heart pounded faster. Anna took a deep breath, chiding herself for the foolish thought. She wasn't interested in falling in love . . . ever. She was interested in finding her necklace. "I better go, before the train arrives."

"Wait." Elise grabbed her arm as she started to walk by. "There's something I need to talk to you about."

Anna furrowed her brow in confusion, noting the radiant shine in Elise's cheeks had suddenly dimmed.

"I wanted to mention it the other night, but we found Sebastian, and then time just, well, sort of got away." Elise hesitated, releasing her hold. She patted one side of her upswept blond hair, then ran both hands nervously down the front of her apron.

Anna had never seen Elise anything but calm and sure. This unfamiliar agitation caused a pit of wariness to form in her stomach. "What is it?"

"Well, I . . ." Elise cleared her throat. "I, um . . . wanted to tell you how much I enjoyed your singing the other night."

Anna nodded, remembering how she had finally succumbed to the girls' coaxing several nights ago to sing with them while Mrs. Harrington played the piano, then being further talked into helping Katie and Patricia practice their musical numbers for a planned extravaganza at the town's upcoming Fourth of July celebration. She also remembered that Elise had told her then how much she enjoyed her singing.

"I even told Wallace's mother how pretty you sounded. And I was wondering . . ." Elise paused, her throat rippling as she swallowed. "Would you sing at my wedding?"

Anna blinked her surprise, then her heart fluttered with honor at the request. She loved to sing, and she liked Elise. Anna wanted to say yes, but she couldn't forget that she was here to hide. Standing before a crowd of people was not the way to accomplish that. She had begged off going to church every Sunday with the others to avoid meeting folks. She didn't want a lot of people to remember her once she was gone, and if the law came looking, possibly connecting her to the woman who used to sing in her father's saloon on occasion . . . and was wanted for murder in Missouri—a murder she hadn't meant to commit. But she couldn't prove that she had only been defending herself.

"I'm sorry, Elise, but—"

"Oh God, please don't say no," Elise begged, her eyes rounding in stricken disbelief. "You can't. I mean . . . well, that is . . ." She sighed; her face grew pensive. "The fact is, I've already told Wallace's mother that you agreed," she admitted, guilt and apology tangled together in her voice. "And she's already mentioned it to her family and friends."

The small hairs rose on Anna's neck. *Oh dear!* She hated to let Elise down, especially after she had been so nice since Anna arrived.

"I know I shouldn't have said anything without asking you first," Elise continued, deep contrition in her tone. "I'm real sorry. I didn't mean to. I was just visiting with Mrs. Sanderson, and telling her about your beautiful voice. Next thing I knew, the words about you singing at the wedding just flew right out of my mouth."

Anna swallowed. She didn't want to hurt Elise's feelings, or cause her embarrassment at being caught in the lie. "Um . . . couldn't you just tell her I changed my mind. I really . . . don't feel comfortable singing in front of a crowd," she hedged.

"It's just going to be a few folks," Elise rushed the words, leaning forward in the chair. "The girls, of course, and the others here at the restaurant, Wallace's family, and just a few other friends. There won't be but about twenty people. You already know most of them. Please, Anna."

Her fervent resolve to say no slowly melted in the heat of Elise's beseeching stare. A bell loudly clanged outside from the station platform in warning to the waitresses of the train's arrival.

Elise darted her gaze to the window, then back. "Please, be a dear friend and do this for me," she pressed.

Friend? Anna's breath caught in her throat. The childhood

years spent roaming with the medicine show, never being around any children her own age for longer than a few days— never enough time to make friends, only acquaintances—and the years of loneliness living above the saloon overwhelmed her in a crushing flood. How many times had she longed for friends?

She thought about the girls at the boardinghouse. She had enjoyed her walks with Elise and Caroline, and had gotten along well with Katie and Patricia, too . . . and, of course, Samantha. Mrs. Harrington and all the girls had been so nice and welcoming, especially Elise.

Anna released a heavy sigh, then bit at her bottom lip. Could it really hurt to do this *one* small favor, she pondered. Elise said there were only going to be a few folks, and she already knew most of them anyway. If she only sang one song, and she made sure not to get herself in this sort of bind again, maybe she wouldn't be taking too big of a risk. It might be all right.

"Yes, I'll do it," Anna quickly whispered before she could change her mind, then sent a prayer heavenward that she wouldn't regret her decision.

Chapter Four

"Sebastian, stop that," Anna scolded as she bent down for the third time to free the kitten's claws from the hem of her skirt. "Now, go back." She waved one hand to shoo the feline away.

The four-legged bundle of energy sprinted through the grass and up the nearest tree.

Anna gathered her skirt and hurried through the stand of cottonwoods and firs behind the station, hoping the kitten stayed distracted long enough for her to escape its notice. The last thing she needed was Sebastian's playful antics while she searched for her necklace. She gained only a short distance before she felt a tug at the back of her skirt, and a bare second later heard the material rip.

She stopped and stared over her shoulder, frowning down at the kitten. "Now, look what you've done."

The gray feline sat back and cocked its head, round, black eyes staring.

Anna narrowed her gaze in silent reprimand, then lifted her

skirt to take a closer look at the L-shaped tear near the hem. The kitten leapt for another hold.

"Oh, no you don't." She hiked her skirt up past her knees, keeping an eye on the kitten as she sidestepped away.

Sebastian gave chase, his spindly paws swatting at her legs.

Masculine laughter resounded at her back. Anna froze, the deep timbre ringing with a familiarity that made her pulse pound faster. She released her skirt and turned around. The sight of Storme standing at the edge of the grove, golden rays casting his tall frame in a soft halo, made her breath catch.

"Can't blame him for chasing a pretty woman."

Storme thinks I'm pretty? Her heart jolted, and a dizzying current swept through her with burning enthusiasm. He wasn't so hard on the eyes himself. She slid an appreciative gaze over the clean denims that hugged his long legs, the blue shirt left partially unbuttoned to reveal a glimpse of his gleaming bronze chest, the beaded leather that was tied around his neck and rested on his strong, handsome face.

He sauntered forward, guiding his horse by its reins.

Sebastian puffed out like a frayed ball of yarn, hissed at the black mount, then darted through the grass and clawed his way up a nearby tree.

Anna chuckled, smiling. "Thanks, I shouldn't have any problem with him now."

"Since you didn't seem to want him along, I'm glad I could help." His hat shaded his eyes, but not the square line of his smooth jaw, or the warm smile that graced his mouth and sent tingles scattering through her stomach.

Storme dropped the reins, ground-tying the gelding, and crossed the last few feet between them. He shifted his gaze over her creamy, oval face, his pulse stirring at the pink flush in her cheeks, his thoughts firing hot with the memory of black stockings and shapely legs as she had dodged the kitten.

"I didn't expect to see you, Mr. Warwick? Are you still out looking for more clues to that shooter?"

Storme shook his head, trailing his stare down the slender column of her neck, along the edge of her simple white collar, over the swells of her—

He swallowed, hard. No sense starting down a road he had no business traveling. No matter how lovely the scenery. "I was on my way to see you. I wanted to make sure you hadn't suffered any ill effects from that scorpion sting."

Her smile blossomed deeper, as captivating as a new flower opening to reveal its full beauty. "No, it's much better." She raised her hand for his inspection.

Storme took a deep breath, and tore his gaze away from her face, pleased to see only a tiny pink dot marring her pale flesh. He resisted the strong urge to take hold of her hand, to feel her smooth, satiny skin again. "Any pain?"

She shook her head. "That's nice of you to be so concerned, though."

Storme's heart slammed to a stop, then kicked up with the speed of a raging river. It had been a long time since a woman thought him nice. A woman he wasn't paying to spend time with him, anyway. "I've also been up on the mountain looking for your necklace."

Her eyes widened, a hopeful glint sparkling in her green depths. "Did you find it?"

The memory of her tears twisted at his gut, as it had throughout the day, and he wished he had better news. "No. I'm sorry."

She sagged like a wilted flower too long in the sun. Storme forced himself not to reach for her, to take her in his arms and ease the sadness that haunted her expression and drooped her shoulders.

To his surprise, she just as quickly straightened and jutted her chin out with determination. "I was just on my way to search. I'm sure you did a thorough job, but I don't suppose it could hurt to have another look, anyway."

Storme admired her persistence, and her tenacity only reinforced how special the necklace was to her. But it was the mention of her intended trip to the mountain that reminded him of the other reason he had been coming to see her. "I don't think you should go up there alone. Not for a while, anyway."

She furrowed her brow. "Why?"

"Whoever shot at me may think you saw more than you did and might feel the need to make sure that you don't say anything."

Her expression grew serious, contemplative. After a brief time, she nodded. "You might be right about that. But I have my gun with me. I'll be fine."

Her cool assurance triggered a slight annoyance in him. *For about two seconds with that tiny thing.* "Have you ever shot it before?"

She shrugged one shoulder. "No, but I've been meaning to practice."

"Do you know how close you have to be to make an impression on a man with that derringer?"

She grinned mischievously. "Well, I don't recall having any trouble impressing you to stop."

"It wasn't your gun, Anna." Storme frowned at her confidence. "I didn't want to harm you."

Her humor faded away. "I would have shot you if you'd tried," she said in a much more subdued tone.

Storme nodded, but he still had strong doubts that she would have followed through. The courage to do so had been in her eyes, but he recalled the hesitation he had seen in her shaking hand, and knew a second's pause was all the time a man would need to disarm her. He considered the possibilities of what could happen if she encountered the shooter, or any man who might happen along up in the mountains, and the need to protect her dug deeper at him. He considered buying her a bigger gun, considered suggesting that she stay locked in her room until he uncovered the shooter's identity and could ensure her safety. He decided on something a little more reasonable.

"If you want to go look for your necklace, that's fine. I'll go with you."

She cocked her head. "Thank you, but that's not necessary."

Storme smiled. "Just consider it another payment toward my debt."

She planted her hands on her hips, and eyed him with challenge. "There is no debt. I helped you, and you've helped me. More than once now. Far as I'm concerned, we're squared up."

Her words nicked his pride. "You must not place much value on a man's life, if you consider tree climbing and searching for a necklace equal to my honor-bound duty to repay you for saving me from that shooter."

She raised her chin in defiance. "I believe value is measured by the importance of the deed, Mr. Warwick, and the honesty behind a man's word."

His pulse raced with increased regard at her matter-of-fact response. He could find no defense against her argument—save one. "You're a noble and generous woman. Should you one day owe me a debt, I give my word you may be the judge of the price paid." He lifted one corner of his mouth in a half smile. "Since this is my day, I shall judge when this debt is done."

She hesitated, her lips pursing as the realization of defeat rose to simmer on the horizons of her spring green eyes. She arched her eyebrows. "Are you always so stubborn?"

Storme chuckled, and shrugged one shoulder. "My brother says so. There are a few others that would agree."

"They would be right, too." She smiled. "But I appreciate the company. I need to hurry, though. I have to be back before dark." She marched past him, and Storme caught the scent of lavender drifting on the air in her wake.

He breathed deeply, then shook his head. *Fool!* He needed to stop torturing himself with wayward desires that he had no intentions of acting on. He fell into step beside her, narrowing his stride to match her pace, grabbing the gelding's reins as he went by, and tugging at the reluctant animal, who wanted to stay and chew on the patch of grass at its feet.

Sunlight coated the path outside the stand of trees. A light breeze brushed against Anna's face, slightly cooling her heated cheeks, warmed as much by the sun as by the man walking at her side. She still couldn't believe that Storme had come back to search for her necklace. Her heart beat joyously at his generosity and his concern about her safety. She could do without his continued determination to repay this debt he claimed, but he struck her as a man strongly driven by pride and suspected that's what fueled his stubbornness, as well. She couldn't help but wonder again why someone would want this kind man dead.

"Why did that man try to shoot you?"

"I'm not sure, yet. I came back home to help my brother. He's been having trouble with rustlers. It could've been one of them . . . or someone who just doesn't like me for one reason or another," he answered low and even, surprisingly without a hint of concern.

She stared up at the bronze tone of his face. "One reason being because you're part-Indian?"

He nodded, his eyes narrowing, his mouth firming into a thin line. "Does my Apache heritage bother you?"

Anna shook her head. Living and working at the saloon, she had learned firsthand how quick folks were to pass judgment on a person. "I judge you only as a man." And so far, Storme had garnered more of her esteem than any man she had ever met.

He smiled. "Thank you, Anna." Her name rolled from his lips like honey, and sent tingles charging through her veins.

"You don't look much like your brother. Is he part-Indian, too?"

"No, we share the same father, but Ben's mother was white, and mine Apache." Storme looked off toward the mountains, but not before Anna saw the sadness that sparked in his brown eyes.

"Where are your parents?" she inquired.

He dipped his head slightly and looked over at her. "Ben's mother died when he was born. My mother was killed in an army raid on our village when I was thirteen. Our father died several years back."

Anna heard the telltale remnants of sorrow in his voice and understood his pain. "I'm sorry. I know it's hard not to miss them sometimes. My mother died from consumption when I was sixteen. We were very close. My father passed away just a few months ago."

Storme placed one fist over his heart. "But the memories will always live on."

She nodded, her own heart swelling with love and a tinge of sadness as she recalled her mother's gentle voice, her soothing words of guidance and encouragement . . . her too-thin frame in the worn calico dress as the lung disease had slowly stolen her strength.

Anna stared ahead at the sagebrush, mesquite, and piñon pines that dotted the valley floor and turned the trail toward the mountain base into a winding maze. Silence stretched between them, but it was a companionable quiet that engulfed her in contentment as they followed the path. She scanned the ground for her necklace, every now and then shifting her gaze to watch the few birds fluttering about from tree to brush, and listened to the scurrying of tiny-footed creatures in search of shelter against the night ahead. A roadrunner darted across the valley. An eagle's shadow crossed their path as it soared high above, then disappeared in the glare of sunset's light. The sun hung half-hidden behind the western arm of wooded mountains that surrounded Pleasant Grove, ribbons of pink and orange streaming a painted path down the higher sloping regions.

Mama would have loved these mountains, she thought, staring at the towering, ragged peaks. *The mountains are nature's greatest gift, my little Annika.*

Anna closed her eyes, hearing her mother's words, seeing her weathered, suntanned hands so warm and gentle against Anna's childish fingers as they walked through the mountains in Colorado so many years ago.

Storme grabbed her arm, jerking her to attention as he pulled her to a halt. Anna sucked in her breath at the sight of the large rattlesnake crossing their path ahead, gauging the fat, spotted brown creature to be at least eight feet long as it slithered on its course, thankfully unaware of their presence. Anna glanced over at Storme, his face set hard as stone, his stare focused where the snake had disappeared. Seconds later, the tension left his broad shoulders, and he holstered the six-shooter she hadn't even heard him draw.

He looked down at her, his face softening back into the natural hard grooves along his chiseled jaw, his easy smile rolling over his firm mouth. He released his hold, surprising Anna with a saddened loss, even as her blood still raced from his touch.

"We should hurry. The sun won't last much longer."

She nodded, resuming her pace beside him. They reached the mountains a few minutes later, and Storme left the horse at the base, then led the way upward along the trail to the cottonwood tree she had hidden behind. Using the toe of her boot, Anna once again searched through the grass and fallen foliage.

Storme walked a wider perimeter around the tree. "Tell me what this necklace looks like."

Anna jerked her gaze up, for the first time realizing that he had come to search with no idea of what he sought exactly, and his persistence and thoughtfulness touched her deep. "It's a silver heart, with a rose etched on the front and an *A* engraved on the back."

He nodded, then walked on farther. Anna spirits sank with

final certainty that her treasured jewelry was gone for good as they worked their way through the forest and circled back to where the gelding stood ground-tied, patiently chewing on a mouthful of buffalo grass.

"I'm sorry, Anna," Storme offered. The dejected set of her shoulders and the tears swimming in her green stare ripped at his gut. "I can see it was special to you."

She nodded, looking off into the distance, where the sun barely peeked above the mountains now in its descent to end the day. "My mother gave it to me for my birthday . . . just a couple days before she died," Anna whispered, fairly tearing his soul apart with the tortured note in her voice.

"I understand your sadness." He reached up and touched his finger to the beaded leather around his neck. "My mother gave me this. She wanted me to always remember who I am, and where I come from. I would not wish to lose it."

"Does the arrow have a special meaning?"

"It's a symbol of my Apache name. Motega. It means New Arrow. My mother believed I was destined to walk a new direction someday."

"And now you walk the white man's ways?" Anna quietly asked, pleased and surprised that he seemed so willing to share such a personal part of himself.

He nodded. "It was what my father wished."

Anna cocked her head. "Is that what you wanted?"

"Yes." There was no hesitation in his response.

Anna could see the love for his parent shining in Storme's eyes, as well as an odd glint of guilt that puzzled her. "Do you have other family besides your brother?"

Storme shook his head. "What about you?"

"No."

The loneliness in her voice pulled hard at his heartstrings. Small and slender, she looked so fragile standing before him with her face flushed and somber, and so pretty with the evening sunlight shining in the reddish gold strands of her upswept hair.

Storme stepped back before he gave in to the desire to take her in his arms and kiss away the sorrow that pulled at her mouth. Not for the first time, he wondered where she came from and what had brought her to town. "If not family, then what is it that has brought you to Pleasant Grove?"

"I . . ." She blinked several times. "Well . . ." She glanced around nervously. "It's getting late. I better get back."

Storme inwardly frowned at her evasion, as well as the sudden wariness that sprang up and danced in her eyes. He wanted to ask what troubled her, but decided not to risk the trust he had gained with her so far. He smiled. "I guess you don't wish to climb that tree again?"

Her sigh of relief told him he had made the right decision. "You're right about that." She chuckled.

Storme grabbed up the gelding's reins. "Would you care to ride back, or walk?"

"You don't need to see me back. I'll be fine. Besides, you've done enough already." The warmth of her smile was a sweet reward and made his blood hum with pleasure.

"I'm meeting my brother in town, anyway." Even if it weren't the truth, Storme couldn't deny that he would have made up any excuse just to stay in her company a while longer.

She bit her lip and glanced toward his horse. He wondered if her hesitation stemmed from memories of their close proximity on the mount this morning. He certainly hadn't forgotten about it.

"I think I'd like to walk."

Storme nodded. *That's probably for the best.* He was having a hard enough time keeping his distance from her. He fell into step beside her, pleased that she didn't stay silent and happy to answer her inquisitiveness about his life with the Apache as they headed back toward town.

* * *

Storme crossed his arms over the saddle horn, eyeing the jagged-edged stain on Ben's white shirt and the crimson handprint that marked his scowling face. "I take it Miss Crowley wasn't happy with your apology, little brother?" He shook his head, laughing.

"Shut up," Ben snapped, then stomped down the steps from the depot platform.

"I tried to warn you." He certainly made no claim to understand women, but he wasn't foolish enough to break his word to one and not expect some fur to fly—no matter how brief the acquaintance. But Ben had been confident his excuse of the council meeting last night, then riding out with Storme and Winston to scout for signs of the rustler's trail that afternoon, would suffice.

Ben stopped. His brown eyes seared the distance between them. "Fine. You were right. But I just met this woman. How was I to know she'd get so upset? And don't get too smug, either. Samantha didn't get violent until I called her childish. Up till then, I had it all under control."

Storme arched his brow, surveying the damage to Ben's appearance. He couldn't picture this control his brother boasted, but Storme knew full well that a man's restraint could be a tenuous hold when sorely tested, especially if a woman was involved. And he knew anger wasn't the only emotion that could make it snap. His thoughts jumped to Anna, to the strong temptation he had had to hold her, to kiss her.

"I could use a drink after . . ." Ben grimaced, waving his hand in disgust toward the restaurant, "that." He unwound the reins from the hitching post and climbed into his saddle. "Feel like moving your little gloating act over to the saloon?"

Storme smiled. "Sure, you can buy me a drink, little brother."

Ben tugged on the reins, backing his mount away from the post. "At least I don't have to worry about some gal slugging me at Slim's place."

"Ben, wait!" A feminine voice called out, drawing their attention.

"Aw shit, this is all I need," Ben grumbled.

Puzzled, Storme glanced from his brother's disgruntled face to the small woman dressed in a black dress and full white apron. She pulled the door to the restaurant closed and hurried toward them, her bootheels clicking along the wooden walk. Twilight's shadows dimmed the shine on the woman's upswept blond hair, but not the anger Storme saw in her eyes.

The woman stopped at the edge of the platform and planted her hands on her slender hips. "I can't believe you're just going to ride away," she snapped.

"What do you want, Elise?" Ben ground out.

She arched one pale eyebrow. "Is that the same mannerless tone that earned you the coffee on your shirt?" There was a touch of laughter in her sarcasm. A bright smile formed on her lips when she turned to Storme. "Hello, I'm Elise Weatherford."

Somewhat startled at her switch, Storme sat back in his saddle, then reached up and tipped his hat. "Storme Warwick, ma'am."

Her eyes widened in surprise. "Ben's brother?"

Storme nodded.

She crossed her arms and glared over at Ben. "You didn't tell me he was home."

Storme pulled his eyebrows together, baffled at why this woman expected to be in Ben's confidence.

"I was going to. He just got back," Ben defended himself, then sat up straight and squared his shoulders. "I'm not in a real good mood at the moment, Elise. So, what do you want?"

His brother's harsh tone further piqued Storme's curiosity. The indignation that flushed the woman's cheeks gave him pause to wonder if Ben was going to fare any better in this argument. Storme crossed his arms and settled in to watch the heated exchange.

"I want you to come back inside," determined insistence deepened Miss Weatherford's low drawl, "and tell Mr. Chesterfield that what happened was all your fault and that *you* spilled coffee on yourself."

"Why would I tell that pack of lies?"

Elise huffed. "Because you and Samantha barely know each other, and this tiff is stupid!"

"Got any other opinions you'd like to toss out?" Ben growled, then rolled his eyes. "Never mind, I don't—"

"No," she raised one hand, palm out. "You asked, now you're going to listen. First, you could have sent word to her that you weren't coming last night. Second, you might consider using more of the brains the Good Lord gave you. You kept her outside talking yesterday and got her in trouble for being late to work. Now, you're about to get her fired." She wagged one finger. "She doesn't deserve that, and you know it."

Ben rubbed one hand over his chin, his stare hard and thoughtful.

Storme recognized the gesture, and knew his brother had conceded his mistake and was only taking a moment to let the resignation of doing right settle in over his anger.

"Besides," Elise continued, "you'll both be at the wedding Saturday night, and I'd prefer that you not be at each other's throats."

"Fine, I'll apologize and take the blame," Ben stated.

"Good." Elise nodded, then hitched one thumb over her shoulder. "You better hurry before it's too late."

Ben dismounted and stared across his saddle. "I'll be right back, Storme, then we'll go get that drink." He climbed the steps, pausing just long enough to accept the kiss Elise placed on his cheek, then walked on.

Storme narrowed his stare, curious why the woman didn't follow.

She cocked her head, and stared at him with bright hazel eyes. "Your brother's a good man."

Storme smiled. "I think so, too, ma'am."

"He's talked about you a great deal. I know he's glad you're home. Are you planning to stay long?"

Storme swallowed, slightly uncomfortable with the disadvantage she held. He shook his head. "Just long enough to take care of some business."

"That's too bad. He's missed having you at the ranch," she stated with a hint of reprimand.

He frowned. "My brother understands."

"Doesn't mean that things can't change, Mr. Warwick." Her voice held more conviction than reproach this time.

Storme wished she was right, but he knew better. He would always be a half-breed, and there would always be people who hated him for it. The shooting and the rustler's threatening note were just the latest proof of that. "Some things are better left as is, ma'am," he responded, not bothering to hide his slight irritation at her interference.

Hesitation danced in her eyes, then she smiled. "All right, I'll mind my own business."

Storme nodded his appreciation. "I *am* grateful for your obvious concern about my brother."

"We've gotten to be good friends over the last year." She shoved her arms behind, and rocked back on her heels. "And he's going to give me away at my wedding. It would be nice if you'd come, too. I know Ben would like to have you there."

Storme inwardly cringed at the thought of a social gathering and the complications a half-breed could bring to a party. "Thank you, but I don't wish to intrude."

"How can you intrude, when you have an invitation?"

He smiled at her tenacity, even as he shook his head.

She frowned slightly. "Well, I hope you'll reconsider. You're more than welcome to come." She glanced briefly over her shoulder. "I'm afraid I need to get back to work. It was nice to meet you."

"Pleasure meeting you, ma'am." Storme tipped his hat, offering no acceptance of her invitation.

She turned and walked away.

He sat, contemplating her insistence that he reconsider, and the genuineness in her tone when she had said he was welcome at her wedding.

'I know Ben would like to have you there.'

She seemed to know an awful lot about his brother, and that burned a hole in Storme's gut. He realized that he didn't care for feeling like a stranger around his own family.

Chapter Five

"One job saved." Ben grinned, descending the steps two at a time.

Storme noted the handprint on his face had faded to near invisible, but the coffee still dampened a dark spot near his shirt pocket. "And was Miss Crowley grateful?"

Ben nodded, lifting one eyebrow in a cocky arch. "Even apologized for slapping me." He gathered up the reins and climbed into his saddle. "Now, let's go get that drink."

Storme nudged his horse into a walk alongside his brother. They rode by the train sitting on the tracks in front of the depot and passed the restaurant where several folks lingered out front, then turned the corner onto Main Street. The half-moon inched its way above the mountain peaks and glowed bright against the velvet sky, shrouding the town in its soft light. Faint sounds of raucous laughter mingled with the tinny piano music that drifted from the saloons at the far end of town. A handful of people stood outside the two-story hotel—another addition like the boardinghouse, the depot, and restaurant, and three new saloons built since Storme had left. He expected the changes, though. Ben had written about them . . . but he hadn't mentioned a word about his friendship with Elise Weatherford.

"Tell me about Miss Weatherford."

Ben tipped his hat brim up slightly and furrowed his brow. "Not much to tell, really. I met her about a year ago when she came to work at the restaurant. We got to be friends, and she asked if I could help her get a divorce from a husband who'd abandoned her. She hadn't been working here too long and didn't have much money." He shook his head, his mouth firming in a thin line. "I just wanted to give her what she needed, but damn stubborn woman insisted it had to be a loan. Anyway, I went with her to talk to the circuit judge when he came through town, then went to Santa Fe to collect the final papers for her."

Storme wasn't surprised at Ben's generosity. His brother had a kind heart and had always helped folks out. He was glad to see that the hate and trouble he had brought to their lives when he moved to Pleasant Grove hadn't changed that in Ben over the years. "Why didn't you ever mention her in your letters?"

"I thought I did."

"No."

"Hmm." He scrunched his face in thought. "Well, we made sure to keep everything real quiet because she was wanting to make a new start here." He shrugged an offhand apology. "I guess I was just being too silent." The corners of his mouth drew up in a smile. "Elise is real nice, though . . . when she's not yelling at me."

Storme narrowed his stare at the gleam of fondness that rose in his brother's eyes. The look burned a little hotter than just friendship, he thought. Since Elise was marrying someone else in a couple of days, he sure hoped he was seeing wrong. "She seems like a nice woman. A little headstrong, maybe."

"Yeah, she can be." Ben chuckled. "I noticed that Elise

stayed behind when I went back inside. What did you two talk about?''

Storme braced one hand on his thigh. ''She invited me to her wedding. Said you'd like me to be there, because you're giving her away.''

Ben nodded. ''Elise doesn't have any family out here, and she's not close with her relatives back East. I'm honored she asked me. And I would like for you to be there.''

Storme's gut tightened. The music and laughter grew louder as they passed the mercantile and various other businesses that lined either side of the street, and rode nearer to the end of town. He wasn't much for parties. He had attended enough social functions to know he never felt comfortable going to them, and more often than not, his presence caused a definite air of tension to hover over the festivities. ''The other guests may not be as welcoming.''

Ben waved a dismissive hand. ''It's just going to be a small affair out at her fiancé's farm. She's marrying into a good family. The Sandersons are real nice folks. I've gotten to be friends with them since they moved here a few months back, and I know they'd like to meet you. Most of the guests that'll be there are friends of mine, too. No one's going to mind if you come.''

Storme paused, finding no easy way to decline and not sure that he even wanted to now. He knew his brother hadn't spoken lightly about wanting him there, and he wouldn't mind meeting Ben's friends and knowing about his life.

A mischievous grin lifted the corners of Ben's mouth. ''Elise invited Miss Alexander and the other girls from the boarding-house. There'll be plenty of single ladies to dance with.''

Storme's heart pounded faster. He wasn't the least interested in the other single ladies, but he certainly wouldn't mind seeing Anna again. Dancing with her was another matter, though. He was already having enough trouble keeping her off his mind without torturing himself further by holding her in his arms. "All right, I'll go."

"Thanks, Storme."

The appreciation in his brother's stare sent warm gratification shooting through his chest. Anna's pretty face floated across his mind, accelerating his pulse and making him doubly glad he had agreed to attend. Maybe he *would* dance with her—just once.

They reined their mounts to a stop outside the Desert Trail Saloon. Smoke-filled light spilled out around the swinging half doors, along with loud conversations and the drifting sounds of a piano player pounding out a tune from the far back of the building. Several men traversed the walkways in front of the saloons, and a dense array of horses lined the hitching posts along the road. Storme dismounted and wrapped his reins around the post, then stepped up to the walkway behind Ben and followed him through the swinging doors.

He noted the looks his presence garnered from several of the men standing at the long mahogany bar and gathered around the tables that dotted the opposite side of the narrow room. Storme recognized only two ranchers among the group. The men met his stare but offered no greeting, though they did wave to Ben. A few patrons shot him looks of annoyance, others shrugged their disinterest after a moment and turned back to their liquor and card games, or the brightly dressed saloon girls, their ruffles and feathers exposing more flesh than they covered. But there were a couple of men who continued to glare the savage-labeling hatred he saw far too often in folks. It was these men that Storme kept in his line of sight as he walked over to the bar and stood beside his brother.

The bald-headed barkeep wiped a damp glass with a scrap of toweling as he made his way to their end. He narrowed his eyes and nodded downward. "What happened to you, Ben?"

Ben glanced at his shirt, a slight scowl pulling at his jaw. "Tangled with a cup of coffee and lost. Decided I better stick to liquor." He braced one elbow against the countertop. "I'd like you to meet my brother, Storme." He nodded toward the barkeep. "This is Slim Hardaway. He owns the place."

The man set the glass down, tossed the towel over his shoulder, and stuck his hand out. "Good to meetcha." He smiled wide enough to show several teeth missing. Thin, blue veins ran in broken lines through the ruddy complexion of his cheeks and across his bulbous nose.

"Likewise." Storme nodded and shook the man's hand, grateful for the affable greeting. He knew from experience that not many saloon owners welcomed a half-breed into their establishments, regardless of whose company he was in.

"What can I getcha, boys?" Slim inquired, nodding toward the ornate cherry backbar that boasted a broad, etched mirror and narrow shelves lined with a variety of liquor bottles.

"Whiskey will work," Ben answered. Pulling his wallet from his pants pocket, he fished out several bills. "A bottle of your best."

Slim reached for a bottle of the rich amber brew and two clean glasses, then placed them on the counter. "You boys enjoy." He scooped up the bills Ben laid out, then headed down to other end of the bar, where a cowboy hollered out above the noise for another round of gut warmer.

"Come on," Ben said, grabbing up the bottle and both glasses. "Elise's fiancé is sitting over there." He pointed toward two men sitting at a table close to the wall and beneath a canvas painting of a nude woman lounged on a red-velvet settee. The broad-shouldered, blond man lifted his drink at Ben's acknowledgment. "You might as well meet him, since you're coming to the wedding."

"Might as well." Storme followed his brother through the weaving path of tables, not bothering to meet anyone's eye directly but not missing the looks shot his way.

"Evenin', Ben. Pull up a seat," the blond man offered, then nudged the dark-headed man next to him with his elbow, and smirked. "Especially if you're willing to share that bottle of sheepherder's delight."

"I think that can be arranged." Ben grinned, setting the bottle and glasses down. "This is my brother, Storme." He motioned toward the blond man. "This is Wallace Sanderson, and this is his cousin, Blaine."

Storme exchanged greetings with the men. Wallace's blue gaze held no sign of contempt at drinking with a half-breed, but Storme didn't see quite the same welcome in the other man's dark green stare, though Blaine Sanderson did reach across the table and shake his hand.

"Just saw your bride-to-be," Ben said as he sat down and pulled the cork from the whiskey bottle. He poured drinks all around.

Storme removed his hat and sat in the empty chair near the wall, where he could keep an eye on the room and anyone who thought to give him trouble.

"How is my sweet thing?" Wallace took a long swallow of his drink, a look of savored pleasure spreading across his face.

Storme wondered if it was the savoring of fine whiskey or the woman that put it there.

"Your *'sweet thing'* just took a verbal chunk out of my ass." Ben grimaced.

Storme sipped at his whiskey, hiding his smile at the memory of the encounter.

Wallace chortled, drawing the brief attention of several patrons around them. "Made her mad, did ya?"

"Let's just say, I don't envy you being saddled with that little spitfire's temper."

"Amen to that," Blaine Sanderson said, lifting his glass in a mocking toast, his jesting grin aimed at his cousin. "I'd rather prod a locoed steer than deal with that woman's anger."

Wallace's smile grew wider. "She's as sweet as apple pie with me."

"Yeah, well, just wait until a few flies walk all over that

apple pie and see what happens," Ben warned with only a half-joking note in his tone.

Wallace shook his head, staring first at Ben, then his cousin. "Treat a woman right, and you don't have to worry about flies ruining the good stuff." He turned to Storme. "Did she give you any trouble?"

"No." He chuckled lightly. "But she was a little . . . disappointed when I didn't accept her invite to your wedding."

Wallace arched his brow. "Elise invited you, huh? Well, she wouldn't have done it if she didn't mean it. I hope you'll reconsider and come."

To his surprise, Storme heard only sincerity in the man's voice. "Thank you. And I have reconsidered."

"I'm glad. And I know Elise will be, too." Wallace took a sip of his drink, then cast a teasing smirk toward Ben. "For some reason that I still can't fathom, she considers this scalawag brother of yours like family."

Scalawag? Storme frowned, as much at the unflattering reference as at Ben's hearty laugh and shrug of acceptance of the title. Again, the realization of how little he knew about his brother's life settled like a sharp thorn in Storme's gut.

"Hope you'll keep that family part in mind, Ben," Blaine grated, his square jaw tightening beneath a day's worth of black stubble. "When we lose the farm and need someplace to go."

Ben's eyebrows pulled together, forming a solid brown line. "What are you talking about?"

Wallace shot his cousin a glaring look. "I told you we could handle our own affairs," he snapped.

"What's this about?" Ben demanded, leaning forward to rest his arms on the table.

Wallace shook his head in disgust. "It's just Dodding again."

Storme sat back in his chair and sipped his drink, his curiosity more than a little piqued at the mention of the rancher.

"Him and some of his wranglers tried to stop us from herding our sheep over to the river today,'' Wallace explained. ''Killed about a hundred head just this side of Caney Trail.''

Storme knew most ranchers felt that sheep tore up the ground, ruining it for future grazing, and were highly opposed to the numerous herds moving in throughout the West, more often than not resorting to gunfire to try to drive them out.

''That bastard's got his nerve.'' Ben shook his head and downed the whiskey, then refilled his glass. ''I thought Elise told me you were buying that section of land that butts next to yours, so you wouldn't have any problem gettin' to water.''

''Haven't saved up enough money.'' Wallace grunted. ''Doesn't matter though, someone beat me to the claim.''

''A man name of Robert Blanchard.'' Blaine sneered. ''Ever heard of him?''

Ben sat in silent contemplation for several long seconds, then shook his head.

Storme rolled the name around in his mind, finding it familiar, but unable to place a face.

''What are you gonna do now, Wallace?'' Ben asked.

The man shrugged. ''Find another section to buy. Pray that water hole on my place doesn't dry up completely before I can get a well dug. See if I can cut some sort of deal with this Blanchard fella and cross his land. Of course, none of it'll matter if Dodding kills much more of my herd.'' Wallace tilted his head back and downed the last measure of whiskey in his glass.

''I could give you a loan—''

''No.'' Wallace slammed the glass on the table and shot his cousin a warning look that said to keep his mouth shut. ''We'll be just fine. Besides, you've got your own troubles. I hear the rustlers hit you again.''

Ben nodded, his jaw pulling taut. ''It just keeps getting worse. That's why Storme came back to help out.''

The conversation turned to the problems at the Lazy W. Storme listened, offering an opinion when solicited, but for the most part just sipped his whiskey and kept his eye on the room. He shifted his gaze to the table beside them where five men sat playing poker, and arched his brow at the high-stakes betting as the play rounded the table and each man upped the large pot by another twenty dollars.

One shaggy-haired wrangler dressed in dusty denims and a sweat-stained blue shirt sat at an angle that Storme could see his cards. Three fives, a nine, and a queen. Storme thought the wrangler was taking an expensive chance on that hand, and had his suspicion confirmed seconds later when a black-suited man sitting across the table laid down four kings. Storme shrugged as the wrangler's money was whisked away, and started to turn his attention elsewhere . . . until the wrangler pulled a thin chain from his shirt pocket, and dangled the silver heart from his grimy hand.

Disbelief pumped through Storme's veins with the force of metal pounded against an anvil. He propelled himself from the chair, anger roaring in his ears as he crossed the short distance.

"Where you going?"

Storme ignored Ben's stupefied inquiry, his focus on the dusty man who tossed the necklace toward the center of the table for his next bet. Storme snatched the delicate jewelry before it had a chance to hit the wood.

"What the hell you doing?" The wrangler rose, meeting Storme at eye level, angry challenge burning in his blurry, red-rimmed stare.

A heavy quiet slowly roamed throughout the room.

"Where did you get this?" Storme held his palm out, the rose-etched heart that Anna had described lying faceup. He flipped it over, glancing at the engraved A on the back.

"If it's any of your business, I found it, Injun. Now give it back," he growled the last, reaching his hand out.

Storme cupped his fingers around the necklace and lowered his arm to his side. "I know who lost it."

The man hesitated, then straightened just a little taller. The hatred in his look turned more degrading as he raked his stare over Storme. "And I'm supposed to take *your* word for that?"

No. Storme was more than willing to offer his fist, as well. He flexed the fingers on his right hand. "I'll give you a hundred dollars for it."

The cowboy smiled, a greedy gleam flaring in his expression. "Make it three," he countered in a tone that said he was ready to bargain down just a bit.

Storme wasn't in the mood for his game. "Done." He stuck the necklace in his pocket, pulled several bills from his wallet, and handed them to the gawking cowboy. He offered a smile to the men around the table he was sure would wind up with his money before the night ended, then walked away.

"What was that about?" Ben demanded. "Whose necklace is that?"

"I'll explain later," Storme answered, grabbing his hat off the corner of the table and settling it on his head. "It was good to meet you Wallace. Blaine." He glanced down at his brother. "See you back at the house."

The low flame flickered beneath the clear lantern globe, dimly lighting the room. A cool breeze fluttered the white-lace curtains drawn back on either side of the window. Anna sighed and pushed herself up off the bed, restless in spite of the solitude she had coveted when she declared a headache and begged off from joining the others for tea. In truth, it was her heart that ached, with despairing certainty that her necklace was gone for good. She choked back the sadness that had fueled her tears earlier, and threatened to do so again.

Samantha had been kind, offering her sincere commiseration of the loss before she had gone downstairs to join the others. The show of friendship had brought a smile to Anna's lips more than once over the last hour, as had thoughts of Storme's generous efforts to help her find her pendant. But each time, the joy had been short-lived, engulfed by the grief that she had nothing left of her past, save the memories.

She yanked open the wardrobe door, pulling her cotton nightgown off the shelf. A short, guttural whistling sounded from outside the window. Anna jerked up straight and froze. Her skin grew clammy as the odd call came again.

What the heck is that?

She spun around, dropping the gown to the floor, then ran to the window. Her eyes rounded in shock; her heart missed its next beat. Standing on the same branch level with the wooden sill, Storme's tall, masculine frame blocked the thick trunk that he leaned against.

"What are you doing out there?"

He smiled, even white teeth shining bright against the night. "I brought you something."

Anna cocked her head, her brow furrowing in curiosity. *What on earth could he have brought me?*

No hat graced his head. The long, straight strands of his hair fell in a thick, onyx blanket and disappeared behind the span of his shoulder. Anna raked her gaze over his moonlit face, down the bronze column of his corded neck, along the line of his outstretched arm . . .

She gasped, her heart pounding with excitement at the sight of the necklace looped around his hand and dangling down. "You found it!" She covered her mouth, realizing how loud she had exclaimed her delight.

He nodded, his grin widening. "The clasp was bent, no doubt the reason you lost it. But I fixed it for you."

Tears of happiness welled in her eyes. "Thank you for finding it, and fixing it," she said in quieter voice, but holding none of her gratitude back.

"You are most welcome, Anna."

His steady gaze was as mesmerizingly soft as a caress, and filled her with an eager affection that confused her as much as it excited. "That was nice of you to go back and look again. But where did you find it? How did we overlook it before?"

He frowned, then reached his free hand up, grabbed the branch above, and took a step away from the trunk. "I saved it from being wagered in a poker game down at the saloon."

Anna wasn't sure whether to laugh, or cry, at the irony that her last possession should have found its way to the same fate that had taken everything else away from her. Poker. "How did it get there?" Her heart lurched as Storme took another step along the branch, and she recalled the groaned threat the limb had sent out the night before. "Be careful."

He nodded his assurance, a sparkle of pleasure at her concern flickering in his moonlit brown eyes. "The man said he found it. And I got it back from him."

"Did you win it back?" The idea that Storme was a gambling man tightened like a cold fist in her gut.

"No, I don't gamble with things that matter. I paid him."

Relief ran swift through her veins, and Anna had a moment's pause to wonder why Storme's gambling habits mattered so much to her. But she didn't have to question his thoughtfulness, or the special place his kind deed found in her heart. She had to pay back him, though. "How much?" Anna chewed at her bottom lip, hoping it wasn't much. She had fled Missouri with nothing more than the clothes on her back and had spent part of the money she had earned so far from her job on necessary items to replenish her wardrobe, leaving her with only ten dollars and twenty-five cents to her name at the moment.

"It doesn't matter." He made his way slowly along the branch.

"Yes it does, I want to repay you." She braced her hands against the window sill as he moved closer, her breath lodging with fear for his safety.

"I don't want your money, Anna."

She sighed at the stubborn lift of his brow. "All right, then we'll consider it the rest of the debt you keep saying you owe."

He shook his head. "This"—he held the necklace up, the silver heart swaying, glistening in the moonlight—"has nothing to do with the debt." He eased his way closer.

Anna waited every tense second for the branch to groan or crack, thankful that it didn't.

"I'm glad to do this for you. I know how much you wanted it back."

His words, as much as the tenderness in his voice, sent a flood of heat rushing into her cheeks. "Why didn't you come to the front door?"

"I gave you my word that I wouldn't say anything about you being late. I didn't want you to have to explain how your necklace got lost. But I wanted you to have it back, so when I saw the light burning in your room, I climbed up."

A man of his word. Anna's regard for Storme rose another notch, as did her estimation that she could truly trust him. She cocked her head as curiosity rifled through her. "How did you know it was me inside, and not Samantha?"

"I just had a gut feeling."

Anna arched her brow at his confidence. "What would you have done if it was Samantha?"

He shrugged. "Climbed back down." He playfully lifted one black eyebrow. "Or waited for you to come upstairs."

She chuckled. "Given your stubbornness, I bet you *would* have waited."

"I bet you're right." He smiled, and winked, sending an unexpected delight shivering through her limbs.

She shook her head and blew out a soft breath. He was definitely a dangerous distraction to her senses.

He stood just a few feet away now, and stretched his arm out, holding the thin chain between two fingers. She leaned farther out the window, reaching her hand toward his, and circling her fingers with welcomed relief around the metal heart, still warm from Storme's touch. He released the chain, and the thin links fell, pooling into the small circled opening of her fist.

"I really appreciate all the tr—"

"Who are you talking to, my dear?"

Anna gasped, her eyes widening at Mrs. Harrington's stern inquiry that came from behind. She saw her own astonishment mirrored in the stunned tableau on Storme's face, and in disbelief saw him move closer toward the window.

Anna spun around, throwing her arms out wide to block as much of the opening with her body as she could. The branch cracked, then the sudden loud cacophony of rustling leaves and snapping twigs filled the night, followed by the muffled thunk of something heavy hitting the ground. Anna bit her lip.

Mrs. Harrington's face tightened, deepening the lines on her aged face. She tapped one hand against the stock of the long-barreled rifle that rested in the crook of her arm.

Anna's heart plummeted with concern for Storme's safety, even as panic for her own precarious situation at the moment made her insides shake.

Good heavens! She was in trouble now.

Chapter Six

"Cats," Anna blurted, hating the way her voice squeaked with guilt. She lowered her arms.

Mrs. Harrington's apple green stare narrowed behind the round lenses of her gold-wire spectacles. "You were talking to cats?"

"Yes, ma'am." Anna glanced over her shoulder at the emptiness where Storme had stood. She strained to hear a movement from below—something, anything that would let her know he wasn't hurt. All she heard was silence. "Two of them. Toms, I think. They chased poor Sebastian right up the tree, and I was trying to shoo them away."

Several worried gasps issued from the girls gathered in the doorway behind the housemother.

"Poor kitty," Elise stated with compassionate concern.

"Frightened to death, no doubt," Patricia added, poking her red head farther into the room.

"Little bugger will probably hide out for a week now," Katie sympathized in her thick British accent.

"Cocky mongrel has to learn to fend for himself sometime."
Silence fell at Samantha's callous comment. "What?" The girl
waved her hands about, glancing around at the piercing stares
turned her way. "Surely you can't expect me to feel sorry for
the runt, not after he attacked me this morning."

"Really, Miss Crowley." Mrs. Harrington's chubby cheeks
pinched into round balls that reminded Anna of rising bread
dough. Raising one finger, the matron shoved her glasses higher
up the bridge of her nose, then rested her hand back over the
butt of the rifle. "Sebastian was only playing. Besides, the
scratches are minor, and you have another pair of hose. I think
you've carried on about it enough for one day."

Twitters and chuckles of agreement filled the air.

Samantha's cheeks reddened. "Fine. I'll not say another
word." Indignation showed in her raised chin. She gathered
her skirt and whirled away, her booted footsteps pounding with
angry force along the short hallway, then down the stairs.

Mrs. Harrington shook her head and rolled her eyes. "Such
theatrics. That girl should be acting on a stage, instead of
waiting tables."

And I should be singing on that same stage, Anna thought,
*instead of facing the termination of my job and worrying about
a man possibly sprawled unconscious on the lawn below.* She
prayed Storme wasn't hurt, but the fall had sounded quite nasty,
and she couldn't help but fear the worst.

"So, where's Sebastian now?" Mrs. Harrington queried,
snapping Anna's attention as the housemother made her way
across the room. "Is the poor thing still in the tree?"

"N . . . no." Anna squared her shoulders and moved forward
to block the woman's progress to the window. "He ran back
down, and that noise you heard was the toms chasing after
him."

More murmured condolences and concerns issued from the
girls.

Mrs. Harrington paused, frowning as she cocked her head

to one side. "Toms? Are you sure? That was a mighty big ruckus."

Anna quickly nodded, then shoved her shaking hands into her skirt pockets, depositing the necklace as she did.

Mrs. Harrington looked over her shoulder, and addressed the girls gathered at the door. "I wish a moment alone with Miss Alexander." The elder woman's tone brooked no argument. "You girls may go down and finish having tea. And close the door."

Curiosity claimed the girls' expressions as they backed away. Elise's confused but sympathetic look was the last thing Anna saw before the door firmly closed. Her nerves rattled like bits of ice pelting a winter ground, as much for herself as for Storme.

"Go on," Mrs. Harrington waved one hand toward the window. "Go make sure your friend didn't hurt himself."

Anna didn't wait for a second prompting, didn't even care at the moment that the housemother had seen through her lies, but turned and rushed back to the window. She scanned the moonlit yard below, her heart stopping when she couldn't find him, then galloping at breakneck speed when Storme stepped into her range of sight.

"Are you all right?"

He looked up, no smile warming his lips this time. "Yes."

A line of blood trailed down his left cheek, but Anna thankfully saw no other signs of injury. The odd desire to reach out and pluck the leafy twig snagged in his hair caught her by surprise, as did Mrs. Harrington's sudden appearance at her side. To Anna's relief, the elder woman no longer sported the rifle but had propped it against the wall.

"Since you're not hurt, young man," Mrs. Harrington called down, "go home."

"Yes, ma'am." In contradiction to his affirmation, Storme made no move to leave. "But first, I would offer my apology for this . . . unfortunate incident. This is not Miss Alexander's fault."

"Your apology is noted," Mrs. Harrington stated in a harsh tone. "And I will deal with Miss Alexander about this. If you wish to call here again, make sure you use the front door." She straightened, pulling Anna back by the shoulder, then in one swift move reached up and firmly tugged the window down into place.

Mrs. Harrington turned and planted her hands on her ample hips. The stance pulled her gray bodice taut across her large bosom, straining a gap between two of the pearl buttons that lined the front.

Anna dug her short nails into her palms, bracing herself for the certain reprimand, and the firing. She could see it coming in Mrs. Harrington's angered eyes, in her shaking head, and the heavy sigh she released . . . and Anna didn't blame the woman. Rules were rules, after all. She had been told that right up front, and had made sure to memorize all twenty so she didn't break any of them.

Rule number one: No missing curfew.

Anna frowned. Failure number one.

Rule number four: No men allowed in the bedrooms.

Anna bit at her bottom lip, well imagining that in Mrs. Harrington's estimation a tree visit would still be considered a serious breach of that rule.

"That was some mighty quick thinking about the cats." Mrs. Harrington's voice held a hint of amusement that Anna noted didn't reach the rest of her tight expression. "I'm also quite disappointed in you."

The words stung. Despite the barrage of rules, Anna admired and appreciated Mrs. Harrington's kindness in hiring her, and was saddened that the housemother now had a reason to question that judgment. "I'm sorry."

"I am, too." Mrs. Harrington peered over the top of her spectacles. "But I've been chaperoning girls a long time, and I do understand the cravings of a young heart."

Anna stiffened. *Cravings?* She didn't crave Storme Warwick.

She willed away the defiant desire that reared up to suggest just the opposite. She liked him, yes. He was a nice man, and she would be eternally grateful that he had returned her necklace. Nothing more. "I promise you, I have no such designs on Mr. Warwick, ma'am. And he spoke the truth, I didn't invite him here."

Mrs. Harrington cocked her head and eyed her doubtfully. "That may be, Anna, but he had *some* reason for climbing that tree, whether you encouraged it or not. And it doesn't change the fact that you've placed us both in a bad spot."

Anna nodded, swallowing.

Mrs. Harrington tapped one finger against her chin, and let the silence drift heavy until Anna thought she would choke from the waiting. She came very close to blurting out the truth about missing curfew and losing her necklace, just to get the inevitable over with it.

"But, you are a good worker." The housemother's voice was calm and thoughtful. "And I'm really not inclined to spend time searching for another maid when I've only just found you."

A guilty pang that she wasn't planning to stay in town all that long nipped at Anna's conscience, but couldn't overshadow the hope that swelled in her chest. "You're . . . you're not firing me?"

"No." A slow smile curved the housemother's mouth.

Anna released a heavy sigh. Relief raced through her like a swollen river. The warm rush comforted her concerns about where she would go, and how she would get *anywhere* without enough money for train fare.

"I like you, Anna. You remind me a lot of myself years ago."

"I do?" she whispered in startled wonder, even more puzzled when Mrs. Harrington stared toward the window, a soft gleam briefly clouding her gaze.

The older woman nodded, then graveness replaced the

relaxed lines of her round, aging face. "Since the girls believe your story about Sebastian, I think we'll leave it at that. But"— she raised one finger, wagging it slightly—"I am warning you that I will only let this sort of indiscretion pass once."

Anna quickly nodded her understanding. "Thank you, Mrs. Harrington. I appreciate this, and I promise I won't let you down."

"I'm sure you won't." Mrs. Harrington offered a warm smile, then retrieved the rifle and headed toward the door.

"How did you know he was out there?" Anna asked, unable to stop herself from voicing the curiosity.

Mrs. Harrington paused and looked back, grinning wide. "Now, wouldn't that be silly of me to tell you girls my secrets?" A crafty sparkle shimmered in her light green stare as she peered over her spectacles. "Just know that I see everything."

Anna chuckled, but given all that she was hiding, seriously filed away the information for future reference.

Storme stood on the front porch, enjoying the cool breeze that brushed against his face, and raised the cup of coffee to his mouth, sipping the hot brew. With a reverence that sprang from his love for the land, he watched the dawn greet the horizon with a golden yawn over the distant hills that rimmed the grass-covered valley. From every corner as far as the eye could see, the Lazy W basked in the brilliant glory of the new day, and a warm contentment slowly eased its way through him.

He had seen this sight at least a thousand times, dreamed of it thousands more since he had been gone; but he never tired of it. A shiver raced up his spine and trembled across his shoulders. He released a deep sigh, knowing it wouldn't be easy when the time came to leave again.

Booted footsteps sounded from the foyer behind, then the

front door Storme had left open when he came outside was slammed shut.

"All right, I'm ready," Ben grated in a voice laced with the thick, after-coated sound of too much alcohol. Dark circles filled the skin beneath his eyes; his sandy hair stuck out in spiky points beneath his hat, and the blue shirt he had thrown on looked as though a good washing and ironing wouldn't be amiss.

Storme arched his brow at the declared readiness and stared at his brother's narrowed, red-rimmed eyes, recalling how he had staggered in after midnight, more than a little drunk and sloppily grinning his satisfaction in losing two hundred dollars to Wallace at poker. "You look like you could use some coffee."

Ben swallowed hard, his Adam's apple sliding slowly along his throat. "Had some already." He squinted against the glare of the morning light and tugged his hat brim down lower.

"Maybe you need something a little stronger," Storme teasingly suggested.

Ben closed one eye and arched his eyebrow high above the one he left opened. "Funny. And those two bottles were for a good cause."

"No argument here, little brother. You did a good thing."

Ben shrugged away any importance to his kindness, then a gleam of remembrance sprang into his stare. "What about you? You gonna tell me about that necklace, and why you ran out of the saloon like your pants were on fire."

Storme frowned. "I don't recall running."

"Wallace's choice of words." A grin pulled at his mouth. "But I concur."

Irritation hardened Storme's muscles, more at his unexplained foolish hurry to return Anna's necklace than his brother's humor at the situation. He had expected the latter. He didn't understand the driving force of the former. But he sure as hell knew that he had gotten Anna into trouble! He worried that she wasn't going to forgive him, either, especially if she lost her job, or embarrassing gossip spread around town.

Ben cocked his head to one side and peered harder. "How'd you get that scratch on your face?"

Storme groaned. "I'll tell you on the ride out." He turned away and headed down the steps, then over to where he had left the two saddled mounts earlier.

They rode past the barn, its red boards washed pale in the burgeoning sunlight. A wrangler waved his greeting from atop the roof, then went back to repairing loose boards. Several horses neighed from the corrals, as two more cowhands prepared to turn them out to pasture to graze. Farther down the road, Storme rode beside his brother as they crossed under the high iron arch, then kept the horses to an easy pace over the dew-soaked buffalo grass that coated the open range.

With reluctant resignation, Storme explained about Anna's lost necklace, briefly mentioning that he had helped her search the mountain last evening, then the harder part of how he had returned it later and gotten caught.

"Lord, what were you thinking?" Ben shook his head in disbelief. "Why didn't you just go to the damn front door if you wanted to call on Miss Alexander?"

"Because I wasn't *calling* on her," Storme defended. "I just wanted to return the necklace. I didn't want to start any talk."

Ben stared incredulous. "Brother, you started 'talk' when you snatched that necklace from the poker game. And getting caught by stodgy Mrs. Harrington is worse than being sentenced by a hanging judge."

"You know this from experience?" Storme challenged in a tight voice.

"Hell no, only hearsay." Ben chuckled, then grimaced and pressed a hand to his temple, issuing a groan. "Besides," he continued when the pain obviously subsided, "I've got more brains than to go climbing into a lady's window at night."

"I wasn't climbing into Anna's window, dammit!"

"Climbing. Visiting. Returning a necklace." Ben shrugged. "Call it what you want. I doubt Mrs. Harrington will stand on too much ceremony about details. Let's hope she doesn't gather the Garden Society ladies together and set up a tar and feathering for you."

Though the words were spoken in jest, Storme still shuddered at the thought. It didn't take much to incite a crowd to a vicious frenzy sometimes, especially if the anger was directed at a half-breed. Get a group of riled-up women together and the outcome could be a virtual shredding of a man's dignity, and various other physical parts.

But at least Anna had her necklace back. A glow of satisfaction warmed his blood, then quickly cooled as he worried about the consequences of his rash hurry to return it. The older woman had looked mad enough to spit bullets with the same explosive force as that Buffalo rifle. Storme had been more than willing to take the brunt of Mrs. Harrington's wrath, especially since the blame for this whole fiasco lay at his feet. When she smartly dismissed him and slammed the window closed, though, he had little choice, save breaking the front door down, except to head home. But he fully intended to return to the boardinghouse today—by way of the front door—and find out what had happened. "I just hope Anna didn't get fired."

"What if she did?"

Storme sighed and shook his head. He didn't know what he would do yet, but he would make sure she was taken care of somehow.

Ben grinned mischievously. "Be careful, Storme, between the life-debt and this, you get in any deeper you may end up having to marry Miss Alexander to set things straight."

Storme stared ahead, deeply bothered that the idea didn't disturb him as much as he thought it should. He wasn't interested in marriage—with any woman. And he had had just about enough of his brother's teasing for the moment.

"Well, at least I only have trees slapping me in the face." Storme tightened his hold on the reins and kicked his horse into a run, wishing he could leave Anna's haunting image behind along with his brother's laughter.

Winston Goff shifted the wad of tobacco in his tanned, freckled cheek. "Found him just after dawn. Swingin' from a rope 'bout a mile upstream."

"Hung?" Ben's incredulous tone rose above the dissonant cattle cries that filled the valley and drifted into the cloud-dotted sky.

Storme glanced down at the blanket-covered figure that had been laid out on the ground at one end of the wranglers' camp.

"Yup." The assistant foreman shifted his lanky frame, placing one booted foot out an angle, then hooked his thumbs in the waistband of his denims. "But it's the bullet to his head what killed the stranger, not the rope. I had Cale and Garcia comb the area, but they couldn't find a track one."

Storme's gut knotted into a hard ball. A murdered man on their property. He didn't like the looks of that.

Winston reached down with one hand and grabbed the edge of the blanket, lifting it from the man's face.

"Sonofabitch," Ben said in harsh surprise.

Storme's heart hammered as he stared at the dusty wrangler that had tried to bet Anna's necklace.

"You know him?" Curiosity blazed in Winston's blue stare.

"Just the face," Ben responded. "Saw him in the saloon last night."

"Throwing away money in a poker game like it was water." Storme found it more than a little disturbing, and too coincidental, that the same man he had encountered last night now lay dead at his feet.

Winston's red eyebrows pulled together in a straight line. "Maybe you two can figure out this note I found on him, then."

"What note?" Storme tensed. He thought about the note the rustlers had left after their last run on the cattle and glanced over, seeing the same memory burning in his brother's eyes.

Winston reached into the deceased man's shirt pocket and pulled out a slip of paper. "Doesn't make much sense," he said. "Something about a necklace."

A spurt of alarm kicked Storme's pulse into high speed. He grabbed the paper from Winston's hand.

*'I wasn't ready for the pretty lady
to get her necklace back yet, Injun.'*

Storme jerked back from the shock. Anger roared in his ears as he stared at the familiar handwriting . . . and an increased fear stomped its way into his soul.

Dammit! How much else does this bastard know about Anna?

The possibility that he had been followed to the boarding-house clogged his throat with worry. Anna could be in more danger than he anticipated. The shooter had come back to cover his tracks . . . and must have found the necklace, Storme thought. The handwriting and the knowledge of Anna's pendant left no doubt in his mind now that the incident on the mountain *was* connected to the rustlers, and this revenge. He glanced down at the dead man, finding nothing familiar about his face. Storme knew he had to be riding with the rustlers, though. How else could he have gotten his hands on the necklace?

"What's the note say?" Ben queried with a hint of impatience.

Storme handed it over as his thoughts rolled one over the other. *Who's behind this vengeance . . . and why?* He also worried just how far these rustlers were willing to go to carry out this grudge.

Ben's face pulled taut with surprised disbelief, then dawning concern. "Shit," he ground out, shaking his head. "It's the same handwriting, and this is about Miss Alexander's necklace, isn't it?''

Storme nodded his agreement with both points, taking the paper back and stuffing it in his front pants pocket.

''Same handwritin' as what? And who's Miss Alexander?'' Winston spit a stream of tobacco juice into the grass, then crossed his arms over his chest. The look in his narrowed stare demanded answers.

Storme admired Winston's backbone in asking right up front. He also knew the time for holding anything back was gone. Quickly, he explained about the threatening note Ben had found, about Anna warning him of the shooter's intent, and his certainty now that it *was* one of the rustlers. Then he explained what had happened at the saloon.

''Well.'' Winston straightened. He reached up and adjusted his hat back farther on his head. His short red hair gleamed a darker shade of orange in the morning sunlight. ''These rustlers are gettin' mighty cocky. I don't cotton much to threats of any sort, especially against the men I work for. I certainly don't like them involvin' an innocent woman. I best go tell the boys to get ready to dig in for war.''

''He's a good man. I'm glad I decided to keep him on,'' Ben commented after Winston had walked away.

Storme nodded. He appreciated the foreman's devotion, and was beginning to understand why Ben had said more than once that Winston was a man to be trusted. He turned his attention back to the dead wrangler. ''Did you recognize any of those men playing poker with him?''

Ben rubbed one hand over his chin, his eyes narrowed in thought. ''No. But they were no doubt just passengers from the train that ended its last run for the night here. They probably stayed at the hotel.''

''I need to talk to them, and see if they can put a name to this man's face. If I know who he is, maybe I can find out who he was riding with and be a step closer to catching these damn rustlers.''

Ben squinted up at the sun, and shook his head. "The train always pulls out early when it stays over. I don't think you can make it to town before it leaves."

Storme frowned. "I'm going to ride in and try. Maybe it'll be running late. If I miss it, I'll see if Sheriff Hadley can help me out. Besides, I think it's time I talked to him about these notes and the shooting, anyway."

Sheriff Hadley shook his gray-streaked head, then glanced up from the two notes flattened out on top of his desk. "And a dead man, too, huh?"

Storme nodded. "A couple of the hands are bringing him in. Need to find out who he is." To Storme's disgruntlement, the train *had* already pulled out by the time he reached town. The hotel clerk had recognized the descriptions Storme gave, and confirmed that the men he sought about the dead wrangler's identity had indeed stayed the night and left that morning on the train.

The sheriff's face pulled taut. "Won't be easy. Since the train came to town, we get strangers passing through all the time." He glanced down at the notes again. "These rustlers are raising more smoke than a wet-wood fire. You got any idea who's sportin' this grudge?"

Storme crossed his arms and sat back in the chair. On the ride in and through the recounting of events to the sheriff, Storme had pondered that very question, raking his memory over the faces of everyone in the saloon the night before. None of the strangers had stood out as an enemy Storme would suspect, and the two ranchers he recognized didn't have any real grudge against him beyond his Apache blood—which he knew was enough for some folks. His gut told him this went deeper, though. He considered his enemies over the years, people he knew who would like nothing better than to see him dead. One man kept springing to the forefront of his thoughts.

"Could be Dodding."

The sheriff narrowed his stare and leaned just a bit farther over the scarred wooden top. "You serious?"

Storme recalled the meeting on Caney Trail, and the word *Injun* that had flown from Dodding's tongue. It was a small connection, but not one he was inclined to rule out altogether given the rancher's hatred. "Maybe. But I do have other enemies."

"Well, rifle through those and see if any ring a bell. See if any of them look like that dead man, too, while you're at it." Sheriff Hadley shoved a two-inch stack of wanted posters across the desk.

Storme took the pile, then propped his ankle up on the knee of his other leg, and started sifting through them. He stopped at the rough sketch of a craggy-faced man with a large nose, and a thousand-dollar reward on his head for the murder of a rancher up near Denver.

"You can toss that." Storme set the poster aside. "I collected the reward on Hawk Johnson two months ago. Watched him hang."

"Anyone else I'm wasting my time on?" Sheriff Hadley asked, wadding the paper and throwing it toward a waste can off to one side.

Storme scanned through the stack, recognizing a few of the more notorious outlaws only by their names. The rest were unfamiliar, their crimes committed in the southwest territory where he didn't roam, finding jobs plentiful farther north.

"Hawk is the only one I know about," Storme answered, setting the stack of posters aside on the desk. "I don't recognize anyone that could be considered an enemy with a grudge or anyone that looks like that dead wrangler, either."

The sheriff sat back in his chair and ran one hand through his hair. "I'll send out wires to several of the towns in the territory, see if any of the sheriffs recognize that dead man's description. I can also wire ahead to the next train stops. Maybe we can find those men who were playing poker with him and get a name. I'm expectin' a new batch of wanted posters in a couple days, too. Stop by and take a look at 'em, if you want.''

''I'll do that. And thanks for the help.'' Storme stood. ''I'll let you know if we have more trouble out at the ranch.''

Sheriff Hadley nodded and shook Storme's hand. ''I'll keep an eye out on things at the boardinghouse. Not that I worry about much over there. Miss Alexander couldn't be in any safer place. That Mrs. Harrington's a damn good shot. She's run off a fair share of men with that Buffalo gun she keeps on hand.''

''That's good to know.'' Storme searched the sheriff's expression, but saw no signs that the lawman was speaking of him as being the latest man run off. He had only told Sheriff Hadley about buying the necklace, not returning it. Storme sure hoped there wouldn't be any gossip spread about his visit to Anna.

He bid the sheriff farewell and crossed the room, stepping out into the morning sunlight. He closed the door behind, then took a deep breath.

Returning that necklace last night was a big mistake. What the hell had he been thinking? He shook his head, then walked over and untied his gelding from the post. He had been thinking about making Anna happy, that's what, and seeing a smile on her pretty face. He recalled that beautiful sight when she had first spotted the necklace in his hand. His pulse raced. That alone had been worth it all.

Storme frowned. Well, not worth the trouble his actions had caused. He could have found the same satisfaction if he had used his head and waited for a more decent time and place to return the necklace.

He mounted, then headed down Main Street, weaving his way around the other riders and wagons kicking up dust along the road. He glanced up at the sun. Half past ten. Still a little early in the day to be paying a call, but he needed to warn Anna about the rustlers, even if he had to brave Mrs. Harrington's rifle to do so.

Worry stabbed at his gut. *Damn!* He sure hoped Anna still had a job, and that she didn't hate him for causing her this trouble and possible gossip.

He started past the mercantile just as the door opened, jangling the bell above. Storme smiled, his heart pounding faster as he recognized the well-shaped bottom backing out of the doorway, then the sunlight caught like fire in her upswept hair.

Chapter Seven

"But we haven't finished telling you about the extravaganza, or how much we could really use your help," Edna Mae Mason protested, the black mole above one corner of her lip more stark against the reddened determination that flushed her slender face.

"Really, Mrs. Mason." Anna smiled at the mercantile owner's wife, and backed another step out the door. "I'd love to stay and hear about this, but I—"

"It won't take but just a minute, dear. And we'd really like for you to reconsider," Sally Hankins insisted. Her upswept cinnamon hair displayed a blue-feathered bonnet atop the mass that bridged the gap behind Mrs. Mason's shoulder and Hannah Montgomery, the middle-aged banker's wife, who also hovered in the doorway.

Like chickens flocking to thrown feed, the three women moved forward, coming at Anna and forcing her to back farther outside onto the planked walkway. Then they quickly hovered around her, blocking an effective escape—just as they had done in the store when they first cornered her about the musical planned for the Fourth of July celebration.

"Mabel Sanderson said that Elise told her you sing like an angel," Hannah declared, the loose black curls dancing around her face as she bobbed her head.

Anna swallowed her groan. Who else had Mrs. Sanderson talked to?

Sally narrowed her brown eyes and wagged one finger. "We could certainly use talent like that in the Garden Society's extravaganza. I still can't believe Harriet Harrington didn't say anything about you."

Anna held her smile. *Mrs. Harrington already knows that I'm not interested in participating.* For the last two weeks, Anna had enjoyed listening to the housemother play the piano as she practiced the numbers planned for the program. Mrs. Harrington had asked Anna about singing in the musical the night she had joined in the parlor music and helped Katie and Patricia with their songs. Unlike these ladies hovering around her, however, the housemother had taken no for an answer.

"I'm sorry, ladies, thank you for asking, but no. I just don't like to sing in front of a big crowd. And I really need to leave now." Anna clutched the string-wrapped bundle in her arms, rattling the brown paper for added effect. "Mrs. Harrington is waiting to get started on these new curtains." She took a step back, stopped from taking another when Edna Mae's clawlike fingers clamped down on her shoulder.

"If you could just come to our practice next Wednesday nig—" Edna Mae's gaze shifted slightly to the left. Her hazel eyes rounded in shock. "Oh, my," she gasped, her whispered tone whipping the other two ladies' attention more effectively than if she had shouted.

Hannah sucked in a sharp breath, black eyebrows lifting high on her forehead. Sally Hankins's face pinched into a hard frown.

Anna shrugged her shoulder out from under Mrs. Mason's hold and turned around to see what had caused their looks of

unpleasant surprise. Her heart pounded with unexpected joy at
the sight of Storme seated on his horse.

He nodded once, reaching up to tip the brim of his hat.
"Good morning, ladies."

"Morning, Mr. Warwick." Anna smiled, her delight at
seeing him tamped only by the concern that had plagued her
during the night. She searched his face, relief unfolding when
she saw only a small scratch that marred his cheek as evidence
of his gallant kindness. But Anna knew the memory of his
sweet efforts would stay in her heart much longer than his
wound would show. "It's nice to see you."

"And you, Miss Alexander." His warm smile sent a flare
of excitement pooling low in her stomach.

"I didn't know *you* were back in town," Edna Mae snapped.

"Neither did I," Hannah stated bitterly.

"Well, this *is* surprising," Sally Hankins bit out in an icy
voice that Anna was sure could rival the temperature of a blue
norther. "I'll have to make sure my Hal prints *this* in the next
edition of the *Pleasant Grove Recorder*."

Anger burned in Anna's veins as she stared at the rude
women, itching to slap the unmitigated disgust from their faces.
She forced a smile instead. "Be sure to tell your husband that
Mr. Warwick is back visiting his brother. He'll need to know
that for the Social News section."

Sally pulled back, blinking her shock. "This isn't social
news. This needs to go on the front page with a big warning."

Anna let her smile fall. "Why is that necessary?" She added
a cool edge to her challenging tone.

"He's a savage!" Hannah exclaimed.

"People need to be warned," Edna Mae added with a sharp
indulgence that said she didn't understand the need for this
explanation.

Anna arched her brow and considered telling these pious
women that if the town needed to be warned of someone, it
was her. Wouldn't these ladies have apoplexy to know they had

practically begged a saloon owner's daughter—and a wanted criminal, no less—to sing in their extravaganza. "Mr. Warwick is here to help his brother with some rustlers. What is there to be warned about?"

"Be sure to tell your husband that I'll only be home for a short time, Mrs. Hankins," Storme calmly interjected.

Anna frowned, wondering why he was so tolerant of these women—except that being polite just seemed to be such a part of his nature. She did admire the way his smile never slipped . . . and the way he casually leaned forward and crossed his arms over the saddle horn, as though he had nowhere better to be than right there staring at her, with an intense regard she found herself wanting to get lost in.

"I'll do that," Mrs. Hankins coldly commented. "Now, move along and let us finish our conversation."

Anna gritted her teeth, bristling.

Storme only nodded, and tipped his hat. "When you're finished, Miss Alexander, I wonder if I might have a minute of your time?"

"I'm sure Miss Alexander has better things to do wi—"

"Actually," Anna cut off Edna Mae's rude reply, "I'm finished right now, Mr. Warwick." She glared back at the women. "Excuse me, ladies."

Heightened displeasure etched the women's faces, and disgruntled huffs of indignation graced their quick retreat back inside the mercantile. Anna shrugged, then turned away and headed down the steps, her blood racing at the sight of Storme swinging his leg over the saddle, corded muscles bunching against his denims. The gleam in his brown stare was as dazzling as the sun after a blizzard.

"Let me carry that for you." He reached his hand out, palm up, his white shirtsleeve rolled back, revealing his strong, bronze arm.

"It's not heavy." Anna hugged the bulky package closer to

her midriff, grateful for the string binding that nipped into her wrists and distracted her from his powerful presence.

He shoved his hand a little closer, his eyebrows lifting in a stubborn arch. "Well, fine." She chuckled. "If you insist."

The corners of his mouth tipped upward. "I do." He took the package she handed over and looped one section of the string around the saddle horn, letting it rest secure on the leather seat. He gathered up the reins in one hand, then gently gripped her elbow with the other, his warm touch seeping through her sleeve and making her skin tingle.

Anna fell into step beside him, noticing that several folks riding by, and others standing on the planked walk across the road, kept darting scowls of surprise and displeasure their way.

"You did yourself no favors back there, Anna."

There was admonishment in his low voice, but she also detected a hint of approval that pleased her. "I wasn't looking for favors. You're a nice man, Mr. Warwick. You didn't deserve that rude treatment."

He nodded once. "I appreciate your opinion." His caressing gaze sent a shudder of excitement rippling through her. "But I've fought this battle around here for a long time. Some things just don't change. And I should warn you that your actions will no doubt be printed in the *Recorder,* along with the warning about this savage's return."

His concern for her reputation touched her, but given the chance she wouldn't take back a single word she had spoken to those ladies. In fact, she wouldn't mind adding a few more. "I've survived worse things than having my name in the paper, Mr. Warwick. And I've met a few men who could truly wear the label of savage. You're not one of them. I wouldn't like you so much if you were." Anna's breath caught. *Good heavens!* She hadn't meant to say that last part out loud.

His fingers tightened around her arm. He stared hard at her for several seconds, then the planes of his chiseled face softened into a smile, and he relaxed his shoulders. "I like you, too, Anna."

Her heart soared. She released the breath she'd been holding, and couldn't stop the smile that overtook her mouth. Heat that had nothing to do with the sun beating upon the valley rushed through her limbs. The depth of pleasure his admission wrought took her by surprise. Anna swallowed and looked down, staring at the dust that issued from beneath her steps and settled in a thin layer on the hem of her brown skirt.

What the hell was he doing? Storme took a deep breath. Walking through town with his hand glued to her arm wasn't going to reflect any better on her reputation than having her name linked with his in the paper. He waited for the freight wagon to pass, for some of the dusty grit it kicked up to settle, then he guided Anna along a path across Main Street.

He glanced over, watching the sunlight dance in her hair, his gaze following the smooth line of her flushed cheek. He had never had a woman stand up to others on his behalf before, and her bold defense had been a nice surprise. Her announcement that she liked him had come as an even bigger shock, and reached a lonely part of his soul he had almost forgotten about. His pulse pounded harder. He *did* like her, more than he knew he should . . . and he needed to keep his hands off her, *dammit!*

They reached the other side of the road, and Storme forced himself to release his hold on her arm. She looked up, disappointment flashing in her green stare. Blood roared through his lower regions. The thought that she wanted him to go on touching her almost undid him. He swallowed and stared ahead, taking several deep breaths.

At the corner of the bank, he turned off the main road and headed down the narrow lane that led to the boardinghouse at the far end. Off to the right, a large grassy section of empty expanse separated the road from the back of the restaurant depot. Muted sounds of banging pots and raised male voices drifted out from the opened back door of the kitchen, but Storme didn't see anyone through the shadowed opening.

Grateful for their relative privacy, he broached the subject that had been bothering him. "Anna, I wanted to talk to you about last night,"

She nodded, smiling up at him, then circled one hand around the silver heart nestled between her breasts. "I want to thank you again for finding my necklace and getting it back." Her eyebrows pulled together, and she moved her hand up toward his face. "And I've been worried about that fall you took. Did you get hurt anywhere else?"

Storme's heart nearly jumped from his chest as her fingers lightly grazed the scratch on his cheek. Her gentle touch seared his flesh with unexpected pleasure. "No," he choked out around the breath lodged in his throat, then took hold of her hand, pulling it away before his desire ran any deeper. "I'm fine. I want to know how much trouble you got in."

She made no move to pull her hand away as they walked down the road, and for the life of him, Storme couldn't bring himself to do so, either.

"Well, Mrs. Harrington *was* mad, and adamant that nothing like that better happen again." A small smile lifted the corners of her mouth. "But I didn't get in any trouble. I'm pretty sure she believed that I hadn't invited you. She knew you had to have some reason for coming, though, but she never asked me what it was." She curled her nose, and her eyes shimmered with a glint of guilt. "So, I didn't volunteer any information about the necklace."

Storme released a heavy sigh of relief. "I'm real glad I didn't get you in any trouble."

"It would have been worth it." Her smile returned full force, rocking his senses. "I really did want my necklace back. Thank you."

"You're welcome, Anna." He forced himself to look away

from the mesmerizing sparkle in her eyes, to ignore the building fire in his loins that he knew he had no business feeling.

Up ahead, he spotted a small gray ball perched on the white-columned porch of the boardinghouse, then it bounded down the steps and darted across the front lawn, disappearing behind the slatted fence row. The kitten's small, round face peeked between the whitewashed fence seconds later. He wondered if the feline had spotted Anna coming up the road, and was preparing for another attack on her skirts.

"I wish you'd let me pay you back. How much did you have to give that man for it?"

Storme's stomach clenched tight at the reminder of the dead wrangler. The rustler's note slammed to the forefront of his thoughts. He stopped and tightened his hand around hers, refusing to let go as she walked ahead.

She jerked slightly to a halt, then turned to face him, confusion pulling her smooth cheeks taut and narrowing her gaze.

"I don't want your money, Anna." He would willingly spend twice as much just to see that happy delight on her face again. "But there is something I do want."

She straightened, tensing. Her fingers stiffened against his palm. "Wha . . . what?"

Storme stared into her gaze, seeing her trust in him start to teeter, and recalled her saying that she had known men who could wear the label of savage. What had her encounter been with these men? What sort of past had she lived? He rubbed his thumb along the back of her hand in a slow, easy circle. He dropped the reins to his horse, and stepped closer, breathing deep as he caught the scent of lavender on the air between them. *Damn!* He had never known a woman who could wear that scent so well.

"I've already mentioned to you that I don't think it's a good idea for you to walk alone to the mountains. What I want is your *promise* that you won't go up there at all for a while, especially not alone."

She relaxed her shoulders and leaned forward slightly. Her auburn eyebrows drew together. "Why are you being so insistent? Has something else happened?"

Storme frowned, wishing there was a better way to tell her what had to be said. "Yes. That man I bought your necklace from turned up dead this morning."

Her mouth gaped open. She blinked her astonishment. "Dead?"

Storme felt the tremors flex in her hand and gently tightened his grip around her fingers. "I don't know who he is or why he was shot. Yet. But it was one of the rustlers who killed him, and I'm certain it was one of them that took that shot at me, too. But the worst thing is, Anna, they know about you." He quickly explained about the note Winston had found. "What I don't know," Storme swallowed, "is who these men are or what they'll do with this knowledge."

She shook her head in confusion. "Why would they do anything with it?"

"Because whoever is behind this has some sort of grudge against me, and he knows you saved my life. It would be easy enough to guess that I'm honor-bound to protect you now. He may try to use you somehow to get to me." Given what he had paid for Anna's necklace, Storme was certain the rustlers would suspect some vulnerability on his part where she was concerned, too . . . and not without good reason—which only added to her danger. "Promise me you won't go to the mountains until I can find these men. I wouldn't ask if I didn't think it important."

She pressed her lips together; her gazed narrowed. He could see her thoughts whirling, absorbing everything he had told her, then settling in accord with his concern. "All right, I promise."

Storme smiled his relief at her agreement and tried to ignore the pulsing knot that formed in his chest at her trust in his judgment. Tried to ignore the burning memory of her declaration that she liked him. His blood surged on a heated journey, pooling low. He released his hold on her hand and trailed his fingers up the thin cotton of her sleeve, feeling the slender limb quiver beneath his touch. Her cheeks colored pink as he followed the narrow line of her shoulder and brushed his hand across her smooth cheek.

"Thank you," he whispered, locking his stare with her pretty green gaze. He circled his hand around the nape of her neck and gently pulled her closer. He captured her startled breath, intending only to express his gratitude with a brief, chaste kiss. But she closed her eyes and pressed her soft lips closer. He moved his mouth over hers, reveling in her sweetness, her warm response. He ran his tongue along the line of her lips. She opened her mouth at the gentle coaxing, and Storme slipped inside, finding himself suddenly lost in a swirling tide he had no willpower to flee.

He slid his arm around her back, and she found the feel of his strength a bit frightening at first as his hand clamped firmly on her waist and pulled her closer. But the fear quickly left in the wake of his slow, thoughtful, probing kiss. Anna shivered with delight, drawn by a force she didn't understand into the comfort of his strong presence, into the intoxicating warmth of his gentle caress. She placed her palms against the hard wall of his chest, felt his heart pounding beneath her fingers.

Her own heart hammered a pace that strongly resembled galloping hoofbeats.

"Half-breed!" A male voice shouted. "Get your hands off her."

Anna froze, her eyes flying open in realization that it wasn't her heart galloping down the road. She jerked back, but gained little space against Storme's continued hold. His narrowed gaze spoke his apology, even as anger rose to darken his brown eyes. She had a moment's hesitation to wonder if he apologized for the kiss, or the interruption, or both. Then he loosened his hold and turned away to stand at her side, but kept his hand firm against the small of her back.

The man reined his horse to a stop, kicking up a cloud of dust that Anna waved away from her nose.

"What do you want, Dodding?" Storme snapped with heated venom.

Anna jumped, surprised at the depth of his temper and grateful it wasn't aimed at her.

Dodding dismounted and removed his hat as he strode forward, his gray gaze riveted on her with deep concern. "This Injun giving you trouble, Miss Alexander?" He cut a disparaging glance Storme's way.

Even besides his judging stare, Anna had no particular liking for the rancher she had met at the mercantile last week. "No. Mr. Warwick is a perfect gentleman." From the corner of her eye, she saw Storme's smug smile aimed at Dodding.

The rancher's jaw hardened. Tiny beads of sweat trailed a path from the side of his black hair down his thick, reddened neck. "Looks to me like he's got trouble keeping his hands to himself." Harsh disapproval tainted his tone.

Anna's anger rose as the memory of her encounter with the rancher flashed across her thoughts. "I could say the same of you, Mr. Dodding."

Storme's fingers dug into her back. His questioning gaze bored into her face.

Dodding arched his brow. "I thought you said at the mercantile you understood that was an accident?"

"I was just being polite." She had been shocked when he bumped into her, then ran his hand over her breast as he had helped steady her. A clumsy accident? *No.* It was all too similar to what she had put up with a hundred times at her father's saloon. "I didn't believe you then. Still don't."

"What accident?" Storme grated through clenched teeth.

Oh dear. Anna swallowed at the tempered growl in his tone, suddenly wishing she hadn't let her mouth run off unattended at Mr. Dodding's arrogant attitude. She glanced between the two men. Hatred thickened the air as they eyed one another. She bit her lip, fearing she had just opened the door to trouble.

"How many times do I have to tell you to stay out of my business, half-breed?"

"And what is your business here, Dodding? If it's with me, this isn't the place. And I don't have time for you right now."

"I can see that." Dodding squared his shoulders, peering down his long nose with contempt, which he then directed toward Anna.

Storme felt the muscles in her back tense. She crossed her arms over her breasts. He lowered his hand, and clenched his fists at his sides, trying not to read anything into her action. But he couldn't help it. His curiosity ate a fiery hole in his gut. He didn't trust Dodding as far as the step it would take to reach his hand around the man's throat right now. He knew him too well. "I'll make time for you, if you want to talk about this *'accident.'* "

Dodding shrugged and crossed his arms over his chest, his hat dangling from one hand. "I've got nothing to say to you. I was just on my way to meet the eleven-thirty train, and thought I was helping out a lady. My mistake." He cocked a half smile and nodded downward. "Hope that kiss was worth three hundred bucks, because you got taken on the necklace, Injun!"

Storme tensed.

Anna gave a start, then turned her rounded stare on him. "You paid three hundred dollars?" she whispered incredulously.

Damn Dodding and his big mouth! "Yes," Storme answered with no hint of apology, then glared at the rancher. "How did you know about it?" He clenched his jaw; the vein at his temple throbbed. Storme knew any one of the wranglers at the saloon last night could work for Dodding and have told him. But unless someone followed him from the saloon, or was connected to the rustlers, they wouldn't have known it was Anna's necklace.

"Why should I tell you?" Dodding sneered, shoving his hat on his head.

The threat against his brother, the note that dared to drag Anna into this vengeance, grated at Storme's anger. "So I don't have to beat you for the information."

Dodding arched his brow. "Try it. I'll ground you in the dust just like I did last time."

Storme's blood surged to his fists as he recalled that night. "Not if you do the honorable thing and come alone this time."

"If you knew anything about honor, half-breed, you'd have left Linette alone. How many other decent women you gonna ruin?"

Storme held Dodding's glare and shook with barely suppressed rage. He could feel Anna's curious gaze burning the side of his face.

A train whistle called out from the distance, white smoke rising above the stand of trees running alongside the tracks north of the depot.

Dodding snorted out a harsh breath, then turned his attention to Anna. "You best take care who you're seen with, Miss Alexander. If you plan to stay in *this* town long, anyway."

"I'll choose my own friends, thank you very much." She squared her shoulders. "And I don't need your advice."

"Really, well think about this." Dodding grinned slyly. "You spend too much time with this half-breed, I won't be the only man in town bold enough to find out just how soft you are."

Anna gasped, tightening her arms over her breasts.

Storme's vision blurred. The roaring in his head blocked out all thought, and fury drove him forward. He plowed his fist into Dodding's mouth with a crunching force that rocked the bones in his hand.

Dodding staggered back several steps, then fell, sending a

puff of dust shooting out from under both sides of his seat. "Shit," he mumbled, and raised his hand to the blood that trailed down from the corner of his mouth. "You'll pay for that, half-breed." The rancher reached for the Colt strapped at his waist.

"You boys just hold it right there," the woman called out with stern authority.

Dodding froze. Storme did as well, then slowly turned his head enough to keep the rancher in his sight and still see Mrs. Harrington standing outside the gate with the long rifle propped against her shoulder. He swallowed, uncertain if he should welcome or fear her presence, until he saw the elder woman's aim led straight to Dodding.

Storme straightened and lowered his hand away from his gun. *Damn! How much had Mrs. Harrington seen before Dodding rode up?*

"Mrs. Harrington." Dodding rose to his feet, dusting at the back of his pants. "I didn't see you out there. I appreciate your help running this half-breed off." He pulled a handkerchief from his back pocket and dabbed at the cut on his lip.

Mrs. Harrington reached her thumb up, and pulled the hammer back on the rifle. "I'm here to run someone off. But it's not him."

The rancher paused, arching his brow. "What?"

Storme took hold of Anna's arm and gently tugged her behind him, then moved his hand within reach of his Colt, his gaze fixed on Dodding.

"You heard me," the elder woman snapped.

"You're making a mistake, ma'am," Dodding stated with arrogant disbelief, thrusting his chin out.

"Not this time," Mrs. Harrington's voice brooked no argument to the conclusion. "And I'll keep in mind not to send my girls to the mercantile alone anymore. If I see your sorry hide around here again, your next stop will be at Doc's with a big hole in your backside."

Dodding glared his dislike.

Storme swallowed down his chuckle, deciding he rather liked the elderly woman. He also knew he might change that opinion when she got through dealing with him, especially if she had seen him kissing Anna. He glanced over his shoulder at Anna's taut face, enraptured with the tension that crackled in the air. He couldn't dredge up a single regret for tasting those sweet lips. But he could find plenty of guilt for causing her more trouble and for the gossip that was sure to spread about this incident.

The train whistle sounded again. The housemother peered over the top of her spectacles. "I suggest you get on out of here, and go meet your train, Mr. Dodding."

Affronted, Dodding jerked up straight, then crossed over and mounted his horse. He rode away toward the grove of trees in back of the depot.

Storme released the tension in his shoulders. Anna stepped up beside him, her pale cheeks and widened eyes tightening the fist over his guilt. He followed her stare to where Mrs. Harrington still stood at the end of the narrow walk, her gun propped in the crook of one arm, and now, thankfully, pointed in the air.

The tightened lines in her face showed her continued displeasure. "I'd like to see you two inside," she commanded.

Chapter Eight

Anna stood outside the front gate, her gaze fixed on the housemother's stiff back as she disappeared inside the house, letting the screen door bang shut behind.

Rule number three: No public displays of affection.

Did Mrs. Harrington see me kissing Storme? Anna sighed, certain she could start packing her things if the woman had.

She glanced over as Storme finished wrapping the reins to his horse around the hitching post, and couldn't stop the smile that rose. She ran her tongue over her mouth, tasting the lingering sensation of his warm lips, her body heating with memories of being wrapped in the secure comfort of his embrace. Hot tingles shot through her stomach. She couldn't find a single regret for kissing him, no matter what was about to happen.

He grabbed the brown-wrapped bundle off the saddle and tucked it under his arm, then quickly crossed the distance between them. "Anna, I'm sorry about this. Are you all right?"

No. She was likely just minutes away from losing her job, as well as her safe haven here in Pleasant Grove, and all she could think about was how much she wished he would kiss her again. His earthy male scent assailed her nose and made her shiver with a strong craving to step nearer, to press her hands against the hard wall of his chest. She nodded. "I'm fine."

He cupped his palm against her cheek, his narrowed gaze burning with concern. "Did Dodding hurt you with his so called *'accident'?*" He snarled the last word.

"No." She pressed her face closer against the warm solace of his strong hand. Humiliation could be as painful as any physical hurt sometimes, but she had experienced anger at the arrogant rancher's bold action more than embarrassment. "I'm glad you hit him, though. He deserved it." Hard and sure, Storme had struck with the speed of an angry rattler and made her blood sizzle with excitement and pride.

"If he touches you again, he deserves to die."

She swallowed, not doubting the fierce promise in his voice or the thrill she found in his assured defense. No man, other than her father when he wasn't too drunk, had ever come to her defense before . . . or gone to such expense on her behalf. Apprehension tightened her gut. Three hundred dollars! His generosity overwhelmed her, but she couldn't in good conscience ignore that large a debt. Goodness, it was going to take her a long time to save that much, though.

"About the money you had to give for my necklace, I—"

"It was worth every penny." He moved his hand from her cheek and pressed one finger against her mouth. "And I don't want to hear another word about you paying me back."

Her pulse pounded at the earnest sincerity gleaming in his molasses gaze. She circled her hand around his wrist, his skin smooth and warm against her palm, and gently pulled his finger from her mouth. "Thank you," she whispered. "But I insist that you consider your debt paid now."

He shook his head; a small smile curved his mouth. "I've

already told you the necklace has nothing to do with the debt. I'm not going to change my mind about that.''

Stubborn man. Anna took a deep breath and released it on a heavy sigh. She liked his honor, though, and his determination.

His slight grin fell into a hard line of remorse. He slid his arm from her grip and took hold of her hand, his thumb circling a path along her skin. ''Anna, I hope I haven't caused you more trouble. I don't know if she saw me kiss you, or not.''

''If I'm in trouble, it's not your fault.'' It was hers. She *had* kissed him back, and *was* the one who provoked matters with Dodding that had brought about the fight.

His jaw hardened. ''Yes, it is.'' He gently squeezed her hand. ''I'm not sorry I kissed you; but I sure shouldn't have done it in the middle of the road, and for that I do apologize.''

Her heart beat faster in response, delight racing through her that he voiced no remorse for their kiss. ''I could have stopped you. I knew where we were. But I wanted you to kiss me.''

His warm smile reached up into his eyes. ''I'm real glad to hear that.''

''You're not going to make me bring my gun back out, are you young man?'' Mrs. Harrington sternly inquired.

Storme released Anna's hand and stepped back, hating the worry that sprang in her widened stare, knowing it was his fault she was in this mess. He turned toward the house. ''No need to do that, ma'am.''

The gray-haired woman stood at the entrance, holding the screen door propped open with one hand, her aged face lined with disapproval at being kept waiting. Storme's smile faded under the intimidating heat of her stringent stare. He almost wished he was about to face a war party without benefit of a single weapon instead of this elderly woman.

He motioned for Anna to proceed him through the gate, then tucked his head down and leaned closer as she started to walk by. ''You stay quiet. I'll figure out a way to keep you out of trouble," he whispered, surprised at the stubborn denial that flashed in her eyes.

"You shouldn't make promises you may not be able to keep, young man. I suggest you get on up here with my housemaid . . . and the curtain material I've waited half the morning for already."

Storme jerked up straight, tightening his arm against the package. "You have good hearing, ma'am." He followed Anna's hurried progress down the walk and up the steps, his longer strides easily keeping him just a pace behind.

"And eyes like a hawk." Mrs. Harrington's gaze softened as she placed her hand on Anna's arm. "I'm just sorry they didn't reach as far as the mercantile, Anna." Her tone was filled with contrition. "I wish you had told me."

"I'm sorry, ma'am, but it would've just been my word against his. And there really wasn't much to be done about it." She glanced over, peeking up at him through her long, dark lashes. "Except what Mr. Warwick did."

Storme's heart pounded harder. He braced his foot against the bottom edge of the door, nudging it slightly to relieve the burden from the older woman.

Mrs. Harrington smiled her appreciation, then crossed her arms over the bodice of her dark blue dress. "I had a feeling there was going to be trouble when I saw Mr. Dodding ride up. Never have liked that man. I appreciate you looking out for Anna and putting that rancher in the dirt where he belongs."

Storme tensed. If the elderly woman saw Dodding ride up, she had to have seen the kiss, too. He looked over at Anna, seeing her distressed gaze, which mirrored his own realization. He shifted his stare back to the elder woman. "I was happy to do it. And he deserved more." Storme intended to make sure the rancher got the full measure of what he deserved, too.

"Well, I'm inclined to agree with you," Mrs. Harrington offered. "But I don't much care for brawls or shootings in front of my place." Her face grew taut. She peered up over the top of her rectanglar spectacles. "I don't care for my girls being kissed out in the middle of the road, either."

Storme wasn't surprised to see his moment of heroism quickly fall by the wayside.

"That was my fault, Mrs. Harrington."

He frowned at Anna's response. "No it's not, ma'am. I'm to blame for that," he insisted.

"Well . . ." Mrs. Harrington arched her thin, gray eyebrows and glanced between them. "This is interesting. Anna, dear, there's fresh coffee made and a pan of gingerbread cooling on the kitchen table. Would you mind fixing a tray of refreshments to bring to the parlor?"

Anna's eyes widened, and her mouth fell open, then she quickly recovered her surprise. "Of course, ma'am." She walked inside, barely passing by the older woman before she looked back over her shoulder.

Storme met her dubious gaze and gave a slight shrug. He hadn't expected the offer of refreshments to accompany the certain reprimand, either. He held her stare as her boot heels tapped a steady rhythm against the pine floor, then she looked away, shaking her head. Storme made the mistake of glancing down and lost himself in the sight of her gently swaying hips, until she disappeared through a doorway near the end of the long hall.

"My mother was half-Comanche. You are . . ."

Storme jerked his attention to the housemother, stunned by her announcement. He searched her face for a sign of her mixed blood, and saw a slight definition in her high cheeks and a faint copper tone in her skin that wasn't brought out by the sun. "Apache."

She nodded, the loose knot of gray hair atop her head shifting slightly with the action. "Folks use to make things difficult for my mother . . . and for me and my brothers. I don't recall many people ever calling my ma by her given name. Heard her called half-breed more than I want to remember, though. I've been labeled the same myself a few times." A look of disgust tightened the edges of her mouth. "I don't care for labels. A person should be judged on his merit. That's why I don't tell very many people about my Indian blood."

Storme was surprised at being singled out to receive this confidence, but attributed part of the revelation to his ability to understand what she had gone through trying to make her way in the white man's world. "I'm honored by your trust, ma'am. Your secret is safe with me."

"I thought it would be." A gleam of amusement hovered in her eyes. "Despite how busy you've been around my place lately, you seem like a decent enough man."

Storme felt the blood rush into his cheeks. Falling out of a tree, kissing the housemaid in public, and getting into a fight weren't the first impressions he would have chosen to make.

"I also think that it's time we were formally introduced. I'm Harriet Harrington."

Storme removed his hat and pressed it against his chest. "Storme Warwick, ma'am."

"It's nice to meet you, Mr. Warwick, and I'm real glad to see you at the front door this time." She turned around and walked into the wide, paneled foyer. "You may leave my curtain material over there."

She pointed toward a small table beside the wooden settee backed against the wall of the staircase. Storme eased the screen door shut behind him, then deposited the package and followed the housemother through a set of sliding doors into a parlor.

"Please, have a seat." She waved a hand toward the long, curved-back sofa, and lowered her broad frame into one of the three rose-patterned Victorian chairs that sat opposite.

A large piano occupied the corner in front of the tall bay windows. Burgundy-velvet drapes were drawn back, giving view to the edge of the grove on one side, and overlooking the front porch on the other. Storme glanced around at the flowers and lace that decorated every table in the room, wishing for the smell of leather or a pair of horns hanging over the fireplace to make him feel more comfortable in this mass of femininity. He sat down and placed his hat on the low table that stood between them.

"You must be Ben's brother," the housemother stated without preamble.

Storme nodded.

"I've heard mention of you around town a few times. And Elise commented this morning that you'd come back home for a while."

Storme nodded again, well imagining the hatred and gossip about him that she had heard around town.

She leaned farther back in her chair, and with one finger pushed her glasses up the bridge of her nose. "I admire your brother. He's done a lot to support the growth in Pleasant Grove since he joined the town council."

"Thank you, ma'am." Storme smiled, pride swelling at the respect he heard in Mrs. Harrington's voice. "He's a good man."

"Yes, he is." The elder woman propped her elbows on the chair arms, linked her fingers together above her stomach, and tapped her thumbs together. "I also know he's the reason Samantha was late for work, and that he nearly got her fired last evening. Does this penchant for getting ladies in trouble run in your family?"

Storme paused, swallowing dryly at the accusation. Regardless of Ben's being slapped, seeing him verbally reprimanded, and called a scalawag all in one night, Storme didn't believe his brother made any sort of habit of it, any more than he did. "Not as a general rule, ma'am. No."

"Hmm . . ." The housemother's green eyes narrowed assessingly. Her thumbs tapped together a little faster. "Well, I do run a respectable home, and I feel a certain protection for the girls staying under my roof. If you don't mind my asking, what intentions exactly prompted you to climb that tree last night''—she lowered her tone—''then find the opportunity to kiss Miss Alexander this morning?''

Storme's gut tightened, and he wished again that he had used his head about returning Anna's necklace, and about kissing her. He didn't misunderstand the elderly woman's meaning about intentions, either, and the guilt settled with the weight of a boulder on his chest. He liked Anna, but he didn't have any plans of letting their relationship go any farther. ''Miss Alexander is a very nice woman, and I can assure you that I have the utmost respect for her. I made some poor choices, ma'am. I never meant to bring any harm to her reputation, or to place her job in jeopardy.''

''That's all well and good.'' Mrs. Harrington cocked her head. ''But it doesn't answer my question, Mr. Warwick. There's some reason you've been turning up around here so unconventionally. If Miss Alexander has encouraged this—''

''No.'' Storme sat up straight. ''I'm the one at fault. She's done nothing wrong.''

''That's not true, Mrs. Harrington.'' Anna gripped her hands tighter around the edge of the silver tray and crossed the threshold into the room.

Storme stood.

Anna saw his confusion and displeasure as he raked her face with his hard stare. Determination pounded through her veins. ''I appreciate what you're trying to do, Mr. Warwick, but you've covered for me long enough. I'm the one to blame for what's happened.'' Anna knew her job was as good as gone, anyway. Rules were rules, and she had broken one too many now. There was no reason to hide the truth any longer. Besides, she didn't want Mrs. Harrington thinking unkindly of Storme. He was the one who had done nothing wrong.

''Well,'' Mrs. Harrington drew the word out in a low, gauging tone. ''Why don't you tell me exactly what it is that's happened, dear?''

Anna set the tray on the serving cart beside the housemother's chair, then took a deep breath and let it out slowly. She slipped her shaking hands behind her back. "I lost my necklace up on the mountain when I took a walk the other evening."

"Would that be the same night you missed curfew, and Mr. Warwick helped you climb the tree?" Mrs. Harrington arched one gray eyebrow.

Anna's heart stopped. How had the woman known? What had Storme talked about while she was in the kitchen? She looked over at him. He shook his head slightly, his expression as bewildered as her own. She frowned. Had Samantha said something?

Mrs. Harrington smiled discerningly. "Don't look so surprised, dear. And no, Miss Crowley didn't give away your secret. Didn't I tell you last night, I know everything that goes on around here?"

Anna slowly nodded, more convinced than ever and strongly suspecting the woman had some mystical ability to read minds. If the housemother knew about the missed curfew, though, why hadn't she said anything?

"Miss Alexander had a reason for being late the other night," Storme stated.

"I'm sure she'll tell me that reason." Mrs. Harrington waved one hand toward the sofa. "Have a seat, dear."

Anna obligingly crossed over and sat down. Storme lowered himself on the cushion beside her, his thigh distractingly inches from her own, his tall, masculine presence making her pulse beat harder.

"Now," Mrs. Harrington shoved her glasses up the bridge of her nose. "You were saying that you lost your necklace."

Anna swallowed. "Yes . . ." She briefly explained everything from the time she had met Storme on the mountain to seeing him again at the mercantile, only omitting the part about pulling her gun. She saw Storme arch his brow slightly at the omission, but to her relief he didn't say anything about it. Anna knew the housemother had plenty of reasons to fire her without giving away that little detail, and she wasn't inclined to have to come up with a lie about why she felt a need to own the gun.

Mrs. Harrington nodded, her face devoid of any expression. "Well, I appreciate your honesty."

Anna's stomach knotted into a hard ball, certain there was no way the housemother would let her keep working here after this confession, especially on the heels of being given a warning just last night. "I understand you have to fire me, ma'am. I don't expect you to give me another chance."

Storme frowned. "That's not necessary, is it?"

"It's all right." Anna appreciated the concern in his voice, but she didn't like the guilt she saw in his eyes. "I broke the rules. I knew the consequences."

"There's no need to fire you, Anna." Mrs. Harrington shoved her glasses up the bridge of her nose. "You did Mr. Warwick a huge favor saving his life, and I understand that you were worried about losing your job. This doesn't change anything. Like I told you last night, you're a good worker, and I don't want to lose you."

Anna paused, fearing she had misheard, but the woman's soft smile sent it sinking in, and waves of relief coursed through her veins, dousing the guilt that wanted to rise at her inevitable departure anyway. "Thank you, ma'am."

"You're welcome, dear. But"—the housemother shifted her stare between them—"from now on, I'd appreciate it if you two would act with proper decorum during your visits."

"You have my word." Strong assurance rang clear in Storme's voice.

Anna quickly nodded her promise, as well, then looked over at Storme, his relaxed smile stealing her breath.

"Good." The housemother's eyes beamed with approval. "Now, let's enjoy our refreshments, shall we?" Mrs. Harrington picked up the silver urn and began pouring coffee into the small, china cups, which she then passed across the table to them, along with plates of the ginger- and cinnamon-scented dessert.

Anna set her refreshments down, her blood pounding faster at the startling realization that suddenly hit her. Had she and Storme just agreed to keep seeing each other? Was that what he had meant? She drew her eyebrows together. She couldn't keep seeing him.

From the corner of her eye, Anna stared at his handsome face and couldn't help but notice how large his hands looked against the feminine china as he set his plate on the table and raised the cup to his mouth. Her wayward thoughts drifted to the memories of his hands so strong and secure at her waist when they had climbed the tree, and so gentle as he had pulled her close for his kiss. She wouldn't mind seeing him again. She sat up straight.

Good heavens! What was wrong with her? She wasn't looking for a relationship. Why did she keep having trouble remembering that?

The housemother took a sip of coffee, then sat back in her chair. "I think it would be a good idea if we discuss a plan of action here, in case Mr. Dodding wants to start gossip about what happened this morning."

Storme set his cup down, and narrowed his stare as he braced his arms on his thighs, clasping his hands together between widespread knees. "I'll make sure Dodding doesn't say anything."

Anna arched her brow at the depth of certainty in his tone, wondering just how he planned to make that happen.

"That might work." Mrs. Harrington nodded, tapping one finger against her chin. "But in case word has already gotten out, I think the best way to handle this is with the truth—that Mr. Warwick did a generous thing returning your lost necklace, Anna, and a small kiss of gratitude transpired." She smiled slyly. "It'll be my word against Mr. Dodding's just how small it was, and I hold a lot more esteem with the folks around town than he does.''

Anna inwardly frowned. She had kissed Storme because he made her blood stir with a craving she couldn't ignore. Gratitude hadn't played any part in it. But she saw the wisdom in the housemother's strategy and swallowed the lump of appreciation that rose in her throat. She had been too worried about her finances, and finding another job, and how long this would delay her getting to San Francisco that she hadn't given any concern to gossip. Now that she was staying, though, she was doubly grateful for the housemother's kindness. ''Thank you, Mrs. Harrington. That sounds like a good plan.''

Storme smiled and nodded his agreement, claiming his cup and lifting it in a gesture of toast. ''You're a wise woman, ma'am.''

The housemother smiled, cocking her head in a slight nod. ''I'm not a bad of judge of character, either, Mr. Warwick.'' She took another sip of coffee. The lines on her aged face deepened with sudden concern. ''Do you have any idea who took that shot at you the other night?''

''No, but I suspect he's one of the rustlers who've been hitting our ranch.''

Anna saw his jaw slowly tighten harder as he explained about the rustlers that had brought him home, their knowledge of her necklace, and the dead cowboy.

Mrs. Harrington frowned. ''Are these rustlers out for cattle, or revenge?''

''Looks like both,'' Storme responded, sending a chill up Anna's spine in increased worry for his safety.

She recalled his demand to know how Dodding had obtained his boasted knowledge of her necklace, and couldn't help but wonder if the rancher was connected to the rustlers . . . and possibly the one who had tried to shoot Storme. She was also curious to know what had caused the obvious bitter dislike between him and the rancher. Was it the woman Dodding had mentioned?

Mrs. Harrington leaned forward, peering over the top of her glasses. "Do you think Anna might be in danger?"

Storme shook his head. "I don't know. I'm being cautious, though. I've told the sheriff everything, and he's going to keep a watch around here." He sat up straight, and Anna could see the determination in his dark gaze as he looked over at her. "I don't intend to let anything happen to her," he confidently stated.

Anna wondered if his concern stemmed from the reason he had kissed her or was solely in response to the life-debt he claimed to owe. She quickly chided herself for the nagging thought and the pang of disappointment that nipped at her heart that it was only the latter. She really needed to stop thinking so much about the man.

"Well, I appreciate your precautions, Mr. Warwick, and I'll be sure to keep my gun handy." Mrs. Harrington set her cup on the cart and picked up the plate of gingerbread. "Tell me," she cut a small slice, then speared it with her fork, holding it partway to her mouth. "Since you don't work at the ranch with your brother, what do you do to earn your way when you're not chasing rustlers?"

Anna looped her fingers through the handle of her coffee cup, her interest piqued at the inquiry, and the memory of her impression when she had first seen him that he might be a gunfighter coming to the front of her thoughts.

Storme shrugged one broad shoulder. "Actually, chasing rustlers *is* part of my job. I'm a bounty hunter."

A bounty hunter! Anna froze. Her blood turned to ice, and quakes of fear surged through her limbs.

"Goodness dear, what's wrong?" Mrs. Harrington exclaimed. "You're spilling coffee everywhere."

* * *

"You want to do what?" Ben ground out incredulously, raking one hand through his sandy brown hair, then shoving his hat back on his head.

"You heard me." Anger pounded through Storme's veins as he pulled his saddle from the lathered gelding, carried it a few feet across the dirt, and tossed it up on the waiting roan.

"Well, I got no likin' for the bastard, myself," Winston commented from where he sat atop the corral rail. He spit a stream of tobacco juice down to the ground. "I'm lookin' forward to watchin' you tromp his britches."

Ben shoved his hands on his hips. Aggravation blazed in his stare. "Yeah, but don't you want to know why we're taking a dozen hands to Dodding's place for this, or *why* we're even going to begin with?"

Winston shrugged. "I know enough. He doesn't want Dodding's men to interfere. If Storme doesn't want to say more, fine. Hell, Ben, you pay good enough I don't need to question something that sounds like fun anyway." He jumped down and spit another stream of black juice, then hitched his thumbs in the waistband of his denims.

"Well, I do," Ben demanded, waving one hand in irritation. "Because we should be concentrating on the damn rustlers."

Storme pulled the stirrup down over the cinched knot, and grabbed the horse's reins, then paused and faced his brother. "Fine. Dodding rode up while I was talking to Anna, and as usual with him, it wasn't a pleasant conversation. I found out that bastard put his hands on her, then had the gall to call it a damn *'accident,'* " he ground out the last word.

"Well, I'm looking forward to this even more," Winston said, his voice now devoid of any humor.

Ben's face pulled taut. "All right, that's reason enough."

"I've got even more reason for you, and this does have to do with the rustlers." Storme swerved his glance to include

Winston. "Dodding admitted to knowing about what happened at the saloon last night. He also knew it was Anna's necklace I bought back. Wouldn't say how, but I'm going to find out."

"This just keeps gettin' better." Winston shook his head, hot anger blazing from his pale blue eyes. "Let's load up the ammo. I wanna see you tear into his hide."

An hour and half later, Storme stared at the sun riding low in the afternoon sky, bright arms of yellow light beaming through the trees that lined the west fork of the Pecos River. In the distance, blue spruce and cottonwoods thickened as the river wound its way toward the base of the mountain and disappeared in the heavy foliage. Nothing stirred above the steady flow of rushing water and the heavy tread of the dozen wranglers riding along the banks.

"Wonder what the hell he's doing way up here?" Winston wondered in a tone that said he didn't expect an answer.

Storme had been considering the same thing ever since they'd left Dodding's place, after forcing the answer about the rancher's whereabouts from a wrangler whose reluctance to part with the information had earned him a broken nose—compliments of Winston's rifle butt.

"Seems a little strange," Ben commented, "that this is the same section of land Wallace intended to buy before the claim got snatched up."

Storme arched his brow, recalling the name of the man Wallace said had bought the land—Robert Blanchard. Again, he thought it sounded familiar, but Storme still couldn't place it.

"You boys can stop right there!"

Storme hauled back on his reins at the shouted warning, scanning the woods ahead for the faceless voice. Ben and Winston stopped on either side, the foreman raising one hand to signal the wranglers riding behind to do the same.

A black-bearded stranger rode out from the group of trees ahead, his rifle aimed at them. "You're trespassing, and you're surrounded."

Several more men emerged from the shelter of the woods with rifles and pistols drawn.

"You best state your business fast, mister."

Ben grunted his displeasure. Winston spit a stream of black tobacco juice into the dirt. From the corner of his eye, Storme saw the foreman ease his right hand along his thigh, close to the Colt strapped around his hips.

"I'm here to see Dodding," Storme responded, wondering if the bearded man worked for Dodding or Blanchard, or both, and why the need for this protection when there was nothing out here.

"Don't know anyone by that name," the guard countered in a harsh tone.

Storme frowned. "I stopped at his ranch and was told I could find him here."

The man paused, eyeing him through narrowed lids. "You fellas that crew he hired?"

Crew? Storme hid his surprise. "That's right," he said, tensing with added caution. He glanced over and saw Ben's scowl at the lie.

The stranger lowered his rifle. "It's all right boys, let 'em pass," he called out. "Come on, I'll show you the way." He reeled his horse around and started up the trail along the river.

Storme glanced from Ben to Winston with a shrug and a silent warning to stay alert, then signaled the men to follow as he kicked his mount into a walk.

"Well, now isn't this mighty hospitable," Winston stated low.

"Wonder what Dodding's up to?" Ben whispered out the side of his mouth.

Storme shook his head. "Guess we'll find out, little brother." He leaned slightly toward Winston. "Keep the men back," he whispered. "I don't know why the need for all these guards, but there may be more up ahead." And Storme had no intention of getting sidetracked from giving Dodding what he deserved, or from getting the answers he wanted about the necklace.

Winston nodded and pulled back on his reins, falling behind with the rest of the wranglers as Storme and Ben held the lead.

The stranger kept to the trail by the river for another mile, riding under the timbered train trestle overhead that bridged the Pecos, then guided them onto what Ben discreetly informed Storme was government land. About a hundred yards up ahead, the base of the mountain began its upward slope, and where the stream split, three men dressed in dark suits stood near the bank.

Storme tensed at the sight of Dodding. He bunched his fists around the reins and scanned the tree-lined mountain. He didn't see any posted guards, but he knew that didn't mean they weren't there. He glanced over his shoulder, seeing Winston motion for the men to spread out, the foreman's stare searching the area with hard intent.

"Boss," their bearded guide called out as they drew closer, "I brung you that crew you've been expectin'."

Dodding turned.

Storme smiled at the shock that dropped the rancher's jaw. The cheroot he had been smoking fell to the ground, and instantly the patch of bunch grass at his feet caught on fire. Dodding quickly stamped it out with his foot.

Storme drew his mount to a stop, and undid his gun belt, looping it around his saddle horn. He spared a glance at the two men with Dodding, noting the look of displeasure from one man, and that the other had turned away and pulled his hat down low over his face.

"You idiot!" Dodding's long stride carried him over to where their guide reined to a halt. He grabbed a handful of the man's shirt and yanked him from the horse. "What the hell did you bring this half-breed here for?"

"He said he was told at the house that he could find you here," the man defended. "He admitted he was the—"

Dodding backhanded the man.

Storme jumped down from his horse. Memories of Anna's accusation, her arms clasped across her breasts filled his thoughts and fueled his steps. Eyes narrowed and focused on the rancher, Storme crossed the distance between them, tossing his hat to the ground.

"I want to talk to you, Dodding," he growled.

"I've got nothing to say to you, half-breed. Now, get the hell out of here." Dodding flapped the opening of his black coat aside, and reached for his Colt.

A dozen gun hammers locking into place resounded on the air. The rancher paused, enough time for Storme to propel himself through the last few feet, blood roaring in his ears and throbbing in the vein at his temple as he planted his fist into Dodding's jaw. His knuckles split with the force, the pain a minor nuisance in the glow of satisfaction at seeing the rancher stagger back, then fall.

Dodding reached for his Colt again. Storme stomped his boot down on the man's hand, hearing the bone crunch above the howl Dodding released. He snagged the gun and threw it where Ben stood off to the side with his six-shooter aimed at their bearded guide.

The rancher grabbed his leg and tugged. Storme reached down and wrapped his fists in the man's coat lapels, then stepped back and hauled him to his feet.

"You need to respect women better, Dodding." He pulled his right arm back, then let his fist fly with another punch, but the rancher jerked his head back, and the blow landed on the man's chin.

Then a fist plowed into Storme's gut, and the air whooshed from his lungs. He stepped back. Dodding swung with his left. Storme threw his arm up, blocking the punch, then shoved his fist into the rancher's nose.

Dodding staggered back, his left hand cupped to his nose, blood running down over his lip. Storme knotted his hand tighter, and rammed it into the man's stomach. He doubled over, then sat hard on the ground.

Storme stepped back, his breaths coming fast as he caught his air, his adrenaline still pumping, his fists itching for the man to get up.

"Don't ever go near Miss Alexander again," he seethed.

Dodding slowly lowered his hand and raised his head, his eyes hard as cold steel in his narrowed gaze. "Or what?" he grated. "You threatening me in front of all these witnesses?"

"No, Dodding, there's no threat. I promise I'll kill you." Storme's insides shook with rage. "And I won't give you the chance to make another trip to the mercantile if you don't tell me right now how you knew about that necklace."

"Ain't none of your damn business." The rancher braced his hands against the ground, and shoved to his feet.

"I want an answer, Dodding." Storme waited until the man was almost upright, then stepped forward, clipping him in the chin with a fast uppercut.

Dodding's head snapped back with a loud pop. He staggered, groaning. Then a lethal growl ripped from his throat, and he charged forward.

Storme jumped to the side, and brought his fist down on the back of the man's neck, sending him facefirst into the ground. Then he planted his foot firmly in Dodding's back, and pressed against his lungs.

"The necklace, Dodding," Storme demanded.

"I'll . . ." he gasped, "kill . . . you . . . Injun."

"You must live through this first. The necklace." He shifted a little more of his weight to the rancher's back, seeing the reddened flesh of his cheek darken.

"Why . . ." he swallowed, then sucked for air, "should . . . I tell . . . you?"

Storme met the man's gray stare, and smiled sardonically. "Because I know you're a coward, and you don't really want to die." He reached down and lifted his pant leg up, pulling the knife from his boot. Then he removed his foot from Dodding's back, replacing it with his knee, grabbed a handful of black hair and jerked up. He placed the knife at Dodding's throat, staring into the man's wide-eyed gaze of surprise.

"Shit," Ben muttered harshly.

"You just can't go around treatin' women wrong, Dodding," Winston called out, a touch of amusement evident in his voice.

Blood dripped from Dodding's nose and mouth. Dirt gritted his reddened face. Storme knew he wasn't going to kill the man, but the thought was tempting. He did enjoy the fear on the rancher's face, though it didn't come close to making up for everything Dodding had done, in the past, or now.

"All right," Dodding rasped.

Storme pulled the knife away and rose to his feet.

Dodding lay still for several seconds, breathing in large gulps of air, then he slowly pushed himself up to his knees and stood. He made a half hearted attempt to brush off the dirt that dusted his coat. His face hardened with contempt.

Storme smiled inwardly at the resignation in Dodding's eyes, but he wasn't foolish enough to think the victory was more than just *this* battle.

"One of my wranglers was at the saloon." Dodding spit a bloody stream in the dirt, close to the tip of Storme's boot. "He followed you as far as the boardinghouse. When I saw you two kissing this morning, I just guessed the necklace was for her."

Storme frowned, hearing nothing but truth in Dodding's tone. It wasn't like he hadn't anticipated this answer, though—even before Ben had commented on the ride out that he had seen a couple of Dodding's hands at the saloon last night. Frustration at the lack of evidence to connect the rancher to the rustlers cooled Storme's temper to a low boil. "Tell your wranglers to stay away from me."

The rancher turned his head to the side and spit a bloody

mass, then pulled a handkerchief from his coat pocket. "You got your answer. Now, get the hell out of here, Injun."

Storme lifted his chin in defiance and narrowed his stare. "You spread one word against Miss Alexander's reputation, I'll be back to finish the job." He turned and walked to where Ben waited, seeing the curiosity in his brother's stare. He scooped his hat up from the ground and strode toward his horse.

Gun still drawn, Ben backstepped at his side. "What the hell were you doing kissing Miss Alexander?" he whispered out the corner of his mouth.

"That was a nice touch with the knife"—Winston shifted the wad of tobacco in his cheek, and grinned—"boss."

Chapter Nine

A warm breeze drifted through the windows, stirring the lingering warmth that permeated the kitchen. Anna leaned one hip against the counter and stared out, watching as the sun dipped behind the mountains and twilight's shadows began its slow claim over the valley. She raised the half-filled glass to her lips, welcoming the splash of iced lemonade against her dry throat, then sighed. If only she could find as simple a balm for her plaguing thoughts.

She closed her eyes, her heart pounding faster as Storme's handsome face filled the darkness. Tingles coursed through her blood at the disarming images of his chivalrous defense, his warm smile, his soft kiss . . .

His job!

The sweet drink turned sour in her stomach. Anxiety shivered through her limbs. *A bounty hunter.* She still couldn't believe it. Anna opened her eyes and set the glass on the counter.

She recalled her shock, and the curious speculation in Storme's eyes when she spilled her coffee at his pronounce-

ment. To her relief, his suspicion had quickly fled, replaced
with a seeming acceptance of her explanation that the mishap
was nothing more than a loose grip on the delicate handle. She
had left the parlor then, under the helpful guise of fetching a
towel to wipe up the mess. In truth, she had needed a moment
to regain her composure and chase away her initial panic that
he knew the truth, had really come to town looking for *her*.
She had calmed her rattled apprehension with logic that he
wouldn't be so kind to her, or worry over her safety and reputation, if he intended to turn her in.

Besides, she didn't doubt his word about coming home to
help his brother find the rustlers. She didn't doubt that if he
suspected something was amiss, his stubborn persistence would
send him searching for answers, either. Anna bit at her bottom
lip. She had carefully marked a phony trail headed east, and
she would just as soon that the law kept searching in that
direction. The last thing she needed was a bounty hunter nosing
around for the truth.

Anna shook her head at her ill luck. She couldn't have saved
the life of just any man. No, she had to find someone connected
to the law . . . and compound the problem by finding him so
darned attractive!

She sighed heavily, finding no regret for saving Storme's
life, or for her unwise fascination with the kind man, but she
knew she would have to be very careful not to give him any
cause for suspicion. Throughout the long afternoon, as she had
wandered the house unable to focus on her chores, she had
pondered the best solution to keep that from happening, and
kept circling back to only one reasonable answer—she had to
avoid Storme Warwick as much as possible.

A sharp pain jabbed at her chest. Anna's shoulders slumped.
So, why did her heart keep protesting the rational thing to do?

Several sets of footsteps resounded at the front of the house,
then the screen door banged shut. Anna smiled at the familiar

noise of the girls returning from their day at the restaurant, their murmured words drifting down the hallway.

"Anna, where are you?" Samantha suddenly called out in an eager rush.

Anna cocked her head, wondering what had her roommate in such an excited state. She gripped her hand around the glass, the beaded condensation cool against her palm, and started across the room.

"Anna, are you upstairs?" A rasp of enthusiasm rang in Caroline's raised voice.

Anna's pulse pounded with growing trepidation at the urgency that heightened the talk among the girls.

"Maybe she's too embarrassed to come down," Patricia commented.

"That's barmy, why would she be embarrassed," Katie exclaimed. "If I had two men fighting over me, I'd be strutting through town like a proud peacock."

Anna stopped. *How did the girls know about the fight? What else had they heard?* She tightened her grip around the glass as it started to slip. Mrs. Harrington had left earlier on a twofold mission of meeting with the Garden Society ladies about the extravaganza and squelching any gossip that had spread. She hoped the housemother was having some success.

"Maybe she's taking a rest; I'll just run upstairs and check," Samantha remarked.

Anna took a deep breath and squared her shoulders, then stepped into the hallway. "I'm right here."

In a quick parade of black and white cotton and curious faces, the girls rushed down the hall, backing Anna against the far wall as they cornered her in a half circle and cut off any means of escape.

"Is it true?" Caroline's black eyebrows rose high, disappearing in her thin fringe of bangs.

"Did you really have two men fighting over you?" Katie sighed with awe.

"Damon said the man who hit Mr. Dodding looked part-Indian." Patricia's brown eyes widened.

Anna groaned. *The chef had seen the fight?* She turned her questioning frown toward her roommate. "Who else saw?"

Samantha shook her head. "Damon just happened to be throwing scraps out to your mangy cat. Everyone else was busy. Was it Ben's brother? It sounded like it from Damon's description."

Anna sighed her relief, grateful that either Damon hadn't seen her kissing Storme or had chosen to stay silent. "Yes, it was Storme Warwick, and yes he's half-Apache." She shifted her stare around at the girls. "But no, the two of them weren't fighting over me. Mr. Dodding said something offensive, and Mr. Warwick hit him, that's all."

"Well, that doesn't surprise me. Everyone knows Mr. Dodding is a rough sort." Caroline cocked her head, smiling. "So, whose honor was Mr. Warwick defending, his or yours?"

"Mine." A thrilling jolt shot through her stomach at the memory of Storme's gallant action.

"And how did this gentleman happen to be in your company to defend you?" Patricia inquired in a teasing voice.

Heated blood rose into her cheeks. "He walked me home from the mercantile."

"He did?" Samantha arched her brow high, her blue eyes promising she was going to demand more details later.

Katie arched her blond eyebrows as well. "Are you two courting?" Ever the romantic, her violet eyes gleamed with dreamy speculation.

"No," Anna ground out emphatically. "We're just friends."

"Then why are you blushing?" Patricia challenged.

"I'm not. It's just hot in here. I swear, I think this is the hottest day we've had so far." Anna fanned her face with her free hand, then took a sip of her lemonade for added emphasis.

"No, Patricia's right, you're blushing," Caroline stated, narrowing her gaze. ''Are you sure there's something you're not telling us?''

''You can tell us,'' Katie coaxed, glancing around at the others. ''We're all mates. We won't say anything. Will we, girls?''

''Of course not.'' Patricia shook her head hard enough to make the red, frizzed curls bob around her thin face.

''Wouldn't dream of it. You can trust us,'' Caroline assured her.

''If you'd rather not talk about it, that's fine,'' Samantha quietly asserted.

Anna hesitated, appreciating her roommate's discretion, even as her heart soared at the declared vows of friendship. When she came to town, she had intended to stay to herself and tend strictly to her work. Instead, she had found herself quickly drawn into the girls' lives, taking walks with them, talking and laughing, and listening to their tales of childhood and their dreams for the future. Anna had wished that she could share more than a few sparing details of her own past during those times, had wanted to talk about her dreams of singing on stage, but she couldn't. She was carting around too much baggage for any depth of truth to be told, and Anna hadn't relished dishing out a bunch of lies. She smiled. But she could certainly tell them about Storme's kiss—at least the shortened version that Mrs. Harrington was using to head the gossip off. She opened her mouth just as Elise bounded through the front door, drawing everyone's attention.

''Anna, where—oh, there you are.'' Elise hurried down the hallway. ''Sally Hankins stopped by Lilah's shop while I was having my wedding dress fitted. She was madder than a wet hen that you left the mercantile with Ben's brother. She even accused you of kissing him in the middle of town. Is it true?''

''You kissed him!'' The other girls exclaimed in shocked unison, swinging their stares back to her. Even Samantha's eyes widened in a demand for answers right now.

Anna drew her eyebrows together, hoping that Mrs. Harrington was at least having some success getting the facts straight. "No, it wasn't the middle of town. It was out front of the boardinghouse."

"Then you did kiss him," Katie's voice held a sigh of awe as her smile spread wide across her round face.

"Yes." Quickly, Anna told them about Storme's kindness in returning her necklace and kissing him in gratitude.

"Well, I've met Storme Warwick," Elise informed the other girls. "Anna's right, he is a gentleman. And if I didn't have my Wallace, I wouldn't mind taking an opportunity to kiss that handsome face of his, either."

"He does seem like a nice man," Samantha agreed.

"You've met him, too?" Caroline questioned, shifting her annoyed stare at Anna.

"When do we get to meet him?" Patricia demandingly asked the same question that blazed in Caroline's and Katie's expressions.

Anna ran her tongue over her suddenly dry lips. "Well, I . . . um . . . I'm not planning to see him again."

"Sure you will," Elise countered, grinning. "I invited him to the wedding, and Wallace told me he's agreed to come."

Butterflies winged their way through Anna's stomach in haunting reminder of the necessity to avoid Storme as much as possible. But she couldn't stop her traitorous heart from beating joyously faster at the prospect of seeing him again.

The man stood behind the tall cottonwood and peered around the thick, knotty trunk. Through hooded eyes, he watched the young woman emerge from the small wash shed at the back of the three-story house. She carried a large wicker basket, piled high with laundry, propped against one hip, and kept darting her gaze back at the gray kitten that dogged her heels as she crossed the lawn toward the clothesline.

His blood raced with expectation, then throbbed in a hot, hardening pool in his loins. It had been a long time since he bedded a white woman, and he intended to have some fun with that pretty lady. The noon sun reigned overhead, bright rays burnishing her reddish gold hair, the same way it had the night he saw her on the mountain—just minutes before she had called out a warning to that damn Injun.

The lady could've saved her breath. He hadn't been aiming to kill Warwick. Not right then. He knew that half-breed would think she *had* saved his life, though, and his Apache honor would bind him to a life-debt. He also hoped the effort and expense Warwick had gone to returning the necklace meant the Injun felt more than just honorable duty toward the woman.

The man traced one finger along the deep scars that crossed his face. The more that half-breed had to lose, the better he was gonna like taking it all away.

The woman reached into her apron pocket and retrieved several wooden pins, then proceeded to secure a white sheet to the line. He saw her glance down at the kitten, could see her mouth moving, but she was too far away for him to hear what she said. A bright sheen glowed on her oval face. Her lips kept moving as she worked to hang the laundry, and he caught the barest sound of a song issuing on the air as she raised her voice. She looked happy, content.

The man frowned. He had been happy once, and quite content . . . until that Injun ruined his life. Thanks to Warwick, he had wound up in Mexico, and later landed in prison. Six years he spent in that tortuous hellhole. He had spent even longer planning his revenge against that half-breed. Promising money and freedom, he had recruited the three Mexican thieves and the Texas cowboy sharing floor space with him in the cramped cell to help him escape and carry out this vengeance. He hadn't anticipated that Warwick wouldn't be living at the ranch anymore, though, or that he would have to waste so much time stealing cattle before his brother finally sent for him. But the Injun was here now.

A sardonic grin pulled at his mouth. He wasn't in as much hurry to kill him now, either. In fact, when the woman interfered where she had no business, he couldn't have asked for a better alteration to his plan. The two notes and his dead cohort were just the beginning.

He shook his head. The cowboy never should have taken the necklace and a good chunk of money from their bank heist in El Paso and slipped away from camp. When he discovered the theft, he had trailed the wrangler into town and was just heading through the saloon doors when he spotted Warwick snatching up the necklace. Even though the theft had ultimately given him more knowledge to use against the Injun, he hadn't thought twice about killing the cowboy. The wrangler couldn't be trusted, and killing him had shown the others to think twice before trying anything similar.

He caught a movement from the corner of his eye and glanced toward the front of the house, stunned to see Storme Warwick drawing a wagon to a halt just outside the gate. He climbed down and sauntered up the walk, disappearing as he gained the porch. The man looked back at the woman. He could see her lips still moving as she bent over and pulled another sheet from the basket. Warwick reappeared at the end of the porch, took the one long step down, then made his way along the side of the house. He hoped Warwick was here to pay court to her. *The more he has to lose . . .*

The man pulled back and turned slightly, grazing the top of his arm against the hard bark. He winced as hot pain shot across his shoulder. The woman's warning had given the bounty hunter a chance to aim true and graze him with a round. She would pay for that. He narrowed his stare. *I have a lot of surprises in store for her . . . and for that damn Injun.*

* * *

Storme crossed his arms and leaned one shoulder against the corner of the clapboard, smiling his enjoyment of Anna's velvety voice as she sang the sentimental ballad. He knew he was taking far more pleasure in this covert opportunity to watch her than he should, but she was a vision to look at, and he wasn't inclined to give away his presence just yet.

A blue kerchief partially covered her head, the edges tucked back behind her small, shell-shaped ears and tied at her nape. Her hair hung in a wavy mass down her back, stirring a heated urge to run his hands through the thick strands. His heart raced as he slid his stare over her slender waist and gently rounded hips. Her white sleeves were folded up to her elbows, revealing her slim, pale arms as she reached down to gather up another sheet from the basket. The brown-calico skirt draped over her nicely rounded bottom and hiked up to reveal bare feet and the pale flesh of her calves. His breath lodged. His pulse soared. Then a strong wave of unexpected jealousy pulled at his pleasure and made him glance around. He certainly didn't begrudge her the impropriety on such a hot day, but he didn't like the idea of any other male eyes watching, either.

He swept his gaze over the shadowed stand of trees, his gut oddly tightening. Storme frowned, staring harder into the shadows. Nothing stirred. Beyond the grove, he heard the train hissing steam as it prepared to pull out, then the muted call of final boarding and the faint sounds of hurried footsteps running along the depot platform. He made another passing sweep along the grove, then shook off the odd sense as nothing more than his guilt at his own clandestine action. He looked back at Anna, his smile deepening at the sweet sound of her voice filling the air, his eyes drinking in the sight of her as she bent to retrieve another sheet from the basket.

She straightened, then lifted one end of the linen to the line beside the row of others and secured it with a wooden pin. Her voice rose slightly as she reached the last of word of the final chorus, then tapered into silence. She glanced down. "How did that sound, Sebastian?"

Storme followed her stare, spotting the gray kitten sitting beside the large basket. The small feline cocked its head to one side, and meowed.

"Well, I'll take that as a compliment." Anna's chuckle filled the air, the melodious sound washing over him in a warm wave. She stretched out another section of the sheet, and shoved a pin over the edge of the cloth.

"If you'd like another opinion, you sounded great."

She jumped, dropping the rest of the sheet as she spun around, one hand pressed against her chest, her green eyes wide.

"I'm sorry. I didn't mean to startle you." Storme uncrossed his arms and straightened.

Her breasts rose with her quickened breath. She pulled her eyebrows together. "How long have you been standing there?"

"Just since the last verse." He removed his hat as he made his way across the yard. "I knocked at the front, but no one answered. I could hear you singing and came around." He smiled. "I hope you don't mind. You have a beautiful voice. I didn't want to interrupt."

She lowered her hand to her side. "No, I don't mind." A soft smile tilted the luscious curve of her mouth. "I was just practicing for Elise's wedding tomorrow night."

"I didn't know that you'd be singing. The guests are in for a real treat." Her nearness made his senses spin. Storme tightened both hands around the brim of his hat. "You sing better than anyone I've ever heard in any performance, and I look forward to hearing you again."

Twin spots of pink filled her cheeks and fired his blood, sending a surge of desire to touch her face itching in his fingers. "Thank you." She arched her thin eyebrows. "Have you seen many musical performances?"

Storme chuckled lightly. "Are you doubting my compliment?"

"No," she quickly responded, her eyes widening at his challenge. "Just curious. My mother took me to the theater a couple of times, and I really enjoyed it."

He nodded. "I've seen a few. My father enjoyed the theater, and would travel to Denver or over to Santa Fe quite often. He was also a firm believer that one should broaden his interests, and insisted that my brother and I accompany him on occasion."

She cocked her head. "And were you glad to have your interests broadened?"

Storme shrugged. "In that particular area, not as much as Ben, I'm afraid." He had enjoyed the time spent with his father and brother more than being confined in one place for hours on end, though there were a couple of plays that had captured his attention. "I didn't mind sitting through the performances sometimes. But I can't say that I've been since I was old enough to tell my father no . . . and get away with it." He grinned, then leaned forward slightly, lowering his voice. "I usually prefer reading instead, though I could sit and listen to you all night."

She tucked her head down and shyly peeked up at him through her thick lashes. "That's nice of you to say."

"It's the truth," he whispered, smiling.

She glanced down, her sweet smile disappearing as she caught her bottom lip between her teeth. She raised one hand to the front of her hair, frowning as her fingers touched the kerchief, then she brushed at the damp tendrils that framed her face. "I wasn't expecting any visitors."

Storme's smile widened at her concern about her appearance in front of him. "You look fine, Anna." His manhood throbbed as he gave her body a raking gaze. *Real fine.* His breath hitched when he met her stare and saw the sparkle of delight at his appraisal dancing in her spring meadow depths. The desire to pull her into his arms tugged hard at his resolve to keep his distance from her. "And I know you have work to do. I just stopped by for a minute to make sure you haven't had any trouble with Dodding . . . or the gossip." And because he had an insane urge to see her again as soon as possible.

She shook her head. "I haven't seen Mr. Dodding, and there was only a short burst of gossip yesterday, a little about our . . . um, kiss." She licked at her lips, making his blood sizzle with a heated fervor to kiss her again, right now. "But Mrs. Harrington and I made sure everyone knew about your generosity in getting my necklace back. Most of the talk, though, was about your fight with Mr. Dodding."

"I was just over at the mercantile picking up supplies. That's all I heard mentioned, too." Which had surprised Storme, just as much as the two farmers who had never spoken more than three words to him before, but had greeted him cordially and offered their opinion that it was time someone put Dodding in his place. Bob Mason had added his agreement, as well, and one elderly woman had even offered him a quick smile. Mrs. Mason and Sally Hankins, however, had showed their usual scowling faces and given him pause to worry that Anna's reputation could still suffer harm.

"The girls think you're a hero for hitting Mr. Dodding. They can't wait to meet you at the wedding."

Storme arched his brow. "The girls?"

"My friends who live here at the house."

Storme nodded, smiling. A warm glow formed in his chest. He liked the idea that she had spoken of him to her friends. Linette had never talked to anyone about him. "I'd like to meet your friends, but they may be disappointed. I'm no hero. I did nothing more than any decent man would have done."

"You're being too modest. It's been my experience that decent men can be in short supply."

Storme frowned at her comment, recalling her words about knowing men who could wear the label of savage. "And what experience would that be?"

A look of haunting anxiety sprang into her gaze. "Nothing," she whispered, then turned away.

Storme reached out and circled his hand around her wrist, gently forcing her to face him. "Has someone hurt you, Anna?"

She blinked back the moisture he saw swimming in her eyes, then lifted her chin slightly. "Life is full of hurts. You just have to learn to live with them."

He certainly couldn't argue that point. Frustration tensed his muscles. But it sure as hell didn't answer his question . . . or quell his curiosity.

"I really do appreciate you coming to my defense."

He took a deep breath, pondering whether to push for the answers he wanted, and decided against it for the moment. He was earning her trust, one slow step at a time, and he didn't want to risk her flying away to retreat from the progress he had made so far. He released her arm and cupped his hand to her cheek. "I'd do it again in a heartbeat for you, Anna."

She lifted one thin, auburn eyebrow. "Because of your debt?"

Storme shook his head. "Because you're a sweet, lovely woman, and you deserve to be treated as such."

"Thank you." Her throat rippled as she swallowed.

Storme's heart jolted. He knew he needed to back away. He wanted to step forward, wanted to press his mouth to the slender column of her neck and slowly work his way up. He took a deep breath and lowered his hand from her face. "I better be going."

She hesitated, glancing toward the house. "Would you like something to drink before you leave? There's some fresh lemonade in the icebox."

Storme shook his head and hitched one thumb over his shoulder. "Thanks, but I need to get those supplies on out to the ranch." And himself out of there.

"I understand."

His pulse hammered in surprise at the disappointment he

heard in her tone. Damn, why did she have be so pretty . . . so tempting? He would like nothing more than to hang around a while longer. He shoved his hat onto his head. "I'll see you tomorrow night."

A hot flame of anticipation torched her eyes, mirroring his own expectations. She nodded. "Bye, Storme."

His heart stopped at the sound of his name, as soft as a gentle breeze whispering from her lips for the first time. His feet stayed rooted to the spot. He glanced at the house, recalling his unanswered knock, then down at Anna. Before he could talk himself out of it, he reached around, cupping his hand to the back of her head, and leaned down. Her warm palms flattened against his chest. She closed her eyes as he pressed his mouth to her full, warm lips. He wrapped his other arm around her back and pulled her closer, kissing her slow, rocked with a powerful sensation as her mouth parted, her tongue eagerly meeting his in an urgent exploration.

Storme ended the kiss, forcing himself to draw back from her sweet, willing response before he lost all sense of where they were. He stared down into her dazed expression, and took a deep breath, then lowered his hands to his sides and stepped back.

"Bye, Anna." He turned and walked away, while he still had the good sense and the willpower to do so.

"No dear, not there," Mrs. Harrington gently rebuked.

Anna froze, the cloth-covered bowl of fried chicken heavy in her hands as she held it above the white linen. She stared across the makeshift table that had been set up between two tall oaks in the Sandersons' side yard.

"More to the center." Mrs. Harrington motioned toward the right.

Anna indulgently moved the large dish, until the housemother stopped making the short, quick wave with her stiffened fingers and nodded her approval, then she gratefully set the earthenware bowl down.

Mrs. Harrington crossed her arms and peered over the top of her glasses, studying the six-foot table laden with food. Anna suppressed her smile at how fussy the woman had been all day—first with Elise's dress, then reminding Mr. Chesterfield more than once that the girls needed to finish on time so they wouldn't be late to the wedding, and trying to oversee Damon's preparation of the food—which, according to Samantha, the chef had loudly refused to allow—and now the presentation of the refreshments. *She's like a worrisome mother hen,* Anna thought.

A warm glow spread through her veins as memories of the woman's kindness flooded in. *A forgiving, worrisome hen,* she amended. Anna knew the housemother had a deep fondness for Elise, and cared about all of them living at the boarding-house, but she had been a little surprised to see the older woman wipe away several tears when Wallace had arrived this morning and loaded Elise's packed belongings into the wagon to be moved out to the Sanderson farm.

A sudden frown firmed Mrs. Harrington's mouth. "We're missing the apple stack cake. Would you run and see what's keeping Samantha? She may not remember that I put it up front under the wagon seat."

"I'd be happy to, ma'am." Anna made her way along the side of the two-story frame house, glancing through the white, wooden beams that supported the porch overhang, and looked over the two dozen people scattered about on the Sandersons' front lawn. She saw Katie and Patricia talking with the minister and two other gentlemen, waved at Caroline talking with Blaine and Wallace's father, then sighed her disappointment when she didn't see Storme anywhere about. Had he changed his mind about coming?

His unexpected visit yesterday had been a nice surprise. The gleam of adoration in his eyes as he had assured her that she

looked just fine still haunted her thoughts, as did his parting
kiss. She scanned the yard one more time, taking note that Ben
Warwick had yet to make an appearance. Her heart beat a little
faster that Storme might still be coming after all.

Anna shook her head and hurried across the yard, chiding
herself for being so anxious to see him again. She knew she
had roused his suspicions with her comment about decent men
being in short supply, and reminded herself that she needed to
be more careful . . . and stay away from him.

She lifted her skirt a little higher as the grass gave way to
dirt. The sun eased behind the distant mountains, brilliant
golden streaks fanning out low to light the last vestiges of the
day. The smell of wool clung in the air, but Anna saw no signs
of the Sandersons' sheep in the large, circular pen set off from
the barn. Out front, a large, square platform had been erected
to serve as a dance floor. From wooden poles that stood at each
corner, lanterns hung ready to be lit once the heat and light
had fled for the day. Anna wondered if Storme would ask her
to dance, then shoved the notion aside. *Fool!* She was supposed
to be avoiding him, not dallying with wayward thoughts of
being held in his arms.

She skirted around the wooden floor, her steps slowing as
she caught sight of someone moving in the gray shadows just
beyond the opened barn doors, her heartbeat picking up when
Storme stepped outside and blocked her path.

"Hello, Anna." A warm, engaging smile claimed his mouth
and stole her breath

She swallowed and smiled back. "Hi, Storme." Shivers of
delight raged through her blood at the handsome sight of his
tall, masculine frame dressed in the black suit. A silver eagle
decorated the buttoned neck of his crisp white shirt, the black
strings of the tie hanging down against his broad chest. No hat
graced his head, and his long black hair was brushed to a
polished gleam and tied back with a strip of leather. "I was

beginning to wonder if you'd changed your mind about coming.''

He shook his head. Nothing short of death would have stopped him from being there. He had thought of little else all day but seeing her again. "We're just running a little late. We saw Miss Crowley when we rode up. She said something about fetching a cake, and Ben went to help her. I was just waiting for them.'' He looked back over his shoulder toward the other side of the barn, where the guests had left their wagons and carriages. They had been gone a while already, and Storme hoped now they would stay gone for a while longer.

Anna took advantage of his distracted stare and leaned a little closer to him, breathing deep of the intoxicating scent of his spicy maleness. She straightened and shook her head. *Goodness.* What was wrong with her? Why couldn't she stay away from this man?

Storme swerved his stare back around, his breath lodging at the sight of her pretty flushed cheeks. Sunlight shimmered in the short, silky tendrils that framed her smooth face, and the long strands that hung in thick waves against her back, tied at her nape with a green ribbon that matched her printed lawn dress. A wide satin sash hugged her narrow waist, and the sheer organdy lace that covered the darker bodice and skirt shone nearly translucent beneath the sun's soft rays, revealing the delicate pale flesh of her slender shoulders and arms. He couldn't wait to dance with her later. His pulse pounded at the thought of holding her close. "You look lovely tonight, Anna.''

"Thank you.'' Her eyes sparkled; her blush deepened.

He couldn't stop himself from reaching over and taking hold of her hand, from circling his thumb along the top of her soft, warm skin. "Are you nervous about singing?''

"A little.'' She ran her tongue over her lips, driving his blood to a heated level that roared in his head and surged to a throbbing crescendo in his loins.

He fought the urge to lean down and capture her sweet, full lips. "Have you sung in front of folks much before?"

Her shoulders tensed slightly. Storme pondered at the hesitation that tightened her face, and the odd gleam that darkened her eyes, as though she weighed the decision of whether to evade or answer his question. Then she sighed, and nodded. "It's been a while, though. When I was a child, my father had a medicine show. I used to sing as part of the entertainment."

Storme arched his brow in surprise. "Really?" Roaming from town to town in search of outlaws, he had come across a few medicine shows, and recalled the musical entertainment and variety acts performed to draw the townsfolk's attention, and the "doctors" who hawked their patent medicines, boasted to cure nearly every illness known to man. A good many of the "doctors" were little better than swindlers. He had even seen one man strung up by angry townsfolk when they discovered his elixirs were nothing more than rat poison and sugar water. "And did you enjoy singing for your father's show?"

"Yes. I'd get real nervous sometimes, though, especially the first night we were in a new town." A light smile tipped the corners of her mouth. "But my mama would always calm me down."

"And what would your mama do?" He sure as hell knew what he would like to do—carry her into the barn, and help take her mind off of singing by kissing her senseless.

She shrugged. "Just talk to me about things that had nothing to do with singing. She'd tell me about her childhood, and we'd talk about traveling to new places, or about how we'd have a house in the mountains someday. A real home, where we could settle down in one place for a while."

Storme's ardor cooled slightly in the wake of his piqued curiosity about her past. He was glad to see her finally opening up about herself, and since she seemed to be in the mood to talk, he wasn't going to pass up this opportunity to learn more.

Maybe he could also find out what she was hiding. "Did you ever have that?"

Sadness dimmed the glow in her green gaze. "We settled down. Not in the mountains, though."

The anguish in her voice tore at his heart. He tightened his hand around hers, offering his comfort, and questioned his insane urge to build her a house in the mountains as soon as the sun came up. "Is that why you came to Pleasant Grove, to be close to the mountains?"

She shook her head. "My mama loved the mountains. It was her dream to be close to them."

He stared into her eyes and rubbed his thumb along her hand. "And what's your dream, Anna?"

She bit at her bottom lip. Storme saw the same look of hesitation on her face, and knew she was deciding whether to answer or not. He held his breath, waiting.

"Anna, where's Samantha? Mrs. Harrington wants her cake."

Storme frowned at the woman's shouted interruption and stepped back, releasing Anna's hand. He turned a hard stare on the black-haired girl making her way toward the barn with Blaine Sanderson.

Anna swallowed and turned to face the approaching couple. "She's getting it right now," she called out, answering Caroline's inquiry, grateful for girl's interruption. *Good heavens! What was it about Storme that made her talk so freely, that caused her to trust him so deeply?* She had opted to tell him the truth about singing in hopes it would assuage some of his curiosity and divert any suspicions. But she hadn't meant for the conversation to turn to her plans for the future. She glanced up at him, meeting his narrowed gaze, seeing his heightened interest in her and a promise that he wasn't through probing into her life. Anna took a deep breath. *Blast it! I don't need a bounty hunter prying into my past.*

"Glad you could make it, Storme," Blaine greeted, coming

to a stop and sticking his hand out for Storme to shake. "Haven't had a chance to thank you and Ben for sending your hands over to ride guard yesterday. Dodding's men gave us a little trouble, but they didn't try to stop us from herding our sheep to the river this time."

Storme nodded, his mouth firming in a straight line. "Good. Just let us know if we can help again."

Blaine smiled his appreciation, then frowned slightly, glancing around. "Where is Ben, anyway? Elise is fit to be tied because he's late."

Storme pointed toward the side of the barn. "He's helping Miss Crowley with that cake."

Anna saw Caroline's raised brow beneath her black fringe of bangs and her demanding nod toward Storme. She smiled, recalling the ride out to the Sanderson's farm, and the girls reminded insistence that they wanted to meet him. "Caroline, I'd like you to meet Storme Warwick." She made the introduction, then glanced up at Storme. "This is Caroline Smythe. One of the friends I was telling you about."

He nodded in remembrance of their conversation yesterday. A desirous gleam of another memory flashed in his stare, fueling her own heated reminders of their kiss before he looked away. "It's nice to meet you, Miss Smythe." He smiled and tipped his hat.

"Likewise." She smiled, then cocked her head. "You certainly stirred up a lot of excitement in town when you hit Mr. Dodding the other day."

Blaine arched his thick, black eyebrows. "You hit Dodding in town? I thought your men said you beat him up out at the river?"

Storme's jaw hardened. "We had an altercation at both places," he stated low and even, without a hint of the deep anger Anna knew he was capable of where the rancher was concerned.

She wasn't too surprised there had been another fight. She

had had a suspicion that might be Storme's intent when he promised to make sure the rancher wouldn't spread any gossip. She glanced down at Storme's clenched fists, noting the slight bruising and small, partially healed cut across his right knuckles. His defense and concern about her reputation sent a renewed thrilling jolt coursing through her veins.

Caroline shook her head and issued a tsking sound. "Well, that man deserves whatever he gets. His manners are worse than an angry bull's."

Anna couldn't agree more.

"What did you two fight about, anyway? Your men never said." Blaine lifted his chin slightly and chuckled. "Not that Dodding doesn't deserve to be hit most days just for taking up space."

No smile graced Storme's lips, though he did nod in agreement with the comment. "This time it was for bad manners."

"Well, I don't consider it good manners for you people to lollygag with my apple stack cake." Aggravation rang clear in Mrs. Harrington's voice.

Caroline and Blaine spun around. Storme straightened, squaring his shoulders. Anna's heart skipped a beat. She bit her bottom lip and glanced toward the side of the barn. *Good heavens, where is Samantha?*

Mrs. Harrington's face pulled taut. She planted her hands on her ample hips. "Where is Miss Crowley?"

"Here I am, Mrs. Harrington." Samantha rounded the corner of the barn, her blue skirts swishing about her ankles with her hurried steps. Anna stifled her groan when she saw that the girl's hands were empty. Was Samantha *looking* for ways to get in trouble?

Ben appeared close on her heels and strode forward, offering a bright smile and tipping his hat. "Mrs. Harrington, how nice to see you again. How are you this evening?"

The housemother frowned. "Well enough that I'm not interested in any lies you're about to concoct over what's taking

Miss Crowley so long." She swept her gaze over the group. "Or why it takes so many people to fetch one cake. Now, you've all dawdled long enough down here. The wedding's about to start." She shoved her glasses up the bridge of her nose and narrowed her eyes. "And just where is my apple stack cake, Miss Crowley?"

Samantha gasped, her eyes widening. She spun around and hurried back toward the side of the barn.

To Anna's surprise, Mrs. Harrington shook her head, chuckling as she rolled her eyes.

Chapter Ten

Anna held the note until her breath grew thin, paused to draw in air, then began the words to the last refrain of "Silver Threads Among the Gold." From the Sanderson's front porch, she had a clear view of the guests gathered on the lawn, but her gaze kept darting to Storme standing up front beside his brother. Her blood raced at the sight of his handsome, bronze face, at the look of admiration in his dark stare.

The man was a distraction to her senses. A distraction she didn't need. But one she definitely enjoyed . . . and which was pulling her fondness to a dangerously deep level.

She glanced away, closing her eyes as she raised her voice another octave to reach the final note, and holding the measured beats strong and steady before trailing into silence. Storme's approving smile was the first thing she saw when she opened her eyes, his appreciative applause rising with the others'. Anna sighed, glad to be finished, happy she had hit every note without fail. She looked up at the purpling twilight sky and wondered if her mother was looking down, picturing the proud smile she knew would light up her face.

"That was very nice. Thank you, Miss Alexander." The Reverend Banks smiled, his pudgy mottled face glowing under a sheen of sweat.

Anna climbed down the two steps from the porch, smiling at Elise as she started to walk by where the bride and groom stood before the minister.

Elise touched her arm, stopping her, deep gratitude shimmering in her hazel eyes. "You're a good friend; thank you," she whispered.

Friend. Anna sighed as a warm glow spread through her heart. "You're welcome." She walked on, glancing over at Storme, his wide smile making her breath catch, then made her way over to where the girls stood, nodding her thanks at their whispered compliments. She took a place beside Samantha and focused her attention front as the reverend began the ceremony.

Mimicking the action of several ladies present, Anna pulled a small fan from her skirt pocket, and waved the spread-out folds past her face in the fading heat. The minister's monotone voice droned on, and Anna soon found her attention drifting from his dry tone to thoughts of Storme's deep voice, his warm kisses, the way he held her hands and always circled his thumb in a gentle caress against her flesh. Leaning forward slightly, she glanced toward the other end of the row. Her cheeks heated with pleasure at finding him watching her. Anna straightened, willing her pulse to slow. Why did he have to be so handsome, so nice . . . so easy to trust?

Why did he have to be a bounty hunter?

She frowned. His job was only part of the reason she shouldn't be getting more involved with this man. She brushed her fingers over the silver necklace gracing her neck. She was grateful to him, but she couldn't let herself feel anything more. She didn't want anything more. She wanted to sing, wanted to travel and see new places. She had wanted that long before she wound up in trouble with the law and had a real need to leave the country.

Anna leaned forward again, staring at Storme's strong, handsome profile as he watched the ceremony. As though sensing her gaze, he turned, smiled, and nodded once. She swallowed and quickly straightened, catching Samantha's curious look. Anna sighed, scolding herself for the wayward attraction, and forced herself to concentrate on the rest of the ceremony. She smiled as the bride and groom sealed their future with a kiss, added her applause with the others, then made her way over with the girls to offer her congratulations to the happy couple.

The guests dispersed after the ceremony, mingling in the yard as they visited with one another and enjoyed the offered refreshments of food and drink. Anna tried several times to make her way over to the side of the house, her parched throat begging for a much-needed glass of lemonade; but she kept being stopped by folks wanting to offer their compliments for her singing, then lingering to chat. As the minutes ticked by and the sun disappeared for the day, she tried to deny the disappointment that nipped at her heart when Storme didn't try to seek her out. She couldn't stop her gaze from occasionally wandering over the crowd in search of him.

Once, she caught sight of him across the yard, shaking hands with Wallace, then he said something to Elise that made her laughter ring above the noisy crowd. Anna also saw Edna Mae Mason standing off to the side aiming a disapproving scowl at him. She saw him again later talking with his brother and the Sanderson men, and a couple other farmers Anna didn't know. Her attention was diverted by the seamstress, Lilah Duncan, and Mrs. Mason, wanting to inform her they were willing to overlook her poor choice of leaving the mercantile with Storme the other day if she would reconsider participating in the Garden Society's extravaganza. Anna politely explained that she hadn't made a bad choice, and still wasn't interested, thank you very much, then left the women with their mouths gaping open. She was just making her way across the lawn toward the refreshment table when she saw Storme again and came to a stop. He was surrounded in a circle of colorful skirts, and smiling so handsomely as he talked with Samantha and the other girls from the boardinghouse. The spark of jealousy that reared up took her by surprise. Calling herself every sort of fool, she quickly turned away from the sight, and found herself facing Wallace's mother.

"Elise wasn't exaggerating when she said you sing like an angel," Mabel Sanderson declared, her high voice bright with excitement.

"Thank you, ma'am."

"That's a beautiful ballad, and I've never heard it sung any better." She cocked her head, evening shadows darkening the tint of her sandy hair. "Have you been schooled in music?"

"Not formally. My mother taught me, but she studied at the Boston Academy of Music for a number of years," Anna responded, seeing no harm in the admission and taking pride in the memories of her mama's talent. Her mother had had a strong, beautiful voice, but her musical love was the piano. As a young girl, she had once dreamed of playing with an orchestra, of traveling to Europe. But that was before she lost her family, her wealth, and her Georgia home during the War, before she met Anna's father and settled for a stage on their traveling medicine show instead.

Mrs. Sanderson nodded. "You mother did a fine job. You have quite a talent. Have you done much performing before?"

"A little. When I was much younger." Anna shrugged, hoping the woman wouldn't delve any deeper, and quelling the stab of anxiety that jabbed at her stomach. She had lied to Storme, as well. But how could she tell him, or anyone, that her last performance had just been six months ago, in her father's saloon?

"My niece likes to sing, and she has a real nice voice. In fact, she's singing a short solo in the extravaganza." Mrs.

Sanderson's face beamed her pride. "She'd really like to meet you."

Anna swallowed despite the dryness in her throat, and smiled. What she really wanted was something to drink.

Without waiting for an answer, Mrs. Sanderson looped her arm through Anna's, forcing her along across the yard. They headed toward the house, where a young girl dressed in blue calico and lace stood near the steps beside a short, slightly plump woman Anna could tell by the round facial resemblance was the girl's mother.

"This is my sister-in-law, Maryanne Sanderson, and her daughter, Belle." Mabel made the introduction.

"It's a pleasure to meet you, Miss Alexander. I truly did enjoy your song." Maryanne's easy, quiet voice was a nice contrast to Mabel's high-pitched, grating tone.

"Thank you, ma'am, and it's nice to meet you," Anna greeted, then turned her attention to the young girl. "And you, too, Belle."

"Likewise." The girl stepped forward and gave a quick curtsy. A bright pink glow stained her cheeks. Thin and gangly, with her long, black hair braided in two neat pigtails, she appeared to be about ten.

"Your aunt tells me that you're singing in the extravaganza."

Belle nodded. "And I'm real nervous. It's my first time singing in front of such a large crowd."

Anna certainly understood the nerves that could plague a child before standing to face a crowd. She was always grateful her mama had soothed her flutters with stories, and a stick of peppermint. She smiled. "I know what you mean. I get butterflies in my stomach every time I sing. Could you tell how nervous I was today?"

"No. How did you hide it so well?" Belle's violet eyes widened with awe.

The look reminded Anna a little of how she had felt when Lillie Langtry was on tour in America and had arrived in the same town where her parents were hawking their wares that week. To Anna's surprised delight, the famous actress had offered her a few words of encouragement about singing on stage someday after listening to her perform in her father's show.

"The trick is not to think about the audience. Picture them as something else."

Belle cocked her head, her thin eyebrows lifting high on her small forehead. "What do you mean?"

"Well, my mama used to have me practice singing in front of my father's horses, and when I would have to stand and sing in front of a crowd, I'd just pretend all those people out there were the pair of bays harnessed to our wagon. I still do that when I get nervous."

"You think of horses?" Belle giggled. "Do you think that would work with sheep? I could practice in front of Blaine's herd."

"I think sheep would work just fine." Anna reached into her skirt pocket and retrieved a half stick of peppermint candy. "And be sure to soothe your throat with peppermint or lemon drops before you get up there."

Belle smiled wide as she took the offered candy. "Thank you, Miss Alexander."

"You're welcome, Belle." Anna smiled. "And I look forward to hearing you sing."

"Miss Alexander was telling me that she was schooled by her mother." Mabel volunteered the information, her eyes widening slightly as she stared at her sister-in-law. "And that her mother attended the Boston Academy of Music for a number of years."

Maryanne raised her brow with definite interest. "Well, that explains your impressive performance today, and why Mrs. Harrington was saying what a fine job you did helping Katie and Patricia practice. I'd really like for Belle to have some lessons, but we don't have much opportunity out here to meet anyone who's had any musical training."

"After hearing you sing today," Mabel added, "we were wondering if you'd consider giving Belle lessons. At least for her performance in the extravaganza."

"We don't have a lot, but Blaine does his best to take care of us since my husband died, and we could pay you a little," Maryanne offered.

Belle's eyes rounded with anticipation, her face beaming. "I'd be real appreciative, Miss Alexander. I promise to be a good student, and I'll practice as much as you tell me." Belle ran the toe of her slipper along the grass in nervous agitation.

Lessons? Anna pondered the idea. She *had* enjoyed helping Katie and Patricia practice, and Belle's eagerness reminded her a lot of herself at that age. She really wanted to help the girl out. Despite her desperation for money, though, she didn't feel right about charging a fee. "All right, Belle, I'll give you some lessons."

The girl clapped her hands and squealed her delight.

Anna glanced over at the girl's mother. "I don't want any money, though. I'd be happy to do it for free."

"Well, that's very kind of you," Maryanne said.

Mabel voiced her gratitude, as well. Several minutes later, they had decided on a time for the first lesson.

Anna declined their offer to accompany them, pleading her desire to seek out something to drink first. She smiled, watching Belle skip alongside the Sanderson ladies as they made their way through the growing darkness toward the barn, where the muffled voices of the other guests filtered on the air, and the faint strains of a fiddle and guitar being tuned in preparation for the dancing mingled with the crickets that chirped their songs into the night.

"Were you really picturing horses?"

Anna spun around at the sound of Storme's deep voice, surprised to see him standing at the edge of the porch. His broad smile warmed her far more than the day's heat had done.

"Yes." Her heart pounded faster as she made her way over

to where he stood. She had pictured him as a wild stallion, though, instead of a docile bay . . . but she wasn't going to tell him that.

"That's nice what you're doing for that little girl. Why didn't you let them pay you for your time, though?"

"Well, I don't know much about giving lessons, so it didn't seem right to take their money. But I know how my mama used to teach me. If Belle has any voice at all, I can help her some."

"I think you've helped her a lot already. I've got a feeling she'll be spending a lot of time with Blaine's sheep."

"You're probably right." Anna chuckled, glancing over her shoulder at the girl's retreating back. "I hope he doesn't mind."

"I'm sure he won't. He was telling me earlier about his little sister singing in the musical. He's real proud of her." Storme held out a glass of lemonade. "I noticed you never had a chance to make it to the refreshment table, so I saved you something to drink."

Anna wasn't sure what thrilled her more, his thoughtfulness, or his admission that he hadn't been ignoring her since the ceremony ended as she had thought. She appreciated his thoughtfulness even more when she glanced toward the moonlit table underneath the oaks and saw most of the food gone, the glass bowls of lemonade empty . . . and not a guest in sight. She swallowed the surprising realization that they were all alone, and tried to chase away the wayward hope that Storme might kiss her again.

"Thank you." She reached for the glass, her fingers brushing against his. A startling warmth swept up her arm. She gripped the glass, welcoming the condensation that cooled her skin and the tart liquid that splashed against her dry throat as she took a long swallow.

"Did you want to get something to eat?" He pointed toward the table.

She shook her head, then raised the glass slightly. "I'm not hungry. This is really all I wanted."

He pushed the edges of his coat aside and rested his hands on his lean hips. "I enjoyed hearing you sing again. You sounded wonderful tonight. Even better than yesterday." His dark stare blazed with the same admiring regard she heard in his low tone.

She felt the blush work its way into her face. "Thank you." Of all the compliments she had received, his touched her more deeply than any other, and more than she knew it should.

"I heard you talking about your mother attending the Boston Academy. Did she have other dreams besides having a house in the mountains?"

Anna nodded, and told him about her mama's long-ago desire to play with an orchestra, and how she had given up the chance.

"What about you, Anna? You never did get a chance to tell me about your dreams."

She bit at her bottom lip. *To sing. To have my freedom again.* She really wanted to tell him the truth . . . but she couldn't. She didn't dare risk telling anyone about her plans, especially someone connected to the law. She didn't really want to lie to him, either. "I haven't really thought about it." She shrugged and turned away, breaking contact with his intense gaze before she foolishly gave in and told him how much she wanted to join a theater troupe.

The strains of music drifted on the clear night. Laughter and voices blended in a soft cacophony from down at the barn. She finished the last bit of lemonade in the glass and set it down on the edge of the porch.

Her pulse beat faster as Storme moved closer to her side, then placed his finger under her chin, and with gentle insistence forced her to look up. "I think you've given it a great deal of thought. But if you don't want to talk about it, that's fine. I won't press." His breath brushed against her face, and sent shivers of delight chasing along her skin. He cupped his palm against her cheek. "I do want you to kiss you, though," he whispered.

She didn't have time to think, to breathe, to see the blaze of desire in his brown eyes before he closed them and covered her mouth, his lips moving slowly and thoughtfully, his warm breath sweetened with the faint taste of lemonade. His tongue traced a scorching line along her lip, firing her blood with swirling sensations that made her long for more. She parted her mouth at his coaxing. The moan that escaped her throat at the heated touch of his tongue to hers, his deepening pressure, was as shocking as her own eager response.

Desire raced through Storme's veins, and quickly gathered in a heated pool that throbbed like a storm-tossed ocean in his loins. He wrapped his arms around her, pulling her close in his embrace.

Anna's senses spun like a tornado. She found herself melting into the comfort of his strength, and wound her arms around his neck, brushing her fingers against the thick softness of his hair.

Her nipples hardened against his chest, igniting the urgent need that swelled lower in Storme. He pulled her closer, reveling in the feel of her soft breasts flattened against him, her slender body molded so perfectly to his rougher contours, the fiery passion of her kiss that matched the boldness he admired in her spirit.

Storme knew he needed to stop, to pull away from the tempting taste of peppermint and lemon that sweetened her delicious mouth before he lost all sense and lowered her down to the grass. But he hadn't expected such a willing response from her, nor the consuming desire that stole all thought and raged unheeded through his veins.

Her soft moans vibrated gently against his mouth, urging him with her warmth, with the soft, lavender scent that drifted from her skin and lingered in his breaths. He ran his hand up

her back, enjoying the feel of her silky hair sliding against his
skin.

Warning bells sounded through the roar in his head, fusing
with the strains of music. Storme reminded himself they weren't
alone. Not for anything did he want to get caught and cause
Anna embarrassment. With a reluctance that surprised him in
its intensity, he broke off their kiss, then couldn't resist pressing
his lips briefly against hers one last time before staring down
into her pretty, flushed face.

"I would stand here all night, if we were alone. But we
should join the others before someone comes looking for us."

"You're right," she whispered, but hot flames raced through
her blood in opposition to rationale.

She didn't want to leave, couldn't make herself break away
from the tingling feel of his hard muscles against her breasts,
her stomach. His hands caressed her back, then slowly slid
along her hips, and pressed her harder against his body. Anna
bit her lip. She hadn't spent years traveling in a cramped wagon
with her parents, then being subjected to lewd whispers and
fighting off unwanted advances at the saloon without learning
what transpired between a man and woman. She could feel the
evidence of his desire, could see his craving to kiss her again
in his narrowed, molasses gaze. And heaven help her, she
wanted it too.

"Kiss me again, Storme. Then we'll go."

Without hesitation, he reclaimed her lips, more demanding
this time in an exploration of warmth that sent new swirls of
ecstasy coursing through her to pool low in her stomach. She
tightened her arms around his neck, lifting herself higher to
press her lips firmly against his, matching every fiery stroke
of his tongue with her own. She had never known such an
intense need as she felt with him—a passion that took her by
surprise as it flowed with a will of its own . . . and she had no
inclination to hinder its path.

She opened her eyes when he pulled back. He leaned down to brush his lips lightly against hers one last time.

"Did Mrs. Harrington bring her gun tonight?"

Anna nodded. "It's in the wagon." She smiled at his arched brow and look of concern.

"In that case, we're leaving now." He released her and took a step back.

She chuckled. "All right. I don't want to see anything happen to you."

He smiled and reached over, lightly running his fingers against her cheek and firing her skin with his touch. "If you wouldn't get in trouble, I'd take that risk."

Anna swallowed at the seriousness in his words, his voice. She reached up and pulled his hand from her face, with a sharp reminder that she had best remember he was a bounty hunter and she a wanted criminal.

So why did she let her hand linger on his? Let him twine his fingers with hers?

Storme rubbed his thumb gently along her wrist. "Do you like to dance, Anna?"

She nodded, trying to ignore the feel of his finger circling her flesh, and failing miserably as her blood stirred to a simmering boil. "What about you?"

He squeezed her hand lightly and smiled. "It's not such a trial with the right woman. Would you like to dance?"

She smiled her pleasure at his inquiry. "Yes, I would. But I better warn you, I haven't had much practice at it. I'm liable to step on your toes." She had never danced with anyone but her father, and she had stepped on him more than a few times.

He leaned closer, his breath brushing warm against her chin. "Well, that's a chance I'm definitely willing to take," he whispered, then kissed her again.

To her disappointment, though, he didn't linger, but quickly drew back. Still holding her hand, he started across the yard. Anna fell into step beside him. As they drew nearer to the grassy edge, she could see lantern light glowing around the dance floor and illuminating a wide circle in front of the barn. The guests mingled about, their conversations lost in the music that filled the night. Several couples were already dancing along the makeshift floor.

Storme slowed his steps, then came to a stop. He stared down at Anna's moonlit face, her full lips that showed every sign of being thoroughly kissed, and a pang of guilt jabbed at his conscience. He had been welcomed by most of the guests, and was glad for the opportunity to meet Ben's friends, but he knew if he came walking out of the shadows with Anna, it would cause a certain scandal, and his acceptance among the group could die a quick death—not to mention the disastrous results that would darken Anna's reputation.

"You go on ahead. I'll take a different path and join you in a few minutes."

She drew her eyebrows together. "I'm not worried about being seen with you."

"I'm glad to hear that." He resisted the urge to reach over and trace the lines in her furrowed brow. "But Mrs. Mason and Miss Duncan haven't stopped scowling at me all evening. They'll be looking for any reason to stir up gossip."

She hesitated, glancing toward the barn. "You're right. We probably shouldn't come walking out of the shadows together. But I do want to dance with you, Storme. I don't care what they think about that."

He swallowed the lump that rose in his throat at her sweet admission. He released her hand and ran one finger along the line of her shapely mouth, then forced himself to lower his arm to his side. "All right, then I'll see you in a few minutes."

She smiled and nodded, then turned and walked away.

He allowed himself a few moments to enjoy the sway of her slender hips and recall her tender, passionate kisses. She had a definite innocent charm about her, and he realized it was pulling him in inch by inch. Storme straightened and blew out a harsh breath.

He had best remember that he owed her a life-debt, not a heartache, a ruined reputation, or a promise of a future that could never be. Anna was a sweet woman, and she deserved a man who could marry her and take care of her . . . not a man who could only offer to look out for her safety for a short time, and nothing more.

His heart pounded faster. But that didn't mean he couldn't enjoy dancing with her. He waited several minutes, watching as she talked with some of her friends from the boardinghouse, then he walked along the edge of grass, staying in the shadows until he was almost past the barn.

Storme paused, his gut tightening with a sense of alarm when Winston suddenly came riding into the circle of light that shrouded the guests. The foreman reined his horse to a hard stop, then jumped out of the saddle and hurried over to talk to Ben.

Storme could tell by the way his brother searched the crowd that Ben was looking for him. He resumed his pace, emerging from the shadows, and waved one hand in signal to his brother. Ben and Winston left the gathering and started toward him.

"We've had trouble with the rustlers again," Ben grated.

Storme tensed and glanced over at the foreman. "What happened?"

Winston's tanned, freckled cheeks pulled taut. "Me and Garcia were looking for some strays just before sunset, when we heard gunfire coming from south of the valley. Went to check it out, and found close to two dozen head dead, picked off with long-range rifles. We spotted where the men were hidin' in the trees along the ridge, and gave chase. They fired on us. Lousy bastards shot Garcia's horse right out from under him. Garcia broke his leg in the fall. I had to give up the chase to get help. Me and a couple of the hands got him to his cabin, and Doc Garrick's out there right now.

"Damn," Ben muttered. "How's it look for Garcia?"

Winston grimaced and shook his head. "Real bad. I ain't never seen a bone stick so far through flesh like that before. I posted a couple guards out by where I lost those bastards."

"Did you get a look at them?" Storme inquired.

Winston's blue eyes blazed with frustration. "Not a good one, but they were dark-skinned and wearin' sombreros, and they were headin' south." He spit a stream of tobacco juice into the dirt, and shifted the wad in his cheek. "You wanna go see if we can pick up their trail?"

Storme nodded. "We'll ride by and check on Garcia first."

"I'll tell Elise we're leaving." Ben turned to leave.

Storme placed a hand on his shoulder, stopping him. "You stay, little brother. This is an important day for your friend. I can handle this."

Ben shook his head. "We may actually have our first solid lead on these damn rustlers. I'm going. Elise will understand."

Storme lowered his hand to his side. "What about Miss Crowley?"

"She's fine." Ben shrugged. "She started talking to Blaine a while ago, and I haven't seen her since." He pointed toward the dance floor. "Except to watch her dance with him."

Storme glanced over and saw Miss Crowley waltzing around the floor with Blaine.

"I'll be right back." Ben walked off.

Storme made no effort to stop him this time, but shifted his stare across the way to Anna. Her pretty face glowed in the lantern light. She stood talking with Caroline Smythe, and chose that moment to glance over at him. Storme's pulse kicked up its pace when she waved at him.

He frowned at the sudden sadness that seeped into his chest. It didn't look like he was going to have that chance to dance with her, after all. Then a renewed fear slammed into his heart as he recalled the rustlers' note about her necklace, and his uncertainty of just how far they were planning to go with this revenge.

"I've got a job for you, Winston." Storme met the foreman's curious stare.

"I thought I was ridin' out with you and Ben?"

Storme shook his head. "I want you to stay here, and keep an eye on Miss Alexander."

Winston straightened, his expression turning serious. "Is that her over with Miss Smythe?"

"Yes. And I want you to make sure she and the girls get home safe to the boardinghouse, too."

"Escort a wagonload of single ladies home?" Winston's mouth curled up in a smile. He crossed his arms over his chest. "I'd be dumber than a stump to turn down this job." He sobered slightly, and nodded once. "Don't you worry, I won't let anything happen to her."

"Thanks. I need to tell her I have to leave. I'll be back in a minute."

Storme headed across the dirt yard, his gazed fixed on Anna. He raked his stare over her shapely body, the soft curves he had thought he would have the chance to feel again. He wondered if she would dance with someone else since he had to leave. The rage of jealousy that reared its head took him by surprise. He thought about turning around and telling Winston to make sure she didn't, then he frowned.

What the hell am I thinking?

He didn't have any right to do something like that. Maybe it was for the best that he had to leave. He was getting far too attached to that woman . . . and if he wasn't careful, he might find himself missing more than just the ranch and his brother when the time came to ride out.

The half-moon hung overhead, glowing bright amid the innumerable stars twinkling their brilliance against the clear black sky. Storme kept his mount to a walk as he rode alongside his brother, and followed the pair of tracks they had found south of the valley where the cattle were killed. They rode for another quarter mile over the dirt-and-grass terrain, stopping beneath the tall, lone oak. Storme's pulse hammered as he stared at the folded white paper tacked to the trunk with an arrow.

Ben sat back in his saddle, his face pulling taut. "That's why they made their trail so easy to follow this time." Aggravation strained his voice.

Storme agreed the trail had been too easy to follow and had suspected something was up. But his thoughts had leaned more toward an ambush, which was why he had six Lazy W hands riding guard a short way out on either side and at their backs. He took a deep breath and dismounted, then walked over and pulled the note free.

I saw your pretty lady doing wash yesterday.
She's gonna die, Injun, right along with your brother.
But not before I have some fun with her first.

Storme's heart stopped with fear for Anna's safety, then fury roared through his veins, his anger directed as much at himself as at this faceless bastard. *Dammit!* He had had a gut sense yesterday that someone was watching from the grove. Why hadn't he gone and checked it out more closely?

"What's it say?" Ben climbed down from his saddle and strode over. "You look like you're about to explode."

He was, and he would . . . just as soon as he had his hands around the throat of the man behind this threat. Storme had a good idea just what sort of "fun" the rustler intended with Anna, too, and there was no way he was going to let that man, or any of the rustlers, lay one finger on her. He handed the note over to Ben and glanced around at the moonlit terrain. He didn't doubt the trail would play out right there. The rustlers had been too careful covering their tracks so far to get sloppy now.

Ben shook his head. "Damn," he muttered, and glanced up. "Don't worry, Winston won't let anything happen to her."

Storme nodded, glad he had had the foresight to have the foreman stay behind. He didn't doubt that Winston would do everything in his power to keep Anna safe, and he was doubly glad that Mrs. Harrington had brought her gun, as well. But there was a part of him that still gave strong consideration to riding back and seeing after Anna himself. The Sanderson farm was only two miles outside of town, though, and Anna had told him that Mrs. Harrington was planning to leave around midnight. He couldn't make it back in time. His gut tightened. Is that what the rustlers had planned?

Ben rubbed one hand over his chin. "You still think Dodding might be behind all this?"

Storme frowned. He was beginning to have strong doubts. None of this rang true with Dodding's nature. He knew from past entanglements that the rancher was a hothead and quick to action. He was surprised that Dodding still hadn't attempted some sort of retaliation for the beating at the river. If not Dodding, though, then who *was* behind this revenge? Storme didn't have a clue, and the annoying lack of evidence was fast eating away at him.

"Dodding doesn't play games like this." Storme nodded toward the note. "And he won't hire *vaqueros* to work on his ranch, I don't see him hiring them to do his dirty work, either."

"Maybe he's just trying to throw you off the trail," Ben suggested.

Storme nodded. "I agree. He's hiding something, but I don't think it's rustling. I'm guessing it has something to do with those two men who were with him at the river."

Ben's eyebrows pulled together. "What do you think he's up to?"

"I've been giving that some thought, and I keep circling back to that one man who didn't want to show his face."

Ben's jawed hardened; his eyes narrowed in thought. "That *was* strange. He didn't even turn to look when you were stomping Dodding's ass."

"My guess is, he didn't want to be recognized." Storme's thoughts raced with suspicion. "I've got a hunch I might know who he is . . . or at least what Dodding might be up to. You feel up to riding over to the river tonight and seeing if Dodding's crew has shown up yet?" Storme figured they could ride through town on their way, and he would just make sure that Anna was safely tucked in for the night at the boardinghouse.

Chapter Eleven

"I want that damn Injun dead!" Dodding slammed his fist on the desk, rattling the lamp and inkwell, then stood, shoving the leather chair back against the oak-paneled wall of his office. "I can't believe I've let you keep me sittin' here like a coward. That half-breed needs to pay for this." He roughly pointed one finger at his right arm trussed in a white sling next to his chest.

Cole glanced at the bandage wrapped around the rancher's broken hand. "I don't care what you want," he ground out, rising from the chair. "He hasn't come back, and I don't want you giving him any reason to. If he gets wind of this operation, he'll make hell for us with the townsfolk."

"That half-breed doesn't have anything to do with this operation, and the town won't find out a thing until we're ready. Next one of my hands that dares to breathe a word to that bastard Injun knows it'll be his last."

"Good," Cole snapped. "You need to keep your cowhands quiet." He huffed out a deep breath and stared at the early-morning sunlight that streamed through the two large side windows, then at the whiskey bottle on the cart across the room. He wasn't a heavy drinker, but the rancher was slowly pushing him to change that pattern. In the three months since he had met Dodding, he hadn't found anything to like about the arrogant man, except that he had the drive for controlling things and the greed necessary to cheat people. But not the brains or the patience to do it right. Dodding was an amateur. Cole had spent years perfecting his livelihood.

"But I know about that bounty hunter," Cole added. And he didn't want to have to tangle with Storme again, recalling that he had barely escaped the last time. Cole placed his hands flat against the smooth wood. "He's like a rabid coyote when he sinks his teeth into something." Cole jabbed one finger toward the rancher's chest. "I don't want you to bring him sniffing around out there again. You hear?"

Mottled rage reddened Dodding's face. He slapped Cole's hand away. "I'm sick of you telling me what to do."

Cole's anger mounted. "Fine." He straightened, and calmly pulled a cheroot from his vest pocket, then took a match and struck it against the desk top, smiling at the rancher's frown. "I'll just take my crew and leave." He lit the end, and took a long draw.

"You son of a bitch, we have an agreement. And I'm the one paying those men." Dodding scowled. "Never mind. Go ahead and leave," he ranted. "I'll find my own damn crew to hire. I don't need you."

Cole arched his brow. He took another draw on the cheroot, then held the cigar between two fingers. He blew the smoke out in Dodding's direction, and lifted his mouth in a half smile. "And where are you going to build at?" He shook his head. "Not on my land."

Dodding straightened; his jaw tightened.

Cole smiled, and puffed on the cheroot again. He didn't really own the land. But Dodding's idea to control the water flow to the valley had brought a nice price from the investors who *had* filed a claim on that section. Those same men were also paying Cole to build the dam. He wasn't one to pass up an opportunity, though. He didn't mind taking Dodding's money. When this job was done, the rancher would learn soon enough that the agreement they had signed was a fake. By then, Cole would be on a train headed east—provided that blasted bounty hunter didn't ruin everything. If the dam didn't get built, he wouldn't be leaving with full pockets like he planned, but sneaking out empty-handed before the investors had a chance to follow through with their promise to kill him.

"You want your dam built, Dodding, you stay the hell away from Storme Warwick." Cole saw the resignation of defeat slowly rise in the rancher's steel glare. Satisfaction pounded in his chest.

Dodding was greedy all right, but Cole knew how to win.

"Oh, sweet heaven, you're a lifesaver, Anna." Samantha snapped the folds of her fan closed, but didn't rise from where she sat with her back braced against the white column.

Anna crossed the porch and set the tray down on the square, wicker table, then reached for one of the three glasses of iced tea she had brought outside.

Samantha grabbed the unbuttoned neck of her white blouse, pulling the cotton away from her skin, and closed her eyes. "Just pour it right down here."

"Let me do it." Caroline chuckled and pushed herself up from the porch swing. "I'm the one who's been sitting out here listening to your complaints about the heat."

Samantha stared hard through one half-open eye. "No, you'll pour it on my head, and I just washed my hair this morning."

Anna smiled as she held the glass in a threatening tip over Samantha's head. "You could wash it again."

Samantha frowned, opening both eyes. "Don't you dare, Miss Tree Climber," she whispered in bold defiance.

Anna arched her brow. "Is that a threat, Miss Cat Hater?" she countered in a lighthearted tone, not feeling the least concerned that her roommate would expose her secret about missing curfew and climbing the tree. Even though Mrs. Harrington knew the truth now, Samantha had still promised not to say anything to the others, and Anna knew she could trust her to keep her word. She shifted the glass slightly and poured a small portion down the front of Samantha's blouse.

"Ohhh," Samantha closed her eyes and tilted her head back. "That feels good. More."

Anna turned at Caroline's nudging poke to her arm and saw Mrs. Harrington standing in the doorway with the screen popped open, a mischievous gleam in her apple green stare and a glass of ice water in one hand. The housemother lifted the glass slightly and nodded toward Samantha.

Anna covered her mouth, stifling her chuckle.

Caroline tiptoed over and took the glass, then hurried back, dumping the entire contents down the front of Samantha's blouse.

Samantha squealed, her eyes flying open wide in shock as she jumped to her feet.

Anna's laughter rang in harmony with Caroline's and Mrs. Harrington's. Katie and Patricia issued loud chuckles from where they leaned out of the opened parlor window at the end of the porch.

"Feeling better now, Miss Crowley?" Heightened humor laced the housemother's voice.

Samantha paused, glancing down at her soaked blouse. A grin spread across her face. "Actually, yes I am." She plucked the glass of tea from Anna's hand and turned to Caroline. "Now, let me return the favor."

Caroline gasped. She set the empty water glass down, and lifted both hands to ward off the attack as she backed away. "It was only water, I swear. Ask Mrs. Harrington."

Anna stepped out of the way as Samantha proceeded to chase

Caroline across the wide verandah. Amid the laughter, and shouted warnings from Katie and Patricia, the dodging byplay continued. Anna's heart bubbled with excitement as she watched the antics, then found herself dragged into the chase when Samantha gave up on catching Caroline and came after her. It had been a long time since Anna felt such freedom, and even longer since she had had so much fun. But it was the mutual esteem, the circle of friendship, that swelled her heart with happiness.

Then everything came to an abrupt halt when Samantha tripped on her skirt and iced tea went sailing all down the front of Mrs. Harrington's gray dress.

Anna bit her lip, and clutched her hands together as the silence hung heavy.

Mrs. Harrington's face pinched into tight lines. She glanced down at the large, wet stain, then slowly shoved her glasses up the bridge of her nose, and smiled. "Nice aim, Miss Crowley."

Anna sighed and chuckled along with the other girls, a tide of joy at the shared enjoyment washing through her veins.

"Well, I suppose I should change now." Mrs. Harrington picked up the sodden front of her skirt, then paused, glancing toward Katie and Patricia where they still leaned out the window. "Give me a minute, girls, and we'll start practicing your song."

"Oh, Mrs. Harrington, this heat's worse to tolerate than being dragged backward through a garden hedge," Katie said with a slight whine in her tone. Then a smile formed on her mouth. "Would it be all right if we make ice cream instead. We'll practice tonight, won't we, Patricia?"

"Twice as long," Patricia added her promise, then waved the fan in her hand a little faster. "And maybe Anna will feel inclined to give us a few more pointers on hitting those high notes."

Anna smiled. "Sure. I'll be happy to."

The housemother nodded. "All right. I think ice cream would

make a nice Sunday afternoon treat. You two go on and get the churn.'' She went inside, letting the screen door bang closed behind.

Amid giggles of delight, Katie and Patricia ducked back inside the house. A few seconds later, Anna heard their footsteps hurrying down the hall toward the kitchen.

''That was fun.'' Anna took one of the two remaining glasses of tea from the tray and crossed over to sit on the white porch swing.

''I enjoyed it, especially since Mrs. Harrington didn't get mad about the tea,'' Samantha stated as she reclaimed her seat on the planking and leaned back against the pillar. She plucked at the wet cotton that stuck to her chest. ''Hopefully, this will keep me nice and cool until they get that ice cream done.''

Caroline reached for the remaining glass of tea. ''Well, if you start complaining again, I *will* dump this on your head.'' She arched her brow, her dark blue eyes sparkling with amusement as she raised the glass.

Samantha lifted her hands in surrender and made a mock show of being afraid. Then her roommate stuck her tongue out.

Caroline burst out laughing, then shook her head as she crossed over and sat beside Anna, setting the wooden swing to a slow rocking motion. A look of melancholy dimmed the humor on her face. ''Seems rather strange not having Elise here to join in the fun.''

Anna nodded. In the last month, she had grown quite fond of Elise and was going to miss her company, as well as their walks in the evening. A sharp sadness pricked her heart. She realized that she was going to miss all the girls, and Mrs. Harrington, when the time came to leave. She swallowed the wistful knot that rose in her throat, then stared off at the mid-afternoon sunlight that illuminated the lane toward town, and sipped her tea.

''She sure had a real nice wedding. I hope I have one just as fine someday,'' Samantha mused, a wistful note in her voice.

Anna glanced down at her roommate, and smiled. "With Blaine Sanderson, perhaps?" She couldn't resist jesting.

"You did dance nearly every song with him," Caroline added, grinning slyly.

Samantha cocked her head, a look of slight indignation tightening her face. "So, I didn't want to dance with anyone else."

"What about Ben Warwick?" Anna asked. "You were all excited yesterday about seeing him, then you barely spent any time at all with him before he had to leave last night."

"Well . . ." Samantha hesitated, frowning, then huffed out a small breath. "Ben's nice, and I'm grateful he spoke with Mr. Chesterfield and saved my job. But I think Elise is right about him not being in any hurry to settle down. He's got more flirt to him than seriousness." She furrowed her brow. "And did either of you notice the way he kept watching Elise?"

Anna shook her head. Of course, she had been too busy watching Storme to notice much of what anyone else was doing.

"I didn't notice anything," Caroline stated. "What are you getting at?"

Samantha pursed her lips in thought. "I know they're friends, but . . . there was something besides friendship gleaming in his eyes when he thought no one was looking. Made me think he might be carrying a torch for her."

"Oh, that's silly." Caroline waved one hand in dismissal. "They've known each other plenty long enough that he could have declared his feelings if he had any."

Samantha's brown eyebrows arched high on her forehead. "Well, maybe he did, and Elise turned him down."

"No," Caroline firmly responded. "Elise would have said something. They've always just been good friends."

Anna hoped Storme's brother didn't have any deep feelings for Elise. She couldn't imagine how painful it would be to watch someone you love marry another. Her heart stopped at the thought of Storme marrying someone. Pain jabbed at her chest and stole her breath. Maybe she could imagine it. She shook her head slightly. She wasn't in love with Storme. What was wrong with her?

"Well, you've known them both longer than I have. I'm sure you're right." The dubious light in Samantha's pale blue eyes belied her full acquiescence. "But that didn't have anything to do with why I spent so much time with Blaine."

"So why did you?" Anna questioned.

"When I started talking to Blaine, I just felt something different." Twin spots of pink filled Samantha's round cheeks. She pulled her knees up beneath her blue skirt and wrapped her arms around her legs. "Have you ever met someone that makes you feel comfortable enough to just talk about anything? A man that you know right off in your heart you can trust, and just makes you feel safe?"

Oh yes. Anna knew a man like that. Her blood raced faster at the memories of Storme that crashed into her thoughts.

"No, I can't say that I have." Caroline brushed at the black bangs that draped across her forehead. "But I did enjoy talking to Winston Goff." She lifted her glass and sipped at her tea.

"Well, I felt that way with Blaine. I had a real nice time with him, and I wouldn't mind if he came to call on me."

"I bet he does," Caroline said, cocking her head to one side. "Blaine looked pretty smitten with you." She shifted her stare over to Anna. "And the way I kept seeing Storme Warwick watch you all through the wedding, I'd say he'll be coming to call, too."

A heated flush crept into Anna's cheeks. She enjoyed Storme's company, admired his honor, his kindness, and she definitely liked the way he worried about her reputation and safety. She trusted him more than she ever had any man, and he made her feel safer than she had in a long time, even despite the fact he was a bounty hunter—that was just an added complication. But there wasn't any lasting relationship destined for their future. "It's not like that between us. We're just friends. Besides, he's just home to help his brother with the rustlers. He's not planning to stay in town." And neither was she.

"Oh, well that's too bad," Caroline commented. "He's a real gentleman."

"I agree with that." Samantha grinned. "I particularly liked the way he handled Mrs. Mason and Miss Duncan."

Anna tensed, frowning. "What did they do?"

Caroline shook her head in disgust. "When we were talking to him, those bothersome biddies had the gall to sidle right up beside us and start talking real loud about a schoolteacher he courted once, and the trouble it caused. But Storme, he just smiled real polite like and excused himself, then walked over and nicely asked them to mind their own business." She chuckled.

"What did they say about the schoolteacher?" Anna queried, more curious than she wanted to admit.

"Well," Samantha sat up a little straighter, her blue eyes rounding. "They mentioned that Storme got in a scandalous fight with Mr. Dodding over this woman. Right in the middle of town."

Anger seeped into Anna's blood. She could well imagine that horrid Mr. Dodding had started it, too.

"And," Samantha continued, "that the schoolteacher left town because her reputation was completely ruined for daring to court a half-breed."

"That's silly. Why should her reputation have been ruined? Storme's a nice man," Anna defended.

"I agree." Caroline nodded with added emphasis.

"Me too," Samantha said. "I don't feel the least bit threatened by him being part-Indian."

Anna smiled her appreciation of their support for Storme, even as she recalled Dodding's accusation the other day. *'If you knew anything about honor . . . you'd have left Linette alone.'* Was Linette the schoolteacher? Had she broken his heart when she left?

"Well, what do you know," Caroline's voice rose a little higher with surprise. She pointed toward the road. "It looks like we have a visitor coming."

"Is it Blaine?" Samantha's face beamed with anticipation as she jumped to her feet and spun around, bracing one hand against the column support. Then her shoulders slumped in disappointment.

Anna's blood glowed with excitement, her pulse pounding faster at the sight of Storme riding up the lane. Caroline nudged her arm.

"I told you he'd be coming to call."

"And I told you, we're just friends." But Anna couldn't hold back her smile as she watched him ride closer. She didn't know what had brought him here. She was certainly glad to see him, though. "Excuse me." She rose from the swing and set her glass of tea on the tray, then headed down the steps and along the walk as he drew his horse to a stop outside the fence.

"Hello, Anna." Butterflies winged their way over her heart at his low, sensuous tone.

"Hi, Storme," she whispered, trying to catch her breath, lost in the wake of the appreciative gaze she raked over the rugged denims hugging his muscled legs, and the gun belt strapped around his lean hips. His white shirt was partially unbuttoned, revealing the beaded leather and the red bandanna tied around his neck, and a deep V-lined view of his smooth, bronze chest.

He shifted his glance toward the house, tipping his hat. "Afternoon, ladies."

"Good afternoon, Mr. Warwick," Caroline called out.

"Nice to see you again," Samantha added.

Anna glanced behind in time to see the two girls walk inside the house, then turned back, watching as Storme dismounted and sauntered toward her, a warm smile gracing his firm mouth. God, he was so handsome. She wrapped her hands around the top railing of the fence, fearing she would give in to the sudden strong desire to press her hands against the firm muscles of his chest, to wrap her arms around his neck, and kiss him.

"I'm sorry again about having to leave the wedding last night. Did you have a nice time?" His dark, compelling stare mesmerized her as much as his magnetic presence.

"Nice enough. I missed you. I was really looking forward to that dance." Embarrassing heat flooded her face. *Goodness.* What was it about this man that made her say such bold things?

Storme's heart broke into a hard gallop. "I missed you, too. And I guess I'll just have to make it up to you about that dance." He smiled, recalling Winston's report last night that the rustlers hadn't made any attempt to get to her, and his pleasure at the foreman's added comment that she hadn't danced with anyone.

She lifted one auburn eyebrow in a teasing arch. "Is this another debt?"

He shook his head, gazing at her pretty face through hooded eyes. Sunlight glistened in her upswept hair. He wished she had worn it down. He had a strong desire to run his hands through the thick, silky strands again. "A promise," he whispered. One he vowed to make sure he kept before he left town, even if he had to hire a whole orchestra to make it happen. He thought he might even talk her into singing again, too . . . this time just for him. "I hope you don't mind that I stopped by."

"Not at all. I've been wondering what happened with the rustlers. Did you find them?"

"No." Concern charged a path over his enjoyment at seeing her. His smile faded. "But they left another note, Anna. They've made a threat against you."

Her eyes widened, and the blood slowly drained from her face. "What sort of threat?"

Storme shook his head. "The details don't matter, because I'm not going to let them to touch you." He placed his hands on top hers where they rested on the fence. "The sheriff's been keeping an eye on things around here, but I'm going to send some of the ranch hands out in shifts to make sure the house is guarded at all times.''

She frowned. ''Is that really necessary? I don't want to worry the girls.''

She had voiced the same concern last night when he informed her that he was having Winston stay behind. He agreed there wasn't any need to worry the others. ''I'll tell the men to keep out of sight. But Mrs. Harrington needs to know. And I want you to promise that you won't go anywhere alone.'' He was glad to see her quick nod of agreement, though he hated that because of *his* troubles she had a reason for the fear that darkened her green depths. ''I also want to make sure you know how to shoot that derringer of yours. Do you think Mrs. Harrington would let you take a ride with me up to the mountains so I can give you some lessons?''

A spasm of hesitation crossed her face.

''It's all right, Anna. I know she doesn't know about the gun.'' He hadn't forgotten about her leaving that part out of her retelling to the housemother. ''And I won't tell her. I just came from the mercantile.'' After finding stakes and strings strung across the river last night, and a dozen men bedded down nearby, Ben had gathered the councilmen together for an emergency meeting this afternoon. Storme had only stayed long enough to relay his suspicion about Dodding possibly scheming to build a dam with a shyster named Cole Hansen— a man Storme had encountered several years ago in Wyoming, who had teamed up with a train robber and two wealthy ranchers and tried to take control of the water rights to a small town; a man who also went by the name of Blanchard on occasion. ''Bob Mason opened up long enough to sell me some shells. We'll just tell her I bought the gun for you, too.''

Anna's smile of gratitude seared a path straight to his heart, and he had to force himself not to lean over the fence and kiss those beautiful, full lips. ''Do you have your gun with you now?''

She shook her head.

He smiled. ''Then run upstairs and get it, while I go talk to Mrs. Harrington.''

Chapter Twelve

The gentle pressure of Anna's hands on his waist sent desire pulsing through him in torturous defiance of his good sense. He frowned. *Why didn't I suggest walking?* Her breasts softly bumped against his back with every rocking motion of the horse's gait and filled Storme's head with fervent notions of pulling her around in front and rubbing several other parts of their bodies together.

Rein in those thoughts. He wasn't in any hurry to face the business end of Mrs. Harrington's rifle.

Once he had explained about the rustlers' latest note, Mrs. Harrington readily agreed to the idea of Anna learning to shoot. Not wanting to worry the other girls over this trouble, the housemother had also thought the mountains would serve as a better place to practice. But she was adamant that they only be gone a few hours and had expressed her expectation to see results of the lesson, promising to have several targets set up waiting when they returned.

Storme wasn't intending to disappoint the older woman,

either. But he was going to have to stay focused on the task at hand to make certain of that, not dwell on passionate possibilities of exploring Anna's shapely curves.

Storme guided the gelding around the mesquite and piñon trees dotting the valley and shifted his stare in a watchful sweep over the wooded mountains ahead.

"Do you like being a bounty hunter, Storme?" Her velvety voice broke the brief silence that had settled in their conversation.

He smiled, his heart pounding with pleasure at her continued curiosity. Since leaving the boardinghouse, he had happily answered her questions concerning his family and the ranch. He was delighted that she had favored his own inquisitiveness about her past, as well. He had also been surprised at the glimpse of loneliness she gave when she talked about being the only child among the small group of entertainers that had traveled with her parents' medicine show. But there had been only joy in her voice and a warm, sparkling reflection of excitement in her pretty green eyes when she talked about singing, and which songs she had enjoyed performing most.

"I don't mind it most days."

"And other days?"

He fought the urge to stop the horse and show her just what he would like to be doing *this* day . . . and it didn't have a damn thing to do with bounty hunting or gun lessons. He looked over his shoulder, swallowing as his gaze settled on her mouth and memories of tasting those full, sweet lips surfaced full force.

"Other days, it can be a little lonely. But there's always an outlaw to hunt, and I believe in seeing justice served."

"Do you always know that the outlaws you bring to justice are really guilty?"

Storme paused. *Odd question.* What puzzled him even more was the slight wariness in her eyes and the feel of her fingers tensing and suddenly digging a little deeper into his waist. Was she challenging his honor . . . his greed for the money, he wondered. *Or does it have something to do with whatever she's hiding?* "I don't waste my time going after them unless I know they are."

She nodded, smiling. Her hands relaxed. "Do you like chasing outlaws more than raising cattle? Is that why you don't stay at the ranch with your brother?"

Storme hesitated, still bothered by what had caused that brief moment of caution in her. He gave strong consideration to pursuing the subject, but something told him not to, that he would only risk this bond of trust building between them if he did. And that's the last thing he wanted to do. He liked her company, far more than he knew he should. He liked her boldness in speaking what was on her mind, too, and her innocent eagerness when they kissed. He would give just about anything to hear her ask him to kiss her, like she had at the wedding last night. He sighed. He wished she had asked anything else at all, besides *this* question. With great reluctance, he shifted his thoughts from Anna and sifted through the painful remembrances that had led to his decision to leave the ranch.

"I'm sorry. I shouldn't be prying into your business," she whispered when he let the silence drag on.

"I don't mind."

"Are you sure?" Anna's smile reached into her gaze and made his heart trip over its next beat.

He nodded, surprised at how much he really meant that. Surprised at this longing she brought out in him to talk about things he hadn't shared with anyone, other than his brother. But Anna was unlike any woman he had ever met. She didn't walk a wide path around him like most folks did, either. And unlike Linette, who had wanted to keep their relationship a secret for fear of what others would say, Anna wasn't worried about being seen with him and hadn't shown any inclination to hide their friendship. Just as she said, Anna judged him only as a man, and that made him all the more determined to live up to her expectations. Her willingness to forsake the opinions and labels people stamped on him only strengthened this draw he felt toward her . . . in spite of the fact that he knew he would have to pull back when the time came for him to leave town.

Storme pushed down the sadness at that latter reminder and faced front, staring at the gray shadows that darkened the forested slope. "I left the ranch seven years ago when my father died."

"Why?"

Storme swallowed, closing his eyes against the grief and guilt that seeped in. "Because he was killed, and the bullet that took his life was meant for me," he answered low, then glanced over his shoulder, seeing her widened gaze, and the sorrow that shimmered. "I don't want to risk the same thing happening to Ben."

"Wh . . . what happened? Who killed your father?"

Storme nudged the horse up the trail between the tall spruce and cottonwoods, welcoming the leafy coverage that filtered the sun's glare and offered relief from the burning rays, though it did nothing to cool the anger that simmered in his veins as the memories unfurled. "A band of renegade Apaches were roaming this area back then, raiding farms and stealing cattle. The army dispatched troops up from Fort Sumner to hunt them down. There was speculation among the soldiers, and the townsfolk, that I might be involved. Of course, I wasn't, and my father and the sheriff helped prove that. But there was a certain private in that company who had once been held captive by the Apache, and his grudge toward my people was strong. He didn't like the idea that I was allowed to roam free instead of being forced onto the reservation, and every time our paths crossed in town, he did his damnedest to provoke me into a fight. But he never would swing at me, and I knew if I swung first, the army would arrest me for assaulting a soldier. But one day, that private said some things against my father and brother that I couldn't ignore, and I did hit him. I didn't stop until he couldn't get up, either."

"Were you arrested?"

Storme shook his head. "Sheriff Hadley saw the whole incident, and he came to my defense. The private was officially reprimanded, which only strengthened his hatred. He stopped me in town a few days after that, and making sure no one but me heard what he had to say, he vowed to see me dead. About a week later, I was out rounding up strays with my father near the mountains north of our ranch. We were just starting back toward home when a shot rang out from the woods. One second, my father was sitting on his horse right beside me. The next, he was lying on the ground bleeding to death."

He heard her sharp intake of breath. "I'm so sorry, Storme."

His throat went dry as she circled slender arms around his middle. The sympathy in her offered compassion, in the feel of her cheek lightly pressed against his back, surprised him as much as it warmed his soul with welcome comfort.

"What did the army do to him for killing your father?"

"Nothing." Disgust burned a hole in his gut. "I saw the private fleeing, but I didn't go after him because I was trying to save my father. He died a few hours later. Without witnesses, the army wasn't inclined to take the word of a half-breed over a soldier's and argued that there were a lot of folks around here who didn't like me and could have taken that shot."

"What did you do?" Anna quietly asked, feeling the tension that tightened his muscles. He didn't say anything for several long seconds, and she wasn't sure that he was going to answer, but he did.

"I served my own justice."

Anna strongly suspected that meant he had killed the private. She didn't blame Storme. She had seen how the townsfolk treated him. She admired the way he managed to hold his temper, and even when he had gotten mad and hit Dodding, it had only been in her defense. She had also seen his kindness, had felt his gentleness. Storme was a decent, honorable man. But she knew that decent, honorable people could be pushed only so far. She didn't sit in judgment of his actions against the private, whatever they were. How could she? She had killed a man, and even though it had been an act of self-defense, she had reacted out of anger and grief, too, and fear. "Did you get into trouble?"

Anna pulled back slightly, pleasantly surprised when Storme stopped her from going far by placing his hand gently over her arms, holding them in place around his middle. She closed her eyes, biting at her bottom lip as her breasts rubbed against the hard muscles of his back, and hot tingles scorched a path through her veins.

"No. There wasn't any proof I was responsible for the private's disappearance. But there was suspicion, and anonymous threats made against me and my brother. I left town before anything else could happen." He shrugged. "That's when I decided to take up bounty hunting."

"I'm sorry you had to leave your home. But you had every right to expect justice for your father's death."

"Thank you," he answered in a low, deep voice laced with gratitude, and a hint of affection that made her heart beat faster. He turned his head, his dark gaze raking over her face and a small smile lifting the corners of his mouth. "Tell me about you? Do you like being a housemaid?"

She smiled. "I need the money, and I like working for Mrs. Harrington."

He arched one eyebrow. "I can hear it in your voice that you'd rather be doing something else. What it is you want, Anna?"

She hesitated, wishing she could be as honest as he had been. There was something about this kind, handsome man that touched her soul with a comforting sense of rightness, that pulled more strongly at her trust every time she was with him. God, how she wished her life wasn't so complicated. Why couldn't she have met Storme sooner? Before her life became a fated twist of hide-and-seek with the law and a desperate race to leave the country before she got caught.

She stared out across the forest, at the sunlight streaking a wavy pattern through the heavy foliage. The desire to share her dream with him burned in her chest, the words rising past the choked concern of revealing too much about herself. "I'm going to join a musical troupe someday, and sing onstage."

"Why haven't you already? You have a lovely voice."

"I will, when I have enough money to move on."

"You're not planning to stay in Pleasant Grove then?"

"No." She didn't offer any insight into her planned destination. Storme *was* a bounty hunter, after all, and it wouldn't be wise to let anyone connected to the law know how to find her, no matter how much she trusted him.

Warmth radiated through Storme at her continued willingness to indulge his curiosity. He thought about the rustlers' threat against her. As much as he liked being around her, he knew it might be safer if Anna could leave town right now. "How much do you need? I'd be happy to—"

"No, I'm not taking your money, Storme. You've done enough for me already. I'll make it on my own just fine."

He admired her pride and determination, but couldn't resist teasing her just a little. "Now who's the stubborn one?"

"You still are." He liked the sound of her soft chuckle. Her green eyes sparkled with a hint of mischief. "I've just been taking lessons from you."

He laughed. "Well, you're a quick learner. Let's see how well you do with that gun." He nudged the black gelding up the steep incline through the tall spruce and pines, onto the spongy ground around the small pool he had taken Anna to soak her hand, then reined to a halt where the stream narrowed and began its snaking decline through the woods. He moved his hand away from hers arms, instantly missing her touch as she lowered her slender limbs from around his waist. He swung his leg over the horse's neck and jumped down, then stared up at her pretty, flushed face. "I thought we'd practice by the water. It'll be cooler." He reached up, circling his hands around her waist.

She gripped her fingers against his shoulders. "It's so darn hot, I may just jump in."

Her raked his gaze over her colorful flowered dress. His breath lodged at the image of her wet, her clothes clinging tight to those nice curves. He lifted her down, letting her soft body slide in torturous rapture along his as he lowered her to her feet. "I won't stop you." In fact, he might just give her a hand jumping in.

She smiled, a fervent glow springing into her eyes, and sending hot currents of desire racing straight to the lower regions of his body. Storme knew he needed to let go of her waist, needed to step back, needed to get on with these gun lessons before he got himself shot with Mrs. Harrington's rifle. But Anna made no move to pull away. She slowly trailed her fingers on a burning path around his neck, and quietly drove him crazy.

Oh, hell! One kiss, then we'll get started on those lessons.

Storme wrapped his arms around her back, and lowered his mouth to hers, his last thread of calm snapping as her lips parted. He crushed her to him, running one hand up her spine and reveling in the feel of her tongue thrusting to meet his with wild abandon. Blood roared through his heart at her gentle moan, her fingers stroking his back, running through his hair. He caressed the smooth nape of her neck, then buried his fingers in the silky strands of her hair and pressed her even closer, deepening his exploration of her warm mouth.

His body hardened. His hands itched to roam over her luscious curves. Storme knew he had to stop before he lost all control. With great reluctance, he left the soft sweetness of her lips, but he couldn't let go, not when she looked up at him with that sparkle of wonderment shining in her eyes. Not when she lifted her mouth closer. He indulged in another quick kiss, then pressed his lips to the smooth line of her jaw, working his way up to the small tip of her nose.

"You're going to make me forget why we're here," he whispered, pleased at the warm gleam of satisfaction on her pretty face.

She smiled with a beautiful candor that seriously threatened his tenuous control. "You make me forget all sorts of things when you kiss me, Storme."

Her words washed over him in heated waves and set his heart to hammering against his ribs. He loved her velvety voice, and the way she said his name so tenderly, so passionately. "I'd like nothing more than to stand here and keep doing it, too. But we have to get busy." It took every ounce of strength he possessed to lower his hands, to stand there as she slowly slid her arms over the front of his shoulders. Her fingers lingered in a gentle caress down the front of his shirt and nearly drove him to pull her into his embrace again.

She lowered her arms to her sides. Storme had to force himself to step away. He reached for the canteen, freeing the strap from around the saddle horn, uncapped the lid, and offered it to her.

She smiled her thanks, then lifted the flask to her lips. He watched her throat ripple as she drank, and forced aside the image of pressing his mouth to the slender, pale column of her neck. She handed it back, and Storme took a long swallow, savoring the refreshing water as much as the taste of her mouth that clung faintly to the rim.

He replaced the cap and looped the strap over his shoulder. He tied the horse's reins around a narrow pine near the water's edge and reached for Anna's hand. "Let's walk upstream a ways, so we don't spook the horse."

She nodded.

Storme headed around the pool and uphill, where the stream narrowed slightly. "I know you said you've never fired your derringer, but have you ever fired any sort of gun before?"

Her steps faltered. Storme tightened his hold, frowning at the haunted look that sprang into her gaze before she looked away.

"Um . . . yes, I fired a six-shooter once."

"When?" He stared at the pinched line of her mouth and jaw.

She shrugged. "It's been a while."

Storme hesitated, puzzling over her reason for not being more exact. What the hell is she hiding? As much as he wanted to know what caused these bouts of sudden wariness, though, he decided not to press. He valued Anna's trust more than he did her secret. He knew that everyone carried a secret of some sort from their past. She had opened up to him on the ride, and he was glad, but he didn't expect her to spill her whole life story. He certainly hadn't, and he was grateful that she didn't ask him exactly what he had done to serve justice on that army private. Storme wouldn't have told her the truth. He didn't want her changing her opinion of him and believing he might just be a savage, after all. "Well, your derringer won't hold the same forceful kick, so it'll be easier. But you have to be close to hit something, which means there won't be any time to spare with hesitation. You have to shoot fast."

"All right, I can do that."

Storme smiled at her confidence, pleased to see the tension drain from her face, and her eyes gleaming bright again. He didn't need her pretty smile to reinforce that he had made the right decision not to question her, but he sure liked looking at it.

Golden rays softened the shadows in streaked lines along the thick, grassy bank. Storme stopped and released Anna's hand. He dropped the canteen near the water's edge, then tossed his hat down beside it. He reached into his front pocket and retrieved her gun and one of the two boxes of cartridges he had bought.

"All right." He handed her the derringer. "Now, your gun

holds two bullets," he explained, "but they both fire at the same time, so you won't get a second chance. You have to make your aim true the first time. We'll start with something simple. I want you to fire right over there." He pointed to the thick trunk of a cottonwood standing about twenty feet away on the other side of the creek.

She nodded, lifted the gun, holding her arm out straight, and fired.

Storme frowned. She hadn't hesitated, but she hadn't hit anything, either. "Try again." He pulled two cartridges from the box and handed them to her, impressed that she at least didn't have any trouble loading them.

She took aim and fired again, missing.

Storme patiently handed her two more bullets.

She loaded them, aimed, then fired, this time barely nicking the edge of the tree. Her squeal of delight made him chuckle.

Not bad, he thought, *but not good enough. A slightly wounded man could still come after her.* He made her do it again, pleased when she hit the tree more in the center this time.

Next he had her aim at the thin trunk of a pine just a couple of yards to the left. Three shots later she hadn't hit it yet. Before she fired the fourth, he stepped up behind her. He breathed deep of the lavender scent that clung to her hair and rocked his senses with a desire to know if she smelled that good all over, then shook aside the distraction. He took hold of her wrist and lifted her arm slightly higher, then slid his hand down over her smooth fingers and pointed toward the end of the gun.

"Use the sight to aim with," he whispered against her ear.

She glanced over, frowning. "I have been."

Her mouth was so close, he would barely have to lean forward and he could kiss those pretty lips. Storme swallowed back the desire. He lowered his hand from hers. "Try again."

She looked away, held the gun out steady, and fired. The bullet went into the center of the trunk. She spun around, her eyes wide with excitement. "I did it."

Storme smiled. "That was good." She stood so close. She looked so pretty. She smelled so damn good. He placed his fingers under her chin, and bent down, claiming her lips in quick, thorough kisses. "Now, do it again," he whispered.

She grinned and lifted her eyebrows in a playful arch. "Kiss you? Or hit the tree again?"

His heart pounded faster. "Whichever you prefer."

To his delight, she kissed him again. Then she turned away and loaded the gun. She took aim and hit the thin pine just slightly off center.

Storme had her shoot more rounds, satisfied when she hit the tree four out of five times. "That was very good." He untied the bandanna from his neck and wiped the moisture that beaded on her brow and glistened on her flushed cheeks. Several strands of her hair had slipped from her chignon, the wavy red strands framing her face. Storme couldn't resist trailing his fingers along them.

He smiled and reached down to grab the canteen. He uncapped the top and offered it to her.

She shook her head and knelt at the edge of the stream. She cupped her hands into the water, then brought the liquid up to splash against her face.

Storme watched with rapture as she doused water over her face twice more, then lifted a cupped handful to her mouth. He drank from the canteen, draining the last little bit, then squatted in the grass beside her, and refilled it from the stream.

She smiled at him, water dripping from her cheeks. "Mind if I borrow that?"

Storme glanced at the bandanna in his hand that she pointed at, but instead of handing it over, he dried the moisture from her face himself. He leaned over and lightly kissed her lips. "You ready to get back to these lessons now?"

"Sure."

He stood and helped her up, letting his hand linger on her elbow. "I want to try something a little harder this time. I want you to put the gun in your pocket." He nodded down toward her skirt. "I'm going to come at you like I intend you harm, and I want to see how fast you can pull it out and fire at me."

The blood drained from her face. "I can't shoot you."

Storme held back his grin. "Sure you can. Just pretend it's the first night we met. You seemed pretty intent on doing me in then."

She frowned. "But that was different. I didn't know you then."

"This is different, too." He let his smile roll full over his mouth, then reached up and tapped one finger against her nose. "We're not going to load the gun this time, little dove."

Storme paused at the endearment that flowed so easily, and unexpectedly, from his lips, seeing the look of surprise that flashed in her eyes, as well.

Her smile came slow. Then, to his astonishment, she lifted up on her toes and planted a firm kiss on his mouth. "In that case, I'll give it a try." She stuck the gun in her pocket.

Storme turned around and walked several yards away, then without any warning, he turned back and broke into a run straight for her. She fumbled getting her hand into her pocket, never had a chance to pull the gun out before he reached her, gathered her in his arms and spun her in a circle, delighting in the sweet laughter that bubbled from her throat.

"That was a poor attempt," he said lightheartedly, loving the sight of her flushed cheeks.

"Well, you didn't give me a chance," she responded, still chuckling.

Storme froze, all humor draining away. He set her down on her feet and cupped her face with both hands. "And neither will the rustlers. Now, let's be serious and try this again."

She nodded, her expression sobering.

Storme walked away, then came at her again. She managed to get the gun out, but didn't have time to fire. He repeated the action several times, until she improved her speed and was firing the empty chambers at him every time. He reached over, sliding his fingers through the long silky hair that had fallen from her chignon, then brushed the soft strands away from her face.

"Now, if someone tries to grab you . . ." He went on, giving her advice about jabbing with her elbows and where to kick a man to disable him. Then he walked off into the woods, made his way where she couldn't see him, and quietly came back, sneaking up behind her and circling one arm around her chest. She squealed her surprise, then quickly punched him with both elbows, which he expected and was ready for. But he didn't anticipate her sharp heel stomping down hard on the top of his boot, then her foot swinging back to ram against his shin, or for her to struggle like a wildcat. *She's done this before,* he thought. He loosened his hold because he didn't want to hurt her, but it gave her just enough room to twist around. She moved like lightning, hauling her knee upward and slamming it into his manhood. Pain shot through his groin in hard waves. Storme groaned out loud, letting go of her as he doubled over and clutched himself.

Anna fell to her knees in front of him. "Oh my goodness, Storme, are you all right? I'm so sorry."

He gulped in air, nodded, then gulped in some more. After several long seconds, he lifted his head to meet her fearful gaze of concern and managed a weak smile. "I'll be . . . fine," he choked the words out, barely above a whisper.

She cocked her head, her eyebrows drawing together in a look of doubt.

He sucked in another lung full of air, taking a minute to catch his breath. "That was . . . very good. I'm proud of you." He *was* proud of her. She was a fast learner, and a spirited woman. Just two of the things he liked so much about her.

"Well, I'm not proud." She frowned. "I didn't mean to hurt you." She reached over and ran her fingers gently along his cheek. "What can I do to help?"

Storme's heart pounded faster as several tempting suggestions popped into his mind and fired his blood. His smile came
stronger this time as he slowly lowered himself to his knees.
"Kiss me," he whispered, nearly losing his breath again at the
passionate blaze that scorched the horizons of her spring green
eyes. He placed one hand to the back of her head, digging his
fingers into her satiny hair, and claimed her lips, savoring the
taste of her warm mouth, her sweet, willing response, before
he drew back. "I'm feeling better now."

"You're sure?" she spoke in a husky whisper. "I don't
mind doing it again."

Storme's pulse raced with hot desire. "I won't stop you."

She smiled, wrapping her arms around his neck, then kissed
him with a hunger that took him by surprise with its intensity,
and made him want to get lost in her forever. He forced himself
not to reach for her when she broke off the kiss and pulled
back.

She glanced toward the creek, then favored him with a mischievous smile.

"I'm going to wade in the stream and cool off a little bit.
Want to join me?"

Storme's heart hammered with stampeding force. He raked
his stare over her, images of wet clothes clinging to her full
breasts, her slender curves, burned across his mind, and fueled
his thoughts on to stripping her out of them. "No, you go on."
He just needed to stay right there for a few more minutes before
he tried to stand up, and he also needed the time to get a hold
on his desire, which was making the pain in his groin even
worse.

"All right." She stood and walked over to the bank, then
sat in the grass and unlaced her boots.

Storme sat back on his heels, watching with intent interest
as she reached under her skirt and took her black stockings
off, tossing them on top of her discarded shoes. His breath
caught and pleasure pounded in his chest as she bunched her

skirt up to mid-calf, revealing her smooth pale skin. The water covered her trim ankles as she stepped into the stream, and rose higher up her legs when she continued on toward the middle, forcing her to lift her skirt up to her knees. He found pure enjoyment in listening to her sighs of relief, in the sight of her shapely limbs. She bent over and scooped a handful of water up to her mouth, then glanced over at him. Storme met her narrowed stare, could read her knowing smile that she had caught him staring at her backside. He smiled back, not the least ashamed. What did it matter if he got caught? She knew he was attracted to her. Hell, how could she not? He couldn't keep his lips off her. With a force that rocked him clear to his soul, he realized that he cared for Anna far more than he wanted to admit. Wanted her more than he had ever wanted any woman. He loved her spirited nature, her quick, teasing wit that popped out unexpectedly at times, and he couldn't recall a single time he had ever had so much fun being with a woman.

Storme rose to his feet and went over to stand at the water's edge.

"Are you feeling better?" Anna's heart pounded faster as she made her way through the water toward him.

He nodded. "But don't let that stop you from kissing me anytime you want."

She smiled. The desirous fire burning in Storme's eyes fanned the blaze of her own heated attraction and sent it crashing into a vibrant pool low in her stomach. She lifted up on her toes, bringing her mouth close to his. "I won't," she whispered, offering no resistance as he settled his lips over hers and circled his arms around her, pulling her from the stream and pressing her close against muscled strength.

Anna buried her fingers in the thick softness of his hair, fervent waves raging through her as his hands stroked her back, then roamed lower in a caressing exploration over her bottom, her hips. Her flattened breasts tingled, her nipples hardening at the contact with his hard chest, at the feel of his heart beating as furiously as her own. His hands glided gently along her waist, and brushed the sides of her breasts. Hot jolts shot through her, stirring the moan of pleasure that rose from her throat, and strengthening her own curiosity, her need to touch him.

Slipping one hand inside the collar of his shirt, she trailed her fingers down the column of his corded neck, fingering the beaded leather, then lower, straining the buttons as she roamed over the smooth warmth of his chest, delighting in the quivers that lightly danced along his skin.

Storme's heart leapt with excitement at her gentle touch, at the feel of her hands gliding over his shoulders, down the front of his shirt. He trailed his mouth along the slender length of her satiny neck and kissed the hollow of her throat, then worked his way back to her sweet, tempting lips. Her delicious moans vibrated against his mouth, igniting his ardor with pure, explosive pleasure, intensifying his need to feel more of her soft curves. He circled her waist with his hands, sliding upward along the slim line and cupping the full weight of her breasts in his palms. With gentle strokes, he kneaded the soft round globes, outlining her hardened nubs with his fingers. She arched against his touch, deepening his arousal. He tore his mouth from hers, kissing a path along her chin, down her neck as he worked the buttons of her bodice loose, pressing his lips to her smooth pale skin, moving lower to the soft white mounds that peeked invitingly above the low cut of her chemise. Tremors of heated enjoyment shot through his fingers as he skimmed the smooth flesh of her chest, her shoulders, pushing the cotton away to slide down her slender arms. Storme lifted his head, gazed into her innocent, trusting eyes, and paused. The realization of how far his desire was about to take him slammed into his conscience.

What the hell am I doing? He had no right to make love to her.

Anna had plans, dreams of singing onstage. He had no right

to compromise those dreams. And she deserved a man who could love her freely, provide a home, children, a safe, stable life. Not one who lived in a one-room cabin when he wasn't roaming the countryside in search of outlaws, and was always watching his back, waiting for the next attempt on his life.

Storme lifted the bodice back in place and pulled the opening closed, then stepped away from her. He raked his hand through his hair, taking several deep breaths to calm his racing heart.

"What's wrong?" she whispered, clutching her arms over her front.

Her confused, pained voice ripped at his soul. He hated that he had caused the embarrassing uncertainty that rose to stain her cheeks and drifted hauntingly into her stare. Storme groaned, shaking his head, wanting to take her in his arms, afraid he wouldn't be able to stop again if he did. "I'm sorry, Anna. I didn't mean to go so far."

Anna couldn't stop the tears that welled in her eyes. Storme didn't want her . . . and why would he? He was a kind, decent man, and he deserved better than a woman who acted just like the trollop she had been labeled by the townsfolk in Missouri. "I understand."

He arched his brow in puzzlement and reached one finger over to brush the tear that slipped from her eye. "And just what is it you understand?" he softly asked.

She swallowed. "That you deserve a woman who knows how to act like a decent lady. I should have been the one to pull back, to say no, instead of acting like a . . . a . . ."

He stepped forward and placed one finger against her lips. "Don't even think that. You're a beautiful, passionate woman who knows more about being a lady than any female I've ever met. You're the one who deserves better, Anna." He lowered his hand to his side. "I care about you, and I have too much respect for you to take advantage."

Anna's heart turned over in response. Her body melted at the impassioned light in his gaze. "I care about you, too,

Storme. I've never met a man more kind and honorable than you . . . or who makes me feel so safe and special."

"You are special. You're gentle and sweet, and I don't want to do anything to hurt you."

She trusted his honesty, and his concern for her settled deep in her soul. He wasn't offering commitment. She knew she couldn't accept it even if he was. But she had never met anyone like Storme before, never knew that she could enjoy being with a man, and had never wanted one so much before. She certainly never thought to meet someone who treated her so kindly, who cared enough to consider her feelings above lustful needs. Storme had given her so much today, a sense of peace and freedom she hadn't known in so long, a sense of being alive instead of scared and always looking over her shoulder, waiting for everything to come crashing down around her. She knew her troubles could come nipping at her heels anytime, knew she had no future with this man. But for just that one moment in time, she didn't want to be anywhere else, didn't want to think about her problems or the future that would take her so far away. She wanted what she knew in her heart she would never find again. She wanted Storme.

Anna bit her lip, pondering the decision that rattled in her mind, and seared her heart. "I'm not asking for commitment, Storme. I know you're not staying in town. Neither am I. But I like being with you. I want to be with you, and I'll be happy with whatever time we have together."

He shook his head, frowning. "That's not fair to you, Anna."

No, what wasn't fair was that she hadn't met him before now, before killing someone and being forced into hiding, before giving up on ever thinking she would meet a man she could trust. She knew it wouldn't be wise to let herself get too close, knew she should walk away from this bounty hunter before he learned the truth about her. But her heart didn't want to go, and her desire for him outweighed the risks she knew she was taking.

"But it's what I want," she stated low, stepping closer to him and reaching up to touch his strong, handsome face.

Shock rippled through Storme. He stared at the sure confidence that glowed in her eyes, his heart leaping with surprise, his fired blood coursing with deepened desire. He had never met a woman who made him feel more alive, or who heightened his protective instincts to such depths . . . and he knew in his heart he would never meet anyone like her again. He wanted her more than he wanted his next breath, but hesitation rang through his thoughts. Did she just want his company, a few kisses? He could settle for that, but had to know for sure. The last thing he wanted to do was make the wrong move.

"What exactly is it that you want?"

"I want you to kiss me," she whispered. She tucked her head down slightly, and peeked up at him through her thick, dark lashes. "I want you to touch me again . . . and not stop."

His heart raced. "Are you sure, Anna?"

She bit her bottom lip and nodded, certainty blazing in her eyes.

The low growl of pleasure sprang from Storme's throat as he pulled her roughly to him, matching her sparring tongue stroke for stroke in an urgent exploration that sent waves of heated passion surging through him. She tightened her arms around his neck, her fingers gliding through his hair. Storme ran his hands along her slender back, the soft hollow near the base of her spine, reveling in the feel of her passionate shivers, her hardened nipples pressed against his chest. He gripped her hips, pulling her closer to the hot, pulsing desire that swelled his manhood, then made a path along the gentle curve of her waist, climbing higher to caress her breasts.

He gazed deep into her trusting eyes as he slipped his hands inside her opened bodice, slid his palms along the smooth line of her slender shoulders, and eased the cotton down her arms once again. His breath lodged when she reached out and worked the buttons of his shirt loose, sliding her hands along his skin as she shoved the material from his body, then she pressed her warm palms against his chest, caressing, driving him wild with fevered desire.

His body hardened with an urgent hunger, but his need to please her raged stronger, and his hands shook slightly as he slowly undressed her, inch by inch, exposing her soft, luscious curves, until she stood naked before him. His breath lodged as the sunlight kissed her creamy flesh in spots he longed to touch with his hands, his mouth. He raked his gaze over her full round breasts, dark nipples puckering invitingly beneath his stare, then lower to the auburn curls that marked her woman-hood, and down the luscious length of her shapely legs.

"You're so beautiful," he whispered, trailing his stare back up to her pretty face. He saw the hesitation in her green depths, and took a deep breath. "We can stop, Anna."

She knew he meant it, and his thoughtfulness only made her want him more. His wide, bronze chest glistened in the sunlight. Her fingers ached to feel his hard muscles again. He was so strong, yet so tender with his touch, so handsome he stole her breath away. With a boldness that surprised her, she reached out and undid the buckle of his gun belt. He took the heavy leather and tossed it to the side, then pulled her to him and sealed his mouth over hers, swallowing her gasp at the contact of her breasts against his heated flesh. His warm, masculine scent assailed her nose and fueled the hot swirls of ecstasy that roared through her veins.

She couldn't stop her moans at the feel of his hands stroking her body, firing her blood as his mouth moved over hers with a hungry passion that rocked her senses. She ran her fingers over his broad shoulders, then along his hard chest, loving the powerful feel of his strength, the gentleness in his touch.

He lowered her onto the soft grass, half-covering her body with his muscular length, and caressed her thighs, her stomach, cupping her breasts in his large, warm palms, making her skin tingle, and her pulse race with a rapturous delight unlike anything she had ever known. Then his mouth left hers, and she leaned her head back, closing her eyes as his lips traced a path down her throat, shooting jolts of staggering desire through her when he moved lower and captured her nipple gently between his teeth, then circled the hard nub with his tongue.

He lavished his attention on her breasts, reveled in the feel of her smooth heated flesh, the tight buds that hardened even more at his touch. Storme's desire throbbed painfully against the confines of his pants as he moved his hands lower, stroking her flat stomach, his mouth following the path his fingers took. He caressed her hips, ran his hands along the silky line of her thighs, feeling the shivers that raced through her limbs. He kissed his way back up to her mouth, swallowing her startled gasp as his fingers moved through her soft curls, then lower. His heart pounded at the wetness that greeted his touch. He slipped one finger inside to stroke her sweet, hot core. He kissed every inch of her face, loving the soft purring sounds she made as she gripped his shoulders and arched against his hand. He felt the pleasure ripple through her body, the liquid fire building hotter, and crashing in a heated wave against his hand. She cried out his name, her eyes flying open in shock, then softening with wonderment.

"Did you like that, little dove?" Storme whispered, smiling as her lips curved upward.

"Very much. Is there more?"

Storme's breath hitched in his throat. The sunlight glistened in her hair, shimmering like rich gold in her dark red waves, and shone in the gleam of her flushed face. His pulse rocketed. He sat up and quickly tugged his boots off, then shed his pants, reveling in the stare she raked over his body before he lowered himself back to her side. He captured her mouth, and ran his hands over her body, stoking the fire in her again, until she writhed beneath him and he couldn't stand to wait any longer. Then he eased himself slowly into her and met the tight barrier of her virginity.

He kissed her long and deep, wincing at the gasp of pain she breathed out as he slowly thrust forward and buried himself deep inside her. Her nails dug into his back. Storme stilled, hating that he had had to hurt her, even for that brief moment, then he caressed her body with his hands until he felt her relax beneath him, felt the heated pleasure build in her once more.

Storme rode the wave with her, a glorious harmony, a beautiful blending unlike anything he had ever known with a woman, and when she reached the peak again, cried out his name, he couldn't hold back any longer and followed her over the edge, soaring in a conflagration of searing rhapsody that nearly made him forget the responsible thing to do, and not risk planting his child inside her.

He held her close until his breathing slowed, then moved his weight from her, and rolled to his side. He propped his head in one hand and gazed into her pretty face, her soft, satisfied stare.

"That was wonderful," she whispered, a shy smile lifting her mouth.

"Definitely wonderful." He leaned down and kissed her lips, soft and slow, then he drew back and sat up.

Anna stared at the corded muscles that rippled across his back, marveling at the exquisite pleasure he had given her. He reached over and grabbed the red bandanna, then stood, and towered above her. She ran her gaze over his bronze, muscular body, touched golden by the sun's soft rays, and it took every ounce of her control not to beg him to take her again.

She smiled when he bent down and lifted her in his arms, wrapped her arms around his neck as he carried her into the stream, then he gently lowered her to her feet. Tears rose in her eyes as he wet the cloth and tenderly began to wash her body. Her heart swelled with deepening affection as he planted light kisses on the spots he cleaned, working his way up to claim her mouth. Her desire fired hot. She took the cloth from his hands, and returned the gesture, wiping the moisture of their lovemaking from his shoulders, and the hard contours of his chest, then boldly dared to move lower. His low growl drew her attention. He stared at her through narrowed eyes, then gently pulled her flush against him and dipped his head to claim her mouth.

Anna's heart soared as he carried her from the stream and lowered her back down to the grass, then proceeded to make sweet love to her again.

Chapter Thirteen

"We need to hurry, Storme." Urgency heightened the tremble he heard in Anna's voice, and flew through her fingers as she laced her kid boots.

Storme stared at her pretty flushed cheeks, her kiss-swollen lips pursed in summoning appeal, and swallowed dryly, torn between his satisfied pleasure and mounting guilt. He looped the gun belt around his hips and strapped it into place. What the hell had he been thinking? He never should have taken her innocence, no matter how willingly she had offered it.

She stood and smoothed the folds of her skirt, then reached up and patted at her hair, shoving pins deeper into the twisted knot at her nape. She lowered her arms, and blew out a heavy sigh, a tremulous smile lifting the corners of her mouth. "How do I look?"

Storme's heart pounded against his ribs. He brushed a loose strand of hair back behind her ear. "Beautiful," he whispered the truth, then cupped her face in his hands and leaned down to place a light kiss on her lips. "And calm down, darling.

We're only a little late." He lowered his hands and fastened the top button of her bodice that she had failed to do up.

She nodded. "I just don't want to see Mrs. Harrington waiting with her rifle and threatening to shoot you. Or worse, actually do it."

Reproach gripped his gut in a hard knot. *It would be exactly what I deserve.* "As long as you hit those targets she promised to have waiting, it'll be fine," he assured.

"You think I can do it?" She worried her bottom lip between her teeth.

"I know you can." Storme took hold of her hand, squeezing it lightly. Uncertainty hovered in her stare, and he couldn't help but wonder if she harbored more than just worry over their timeliness and the targets. Was she having regrets, as well? He sure as hell was, but only because he would rather cut his heart out than do anything to hurt her. Anna was young, and sweet, and innocent . . . and *he* had taken advantage. Oh sure, he could sugarcoat his actions with truthful convictions that he cared deeply for her, that he had been honest with her about making no commitment, that she had wanted him as much as he did her, and she was a grown woman capable of making her own decisions. But it didn't change the facts, or ease his mind any. She deserved so much more than he had to offer, and far more than she was willing to settle for with him. He should have stayed his distance. "Anna, about what happened between us . . ."

Her body stiffened. The sudden hurt that leapt into her eyes tore at his heart, and ripped a wider hole in his conscience. Her thin eyebrows drew together. "If you're going to tell me you're sorry, I'd really rather not hear it."

He tightened his hold when she tried to pull her hand free. "I wasn't . . . not yet. I was going to ask if you have any regrets. If you tell me yes, then I'll start apologizing."

She lifted her chin; the bold defiance he admired in her spirit flashed across her stare as a soft smile curved her mouth. "I don't have any regrets, Storme. I knew what I was doing, and I meant every word I said. I'm happy for whatever time we have.''

He released the breath he had been holding, and smiled. He had almost forgotten about her plans to move on, to join a theater troupe. She wasn't looking for a commitment, but a career. Still, his conscience was only slightly eased. Anna deserved so much more that just a few stolen moments . . . especially with a man who had brought nothing but trouble into her life so far. It didn't stop his pulse from beating faster, though, or his desire for her from raging hot. If she wanted to spend time with him—for however long they were both in town—he wasn't going to object. "And I'm happy to spend that time with you.''

A warm gleam sparkled in her eyes. "I'm glad to hear it.'' She furrowed her brow in seriousness and marched passed him, tugging at his hand. "Now, let's go before we're even more late.''

Storme stood his ground, chuckling lightly at the frown she shot over her shoulder at him. *She has some nerve calling me stubborn.* But he really liked that she wasn't afraid to be a little bit bold, and didn't take an excessive amount of time to make a decision about something. Linette had always waffled for days over the least little thing. He gently pulled Anna back to him, capturing her in his circled embrace and pressing her soft curves flush against his torso.

"What are you doing? We need to leave.'' The laughter mingled in her low, velvety voice excited him as much as her weak attempts to squirm from his hold.

Storme smiled, then dipped his head and sealed his mouth over hers. She parted her lips, her tongue meeting his with an eager, passionate response, and slid her hands across his shoulders, firing his skin with her soft touch. Desire roared through him in luxuriant waves. With great reluctance, Storme broke off their kiss, then placed his forehead against hers, and stared into her pretty green eyes.

"We need to go, Storme," she whispered.

He didn't want to leave . . . ever. The realization slammed hard into his soul, and cooled his blood. He *was* leaving, and so was she. He didn't need to let himself fall any harder for her. It was already going to be tough enough to walk away. Storme lowered his arms and straightened. "You're right."

He fell into step beside her as they followed the stream downhill and skirted the small pool. Storme untied the gelding, then helped Anna into the saddle, and climbed up behind. He reined the horse around and headed through the woods, then down the mountain trail. Anna leaned back against him, searing his blood with her soft feel. She tilted her head slightly to look up at him. The happy glow on her face lit up her eyes, as well, and sent his pulse racing. He circled his arms tighter around her waist, enjoying the smile that stayed on her lips as she faced front again.

"I had a real nice time this afternoon. Thank you for the gun lessons . . . and everything."

He smiled at the shy note that sounded in her tone. He reined the horse to a halt where the mountain trail met the valley, then shifted slightly to the side. Placing one finger beneath her chin, he turned her to face him. "I had a real nice time, too, Anna," he whispered, then leaned down to kiss her with a thorough hunger that threatened to chase every responsible thought from his mind.

Anna's heart pounded so hard she thought it would surely leap right from her chest. Oh, how she loved the way he kissed her, how she cared for this gentle, handsome man. In the last few days, he had brought more joy and peace into her life than she had known in a long time. But she also knew what they had shared today didn't change anything between them. He would still be leaving town. And so would she. That didn't mean she wasn't going to enjoy every single minute of what time they did have together, though . . . or ever stop cherishing the memories.

He ended the kiss, and smiled, then in the way she was coming to expect, he leaned down again to briefly press his mouth to hers one final time. He loosened his hold around her waist and gathered up the reins. "All right, Anna, we do have to hurry now. Hold on." He whispered the last in her ear a split second before he kicked the horse into a hard run.

She grabbed the saddle horn with both hands and leaned forward some as they raced across the desert valley. The wind whipped against her face. Anna couldn't stop the laughter that bubbled in her throat and sprang forth at the sense of freedom that swept through her. She wished they could just keep riding forever. But all too soon the boardinghouse loomed ahead, then Storme was reining the horse to halt near the back gate. Anna saw the empty cans and bottles lined up along the fence, the ice-cream churn sitting unattended on the back porch. She was thankful that Mrs. Harrington and the girls were nowhere in sight, giving her another few minutes alone with Storme.

He jumped down from the horse, then reached up and circled his hands around her waist. To her disappointment, he didn't pull her close when he lifted her down, but she could see the desire to do so blazing in his eyes. Butterflies winged their way through her stomach. On impulse, she rose on tiptoe and kissed him briefly, loving the smile that graced his lips at her action.

"Looks like Mrs. Harrington has everything ready for you." He nodded toward the targets. "You need any last-minute reminders before we go find her?"

Anna shook her head. "I remember everything you taught me up there." She batted her lashes innocently, teasingly, reveling in the easy comfort she found in his presence.

He raised one black eyebrow in a playful arch. "You are talking about the gun lessons, right?"

She stifled the chuckle that bubbled in her throat, and furrowed her brow in confusion. "What gun lessons?"

Storme tilted his head back and groaned. "I'll be leaving here and headed to Doc's with a big hole in my backside. I can see it now."

"No, you won't." She smiled, swatting at his chest, then letting her fingers linger in a slow caress down his shirtfront. "Your backside's too fine to be putting holes in it."

He grabbed her arms and pulled her roughly against him, grinning down at her. "Glad you like it. But if you keep talking like that, I'm going to throw you on that horse and head back for the mountains."

His words sent a rush of excitement coursing through her veins and stirred the familiar pool of desire low in her stomach. She wrapped her arms around his waist. "That's hardly a threat," she whispered. "Since I wouldn't put up a struggle if you tried."

A low growl rumbled in his throat. He glanced toward the house, then claimed her mouth in a quick, cruel ravishment that sent swirls of ecstasy raging through her heart and left her breathless when he ended and stepped back.

"Come on. Before you steal away all my good sense, and we both wind up in trouble with Mrs. Harrington." He captured her hand and walked toward the fence. The hinge squeaked as he lifted the latch, then he pushed the gate open and stepped aside for her to lead the way.

"Would you like something to drink?" Anna asked as they walked across the yard and climbed the back steps. "We have iced tea and lemonade in the icebox."

"Lemonade would be nice." Storme held the door open, then followed her inside. He stopped, removed his hat, and set it on the edge of the counter, then watched her enticing stride across the wide kitchen. She opened the icebox door and bent over.

Storme smiled. So, she liked his backside, did she? His heart thumped erratically. Well, he liked hers, too. She straightened and crossed over to a long counter, then poured lemonade from the pitcher into two tall glasses. Storme slid an appreciate gaze over her shapely curves. He liked every inch of her perfect body. In fact, he loved everything about her, and he was going to have to be careful about that . . . or he would wind up getting his heart broken when they had to part company for good. Something told him that this time he might not recover from the pain, either.

"Thanks." He took the glass she handed, letting his fingers brush against hers and seeing the sparkle in her stare that said she had felt the same thrilling jolt at the brief contact. Then he took a long swallow of the cool drink and shifted his gaze over the oak table that filled the center of the spacious room, the yellow-painted walls that added a sunny cheer, brightened by the late-afternoon sunlight that gleamed through the windows.

"It's awfully quiet inside. Everyone must be out front."

Storme arched his brow. "Should we go join them?"

"I suppose we should." He heard the reluctance in her voice, in her sigh, and it mirrored his own wish that their time alone wasn't about to end. "Especially since Mrs. Harrington *is* expecting us back."

Storme nodded, then followed her from the kitchen and down the hallway. He could hear soft, female laughter filtering through the screen door, then growing slightly louder as they crossed the foyer. Storme pressed one hand against the wire mesh, waited for Anna to step outside first, then nearly collided against her back when she came to an abrupt halt.

Hannah Montgomery and Lilah Duncan screamed in alarm and backed up several steps from where they stood at one end of the porch.

For half a second, Storme wondered if they were going to walk off the edge, but they didn't . . . and he wasn't quite sure if he was disappointed about that or not.

"What are *you* doing here?" Edna Mae Mason snapped, her

slim face tightening in hard lines as she rose from the white wicker chair.

"Afternoon, ladies," Storme offered in greeting.

Sally Hankins shot up from the porch swing. "Where's your gun, Harriet?"

Anna squared her shoulders, and walked out onto the porch. Storme followed, letting the door close behind, and wondering if she was about to come his defense again. But she didn't get a chance.

"What do I need my gun for?" Mrs. Harrington frowned at the women but stayed seated in the high-backed wicker chair.

"You have an intruder. He needs to be shot," Hannah protested, her blue eyes widening.

"Looks to me like Mr. Warwick's doing nothing more than drinking a glass of lemonade. If I shot him for that, I'd have to shoot all of you for drinking my tea."

Storme smiled and lifted his glass in salute toward her. "It's the best lemonade I've tasted in a long time, too."

"How can you let him in your house?" Sally harshly questioned. "He's a savage and shouldn't even be allowed to set foot in town. I'm surprised we're all still alive as it is."

"That's hogwash!" Anna grated. She planted her hands on her hips. "He has every right to be in town. And he wouldn't hurt anyone."

"Well of course, *you* would think that," Lilah retorted, raising her chin and staring arrogantly down her long nose. "I noticed that you two didn't come right down for the dancing with the rest of the guests last night. You obviously don't care who you're seen with, or what kind of scandal you cause around town."

"Well, that's certainly the truth," Edna Mae stated.

Storme's anger started to boil.

"You all are being unfair," Mrs. Harrington strongly protested. "Anna's a nice, decent young woman."

"Decent?" Hannah exclaimed. "Then why is she constantly in the company of this savage?"

"We're friends," Anna defended. "And the only savages I've seen in town are you ladies."

A chorus of gasps filled the air.

"I swear, it's Linette Lewis all over again. She at least tried to keep it a secret, though." Sally shook her head in disgust, the feathers on her brown bonnet bouncing wildly with the movement. "But that woman didn't have a shred of decency, either. That's why she was run out of town."

"And you will be, too, if you're not careful," Lilah declared.

Storme's anger rose. He hadn't been able to stop what happened to Linette all those years ago, but he wasn't going to let the same thing happen to Anna. "You ladies try to run her out of town, and I might just turn into that savage you're so worried about."

Anna favored him with a look of gratitude that set his heart pounding faster.

"Did you hear that, Harriet?" Edna Mae shook one long finger at the housemother. "He's threatening us."

"Well, what did you expect?" Mrs. Harrington countered in her deep, authoritative tone, shifting her stare around at the women. She lifted her plump frame from the chair. "You're acting like a bunch of guinea hens jumping all over him. Anna hasn't done anything wrong, and Mr. Warwick is more than welcome in my home. If you ladies don't like it, then I suggest it's time you leave."

Sally's nutmeg eyebrows shot upward on her wide forehead. "You're dismissing us?"

Storme hid his smile behind a sip of lemonade.

"What's gotten into you, Harriet?" Hannah's voice held a high note of shock.

Mrs. Harrington shrugged one shoulder. "I've never been real fond of guinea hens. Besides, you ladies have told me what you came to say about the extravaganza, and now I've got some business I need to discuss with Mr. Warwick.''

"What sort of business could you possibly have with him?" Edna Mae shot him a snobbish stare.

Storme glared back. Enough was enough, *dammit!*

"Gun business," Mrs. Harrington responded. "We're going to do some target practice out back." A sly smile curled the corners of her mouth. "You ladies are more than welcome to come along and give us something to aim at."

Anna chuckled. Storme didn't bother to hide his amusement either as Edna Mae's mouth fell open. Hannah gasped her indignation, gathered her skirts, and headed down the steps, followed by Lilah.

"You're going to regret this Harriet," Sally sternly warned.

"Oh, at my age, there isn't any time left for regrets," Mrs. Harrington countered. "You ladies have a nice day."

Sally huffed her indignation, then headed down the steps beside Edna Mae and followed the other two women along the narrow walk and through the front gate.

"Sorry about that bit of trouble, ma'am," Storme offered.

"It's not your fault." Anna and Mrs. Harrington both stated at the same time, then shared a smile they turned on him, fairly warming his heart and raising his admiration for both of them.

"They're a bunch of narrow-minded biddies, and frankly, I'm glad they're gone. I'd have much rather gone over to the restaurant with the girls for a sarsaparilla," Mrs. Harrington stated.

Anna arched her brow. "I thought they were making ice cream."

Mrs. Harrington rolled her eyes. "Katie decided it was too hot to sit at the churn, and Samantha started complaining about the heat again and wanted something besides tea and lemonade. Of course, she cheered right up when Blaine Sanderson came to call, and invited him along, too." The housemother smiled wide. "Now, Anna, let's go see what you learned about shooting a derringer."

The early-morning sunlight spilled through the opened bay window. The scent of lemon oil filled the growing warmth in the parlor as Anna wiped the dust cloth over the table. She smiled as she worked her way around the room, dusting the wood to a polished gleam, and humming along softly while Mrs. Harrington sat at the piano and practiced the various tunes planned for the extravaganza.

The music fondly reminded Anna of the years spent traveling with her parents, singing together to pass the long hours on the trail as they headed for the next town, her father's smile when sales were good, her mother's hands gracefully gliding over the piano keys when they made camp at night. She could still recall her gentle voice encouraging Anna to practice, to control her breath just a little longer as she drew out the higher notes. There had been so many happy days then, so much love.

Then her mother took ill, and her father bought the saloon . . . and everything had changed.

Anna shook away the sad memories that knocked at her mind, the haunting reminders of all she had lost, and the trouble she had wound up in. She was much too happy today to let her mood be tempted with painful reminders of the past. Storme had promised to come by later around noon, and she couldn't wait to see him.

Mrs. Harrington began a new song, her fingers deftly moving along the keys in the opening refrain of "Listen to the Mockingbird."

Anna sang along and tapped her foot to the lively beat as she ran the dust cloth over the empty tea cart. But she soon drifted back to a hum as memories of Storme crowded the words from her thoughts.

She could still see the pride in his dark stare, the smile that softened his strong, handsome face when she had hit all but one of Mrs. Harrington's targets the day before. Even the housemother had expressed her admiration at the skill. Anna had assured her it was all due to Storme's astute teachings . . . and he had certainly taught her a great deal. Her blood heated as the memories of his warm kisses, his passionate tenderness came rushing in. A flush crept into her cheeks. She had never wanted a man the way she had wanted him, never thought she could ever give herself and her trust that completely, never thought she could ever feel such a strong affection for someone.

She hadn't known that she would meet Storme, though, or that her heart would wage a mutiny against those judgments. But she knew it wouldn't be wise to let herself get too lost in this uprising of emotion, this happy contentment she had found with him, and risk falling harder than she could handle when the time came for them to part. She knew in her soul that she would never meet anyone else like him again. A tight lump rose in her throat.

Anna swallowed. *No.* She wouldn't think about that. Storme wouldn't be in town for long. She would have plenty of time for sorrow after he was gone.

Mrs. Harrington began the refrain to a new song, and Anna turned her thoughts to the music and sang along. Reaching down, she grabbed the bottle of lemon oil and crossed the room, pouring a fresh dab on her cloth and running it over the top of the piano.

Mrs. Harrington smiled, then suddenly stopped playing midbeat. Anna gave a start of surprise, as much at the action as the odd gleam that danced in the housemother's stare.

"You have such a lovely voice, dear."

Warm pride spread through Anna. She had grown quite fond of the housemother over the last few weeks and valued her opinion. She admired the woman even more after her defense of Storme with the Garden Society ladies. "Thank you, ma'am."

Mrs. Harrington cocked her head to one side. "Do you like to sing for folks?"

Anna's hand tightened around the cloth. "Oh, on occasion I don't mind." A pang of guilt clawed at her conscience. She hated having to lie to her.

"Like for a friend's wedding?" The housemother grinned, deepening the lines in her aged face.

Anna nodded, tensing with a strong sense that this conversation was headed in a direction she wasn't going to like.

Mrs. Harrington arched her gray eyebrows. "Or maybe as a favor to an old woman?"

Anna sighed, and relaxed her shoulders. She smiled. "Sure, I'd be happy to sing something for you. What would you like to hear?"

"Do you know 'Come Home, Father'?"

A bittersweet nostalgia nipped at Anna's heart. "Yes." Her smile slipped as she recalled the lyrics about a child who goes to the saloon to beg her father to come home because her little brother is dying in his mother's arms, and *'there's no one to help me.'*

Sad and alone, Anna had held her mother as the woman took her last breath, and just like the father in the song who was deaf to his child's tearful request, her own father had sat in the saloon below, steeped in alcohol. "It was my mama's favorite song." Anna whispered the truthful irony, remembering the many times they had sung it together.

"It's one of mine, too." Mrs. Harrington smiled, peering over the rim of her spectacles. "And it would mean a lot to me if you'd sing it in the Garden Society's extravaganza next week."

A cold knot tightened in Anna's stomach. *Good heavens!* She couldn't sing in front of the town. She was supposed to be lying low, not drawing attention to herself—though she had been doing a lousy job of the latter ever since she'd come to Pleasant Grove. "Why do you want me to sing?"

Mrs. Harrington shoved her spectacles up the bridge of her nose with one finger. "Well, the fact is, much as I don't cotton to the Garden Society ladies personally, I do like to reap the benefits of some the organization's good works. And the reason those ladies came by yesterday had to do with some rather good news. Seems there's a Denver investor who's thinking of building an opera house here, and he's coming to the Fourth of July celebration to see the extravaganza. This musical needs to make a good impression on him. He needs to see that the townsfolk are interested in providing some culture here." Her hazel eyes glowed with a bright excitement that Anna had never seen before. "I've always loved the theater myself, and I'd greatly welcome some decent entertainment in Pleasant Grove. I also know that your lovely voice would certainly add a nice impression to the program."

Blood surged through her veins in heated panic. *How did I get myself into this mess? Oh, blast it!* She knew how. She never should have sung with the girls that night, or at Elise's wedding. Anna frowned. She didn't want to sing in the musical, either, but she *did* want to help Mrs. Harrington out, wanted somehow to repay the continuing kindness the housemother had shown. She wasn't sure she could find it in her heart to say no, despite the risks she knew she would be taking with her future. Anna bit her bottom lip, pondering. *Maybe I won't have to say no.*

"Well, given my friendship with Mr. Warwick, and the words I've had with the Garden Society ladies, I'm not so sure they'll want me to participate, ma'am."

Determination rose in the housemother's eyes. "You let me worry about those guinea hens. They'll see reason. They want this opera house as much as I do." Then her face relaxed into a smile. "So, does that mean you'll agree to sing?"

Oh, dear. That hadn't gone the way she had hoped. How could she say no now?

* * *

The train whistle shrilled, sending a cloud of white smoke billowing into the clear azure sky. The rotund, black-suited conductor bellowed the final boarding call, shoved a silver watch into his vest pocket, and climbed aboard the train.

Storme crossed his arms over his saddle horn and stared over where Ben stood on the depot platform with a train ticket and a small valise gripped together in one hand. "Give my regards to Sal."

"I will," Ben responded. "I'll be back as soon as I get that information and talk to the judge. Wire me if there's any more trouble with the rustlers."

Storme nodded his assurance, then watched as his brother grabbed the railing of the Pullman car and hauled himself aboard.

The town council was grateful for the information Storme had provided, but had also decided they needed proof about Dodding's actions at the river before they made any moves. They didn't want to tip the rancher off that they were looking into it, though, fearing he would just hire his fancy lawyer to fight them like he was doing over Caney Trail. So Ben had volunteered to go to the land office in Santa Fe and check out any recent claims or lease agreements on that government section where Dodding's crew was building the dam, as well as the claim filed by Robert Blanchard on the section of land just below it.

The metal wheels turned in a slow, clacking racket that grew faster and louder as the engine picked up speed and pulled out of the station. The train whistle shrilled a final announcement of the departure, then fell into silence. Much as he hated to admit it, Storme was almost relieved to see his brother go. With Ben out of town, he wouldn't have to worry about the rustlers' threat to kill him and could concentrate on keeping

Anna safe, and putting an end to the trouble at the ranch—
hopefully before his brother returned.

Storme frowned as sadness jabbed his heart. Once the rustlers
were caught, it would be time for him to leave again. He
swallowed, watching the train head west toward the mountains.
He was going to miss his brother. A sharper pang stabbed his
chest. He was going to miss Anna. But he wasn't gone
yet . . . and neither was she. Storme thought about his promise
to drop by the boardinghouse, and couldn't stop the slow smile
that curved his mouth. He was damn anxious to see her again,
and he would, too, just as soon as he took care of one more
errand.

He guided his horse away from the hitching post and, leading
the saddled sorrel Ben had ridden into town, made his way
past the depot and restaurant, then turned onto Main Street.
The sun beamed brilliantly overhead. Several women milled
about the walkways, immersed in conversations beneath the
protection of lace-trimmed umbrellas, while other folks maneu-
vered their way along the planking, intent on whatever errands
took them to the various businesses that lined both sides of the
dirt road. Storme dodged the wagons and horses as he made
his way toward the other end of town, then reined his gelding
to a halt in front of the sheriff's office.

Sunlight streamed inside the small, square confines when he
opened the door, a shaft of yellow rays settling on the scarred
desk top and the empty chair that sat behind.

"Sheriff, you here?" he called out, making his way toward
the back room where he knew Sheriff Hadley kept a bed and
small stove for the nights he stayed in town.

Silence.

"Sheriff?" Storme poked his head through the doorway,
finding the room empty save for the sparse furnishings, then
shrugged, resigned that he would just have to check back later
to see if the sheriff had received any word yet on that dead
wrangler's identity.

Storme smiled. Since it looked like he was staying in town a while longer than he thought, maybe he would see if Anna wanted to have lunch over at the restaurant. He retraced his steps across the office, a lighthearted spring of anticipation lengthening his strides, but he pulled up short when a small form appeared in the doorway.

"Sheriff Hadley, I brung you the— You're not the sheriff," the childish voice accused.

Storme smiled at the boy, gauging him to be no more than about eight, his thick head of blond hair neatly combed, his eyes as round as the bottom of a tin cup, and his mouth hanging open wide.

"You have a good eye," Storme responded in a light tone. He closed the narrow distance between them and stuck his hand out. "Name's Storme Warwick, what's yours?"

The boy hesitated, then placed his small hand in Storme's. "I'm Joshua Hankins. I deliver newspapers for my pa. Are you that Injun my ma is all mad about cause you came back?"

Storme arched his brow. "I guess I am. But your ma has no reason to be mad. Mind if I have one of those?" He nodded at the half dozen folded newspapers tucked under the boy's left arm, curious at the rolled-up bundle of papers hitched higher under his armpit.

"Cost you a nickel." Joshua held out his hand.

Storme nodded and pulled a handful of change from his pocket, sorted through the coins, then placed two five-cent pieces into his small, pale palm. "Might as well let me pay for the sheriff's copy, too. We can leave it on his desk."

The boy scrunched his round face into a scowl. His blue eyes narrowed, his thin, pale eyebrows pulling together above a small, straight nose as he stared down at the money in his hand. "I can't take that other nickel. My pa gives the sheriff a copy for free."

Storme admired the boy's honesty, even as he could tell the

lad wanted to hang onto that extra nickel. "Well, I don't mind paying double for a copy. You just keep that money."

Joshua shook his head. "I can't do that; my pa will tan me good for cheatin' folks. He says it ain't right."

Storme couldn't find a single argument to that one. He knew Hal Hankins was a decent man who had been good friends with Randolph Warwick, and one of the few who hadn't shared his wife's, or most of the town's, unfettered dislike of the half-breed who came to live at the ranch. Storme also knew it wasn't his place to interfere with what the man was trying to teach his son, especially since Ben had mentioned that Hal refused to place a big warning notice about Storme's return like Sally had wanted. He reached for the extra coin, but to Storme's surprise, the boy closed his fist over the money.

"Are you friends with the sheriff?" Joshua asked, cocking his head to one side.

Storme nodded and drew his hand back to his side. He puzzled at the wheels of thought he could see spinning in the boy's eyes.

"Sheriff Hadley pays me a dime to deliver the wanted posters to him when they come in on the train. My pa lets me spend it on candy at Mr. Mason's store."

"Is that the new wanted posters you've got there?"

Joshua glanced at the rolled up bundle and nodded. "I picked 'em up when I delivered papers over to the depot. I reckon I could leave these with you."

Storme smiled. "That'll be just fine." He took another nickel from the change in his hand and shoved the rest back into his pocket.

Joshua looked up, serious hesitation drawing his small cheeks taut. "You promise to get your dime back from the sheriff?"

"You have my word." He wasn't the least concerned about that dime, but Storme decided he would follow through on his promise and make sure the boy didn't risk suffering any repercussions from his pa for taking the money. Though he couldn't be sure the boy's ma wouldn't take a switch to him for talking to a half-breed.

Joshua's face spit in a wide grin as he took the extra coin, then shoved the money into his front pants pocket. He pulled the rolled-up bundle from underneath his arm and handed it to Storme, then plucked out two copies of the *Pleasant Grove Recorder*. "Thanks, Mr. Warwick." The boy turned to leave, then stopped and glanced over his shoulder. "My ma says that Injun blood you've got is liable to make you scalp someone right in the middle of town."

Storme's pulse pounded with grating annoyance. He had never scalped anyone, but Mrs. Hankins was fast becoming a prime candidate as his first. He held back his frown. "I'm not here to hurt anyone, Joshua. I just came back to help my brother with some rustlers."

The boy nodded. "That's what my pa says." Then he bolted out the door.

Storme smiled as he watched the lad make his way across the road and head straight for the mercantile—no doubt to purchase candy with his dime—then he turned and headed over to the sheriff's desk. He tossed the newspapers to one side, then sat in the lawman's chair and unfurled the batch of wanted posters, hoping he could spot a familiar face that might give him a lead as to who was seeking this revenge against him.

He set the first three aside, not recognizing the men wanted for train robbery. He skimmed through a couple faces he recognized, but had never crossed paths with before, then rifled through the rest of the stack with the same lack of results, pausing when he reached the last one.

Annika Olsson.

He arched his brow in surprise. Wasn't often he saw a woman's name listed on a poster. The charge of murder in bold print right below it was just as startling, but it was complete shock that stopped his heart when he glanced down at the sketch and saw Anna's face.

His jaw dropped open. Blood roared in his ears. Storme shook his head and blinked several times, certain she had just been occupying too much of his thoughts, and he was only imagining things. He snatched the poster off the desk, staring hard at the drawing as he sat back in the chair. Confusion pounded in his temples.

It couldn't be her.

But the woman had the same oval face and round eyes. The same shapely lips. *'Light reddish hair and green eyes'*, the description read. Storme's gut tightened. *Is this the secret she's hiding?*

No, there had to be some mistake! Anna wouldn't kill anyone. Not the sweet, gentle woman who had called out and saved his life, who kissed him with such passion . . . who had made love to him beside the stream with tender innocence and heated desire. Not the woman who had stolen his heart. Storme stared at the poster. From the moment he met her, though, he had sensed she harbored a troubling secret. But murder? He shook his head in disbelief.

Wanted for the murder of a wealthy Missouri man, the handbill read. Storme frowned. Anna had never mentioned being in Missouri. He thought back to what he knew about her.

She had traveled with her parents and sung in a medicine show, but he realized that every time she had mentioned that it was always in reference to when she was a child. He didn't know a damn thing about where she had been or what she had done since.

He recalled her threat to shoot him the night they had met, and how she had spilled coffee everywhere when he mentioned being a bounty hunter. He had brushed off the former as nothing more than finding herself alone with a stranger and had accepted her explanation of the latter as being just a simple accident. Had it really been shock, and maybe fear of him, that had caused her actions?

'Do you always know the outlaws you bring to justice are

really guilty?' He had thought her question odd at the time. Had there been more behind her inquiry than curiosity? Was Anna really guilty?

He thought about their time together in the mountains.

' . . . have you ever fired any sort of gun before?' He recalled how she had tripped over her own feet, and hesitated before giving an answer. An answer that now rang through his thoughts like a ricocheting bullet.

'Yes, I fired a six-shooter once.'

Storme's heart hammered against his ribs as he folded the poster and stuck it in his shirt pocket, then stood and headed for the door.

Chapter Fourteen

The mountains loomed majestic, jagged peaks greeting the azure sky and kissing the soft, shimmering rays that radiated down from the late-morning sun. The shadowy slopes beckoned their picturesque promise of a cooler respite amid the forested haven. Anna stared out the kitchen window, pulled by the call of nature's peaceful refuge, her expectations heightened with memories of the stream gurgling along its winding path through the woods, the cold water lapping against her bare legs . . . Storme so tenderly washing her after making sweet love to her.

She smiled, her heart pounding faster with anticipation at seeing him again. Then a wary nagging nipped at her conscience, dousing her excitement. Anna raked her teeth across her bottom lip and glanced over at the wicker picnic basket sitting on the kitchen table. Perhaps she had been just a bit hasty with her plans.

She still had grave reservations about singing in the extravaganza, but when Mrs. Harrington left to have lunch with the Garden Society ladies and discuss Anna's participation in the musical, she had welcomed the unexpected gift of having several hours all to herself. Prompted by the housemother's added intentions to spend the rest of the afternoon visiting with friends in town, promising to return at four to play piano for Belle's first lesson, Anna had rushed through her work, all the while making plans to sneak off to spend the afternoon with Storme.

Heat flooded her cheeks. What would he think of her for being so bold?

They had agreed to enjoy what time they had together, but that didn't mean she should be so eager to be alone with him again. She certainly didn't need to be throwing herself at him. Her eyebrows knit together. *Maybe I should unpack that basket.* For all she knew, Storme might be too busy to spare time for her right now, or maybe he didn't want to spend time with her today. He had only said he was stopping by, not staying. He was no doubt just coming by to check up on her, to talk with the hands posted around the house and make sure there hadn't been any signs of trouble with Dodding, or the rustlers.

Anna frowned. She was being too anxious. She needed to slow down, step back. Storme was kind and caring and made her feel more alive than she had in years, but she couldn't forget that there was no commitment between them. That's the way she wanted it, too. A dull ache stabbed the center of her heat in sharp defiance. That's the way it *had* to be . . . despite the growing fondness she couldn't stop from embedding itself deeper into her soul. She was leaving town, and so was he.

She was going to miss him, though . . . a lot more than she wanted to admit. Anna sighed. All the more reason why she shouldn't be snatching opportunities to spend time with him and adding to the memories that already threatened to haunt her the rest of her life. She had best just forget her foolish plans for the day.

Anna pushed away from the counter she leaned against, and crossed over to the table, pulling the handles away from the top of the basket and reaching for the lid. A loud knocking sounded at the front door. She froze.

Storme!

Her heartbeat stirred, then pounded with renewed delight. She stared at the basket. The knocking sounded again. Tingles swirled through her, journeying on a heated path that converged low in her stomach. *Now what?* Anna swallowed. *Stop being so eager. And don't mention the picnic, that's what.*

She gathered her skirt and hurried from the room. As she made her way down the hall, she saw him standing on the other side of the screen door, her gaze devouring the long length of his denim-clad legs, his lean hips, the white shirt that hugged his broad shoulders. Solid strength and masculinity, the sight of him made her blood heat with a craving too strong to ignore.

"Hello, Anna."

His deep voice and wide, engaging smile stole her breath, further chasing her good sense right out of her head. "Hi, Storme, I've been waiting for you. I was hoping you might have time for a picnic."

Storme straightened slightly, and arched one eyebrow in surprise. *Well, that had been easy enough.* All the way over from the sheriff's office, he had pondered an excuse for getting her alone to confront her about the wanted poster. He stared through the wire meshing, his heart pounding faster at the warm, desirous gleam that sparkled in the green depths of her eyes and spoke volumes of her thoughts to do more than enjoy a meal together. His manhood throbbed in instant revolt to his real reason for wanting her alone right now. He swallowed. "I take it Mrs. Harrington has agreed to this picnic?" The last thing he needed was the housemother tagging along as chaperone.

Hesitation dimmed the shine in her eyes. "Well, Mrs. Harrington is gone for the day, and the girls are working. I've finished my chores already. I just thought we could . . ." She waved one hand about nervously.

"Sneak off for a picnic?" He wasn't sure what excited him

more, her shy smile and the way she glanced up at him through her thick lashes, or her obvious desire to spend time with him.

She nodded. "If you're not busy . . . and you want to."

If he wanted to? Hell yes, he wanted to. Storme's pulse raced with the force of a tornado sweeping across the prairie. "I'm not busy at all, and I'd like nothing better."

Her smile blossomed full force, reaching up to bring a sparkle like jewels in her eyes. "I'll meet you around back, in the woods behind the depot." She turned and hurried down the hallway.

Storme took a deep breath and headed down the steps. The wanted poster sat like a damning weight in his shirt pocket. Guilt nagged at him over his deception. He would like nothing more than to make love to Anna again, had thought of little else since their time together in the mountains yesterday, but he had a strong suspicion his confrontation about this newfound knowledge would put a screeching halt to that possibility. He had no doubts that she was going to be upset. How upset, and what she would do, he wasn't so sure about.

He gathered up the reins to both horses, then mounted the gelding and rode off toward the stand of trees. For half a second he considered not bringing up the wanted poster, until after they had a chance to enjoy the picnic Anna had planned. He couldn't let his desire rule, though, not in good conscience. Besides, he needed answers. He needed to know just how much trouble Anna was in. He refused to believe she was capable of murder, but he was determined to find out the whole truth of what she was hiding.

He reined to a halt beneath the shade of a tall cottonwood near the edge of the grove, then dismounted. He ground-tied both mounts, frowning as he pondered the wisdom of letting Anna ride the sorrel. He didn't want her having an easy means of trying to escape him when he brought up the wanted poster. Maybe he should leave Ben's horse behind. Through narrowed eyes, he scanned the tree line at the far end of the stand where he knew Cale was taking a turn at guard. He spotted the wrangler, and started to return Cale's wave with a motion to come over, but caught movement out of the corner of his eye and turned as Anna hurried toward him.

He couldn't stop his smile at the sight of the gray kitten following in her wake and swatting at her hem every few steps. Anna drew closer, her brown skirt swishing lightly against the grass. Storme took the wicker basket she carried and set it on the ground.

The kitten stopped, arched its back, and hissed at the horses. The black mount reared its head high and snorted loudly. The tiny feline bolted the other way.

Anna chuckled. "I don't think they're destined to be friends."

Storme added his agreement in the form of soft laughter, watching as the kitten darted back across the expanse and slipped through the slatted fence row, not stopping until it had reached the safety of the back porch.

"Why'd you bring a second horse?" Anna queried, pulling Storme's attention. "Did you have something else you were planning to do?"

He shook his head, as much in answer as to ward off the guilt that plagued him. He had something else planned, all right—a sneak attack on her trust. "It's Ben's horse. We rode into town together. He caught the train to Santa Fe this morning."

"What did he go to Santa Fe for?"

Storme helped her climb onto the sorrel's saddled back. "To check on something that Dodding might be involved in."

Her eyes widened with piqued interest. "Something to do with the rustlers?"

"No." Storme grabbed the basket off the ground and mounted his gelding, settling the large wicker in front of him. "Something to do with a dam and controlling the water flow to the valley. The town council's keeping quiet about it, though, until they have some proof.''

Anna pursed his lips and shook her head in slight disgust. ''Wouldn't surprise me if Mr. Dodding's involved in something underhanded. Men like him usually don't know how to be honest about much of anything.''

Storme tensed. Her comment about knowing men who could truly be labeled savages and decent men being in short supply when needed sprang to mind. Not for the first time, he wondered what sort of past she had lived. What had happened to her? Why was she wanted for murder? ''What do you mean men like him?''

She hesitated. He saw the flash of wavering indecision hovering in her gaze, then she blinked, and just as quickly the look was gone. She squared her shoulders. ''Nothing really, just arrogant. The type that thinks just because they have money, it gives them the power to control whatever they want.''

''Have you known a lot of men like that, Anna?''

''I've met a few.'' She shrugged, offering him a look of nonchalance, that Storme wasn't buying for a second.

In Missouri? He held back the question burning the tip of his tongue. He didn't want to start this conversation until they were much farther away from town, and she wasn't sitting on an easy means of escape. Storme reined his horse around and nudged the mount to a walk through the grove.

''Have you had more trouble with Dodding?'' he inquired when Anna brought the mare up alongside.

''No, I haven't even seen him since that day you hit him.''

Storme smiled, glad to hear that. If Dodding dared to touch even a single hair on her head, he wouldn't hesitate to follow through on his threat to kill the rancher. ''If he's smart, he'll continue to keep his distance.''

She lifted her brow in a half-teasing arch. ''If not, I do know how to use a gun now.''

Storme paused, recalling the gun lessons he had given her,

and the fighting struggle she had put up. "Did you bring your gun with you?"

She shook her head. "I didn't think I'd need it since I was going to be with you.

Storme released a sigh of relief. At least he didn't have to worry about wrestling it away from her later and risk her getting hurt in the tussle. Although the thought of wrestling around with her wasn't half-bad.

Storme reined his mount to halt at the edge of the grove, long enough to introduce Anna to Cale, and tell the hand he and the other guard could go back to the ranch for the afternoon, but to make sure that Lazaro and Corky returned later for their turn at guard. He had the hands taking shifts watching the boardinghouse day and night. He wasn't taking any chances with the rustlers. And none of the wranglers seemed to mind the additional responsibility, especially since Storme was throwing in extra pay for the added work.

He kicked his mount into a canter and headed for the mountains. Anna nudged her horse into a faster pace. Storme let her ride ahead, sensing her need to feel a touch of freedom, his pulse stirred by the sight of her fiery hair flying loose against her slender back, her bottom bouncing against the saddle, her brown-calico skirt waving like a flag over the sorrel's hindquarters.

She reined the mare to a stop at the base of the mountain and reeled the horse around. Storme was still a good distance away, but he could see her smile, her pretty flushed face, and a hot flash of burning passion flared through his enchantment. He couldn't deny how much he wanted her, or the growing affection that engaged his heart. He almost wished he had never found the wanted poster, that he wasn't going to have to spoil her good mood—at least for a while. But he knew she was far better off that *he* had been the one to learn the truth. She was carrying a thousand-dollar reward on her head. That kind of price was usually posted for the most notorious of outlaws.

Lawmen and bounty hunters alike would be looking hard for her, and not many men in Storme's line of work would worry about whether she was innocent or guilty, not for that kind of money.

He kicked the gelding into a run and quickly reached her side.

"Do you mind if we have our picnic by the stream?"

"Not at all," he responded, trying not to let the image of their time spent there before crowd out what he knew he had to do. He nudged the horse into a walk and led the way up the mountain.

"Can I ask you something, Storme?"

He puzzled at the frown that creased her brow and dimmed the shine in her eyes. "Ask me anything you want."

"Will you tell me about Linette?"

He grimaced, and his stomach contracted into a hard knot. He really didn't want to think about Linette, let alone talk about her, but he couldn't say that he was overly surprised at Anna's inquiry. He had been half-expecting it ever since Dodding accused him of ruining Linette's reputation in front of Anna, and he was sure gossip had spread about his former courtship at the wedding—thanks to Edna Mae and Lilah. "What do you want to know?"

She shrugged, but her narrowed speculation belied the casual indifference of the action. "Did you really get in a fight with Mr. Dodding over her?"

"We got into a fight, but it had more to do with his threats to ruin her reputation than anything else."

"Was it true what Mrs. Hankins said about her being run out of town?"

"More or less." Storme leveled his stare across the distance between them. "She left before that could actually happen, though. She wasn't like you, Anna. She didn't stand up to folks or speak her mind."

Anna frowned. "Then she obviously didn't care enough about you."

Storme arched his brow. Linette had vowed her undying love for him, and he had believed it with all his heart. But after seeing the way Anna had jumped in to defend him, and their friendship, added to her willingness to ignore the opinions of others where he was concerned, Storme wasn't so sure anymore. "Maybe not," he acquiesced. She sure as hell hadn't had any trouble leaving him.

"Are you still in love with her?" She spoke so low that he almost didn't hear her, but there was no mistaking the burning curiosity that blazed in her eyes, nor the glint of jealous pain that flashed across her spring green horizons.

Storme shook his head. "I haven't even seen her since she left town eight years ago."

Anna's smile warmed his soul. Then his own curiosities got the better of him. "What about you? Have you ever been in love with anyone?"

She hesitated, then shook her head.

Storme wondered at the sparkle that glowed in the stare she raked over him. His pulse raced. Was Anna in love with him? Just as quickly, his blood cooled. *Don't be getting any foolish notions,* he chided himself. He knew she liked him, but nothing had changed. When everything was said and done between them, they would both be leaving town, and not together.

"How old were you when you quit singing for your father's medicine show?"

"Fourteen."

"How come you don't talk about what you and your family did after that?"

She shrugged, and faced front, but not before he saw the troubling gleam that darkened her eyes. "Nothing much to tell. My mama was really ill for a long time, then I ended up losing both my parents and came out here."

Storme had a whole passel of arguments to her comment

about nothing much, but held his tongue. He still hadn't quite figured out how to bring up the subject of the wanted poster. He thought about just being straightforward. *You ever killed anybody, Anna?* No, that was too direct, especially while she was still riding Ben's horse and could bolt away. Not that he didn't think he could catch her, but he didn't want to take a chance on her getting hurt in the process.

Storme reined the gelding to a stop beside the creek and dismounted, setting the basket on the ground. Anna swung her leg over the sorrel's neck. Storme circled her slender waist and helped her down, and to his delighted surprise, she snaked her arms around his neck and kissed him with a searing passion. All thought fled his mind as his body instantly reacted to her touch, her nearness. He pulled her tight against him, and plundered the recesses of her warm mouth, drinking his fill of her sweetness. Then the guilt started to seep in, and he forced himself to draw back, to step away.

He tied the horses to a pine tree near the edge of the water, then snatched up the basket by its handles and headed upstream a short way, stopping in the shade of the willow trees where the stream widened to form the small pool. Anna pulled a blanket out of the wicker confines and spread it over the grass, then plopped down and started to undo the laces on her black-kid boots.

"I'm going to wade in the water and cool off." She paused, and smiled up at him. "Want to join me?"

Storme took a deep breath as his mind wandered over several things he would like to join her in doing . . . and taking her clothes off was first on that list. "No, you go ahead."

She removed her stockings, then stood and stepped into the slow flowing stream. Storme walked to the edge of the bank and crossed his arms over his chest. The wanted poster burned through his shirt pocket in scorching reminder. He watched her for several minutes, enjoying the soft sighs of pleasure that escaped her lips as she hiked her skirt high and waded through the narrow stream. He forced himself to ignore the sight of her pale, shapely legs while he pondered how best to broach the subject. Then it came to him.

He waited until she turned her back on him. "Annika?" he called out.

She spun around. "Yes?"

He knew the instant she realized what she had done. Her smile fell; her eyes rounded in shock, and her mouth started to tremble. But what tore at his heart was the betrayal that flashed across her expression before she turned and bolted across the narrow creek.

Storme tossed his hat on the ground and hit the water just as she climbed the bank on the other side and took off through the woods. "Anna wait!"

She kept running. *Oh God, he knows who I am. What I've done!* She had seen the certainty of that in his eyes when she responded to her real name. Anna's heart raced with panic. Rocks and thorns dug into her bare feet as she ran through the trees. Tears blinded her eyes and coursed down her cheeks. *How did he find out? How long has he known?* Had he planned to arrest her yesterday, then changed his mind when she practically begged him to make love to her? The thought tore at her heart and sent fresh tears rising to scorch her eyes.

His booted steps pounded the ground behind her, drawing ever closer. Fear and anger knotted Anna's stomach and spurred her quickened flight. He had tricked her. He had let her think they were coming up here to enjoy a nice picnic, spend time together. How could she have trusted him?

The scream rushed from her throat when he snaked one arm around her waist and jerked her to a halt, then hauled her back against him. Blood roared through her head, pounded in her ears. She beat at his hold with her fist, kicked and twisted trying to free herself.

"Let go of me!" She shoved her elbow into his gut, hearing his grunt, feeling his warm breath rush out against her face.

"No," he grated. "Not until you promise to calm down and stay put so we can talk about this crime you're wanted for."

Calm down? How could she be calm? Her worst nightmare was about to come true. She didn't want to go to jail. She didn't deserve to hang! She had brushed off his inquiries about her life when she had stopped singing for her father's show as nothing more than a simple curiosity stemmed from the trust and friendship building between them. How could she have been so foolish? So gullible? Well, she wasn't going to give up without a fight, not even for Storme.

Anna forced herself to be still and wiped the tears that streamed down her face before glancing over her shoulder at him. "How long have you known?"

"I found out about an hour ago, when a wanted poster for Annika Olsson was delivered to the sheriff's office. The sketch looks just like you."

A sickening wave of terror welled in her stomach. "The sheriff . . . knows, too?" Her voice cracked as renewed fear surged through her veins.

He shook his head. "I'm the only one who saw it." He loosened his hold and reached into his shirt pocket.

Anna stepped away until she was out of arm's reach, then broke into a run. She had barely managed three steps before his large hand clamped down on her shoulder. She fisted her hands and swung around, plowing into his side, then shifted and rammed her knee upward, slamming into his thigh.

He grabbed her by both arms and pulled her flush against his chest. "Dammit, would you stop fighting me? I just want to talk!"

"Why should I believe you?" She kicked his leg, wincing at the pain that shot through her bare foot and up her shin.

He dug his fingers deeper into her arms, and glared down at her. His jaw was set hard as granite, but the anger in his face, in his tight grip on her, was contradicted by the sad glint that steeled his stare. "Because I thought you trusted me."

"I did trust you," she snapped. "And look where's it got me. You lied to me. You brought me up here to arrest me, not spend time with me, didn't you?" She hated the telltale fear that shook her voice, her body. Tears of panic, as well as from the pain of Storme's betrayal, filled her eyes and flowed unchecked down her cheeks. "Or were you hoping for another quick tumble before you hauled me off to jail?" she angrily accused.

Quick as lightning, he released her and stepped back, fire blazing in his eyes. "If I wanted to arrest you, I'd have done it at the boardinghouse and brought the sheriff along. And if I wanted to tumble you first, then I would have." Harshness grated at his tone. He raked one hand through his hair. "What I wanted was someplace quiet where we could talk this out without any interruptions. You offered that, by suggesting this picnic. But I'm not going to fight you, Anna, or take your insults. If you think running is the answer, then you run. You've got a thousand-dollar bounty on your head, though. How far do you really think you're going to get?"

Anna bit at her bottom lip. A thousand dollars! *Good heavens.* Every bounty hunter in the country would be looking for her. And if the wanted posters were circulating this far west already, chances were that every lawman between here and California would be searching, as well. What was she going to do? "I'll manage. I've gotten this far."

He shook his head and released a heavy sigh. Anna flinched when he reached out one hand and touched her face, but stood her ground as he did nothing more than brush away her tears with the soft pad of his thumb. "Anna, you can trust me. I've told you the truth about wanting to spend time with you." The harshness was gone from his voice, replaced with a tenderness that threatened to draw her into his confidence. "I've been honest with you about everything . . . and now I'm honestly telling you that I want to help you."

Oh God, how she wanted to believe he meant that, wanted

to believe the trust she had felt with him was real. But the lonely, empty ache she had been carrying for months gnawed at her soul. No one had believed in her innocence. How could she be sure that Storme would? "Are you going to help by slapping handcuffs on me and taking me to jail?"

He arched his brow. "Is that where you belong?"

Trembling quakes coursed through her limbs. "N . . . no." A hard lump clogged her throat.

"I didn't think so, little dove," he whispered, trailing his hand from her face around to the back of her neck. "I told you that night we met that you didn't wear the look of a killer. I still believe that."

She didn't fight when he pulled her into his embrace, but buried her face against his shirtfront, absorbing his comforting strength, the feel of his hands stroking her back.

"You're in a lot of trouble, Anna." He spoke low, his warm breath brushing against her hair. "Tell me what happened. Why are you accused of killing that man in Missouri?"

She leaned back slightly to look up at him, and blinked against the tears that welled. She swallowed, praying her trust in this man wasn't misplaced, and feeling in her heart that it wasn't. "Because I did kill him." A sharp ache twisted her heart at the shock that flashed in his narrowed, brown gaze. "But I didn't mean to. I just wanted him to leave me alone."

"What happened?" The warmth in his low tone held more concern than demand.

The pleading regard in his worried stare helped bolster her courage, her trust. She sighed, her breaths coming in ragged stages as she worked to stem her fear and sort her thoughts into some semblance of order. "My papa gave up the medicine show when my mama took ill, and we moved to Missouri. When the doctors in St. Louis told us there was nothing to be done about mama's consumption, papa headed south and bought a saloon in the small town of Copper Point. We moved into the living quarters above, and I took care of my mama.

We knew she was going to die, and my papa just couldn't handle the grief of watching her waste away. He started drinking real heavy, then he started to gamble with the saloon profits. When my mama passed away, papa's drinking and gambling only got worse. I took over running the saloon and tried to salvage what little we had. I kept the creditors away for almost four years, but it was tough, because every time I turned around there was some man, either from around town or just a stranger passing through, slapping an IOU in my face, and demanding I pay off Papa's gambling debts, as well.'' She shook her head and closed her eyes.

Storme's heart broke at the anguish in her voice. He couldn't begin to imagine this sweet woman even being in a saloon, let alone trying to run one. He knew she had only been sixteen when her mother died. Barely more than a child trying to hold on to the fragments of her family, and their livelihood. Not even as old as Ben when he had left him to run the ranch alone. But Ben hadn't been alone. Sal had been there to help. A trustworthy support, not a neglectful parent. Storme tightened one arm around her waist and, with his other hand, reached up and smoothed the loose strands of hair away from her face.

Tears shimmered in her opened eyes. She took a deep breath. ''My papa died five months ago. I closed the saloon and settled what I thought were all of his debts. I was planning to sell the place and use the money to go to New York.'' A wry smile curved the corners of her mouth. ''I was going to join a musical troupe. I was going to sing on a real stage like I always wanted to do, like mama always wanted me to do. But . . .'' Her smile dropped and she frowned. ''Then I learned about the staggering poker debt my father owed a local rancher. I tried to argue with the man, but he showed me the IOU. It . . . it was my father's handwriting.'' She paused, her throat rippling as she swallowed. ''This rancher didn't need the money. He was the wealthiest man in the county, and even more arrogant than Mr. Dodding. But he demanded payment, anyway. I offered him the saloon, but it wasn't worth enough to clear the debt, and he wanted more. He wanted . . . he wanted . . ." She tucked her head down.

Storme's pulse hammered with his own suspicions. He placed one finger under her chin and gently forced her to look up, then ran his thumb along her trembling bottom lip. "What did he want?"

"Me," she whispered. "Just for one night, he said. I told him no, and he made my life miserable until I agreed. With his power and money, he chased off every potential buyer for the saloon and told everyone in town about my father's debt and that I refused to pay off the IOU. We weren't well respected as it was, because of the saloon, and that only added to the townsfolk's dislike of me. I was just going to leave town, forget about the saloon, that rancher, and the debt, but he threatened to hunt me down if I did, and badgered me daily until I finally agreed to his demand. I wanted to leave so bad, to start over somewhere else, that I was willing to agree to anything at that point."

Anger at her father, at the faceless bastard who dared to make her clear the debt raged through him. He was almost sorry Anna had killed the man. Storme would have welcomed the opportunity to hunt the rancher down and do the job himself.

"But I couldn't go through with it. The night he came to the saloon to collect the debt, I gave him the deed, and told him that was all I would do. When I tried to leave, he . . . he wouldn't let me go." She blinked, and the tears spilled out, rushing down her cheeks and ripping Storme's heart in two. "He forced me into the back room, where we kept the liquor supplies. I fought him as hard as I could, but he kept hitting me." She closed her eyes. "Then he started to tear at my clothes."

Storme felt the shudders course through her body. Fury burned through his blood.

She sighed, and opened her eyes. "I wouldn't give up. I

kept struggling until somehow I managed to get his gun out of the holster. And God help me, I fired it without even a moment's hesitation, right at his chest.'' She shook her head, tears coursing unchecked down her face. ''I just wanted to start over . . . to sing.'' She choked on a sob.

Storme wrapped his arms around her and pulled her close. She buried her face into his chest, her shoulders shaking as she cried. His heart wept with her for the pain she had been forced to endure, the fear she had lived through then, and since. ''It wasn't your fault,'' he whispered into her ear. ''You had no choice.''

She lifted her head to stare up at him. ''I didn't, Storme. I really didn't. I begged him to take the saloon . . . and leave me alone. I pleaded with him. I—''

''Shhh.'' Storme placed his finger against her mouth. ''I know. It's all right.'' He scooped her up into his arms, holding her close to his chest, wanting her to feel the same safe comfort she had once told him she felt in his presence.

She wrapped her arms around his neck and pressed her face against his shoulder. He carried her back through the woods and across the creek, then he lowered himself down to sit on the blanket, holding her in his lap, keeping her close against him.

Anna tightened her arms around his neck, pressing herself deeper into the strong comfort of his embrace. Oh, how she loved this man, needed him, needed the secure feel of his arms, his trust. His belief in her innocence, his words that she wasn't to blame, and that she had had no choice in her actions meant more to her than anything. Her heart swelled to overflowing. She couldn't deny any longer that what she felt for him was more than just a caring friendship. She loved him. He was kind and handsome, and she knew in her heart she could always trust him. Storme made her feel safe and gave her strength to draw from, made her wish for things she had never longed for before. A husband. A family.

Anna took a deep breath, her tears fading. She sat up, meeting his concerned, warm stare. "Storme, I'm sorry I ran from you."

He shook his head. "You don't have to be sorry. I knew you were going to be upset. That's why I wasn't sure how to bring all this up." He smoothed the hair back from her face. "But, Anna, you don't ever have to be afraid of me. I would never do anything to hurt you."

"And I won't ever doubt that again." She placed her hands to his smooth, firm jaw. "I promise." She pressed her mouth to his, sighing at his soft caress, his gentle command for more. She parted her lips, his tongue meeting hers in a slow, thoughtful exploration that sang through her veins.

He broke the kiss off much sooner than she wanted, then lightly rested his forehead to hers. "Are you feeling better?"

She gazed into his dark, intense stare. "Yes."

"Enough to talk about this some more?"

The glow inside her dimmed. She wished they didn't have to talk about it anymore, wished she could put it behind her forever, but she knew there were still things that had to be explained. Just as she knew this trouble would always haunt her . . . and that her time in Pleasant Grove was going to have to end much sooner than she had planned now. She slowly nodded.

"Tell my why you're charged with murder, when this is clearly a case of self-defense."

Anna took a deep breath and unwound her arms from his neck, resting her clenched hands in her lap. "That rancher's son knew about our bargain. A few other men around town did, too. All friends of that man I killed. Men who didn't like me because I'd fought off their advances at the saloon. I knew none of them would help, especially the son—he had wanted in on his father's bargain. And there weren't any witnesses to back me up about just defending myself. I was so afraid after I shot him. I knew I had to leave, or I'd hang. So I took the money out of his wallet, left the deed, and ran away."

"Where did you go?"

"North, to St. Louis. There was a posse on my trail, though, and I was afoot, so it took a couple of weeks for me to get there. I hid out from the law and bought a train ticket for New York using my real name, Annika Olsson. I boarded at the last minute, when I didn't see any lawmen at the depot, then I made sure the conductor and several others saw me on the train. A few miles outside of town I jumped off."

Storme's heart slammed to a stop. "You jumped off the train?"

Anna nodded. "Nearly broke my leg doing it, too. I headed farther north after that, and met a nice, older couple who let me ride with them to Illinois. Of course, I didn't tell them my real name. Then I disguised myself as an old woman, bought the derringer, and used the last of my money to buy a train ticket as far west as I could get, which was here. As soon as I stepped off the train, I headed straight for the mountains and took off that disguise. After I burned it, I walked back to town. I called myself Anna. And Alexander is my mama's maiden name. I was lucky enough to have Mrs. Harrington hire me that same day."

Storme shook his head, an incredulous look glazing his stare. "That's some smart thinking. I'm not sure I could have kept up with that trail, and I'm a fair tracker."

Anna swallowed. "It obviously wasn't good enough if my wanted poster has made it this far. I thought for sure they'd just keep looking for me back East."

"Well, once we talk to the sheriff—"

"I'm not talking to the sheriff." Anna jerked back. Panic pulsed through her limbs.

"You have to. We need to get this cleared up. You're not guilty."

"I know that, and I'm really glad you believe me, but we can't tell anybody about this."

Storme frowned. "Anna—"

"No." She pushed at his arms and scooted off his lap, then stood. "The law will send me back to Missouri, and I'll hang. No one back there believes I'm innocent. If they did, there wouldn't be wanted posters on me. They wouldn't still be looking."

Storme slowly rose to his feet. "I'll go with you. I'll help prove your innocence."

"How? I killed him. And I ran away. Besides, my father owed everybody back there money at one time or another. The ladies around town all accused me of being a loose woman because I worked in the saloon. They hated me. I can't go back, Storme. Who's going to believe I was only defending myself, especially now?"

He could see the tears welling in her eyes again, the fear shaking her slender limbs. Frustration ate at his gut because he didn't have an answer for her. He wasn't sure how they could prove her innocence, and he feared if he pressed her into talking to the law, she would only take off on him. As good as she was at hiding, he couldn't be certain he would find her before some other bounty hunter did, either.

"If you really want to help me, Storme, you'll keep my secret."

He shook his head, and blew out a weighty sigh. "What are you going to do, Anna? You can't run forever. What about your dreams to sing?"

"As soon as I have enough money, I'm going to California. Then I'll get on a boat and leave here for good. I'll change my name again. I can join a theater troupe in Paris, or London, or somewhere else." she insisted. "Storme, you said you owed me a life-debt. Well, I'll tell you how you can repay it. You can give me your promise of silence about this. If you care anything at all about me, you'll give me this chance at freedom."

Damn! She wasn't afraid to get right to the heart of things. He did owe her a debt, and he cared for her deeply. He also knew he couldn't fully promise her freedom if she went back. If she was right, and no one believed her, the best he would be able to do was break her out of jail before she did hang, and then she would be worse off than she was right now. At least she was safe here—for a while. He had the wanted poster, and he knew another one wouldn't show up, not in Pleasant Grove, anyway. As far as the law knew, the sheriff had it. There wouldn't be a reason to send another one.

He thought about offering her money again to get her out of town, but his heart didn't want to let her go, not yet. He wanted her here, where he could keep a close eye on her, until he could figure out a way to either fix her problem or make sure she could safely follow through with her plans to leave the country.

"All right, you have my promise," he reluctantly agreed. "We won't tell anyone."

She hesitated, blinking away the fear that had hovered so deep in her gaze, then sighed heavily. Her shoulders slumped forward. "Thank you," she whispered. Then a slow smile curved her full, luscious lips. "I knew I could trust you."

He wanted her trust, as much as he wanted her, and the reward of hearing it spoken with such sincerity and certainty made his heart pound faster. "Always." He smiled, raising one hand to her face, trailing his finger along the tear-streaked lines on her reddened cheeks. He still couldn't believe what she had been through. She was definitely a survivor. Her fortitude and determination only made him love her more, and her troubles added to his worry about her. But she was much safer now that he knew the truth, and knew what to watch for to keep her that way.

Storme pulled the wanted poster out, then reached into his front pants pocket and retrieved a match. "Come on." He took hold of her hand and led her over to the creek.

"What are you doing?" she asked.

Storme squatted down, tugging at her hand until she did the

same, then he struck the match against his boot heel. "We're going to burn this." He held out the flaming match. "You want to do the honors?"

Her eyes widened. Her smile spread across her face. "You are the kindest man I've ever met. Thank you."

She took the match and touched it to one corner of the folded poster. Storme held the folded edge as the paper burned. When there was nothing but charred parchment, and the flames seared his fingers, he dropped it into the water, then stood. He reached down one hand, cupping her elbow, and helped Anna to her feet. Storme was real glad to see the smile that brightened her face.

"What time do you have to be back at the boardinghouse?"

"I'm giving Belle Sanderson a music lesson at four."

Storme nodded, then glanced up at the sun. "We have a few hours. You still interested in having that picnic?"

She arched one thin, auburn eyebrow. "Are you talking about eating lunch . . . or did you have something else in mind?"

Storme swallowed at the soft gleam that sprang into her gaze, at the way she ran her tongue across her mouth. "Well, darling, that's up to you."

She circled her arms around his neck. "Then I'm definitely interested in the something else part." she whispered close to his mouth.

Storme pulled her into a tight embrace and kissed her with a hunger that reminded him just how hard it was going to be to let her walk out of his life.

Chapter Fifteen

Anna tapped her foot in time to the music as Belle finished the last refrain to "Where, O Where Has My Little Dog Gone?" It was such a cute, simple song, and Belle sang it beautifully. But after working with the girl for the last thirty minutes, Anna couldn't help thinking that with Belle's impressive vocal range, she should be singing something that would better show her voice, as well as add a little more strength and fun to the extravaganza's program.

The music ended. Mrs. Harrington sat back on the piano bench, smiling as she adjusted her spectacles. Maryanne Sanderson clapped her approval from where she sat on the parlor sofa.

"How was that?" An anxious gleam shimmered in Belle's round, violet gaze.

"Just fine," Anna assured her, placing one hand on the girl's slender shoulder. "I can tell you've been practicing. Are you singing anything else in the musical?"

Belle frowned and shook her head, sending her black pigtails skimming along her back. "I wouldn't mind singing something else. This song's so short, I'll hardly get a chance to even be onstage."

"Don't complain, Belle," Maryanne lightly scolded. "This is the song the Garden Society ladies asked you to sing."

"I'm not complaining," Belle whined in direct contrast to her words. "I like the song. It's just . . ."

Anna recognized the discouragement that registered in the girl's taut expression. She had always liked trying out new tunes for the medicine show, but her father had wanted her to keep singing the same simple songs he thought appropriate for a child. Thank goodness her mother had understood. Anna had appreciated her mama's encouragement to broaden her musical knowledge, and to sing the songs she enjoyed. "You'd just like something more challenging, is that it?"

Belle nodded, then jutted her chin out. "And much longer."

Anna smiled. "Well, you've a good, strong voice," she offered the honest encouragement. "And I think you could sing any number of songs. Certainly something that would be more fun and appealing to the audience, as well as that Denver investor."

Belle's face brightened with delight at the prospect.

"I would like her to be able to show off her talent," Maryanne interjected, pride ringing in her soft voice. "She might not get the chance to perform in such a big event again. Not for a while, anyway."

"Did you have something in mind, Anna?" Mrs. Harrington inquired.

Yes, she did, but Anna wanted to talk to the housemother alone about it first, before she got Belle's hopes up. "Nothing specific. Why don't you let me think about it, and we'll try out something different when you come back tomorrow for your next lesson."

Belle nodded her excitement. "I'd like that a lot."

"You think that's a good idea." A look of discomfort crossed

Maryanne's face. "I don't want to upset the Garden Society ladies."

"Oh, don't worry about them." Mrs. Harrington waved one hand in a dismissive gesture. "They're all for putting on a good performance, and bringing that opera house to town. They'll do whatever is best for the program."

Anna knew that was true. The housemother had returned this afternoon bearing news that the Garden Society ladies indeed *had* agreed to let Anna sing in the show. She was still dubious about the wisdom of singing for so many people and risking being identified, but Anna knew if the Garden Society ladies were willing to overlook their dislike of her because of Storme to ensure a good show, there was a definite chance they would also let Belle sing something else.

Maryanne lifted her plump frame from the sofa and retrieved her reticule from the table as she and Belle prepared to leave. Anna walked outside on the front porch with them, and bent down to receive the girl's offered hug. A warm glow of satisfaction flowed through Anna's veins as she watched Belle skip down the walk beside her mother. She hadn't expected to enjoy giving lessons so much. She hadn't expected Belle to be so talented, either.

Mrs. Harrington came out onto the porch and waved as the Sandersons drove away in their wagon. "I saw Storme riding through town this morning. Looked like he was headed to the sheriff's office. Did he come by here and see you, too?"

Anna nodded. "But just for a short while." She swallowed, chasing away the guilt that knocked at her conscience. It was the truth. Storme *hadn't* stayed at the house long. "We had a nice visit, though." A blush worked its way into her cheeks as the memories of their afternoon together flooded in. It had been a long time since she had felt such an invigorated freedom. She was glad Storme knew about her trouble with the law, lifting the weight of worry about when he would find out and what he would do. She loved him for never doubting her innocence, for wanting to help her, loved him even more for making her feel so relaxed and secure in her trust for him. They had talked and laughed and teased as they feasted on the lunch she had packed, then Storme had taken her in his arms and guided her on a sweet, passionate journey that still had her blood singing.

"Well, I'm glad, dear. He's a nice man."

Anna sighed, smiling. "Yes, he is, ma'am."

Mrs. Harrington cocked her head to one side, her loose knot of gray hair shifting precariously. "Now, tell me dear, I think you did have a song in mind for Belle to sing. What is it?"

Anna pushed her musings of Storme aside. "Are you familiar with the ballad about Billy the Kid?"

"Why, yes I am. I've played that tune a couple of times myself." Mrs. Harrington pursed her mouth, and her eyes narrowed in thought. "You're right, that would be a good song for Belle to sing. And it would certainly attract the attention of the male audience far more than that little tune about the dog."

"That's what I thought, too. Think we should let her give it a try tomorrow?"

"I do. And I also think it'll give the Garden Society ladies fits." The housemother tilted her head down and peered over the rim of her glasses. "You seem to be pretty good at doing that to them, Anna." Her smile widened in approval. "Must be why I like you so much."

Storme blew out the candle as the first rays of dawn spilled through the bank of windows, golden beams splashing across the wide mahogany desk. He leaned back in the black-leather chair and drinking his coffee, his gaze sliding over the open ledgers, cash box, and papers scattered across the surface. For the last couple of hours, he had contentedly worked, reading through correspondence, making various entries for the bills that needed to be settled, and counting out the cowhands' monthly pay to give them later in the day. The clutter reminded him of the many times he had seen his father sitting here doing the same thing, while Storme had sat across on the other side and eagerly absorbed every word the elder man had to say about running the ranch.

He could still hear his father grumbling over the rising cost of supplies, the drop in cattle prices, the concerns about drought that often plagued the desert town. His father should be the one sitting here now, still handling the ranch's affairs. Storme sighed, chasing away the sadness that threatened to settle in. He took another sip of coffee, then swiveled the chair around to stare out the window, drinking in the sight of the hills and pastures that gently rolled across the land, and not for the first time wished like hell he could stay.

He didn't mind hunting outlaws. He could find a decent amount of satisfaction in knowing he was good at his job, too—he had a substantial amount of money in the bank to prove that—but he hadn't realized just how tired he was growing of always being on the roam . . . until he had come back home. Every morning that he woke up to the sight of the land, the ranch, the more time he spent with Ben and the hands, were all making it harder for him to accept his inevitable departure again.

Storme sipped the lukewarm coffee and stared out the window, watching as the daylight grew stronger, broadening his view of the land. In the distance, he could see the creek that wound its way through the southern portion of the ranch. He smiled as his thoughts drifted to a different stream, to the beautiful, passionate woman he had held in his arms. His heart skipped a painful beat. He was going to miss Anna—more than Ben and the ranch. A hard knot rose in his throat.

She had found her way into his affections more deeply than he had expected, and awakened a need in his soul he hadn't known existed until she walked into his life. He knew the land would always be here, and he might even take the risk of coming back home sometime to visit Ben, but once Anna left town, he would never see her again.

Storme couldn't stop the sadness this time as it came crashing in with brutal force. He closed his eyes as the pain ripped through his heart with a greater intensity than he had ever felt at Linette's sudden departure. Anna was right. Linette hadn't cared enough about him, and Storme realized he hadn't loved her as much as he thought he had . . . or he would have gone after her.

Booted footsteps approached heavily outside the office, jerking Storme's attention. He opened his eyes and swung the chair back around to face the desk as Winston came hurrying into the office.

"The rustlers have hit again," the foreman grated. A muscle twitched in his tightened jaw.

"When?" Storme set the tin cup down and stood, angered adrenaline pumping through his veins.

"About two hours ago." Winston slapped his hat against his thigh. "Damn thieves hit in the south part of the valley again. Came in with guns ablazin' and made off with at least another hundred head."

"Anybody hurt this time?" Storme questioned, thinking about Garcia's broken leg.

"No. Tom and Jasper were riding guard down at that end. They've picked up a trail, and they're out there waiting for us to join 'em. Cale's down at the barn saddling your horse."

Storme nodded, then closed and locked the cash box, and grabbed his hat off the end of the desk, shoving it on his head. "Let's go." He snagged his gun belt off the cowhide sofa and strapped it on as he headed out the door.

The midmorning sun blazed its heated glory over the sagebrush and cactus dotting the flat, desert stretch. Storme reined his horse to halt beside the dead longhorn, and stared his disgust at the bullet wound that had brought the animal down. Blood had already pooled and dried in a wide circle around the steer's head, darkly staining the sandy terrain.

"What the hell you think they shot it for?" Winston queried with heated aggravation.

Storme shook his head. He didn't know what to make of it. Since meeting up with Tom and Jasper two hours ago, he and the others had been following the trail that the rustlers had made no effort to hide. He glanced up at the two buzzards circling overhead, then ahead where the trail continued on its south course. He couldn't help but wonder if this trail was going to lead him to another note . . . and what the message would say this time.

"Damn waste of good meat," Cale shook his head, the cleft in his chin more prominent as annoyance tightened his jaw.

"You want me to ride back and get the sheriff, Storme?" Tom Galloway inquired in a tense tone.

Storme shook his head at the lanky cowhand. "Let's keep going." He kicked his horse into a trot.

Winston rode up beside him, while Cale, Tom, and Jasper fell in behind. They rode for another thirty minutes, then the trail took a sharp turn westward and before long Storme spotted more buzzards circling against the blue sky in the distance.

"Reckon we're about to find another dead steer?" A cold edge tainted Winston's voice.

"Looks like a good chance of it." Storme swallowed, and stared into the heat shimmered horizon ahead.

Their suspicions were confirmed several minutes later when they rode up on the second dead longhorn—also shot in the head. They continued until early afternoon, stopping several times to rest and water the horses, and finding six more carcasses left to rot in the sweltering heat. The trail had taken them a good way off Lazy W land, and deeper into the scorching desert. Storme's trepidation increased with each dead steer they found, and with every mile they covered toward the destination he feared where the trail was leading.

"There's a canyon about four miles up ahead." Winston untied the bandanna from his neck and wiped the beaded moisture from his brow.

Storme nodded. "Shadow Canyon." He knew it well. The last time he had ridden out there was seven years ago, and he hadn't come alone, either . . . but he had left alone.

The three-sided canyon rose like a fortress from the desert floor. About a mile out, Storme reined his horse to a halt and stared at the flock of buzzards circling above the tall, rock walls.

"Well, that's about as noticeable as a new saloon butted up to a church that we're gonna find some more dead cattle," Winston stated, shaking his head.

"I'd say you're right. But it's the unnoticeable that I'm worried about." Storme signaled to the three wranglers riding guard a way out to come in so he could talk to them. "Tom, you and Jasper skirt wide around and head toward the outside of the west wall. About hundred yards from the opening there's a trail you can follow up to the top. Winston, I want you and Cale to do the same on the east side. The climb will be a little harder, though. You won't be able to take the horses. There's very little cover on the outside, but there's plenty of hiding spots inside. You boys keep a close watch and your guns handy."

Winston arched one thick, red eyebrow. "What are you plannin' to do?"

"I'm going to head straight into the canyon."

"That's crazy, Storme," Cale ground out, his narrowed gaze burning with the same incredulous concern that rang in his voice. "You'll be a sittin' target for 'em."

"He's right," Winston added, frowning. "We're ridin' in with ya."

"No." Storme shifted his stare between the four men.

"These rustlers want me dead. The notes they've left prove that. But they're not through playing games yet," he stated confidently, thinking about the threats made against Ben and Anna, and the rustlers' words that Storme would watch his brother die. "And I'm not going to have them picking you boys off like they've been doing the cattle. I'm riding in alone."

Winston grunted his displeasure. The other wranglers expressed their dislike with concerned looks and muttered objections, but no one offered any further argument.

Storme stayed put as the men rode off, and waited until they were almost out of sight as they skirted the canyon, then he nudged his mount forward into a trot. Still several hundred yards from the entrance, Storme reined back to a walk, frowning at the pungent stench of blood and death growing heavy on the air. More than two dozen buzzards circled the clear cerulean sky, and Storme watched as every now and then several would dip down inside the canyon walls. He saw the makeshift fence of boards and brush stretched across the wide entrance, and a growing sense of dread settled in the pit of his stomach. He had little doubt of what he was about to discover. But what else would he find, Storme wondered, drawing his gun out of the holster.

Through narrowed eyes, he scanned the rocky walls for any sign of movement or the flash of sunlight glancing off an aimed rifle on the east side. Nothing. The sun was well into its afternoon descent, its rays blocked by the west ridge, casting the rough-edged surface in gray shadows that stretched out over part of the canyon floor. Storme reined the gelding to a halt several yards from the barrier that blocked the entrance. The stench nearly gagged him as he stared at the hundreds of dead cattle that littered the ground inside.

Caution on high alert, he dismounted and slowly made his way closer, scanning the craggy rocks. He caught a movement out of the corner of one eye, and spun to the left, cocking his gun. He jerked the barrel up toward the sky when he saw

Winston pressed back against the wall at the edge of the entrance.

The foreman smiled, spit a stream of tobacco juice into the dirt, then waved his gun, motioning for Storme to continue on. Much as he appreciated Winston's devoted support, and the coverage, Storme couldn't help but worry. He didn't want any more Lazy W hands getting hurt, or worse, killed. He glanced up toward the ridge, and saw Cale's blond head barely peeking over the top of a large boulder, then over to the other side where Tom and Jasper lay flat on their stomachs near the edge.

Storme walked on, reaching the makeshift fence. The cattle stolen before dawn had been shot down just on the other side and the buzzards were busily picking away at the fresh carcasses. Deeper inside the canyon, cattle were scattered everywhere on the sand-coated floor, lying in varying stages of rot from the blistering desert sun. He shoved one foot against the fenced barrier, splitting the wood. Startled by the movement, the birds lifted their wings and voices in a loud, flapping cacophony as they flew off. Storme paused, waiting, scanning the canyon with watchful eyes, but nothing else stirred. He wasn't surprised. The feasting scavengers had been indication enough that there wasn't anyone lurking close by, and he was certain he had found what the rustlers wanted him to find—the stolen cattle. A good number of them, anyway.

His anger rising as he stared at the senseless slaughtering, Storme wondered what they had done with the others, and if the rustlers planned another trail of dead cattle for him to follow. Deciding there was nothing else to see, Storme turned away from the fence and started over toward the foreman.

Winston met him halfway. "What do you make of all this, Storme?"

He shook his head. "That the rustlers are set on playing a destructive game, and I'm getting damn tired of it," Storme ground out furiously. "It's probably a waste of time, but let's search around and see if we can find any tracks that'll tell us which way they headed from here.''

Winston nodded, then signaled to the men to come down from the ridge. Minutes later, Cale came running around the side of the east wall, his eyes widened in shock, and his face flushed red from the heat.

''Good Lord, that stink is bad.'' He waved his hand in front of his face. ''But we're gonna have to go inside, Storme. I spotted a dead man sprawled out in the middle of those carcasses.''

''Where?'' Storme turned back to search the canyon floor again.

''Down a way,'' Cale pointed. ''Near the back wall.''

Tom and Jasper came around from the other side, bearing the same news.

The wranglers tore a section of the fence away. Storme pulled the handkerchief from his pocket and tied it over his mouth and nose as Winston and the others did the same, then he led the way inside the canyon, weaving a path through the fly-infested cattle.

Three-quarters of the way through the canyon, Storme spotted the dead man. His heart stopped mid-beat. Though the round, brown face of the Mexican was unfamiliar, the haunting sight of his hands and legs tied to the stakes driven into the ground wasn't, and it jerked Storme's thoughts back into the past. His blood pumped faster. He thought about the army private who had killed his father, and the trail that led to Shadow Canyon. Was this just a coincidence, or did this revenge have something to do with that soldier?

Storme glanced to the far east corner of the canyon, to the bleached-out cattle bones that covered the ground and any evidence that would have possibly remained after all this time. No, no one knew what he had done, not even Ben. He had only told his brother that the private was dead. Besides, the army would have arrested him if someone had proof, and as far as Storme knew that soldier hadn't had any family, not around these parts anyway. So who the hell was behind this vengeance? And why?

"These thievin' bastards sure ain't showin' much loyalty to each other." Winston narrowed his gaze. "Wonder why they're killin' themselves off for us?"

Frustrated, angry, Storme shook his head and stared at the bullet hole in the man's forehead, then down at the note held in place by the arrow stuck into his chest. He reached down and tore the paper free.

> *It's almost time, Injun. Get ready to*
> *lose everything you care about.*

* * *

The sun crested over the eastern horizon, and slowly began to chase away the dark clouds that had rolled in during the night. Storme frowned his displeasure that the threatening clouds hadn't produced a single drop of much-needed rain on the valley as he reined his gelding to a halt outside the sheriff's single-story clapboard house. Dismounting, he spared a quick glance at the blanket-clad man draped over the spotted mare, then climbed the steps, gaining the porch just as the front door opened and the sheriff stepped outside.

"Well, what a surprise. Mornin', Storme. What brings you—whoa." Sheriff Hadley glanced toward the horses and arched his brow. "Another dead body?"

"Yeah." Storme frowned. "Found him yesterday in Shadow Canyon. Along with a good number of our stolen cattle. All dead." Quickly, he recounted the details of the latest theft and the discovery he and the men had made, finishing with the recent note that had been left.

Sheriff Hadley scratched the top of his gray-streaked head, his face taut with disbelief. He hitched one thumb over his shoulder. "You wanna come inside and have some coffee?"

"Thanks, but no. I just came by to drop him off." Storme

nodded toward the prone figure draped over the horse. "And see if you had any news on the dead cowboy's identity yet."

The sheriff hooked his thumbs beneath the suspenders looped over his white shirt. "Nope. None of the other sheriffs I wired recognized the description, and those men he was playing poker with didn't bother to get his name, just his money. I did hear about a bank robbery in El Paso, though. It's possible the rustlers hit that bank, then crossed the border into the territory here. I wired the sheriff down there, but haven't heard anything back yet."

Storme nodded. "A bank robbery would explain where that cowboy got the money he was throwing away at the saloon."

"That's what I'm thinking, too." Sheriff Hadley's jaw hardened. "You still ain't got any idea who's sportin' this grudge against you?"

Storme frowned and shook his head. Just as he had suspected, they hadn't been able to pick up a trail showing which way the rustlers had headed from the canyon. But nagging suspicions that the grudge might have something to do with that private continued to plague him. There had been speculation all those years ago about the private's disappearance, but Storme had been careful, and no one had ever questioned his involvement, and besides Ben, Anna was the only other person he had ever breathed a word to about seeking justice.

"If you think of anyone, you let me know."

"I'll do it." Storme nodded once, then paused, a slight smile lifting his mouth. "By the way, sheriff, you owe me a dime."

Sheriff Hadley arched his eyebrows high on his forehead. "What for?"

"I paid Joshua Hankins for delivering those wanted posters the other day. He made me promise I'd get my money back."

The sheriff chortled his amusement as he reached into his pocket. "Sounds like Joshua. He's a good kid." He tossed the dime in the air.

Storme grabbed it and stuck it in his pocket. He bid the

sheriff farewell, then mounted his horse and headed back to the ranch.

After checking on Garcia and learning the wrangler was starting to feel better, Storme met up with Winston and told him to move the cattle to closer pastures south of the house, then he rode into town, stopping first in the grove of trees behind the depot to talk with Jasper Riley standing guard. Storme was glad to learn there hadn't been any signs of trouble around the boardinghouse, and Jasper's recounting of Anna hanging up wash earlier and playing with the kitten for a while only added to Storme's eagerness to see her again.

He had missed her very much since their picnic and had wanted to ride in and see her last night, but by the time he and the men had returned from the canyon, it had been too late to come calling. Storme rode on into town, and by the time he took care of settling the ranch's account at the mercantile and sending a wire to Ben in Santa Fe about the latest trouble, telling him to stay put up there for a few more days, the clouds were gone completely and the sun was hanging close to the noon hour and burning its heated brilliance over the valley. He headed his horse down the lane toward the boardinghouse, intent on his next mission—Anna.

As he reined his horse to a stop out front, he heard her lovely voice drifting out from the open bay windows. He sat and listened as she sang a sad song about a child begging her father to come home from the saloon. Memories of everything she had told him about her life in Missouri sifted through his thoughts, and the reminder of the crime she was running from strengthened his resolve to keep her safe. He had a plan for making that job a little easier, but he wasn't sure if she would agree to it or not.

He dismounted and made his way up to the front porch, surprised to see her appear on the other side of the screen door before he even had a chance to knock. Her bright smile stole his breath.

"Hi, I saw you ride up. I was beginning to think you were just going to sit out there all day."

"I was just enjoying listening to you sing."

She curled her small nose up slightly. "I was just practicing the song I'm going to sing in the extravaganza."

Storme nodded. She had told him about Mrs. Harrington's request, and her reluctant agreement to sing in the musical evening. He had tried to allay Anna's worry about being recognized with assurances that there wouldn't be any lawmen traveling to the small town for the celebration and his promise that he wouldn't let anything happen to her. Storme hoped he was right about the former, and as for the latter, he would do whatever it took to keep that promise.

She pushed the door open. "You want to come in?"

Storme grabbed the edge of the door, holding it open. He smiled, unabashedly raking his stare over the white blouse and brown-calico skirt that gently hugged her shapely curves and fired his blood with a strong desire to peel her clothes off and make love to her. "Actually, I was hoping you might like to have lunch with me over at the restaurant."

"I'd love to. I just need to make sure it's all right with Mrs. Harrington if I wait and finish my chores later."

"It's fine, dear."

Storme glanced over where Mrs. Harrington stood in the parlor doorway. "Morning, ma'am."

The housemother nodded. "It's good to see you again, Storme. You two have a nice time. Oh, and Anna, I'm going over to the church to help the ladies make banners for the Fourth of July celebration, but I'll be back in time for Belle's lesson."

Anna nodded, her heart pounding faster at the news, and her mind whirling with possibilities of how to spend the unexpected free hours, all of them having to do with being alone with Storme. She felt the blush work its way into her cheeks. *Good-*

ness. She was becoming a truly wanton woman where he was concerned. She hoped he didn't mind.

Anna stepped outside and walked beside him as they headed down the steps.

He leaned down close to her ear, and whispered, "I'd certainly like to know what thoughts were running through your mind just now and brought that pretty flush to your cheeks."

Her face burned hotter. Her pulse raced as his spicy masculine scent assailed her nose. She glanced back toward the house as Storme opened the gate for her, then she stared up into his strong, handsome face. "I was thinking how to fill the hours this afternoon."

He smiled. "Just so happens I was thinking the same thing."

Anna walked through the gate. "And what did you come up with?"

"I'll show you."

Her blood heated with anticipation as Storme took hold of her hand and led her toward the woods behind the depot.

When they were well hidden in the shadows of the trees, he pulled her behind one of the tall cottonwoods and wrapped his arms around her, a bright gleam shining in his dark eyes. "I missed you." He claimed her mouth in a hard, searching exploration that sent wild heat swirling through her stomach.

Anna wound her arms around his neck, gliding her fingers through his soft, thick hair, kissing him back with just as much urgency and building desire. He left her mouth and pressed light kisses along her cheek, then rested his forehead against hers, his hat brim brushing against her hair.

"I missed you, too," Anna whispered. "I thought you might come by yesterday."

He frowned, and drew back, but kept his arms tight around her. "We had more trouble with the rustlers."

"What happened?" She trembled slightly, and the small hairs on the back of her neck stirred as he recounted the attack and finding the dead cattle. Anna feared even more for his safety when he mentioned the discovery of another dead man. "Are you any closer to finding out who they are?"

He shook his head. "But I *will* find out. And I did come by to take you to lunch, but I also wanted to talk to you about moving your things out to the ranch so I can keep a better watch over you until this trouble is over."

Excitement rippled through her at his concern, at the thought of being at his ranch, seeing him every day, and night. Then all the reasons why she couldn't came crashing in to squelch the thrill that coursed through her veins. "I can't do that, Storme. What about my job with Mrs. Harrington?"

"I can bring you to town every day."

She shook her head. "Mrs. Harrington would never agree to that. Can you imagine the gossip that would spread? I couldn't put her through that. She's trusted me, and been so kind to me."

"I'll hire a chaperone."

"I don't want a chaperone. I have a house full of those right here. Besides, now that I've agreed to sing in the extravaganza, I have to attend the practices, and I'm giving Belle Sanderson music lessons almost every day. You have enough to deal with trying to find the rustlers. You don't have time to be hauling me to and from town."

His black eyebrows pulled together. "Darling, it would be my pleasure to haul you anywhere you need to go. But does any of this really matter, since you're planning to leave town anyway?"

"Well, I can't leave until I have enough money."

"I'll give you the money."

"No."

"You're being stubborn."

She cocked her head. "So are you."

He hesitated, staring at her through narrowed eyes, then a slow smile curved his firm mouth. "No, I'm being selfish, because I'm worried about you, and I want to spend more time with you before either one of us has to leave."

She smiled, joy sang through her heart at his words, strengthening the love she had for this man, even as sadness settled in at their pending separation. "And I want to spend time with you. I appreciate your concern, really I do. But I can't move out to the ranch."

He sighed, his warm breath brushing against her cheek, then slowly nodded. "I understand. But promise me again that you won't go anywhere alone, and you'll always take your gun. Better yet, promise me you'll stay locked in your room and won't go anywhere at all."

Anna chuckled. "Well, if I do that, how am I'm going to see you?"

"I'll climb up the tree."

She arched her brow. "I already told you that I don't want to see any holes in your backside. And what would we do with Samantha?"

"Do you have an argument for everything?" he countered teasingly.

"No." She wrapped her arms tighter around his neck and brought her lips close to his. "I'm not going to argue at all if you want to kiss me, or take me back up to the mountains."

He kissed her long and deep, his hands roving seductively along her back and hips, heating her blood to a roaring tide of ecstasy. She ran her hands along his shoulders, down the hard contours of his muscled chest.

He suddenly broke off their kiss, and took a deep breath. "We have to stop before I cause a real scandal by doing all the things I want to do to you right here." He stepped back, and took hold of her hand. "Come on, I promised you lunch. Then we'll find someplace where we can get back to this."

Anna fell into step beside him. They left the woods and headed toward the depot as the train whistle sounded, announcing the noon arrival of the Atchison, Topeka, and Santa Fe

Railway. They climbed the depot steps up to the platform as the engine pulled past the station, slowing with a loud grinding of metal and a hissing blast of steam. She felt a stark disappointment at the loss of his touch when he released her hand to open the restaurant door, then sternly reminded herself that she had better be careful about getting too attached to Storme.

As soon as they walked inside the restaurant, Anna saw Blaine sitting at the counter talking to Samantha and Caroline. Across the room Katie and Patricia waved a discreet greeting as they waited on the few townsfolk already seated at the dining tables, then Anna spotted Sally Hankins and Hannah Montgomery. Their shocked stares turned to hard glares as they looked first at her, then Storme.

"Let's sit at the counter," Anna suggested, glancing up at the frown that pulled Storme's jaw taut.

He nodded his agreement, then hung his hat on one of the pegs on the wall beside the door. They walked over and sat down, exchanging greetings with the girls and Blaine. Then the crowds from the train filed in, and the noise of conversations and clattering dishes filled the room.

To Anna's relief, the Garden Society ladies paid them no further attention, and soon left. For the next hour Anna enjoyed her meal and Storme's steady flow of talk, ranging in topics from the ranch to politics, and even a couple of musical shows he had seen up in Denver. Blaine also spent some time visiting with them, and Samantha and Caroline did as well after the crowds had filed out to reboard the train.

"Thank you for lunch, Storme," Anna offered as soon as they stepped outside onto the walkway. "I had a real nice time. I've never done anything like that before."

Puzzlement furrowed his brow. "You've never eaten in a restaurant before?"

Anna chuckled. "Yes, I have. With my parents. Never at a man's invitation, though, and not talking with friends like we did with Blaine and the girls."

Storme smiled down at her, taking hold of her hand as they walked past the depot station and down the steps. "Well, I'm glad you had a good time, Anna. I did, too."

His thumb circling softly over the top of her hand sent a giddy surge of elation swirling through her stomach. Oh, how she loved the way he touched her.

When they reached the woods behind the train station, he stopped and pulled her into his embrace. "I'm sorry about this afternoon. I hated to tell Blaine no when he asked if I'd bring some of my wranglers over to give him a hand again making sure Dodding doesn't stop them from herding their sheep to the river."

Anna shook her head. "It's all right. That was nice of you. Besides, I still have some chores to finish, and Belle's coming over at three, so I don't have that much time anyway."

"I'll stop back by later. But . . ." A mischievous gleam darkened his stare and set her heart to racing. "I've got a few minutes right now before I need to head to the ranch." He leaned down close and whispered against her lips. "Could I interest you in spending that time kissing me?"

Anna circled her arms around his neck, letting her fingers glide through the thick, softness of his hair. "Why yes, Mr. Warwick. I believe I would be interested."

Chapter Sixteen

The moon burned bright against the star-dotted sky, and a light breeze whispered across the night, stirring the flames that struggled to stay alive in the smoldering campfire. The man tossed his burnt cheroot into the low blaze, then reached for a narrow stick of wood and added it to the glowing embers. Across the way, his two remaining cohorts were bedded down in the shadows, their low snores rising above the crickets' noise. The man took a deep breath, relishing the fresh smell of freedom that sweetly scented the air. Six years in that Mexican prison had clogged his throat and lungs with the stench of unwashed inmates, human waste, and food so rotten that even the rats wouldn't touch it—but the prisoners had, welcoming whatever nourishment was offered for their only meal of the day.

Anger simmered in his veins. He ran one finger over the scars that marred his face. Because of Warwick, he had been condemned to a life of hell all those years ago, and now that Injun was going to pay.

The man rose from the bedroll where he sat, cursing the

adrenaline of anticipation that made him restless. It wouldn't be long now. Just a few more days to let Warwick stew over when the next move would come, to worry whether the strike would be against his cattle, his brother, or his woman this time. Lust reared with hot, throbbing expectation as he thought about the pretty lady, and the plans he had for her. He intended to make sure Warwick watched it all, too, and wouldn't be able to do a damn thing to stop it.

Since Warwick had posted guards around the clock at the house where she lived, it was getting harder to sneak into town to watch her, but the man had learned a great deal about being devious while he was in prison, and about patience. He made his way along the packed-dirt bank of the Gallinas River, moonbeams reflecting like shimmering glass against the stream. He pulled a cheroot from his shirt pocket, struck a match against his boot heel, and lit the end, then took a long draw.

What had gone through Warwick's mind as he followed the trail of dead cattle to Shadow Canyon, he wondered. Had the past come back to haunt him? Added a touch of fear to his curiosity about the reason for this revenge? He would liked to have seen the look on that half-breed's face when he discovered Miguel staked out among the carcasses, and hoped the disturbing reminder had shaved a few years off Warwick's miserable life.

He took a long draw on the cheroot, then slowly blew the smoke out, watching it fade into the night, blending with the hazy moonlight. He had needed the help of the three Mexicans and that cowboy to get this far with his revenge, but he never planned to pay them the money he had promised, or let any of them live once this was over. His remaining cohorts hadn't questioned his explanation that Miguel had skipped out on them, happily assuming that their portion of the bank loot had just increased. But as soon as he was done with Warwick, he would finish off the two Mexicans. Then he could take the rest of the money from their bank heist and finally start building a life for himself again . . . as far away from the Mexican border, and this blasted desert heat, as he could get.

Storme reined his gelding to a halt atop the wide mesa and waved a greeting to Cale and Tom riding guard farther down along the ridge. Leaning forward, he crossed his arms over the saddle horn, shifting his sight over the thousands of motley longhorns that littered the grassy valley for miles. Dissonant bellows rose to fill the clear, azure sky as the morning sun crept high above the horizon, washing golden rays over the alder and willows that sparsely lined the banks of the distant stream.

Contentment settled like a warm blanket over his soul at the sight and sounds of the land, his home. Then a smile curved his mouth as he stared at nature's display of beauty that reminded him so much of Anna's green eyes and the gold fire that lit the strands of her silky red hair.

When they had stopped in the woods to share those wonderful, heated kisses, the thought had been tempting to forget food and take her up to the mountains. Then the temptation to forgo lunch had come again when they walked into the restaurant, and he saw the scowls on the two Garden Society ladies' faces. But the glow of happiness that had radiated on Anna's pretty face at spending time with him and her friends had made Storme glad that he hadn't given in to his selfish desire, or his concern about the gossip.

He had kept his promise to come by the boardinghouse after helping Blaine, and had gone over to see her again last night. But the more time he spent with her, the more Anna filled his heart with deeper admiration and love, making it harder each time to part from her company.

She was unlike any woman he had ever met before. He enjoyed her sharp mind and wit. He liked the way she had no qualms about being seen with him. Liked her dauntless defense of their friendship, and her bold, sweet passion that had her whispering in his ear about going to the mountains every time they were together. She was soft and delicate, and as pretty as a spring morning . . . and she had stolen his heart.

He couldn't deny it. His little dove had walked into his life and shattered into a million pieces his vow never to get involved with another white woman. He was very much involved with her, and several times he had come close to telling her how he felt, wanting to stray away from the safe, honest declarations of how much he liked her, cared about her, and just tell her the real truth—he loved her, wanted her with him always. But the cold reality that there could never be more between them than what they shared right now kept holding him back.

He wished things could be different for them, wished he wasn't a man always on the roam with danger and trouble blocking his path at nearly every turn. *And Anna has troubles of her own.* Unless he figured out how to prove her innocence concerning the murder charge, he knew the only way she could stay safe would be to move on and follow her dream of singing somewhere far away from here, as she planned. Storme swallowed the lump that rose in his throat. When the time came for them to part, he knew his heart would go with her, leaving him behind to spend the rest of his life walking through a lonely hell.

He released a deep, sad sigh, then straightened when he heard the approaching hoofbeats climbing the rock-scattered hill behind him. Storme shifted in his saddle and glanced over his shoulder, frowning at the rider who topped the mesa.

"What are you doing here?" he grated.

"Last time I checked, this is where I live." Ben rode up alongside and reined the sorrel to a stop.

"Didn't you get my wire?"

"Yeah, I got it."

"Then why the hell didn't you stay put like I told you to?"

Storme snapped, worry for his brother's safety adding a harsher note to his voice than he intended.

"Because I can take care of myself, dammit!" A proud independence burned like summer lightning in Ben's narrowed, brown stare. "I'm not a kid anymore, Storme. I don't need you always trying to protect me. I've been making my own decisions for a good long time now, and I came back here where I'm needed, just like you did."

Storme paused, slightly irked that he couldn't find a single argument to counter Ben's vehement declaration. But it didn't lessen his concern about the rustlers' threat. "It's good to have you home."

Ben's smile relaxed the hardened line of his jaw. "Thanks. Does that mean you're through jumping my ass?"

Storme furrowed his brow. "Unless the rustlers get ahold of you. Then I'm going to kick the shit out of you."

"Fair enough." Ben chuckled, then a cloud of seriousness settled over his humor. "Now, give me the details about what happened."

Storme recounted finding the slaughtered cattle in Shadow Canyon, the dead man staked out, and the rustlers' latest note, ending on a frustrated complaint that they hadn't been able to pick up any definite tracks leading away from the canyon.

Ben rubbed one hand over his chin, a somber contemplation garnering his expression. "You getting any closer to figuring out who might be behind this?"

Storme shook his head, even as he pondered the coincidences, and his continued suspicions that this revenge *might* be connected to the army private's death. But Storme had raked through his memory, trying to figure out who could possibly know what he had done all those years ago, and the same answer kept coming back—no one. "So, tell me what you found in Santa Fe, little brother."

"Turned out to be quite an interesting trip." Ben shoved his hat brim up slightly, then leaned forward, resting his crossed arms over the saddle horn. "There wasn't a claim filed on that section of government land, but it *was* leased out. Not to Dodding, though. Two men up in Colorado Springs filed the charter, for the purpose of timber mining, not building a dam. The judge recognized their names, said they're as crooked as a coiled snake, and promptly issued an injunction to stop work on the project. Got it right here." Ben patted one hand over his shirt pocket. "Then he sent word to Washington about your suspicions of them trying to control the water to the valley, and set the paperwork in motion to revoke their lease agreement."

"That's good." Storme nodded his satisfaction at the news, then drew his eyebrows together in curiosity. "Did you find out Dodding's connection to all this?"

"Not to the investors." A faint look of amusement crossed Ben's face. "But when I talked to the land office clerk about that section bought by Robert Blanchard, he described the man who came in to file the claim, and the description fit Dodding, right down to his short temper. I told Judge Johnson what you knew about Cole Hansen using the name Blanchard before, and possibly being in cahoots with Dodding. The judge was happy to issue a court order negating the fraudulent purchase. Before I left, I filed a new claim on that section—in Wallace's name."

Storme nodded; proud approval at Ben's influence and handling of the situation swelled in his chest. It crossed his mind that Ben and this judge might be able to help Anna. Storme knew that Missouri was a long way out of the circuit judge's jurisdiction, though, and murder a far cry more severe than land fraud. He trusted Ben to stay silent, but if the judge couldn't, or wouldn't, help, he also knew that revealing Anna's secret, and her whereabouts, could place her in more immediate danger. He had given Anna his word that he wouldn't tell anyone, and he wasn't going to break his promise. He *was* going to talk to her about this, though, and if she agreed, he would see what his brother could do to help. "He and Blaine will be glad to hear about the claim.'' Storme briefly explained about taking some of the hands over the other day to help herd their sheep to the river again.

"Yeah, this should take care of their troubles with Dodding. All that's left to do now is relay this information to Sheriff Hadley, then we can ride out there and serve the papers to stop Dodding's dam. I thought you might want to come along with us this afternoon."

Storme cocked his head, and grinned. "I won't pass up an opportunity to see Dodding get what he deserves."

"Didn't think you would." Ben chuckled, then his expression turned serious once again. "I also went by to see Sal."

"How's he doing?"

"Fine. He sends his regards to you. His son-in-law is up and around now." Regret rose in Ben's stare. "But Sal's decided he's not coming back."

Storme sat up in his saddle, and arched his brow in surprise. "Why not?"

"Says he's ready to give up ranching and spend what remaining days he's got left with his daughter and grandchildren."

Storme recalled Ben's reminder that first night he was home about the foreman's advancing age and his rheumatism getting worse. After all the years Sal had devoted to the ranch, Storme couldn't begrudge the man's decision to settle down to an easier life. "He'll be missed, but it's good that he can be with his family while he still has the chance to do so."

"Well, I'm real glad to hear you say that," Ben responded in a low, odd tone that puzzled Storme as much as the comment. "Because I've been wanting to talk to you about staying at the ranch, instead of heading out like you're planning when the rustlers are caught."

A sharp pain ripped through Storme's gut as the memories of his father's death came charging in with full force. "You know I can't do that. I won't risk bringing trouble to the ranch, and that's just what'll happen."

"Maybe." Ben shrugged. "What I do know is that you left as much out of guilt over pa's death as you did to protect me." He narrowed his stare. "But trouble came calling without you even being here. And if more comes, we'll fight it together, just like we're doing now."

Storme appreciated Ben's confidence, even as it bothered him that his brother was right—he hadn't been here, and still trouble came. But Storme couldn't erase past experience. This was just an isolated incident. If he stayed, things could escalate even more. He shook his head. "I won't take that chance. Nothing's changed. Folks aren't happy about me being back, and you know it. Besides, I have a job."

Ben's mouth firmed into a thin line of displeasure. "I won't argue there's a few people that would just as soon you hadn't returned. But you're wrong about nothing changing. There's folks around here that like you. And the council is appreciative that you figured out the dam situation and brought it to our attention. As for your job, are you going to tell me you'd rather be a bounty hunter than here working at the ranch?"

Storme swallowed dryly, then shifted in his saddle to face front. "No, being a bounty hunter is just what I do, you know that." He stared down at the cattle dotting the valley, at the ranch hands riding guard along the outer edges of the herd and along the mesa, at the land that called to him, pulled at him. He wanted to believe that Ben was right and folks might be willing to accept him, but he couldn't ignore the grave doubts that lingered. "And it could be that folks are only tolerating me because I've made it clear that I'm not staying."

"I suppose that's a possibility with some," Ben agreed with a tight edge in his voice. He squared his shoulders back. "But there's something else that's changed around here, brother. Me."

Storme stared, disconcerted. He couldn't deny that he had

noticed a restlessness in Ben. His brother was different, in his physical appearance as well as this reputation of being a rogue that he had managed to garner. But Storme's gut told him this concerned something a little more serious than growing up, or not wanting to settle into a relationship. "What do you mean?"

Ben didn't say anything for a few seconds, just stared off into the distance. Then he took a deep breath and slowly released it. "For the last couple of years, I've been getting more and more tired of running the ranch."

Storme couldn't hide his stunned surprise. Ben had done a fine job of running the ranch, and Storme had always thought that he was content to do so.

"I don't find the same enjoyment in the daily grind that I used to," Ben continued. "That's part of the reason I decided to sit on the council, and have been so involved in the town's affairs." A glint of excitement sprang into his brown gaze. "To tell you the truth, Storme, I've been thinking about getting into law work. I've handled a number of matters on the town's behalf, and Judge Johnson thinks I'd make a good lawyer."

Shock slapped Storme in the face, dropping his jaw. "A lawyer? What about the ranch?"

Ben sighed, his shoulders slumping as though a heavy weight settled on them. "I'm still just thinking about it. And this ranch means as much to me as it does you. I won't do anything to jeopardize all the hard work Pa put into building this spread. But we both own this ranch, Storme, and all I'm asking is that you give some thought to staying and giving me a hand . . . and the opportunity to think about what I want to do with my life."

A new guilt seeped in, settling in Storme's gut. He loved his brother and didn't want to stand in the way of his future. He also had to admit that Ben had done a fine job of handling things in Santa Fe, and just might make a damn good lawyer. It didn't lessen his concerns, though. He didn't want to do anything that would jeopardize the ranch, either. If folks *were* just tolerating his stay, he knew things could get worse if he didn't leave. But for his brother's sake, Storme knew he would have to give it some serious consideration . . . and deep down he would like nothing better than to come back home for good. "All right, I'll think about it."

Ben grinned. "Thanks, Storme. That's all I'm asking for right now."

Midafternoon sunlight glistened through the thick line of blue spruce and cottonwoods, and bright yellow beams danced over the swift flow of the Pecos River. Up ahead the timbered train trestle rose high above the water and just beyond where the base of the mountain began its upward slope, the sounds of hammers and saws and muted voices drifted on the air.

A rush of adrenaline heightened Storme's anticipation as he spotted the black-suited rancher and mingled with a complacent satisfaction when he saw the white sling holding Dodding's right arm close to his chest and the bandage wrapped around the hand he had stomped on. The rancher stood several yards out from the bank of the river, a cheroot dangling from his mouth as he watched the crew haul logs into the water.

"Doesn't look like he's had time to get much done on that dam," Sheriff Hadley commented.

"Won't take long to bring it down." Storme grinned, glancing over at the sheriff, then at Ben riding on the other side of the lawman. "I think we should send that crew on their way and let Dodding tear it down himself."

Ben chuckled and shook his head. "Since when have you known Dodding ever to do a lick of work himself?"

"All the more reason I'd like to see it," Storme responded with an edge of seriousness that drew the sheriff to look over.

"Don't go looking to start trouble," the lawman cautioned. "Dodding's going to be hot enough as it is when we serve this injunction on him."

Injunction? Shit! Cole peered around the tree, watching as the three men rode closer to the work site. He had been surprised to find the posted guards packing up their gear when he rode by a short time ago. His anger mounted when they told him the sheriff had been there with papers proving the land didn't belong to anyone named Robert Blanchard, and said they were trespassing and had to leave.

Damn that bounty hunter. Damn that blasted Dodding!

Crouching low, Cole stealthily made a path through the thick trees and underbrush. He saw Dodding turn to face the riders, a look of surprise hardening his long, angular jaw and widening his eyes. Cole was doubly glad now that he had stayed back at the ranch to avoid Dodding's company for a while and more than willing to let the arrogant rancher take the brunt of what was about to happen. But it didn't lessen Cole's fury over the discovery of their scheme or at Dodding for causing trouble with Storme Warwick and bringing his attention to the dam. Cole needed to know just how much the sheriff and that bounty hunter knew about the deception, though. Hopefully, it was only Dodding they were after.

He crawled on his belly several feet behind a short patch of scrub, then knelt in the grass behind the thick trunk of a cottonwood. He placed his hat on the ground beside him and peered around the tree. Dodding stood several yards away, glaring up at the three riders who came to a stop.

"What do you mean an injunction?" the rancher bellowed.

"This is government property," the sheriff said as he pulled a piece of paper out his pocket and handed it to Dodding. "You can't build a dam on it. You tell these men to start tearing it down."

"This isn't government property. It's privately owned," Dodding argued, snatching the paper and glaring over at the bounty hunter. "What the hell are you trying to pull here, half-breed?"

"Just serving justice, Dodding," Storme countered in a smug tone.

Cole groaned his displeasure as he listened to the three men explain to Dodding about the crooked investors, the revoked lease, and that the government had been informed of the scheme to control the water flow to the valley.

Damn! He was going to have to flee fast before the investors came looking to kill him. But Cole's temper rose to new heights when Dodding disputed the facts, saying that his partner owned this land, then had the audacity to give them his name and produce the fake document of their agreement.

Cole saw Storme sit up straight in his saddle, and listened as the bounty hunter confidently told Dodding that he had hooked up with a low-down scam artist.

After several more minutes of arguing, Cole could see the realization of being duped slowly register on Dodding's face. But it wasn't until Dodding informed the sheriff that his no-good partner could be found at his ranch that Cole made the decision to handle one last job before he left the territory for new parts . . . and new schemes.

"I'll sing you a true song of Billy the Kid . . ." Belle's voice rang loud and clear through the Meeting Hall as she continued on with the series of verses.

Anna stood between Sally Hankins and Edna Mae Mason, and smiled her encouragement to the young girl standing on the makeshift stage that had been erected for the musical. Hannah and Lilah stood off to one side with Maryanne and Elise. The extravaganza practice had ended a short while ago, and Anna waited until most of the people had left before she approached the Garden Society ladies about letting Belle change her song. Of course, their first reaction had been a flat no, along with their reproach that they didn't appreciate her trying to interfere with the program, especially with a song about an outlaw.

Anna had countered that she was only trying to enhance the

show's presentation to impress the investor and help bring the opera house to town. She also used the argument that it would fit nicely as the opening song to the parody that Katie and Patricia were participating in about four women who go on a picnic, and the encounters they have when they find costumes in their basket—one of the musical farces included a train robbery. But it was Mrs. Harrington's added support, and suggestion they at least listen to Belle sing the tune before they said no, that had finally prompted this audition.

Anna tapped her foot in time to the music, pride swelling as she listened to Belle hit every note just right. When Anna suggested this song at Belle's second lesson, the girl had been delighted, and knew she would have to do a good job if they hoped to convince the Garden Society ladies to let her sing it. Belle had practiced diligently, mentioning more than once at each of her lessons how often she was singing it in front of Blaine's sheep so she wouldn't be nervous.

The thought of Belle's brother reminded Anna of the recent buzz of news that had started around town yesterday. The councilmen were freely talking about how Storme had figured out Mr. Dodding's scheme to build a dam and control the water flow to the valley and how Ben had managed to get an injunction to stop it. The townsfolk were extremely grateful, and more than a few people were saying nice things about Storme. Even the Garden Society ladies had grudgingly expressed their approval, though their acceptance hadn't stretched any further. But no one was happier than Wallace and Blaine when Ben also learned that Dodding had fraudulently claimed a piece of land they needed for watering their sheep and had secured the claim for them. The bigger surprise had come this morning, though, when the sheriff found Mr. Dodding dead out by the dam site.

Anna feared that folks would suspect Storme because of the obvious dislike between the two men. But he had come by the house earlier in the day and, to her relief, had told her that the suspicion was on a man named Cole Hansen, who had no doubt skipped out of the territory by now. She was sorry that Storme had to leave shortly after he returned again this evening, instead of coming to the practice with her, but when one of his ranch hands came to tell him that the rustlers started a stampede, she had understood his need to head home and check on things.

She turned her full attention back to the audition, glancing over where Mrs. Harrington played the piano. Their eyes met, and they exchanged a silent look of pride at how well Belle was doing. Anna shifted her stare over toward Hannah and Lilah, pleased at the smiles that graced their faces, then covertly glanced at Sally Hankins. The woman wasn't smiling, but when Anna looked down, she saw Sally's dark blue hem fluttering as she tapped her foot.

Belle sang the final verse of the ballad:

> *There's many a man with a face fine and fair*
> *Who starts out in life with a chance to be square,*
> *But just like poor Billy he wanders astray*
> *And loses his life in the very same way.*

To Anna's delight, the Garden Society ladies applauded heartily. Belle's mouth parted in a wide grin.

"That was very nice, Belle." Edna Mae offered the compliment.

"Yes, it was. I do believe this *will* make a nice addition to the program," Hannah stated, and Edna Mae and Lilah nodded their agreement.

"You're right, Hannah," Sally commented, then turned her attention toward Mrs. Harrington. "I think we will change Belle's number for the musical, Harriet."

"I'm glad to hear it." The housemother smiled her approval.

Belle squealed her delight, hunching her shoulders up around her face. "Thank you, ladies." Round, pink circles of flushed enthusiasm stained her cheeks.

Sally nodded, smiling at the girl, then she gathered up her skirt. "Well, we really must be going now." Sally turned on one heel and headed toward the door, the other Garden Society ladies following in her path.

Anna was too happy at Belle's excitement and success in being allowed to sing the number to care that the ladies had totally ignored her and the fact that it had been her idea. "You sounded wonderful, Belle. I'm proud of you."

Belle climbed down the short flight of steps. "I owe it all to you, Miss Alexander. Thank you."

"Yes, thank you, Anna," Maryanne strolled over, slipping one arm around her daughter's shoulders. "We really appreciate how hard you've been working with Belle."

Anna smiled. "I've enjoyed it." She truly had. Belle was a sweet girl, and she had a wonderful voice. Anna had also enjoyed participating in the extravaganza, surprised that she found as much enjoyment in thinking of ways to better the musical, and offering direction for changes to the order of the numbers—through Mrs. Harrington, of course. Even now she was thinking of suggesting another change—keeping Belle's old number, but having the six-year-old Holley twins sing it instead. Their mother was singing in the parody with Katie and Patricia, and the little girls had been coming to the practices. More than once, Anna had overheard the blond, blue-eyed twins beg their mother to be included in the show. She thought the audience would find them adorably cute singing the tune about the little dog, and decided she would talk to Mrs. Harrington about it later that night.

"I can't believe how rude those ladies were." Elise frowned, her hazel eyes narrowing with displeasure. "They could've at least acknowledged that it was your idea, Anna, even if they didn't want to say thank you." She shifted her pinched glare toward the front door. "I've got a notion to go out there and give them a piece of my mind."

"It would just be a waste of your good mind, dear." Mrs.

Harrington shook her head in disgust as she ambled down the steps from the stage. "Those guinea hens don't appreciate anything."

"Mrs. Harrington's right." Anna chuckled slightly, the mention of hens reminding her of the housemother's defense of Storme and the women's appalled faces at the reference. "And it doesn't matter. The important thing is that Belle gets to sing the song in the musical."

"That's very gracious of you, Anna," Elise said, her voice tinged with the annoyance that still shimmered in her stare.

The others voiced their agreement about her kindness. Anna voiced her appreciation at their words of support and show of friendship. Then Mrs. Harrington suggested they head over to the boardinghouse for refreshments. The Sanderson ladies agreed, since Blaine was there visiting with Samantha and Caroline while he waited for the practice to end so he could escort his family home. They left the Meeting Hall, walking outside into the early twilight, and found Katie and Patricia talking with Wallace. Elise begged off from the invitation when Wallace informed her he had come to give her a ride home so they could spend some time alone together.

Anna headed down the narrow lane behind the mercantile with the others, and had almost reached Main Street when she realized that she had left her reticule behind. Mrs. Harrington offered to return with her, narrowing her apple green stare in concern that Anna knew had to do with Storme's caution about her being alone. The girls still didn't know about the threats that had been made against her, and Anna didn't want to cause a fuss about going back, certain that since the rustlers had struck out at the ranch again she would be fine. She assured the housemother it wouldn't take but a minute, lightly patting her skirt pocket where the derringer rested. Mrs. Harrington hesitated before relenting about letting her go alone, but was adamant that they would wait right there for her to return.

Anna hurried back as the sun dipped lower behind the western mountain range, surprised to see that Elise and Wallace hadn't left, but were still standing beside their wagon, holding hands and talking. She spoke briefly to them, explaining her return, then made her way inside where evening shadows were beginning to overtake the large interior. She walked up the aisle between the long rows of bench seating and found her reticule up front where she had left it. Snatching it up, she looped the strings around her wrist, then started retracing her steps toward the door.

She barely had time to register the sudden footsteps that sounded at her back before a large, male hand came snaking around from behind, clamped down over her mouth, and jerked her to a halt. Her head snapped back. Her heart stopped, and her eyes widened as a cold chill crawled up her spine. She stared down at the broad, dirty fingers. *Who is this man?* Her pulse raced. Panic rose full force and spurred her into action. She rammed her elbow back, connecting hard enough with his muscled midsection to send needles jarring through her arm, and a low grunt issuing from her captor. The man circled his free hand around her waist, pinning her arms down at her sides, then hauled her back against his chest. Anna kicked at his legs, twisted and struggled to free herself.

"Stop fighting, pretty lady," the stranger whispered in her ear. "I'm not gonna hurt you."

Anna stilled. It crossed her mind that he might be a lawman who had found out about her. But why didn't he just pull his gun and tell her she was under arrest? She turned her head slightly, cutting her eyes to look at him and catching only a glimpse of black hair beneath his hat, one dark blue eye, and the red bandanna tied around his face before his fingers dug like a painful vise into her cheeks, and he jerked her head toward the front again. She swallowed.

Good heavens! He's definitely not a lawman. A cold knot fisted in her stomach. Bile rose into her throat, as much from the stale dirt and sweat that wafted up from his hand pressed firmly against her mouth, as from her nagging suspicion he was one of the rustlers. Her right hand shook as she slowly eased it along the side of her skirt, slipping inside the pocket and circling her fingers around the pistol.

The man tightened his hold, crushing her ribs until tears rose in her eyes. She tried, but couldn't bend her elbow enough to get her hand out her pocket. Then quick as a striking snake, the man lowered his arm and shoved his hand inside her pocket, ripping the opening wider. He clamped his fingers around hers and jerked her hand out. Anna held on to the wooden handle for all she was worth, slapping at his arm with her free hand as he tried to yank the derringer from her grasp. He wrapped his hand around the small barrel and pulled hard. Sharp pain jarred her joints, and loosened her grip. The pistol slipped from her hold. Anna's gasp of alarm was squelched behind the man's hand over her mouth.

He cupped the gun in his palm and twisted his hand free of her clawing desperation, then pinned her arms at her sides again as he reclaimed his tight hold around her waist.

"I can't wait to find out what else you've got hiding under them skirts, pretty lady," he whispered, his warm, tobacco-stale breath brushing across her cheek. There was lustful insinuation in the low chuckle he issued in her ear that sent increased fear coursing through her blood. He lifted his arm higher, pressing against the underside of her breasts. "But we'll wait until that Injun can watch what all I've got planned for you."

Tremors rippled through her limbs and repulsion swirled in her stomach. The man lifted her off her feet and moved backward, deeper into the shadows that slowly crept in to claim the room. Anna's panic escalated, as did her efforts to fight her way free. She had to do something. She couldn't let him take her. She couldn't let him use her to get to Storme.

Through one set of tall windows that bordered either side of the front door, she saw Wallace helping Elise up into their wagon. Her heart pounded faster. *Oh God, they can't leave.*

They can't leave! Anna parted her lips and sank her teeth into the man's palm, gagging on the salty sweat that bit at her tongue.

"You bitch." Her captor growled deep in his throat, then Anna felt his flesh tear as he jerked his hand away.

She screamed, her loud cry cut off as he slammed his palm over her mouth again with enough force her teeth cut into her lip, but a small measure of relief washed through her when she saw Wallace glance toward the Meeting Hall, then walk away from the wagon.

"Damn you," he whispered, and Anna realized he must have seen Wallace heading this way, as well. "This isn't over, pretty lady. I'll be back for you."

Before she had a chance to fully register what he said, or give thought to his intent, the man released her and shoved her forward. Anna screamed as the floor rushed up to greet her with a hard impact that sent the air rushing from her lungs and blinding tears flooding her eyes.

"Anna, what's wrong?" Wallace rushed through the front door, his booted steps pounding across the planking.

She pushed herself to her knees, gulping in air, her shoulders heaving with her labored breaths. Then she sat back on her heels, and rested her palms on her thighs, tears coursing down her face.

He squatted down beside her, and placed his hand on her shoulder, his eyes narrowed with grave concern as he raked his stare over her face. "What happened?"

"A . . . man . . . rustlers." Anna swallowed. She lifted her shaking hand and pointed toward the blackened shadows at the back of the building. "That way . . . hurry."

Wallace nodded and was up like a shot, his gun drawn as he bolted across the room.

Anna!" Elise came running through the front door and hurried over to kneel at the side. "Oh, my goodness, you're bleeding.'' She pulled a small handkerchief from her reticule and dabbed it against Anna's mouth. ''What happened?''

Anna took several deep breaths, trying to catch her air. Her body shook as hard as leaves in a spring wind as she told Elise about the rustler who had tried to kidnap her. Elise was just helping her up to her feet when Wallace came hurrying from the back of the room.

He shook his head, his eyes filled with anger. ''He's gone. No doubt had his horse waiting right out back. As soon as we get you over to the boardinghouse, I'll go find the sheriff.''

''N . . . no.'' Anna bit at her trembling bottom lip, her heart racing with leftover fear from the attack, and added worry for Storme.

Elise frowned, and gently looped one arm around Anna's shoulders. ''Honey, the sheriff needs to know about this, so he can pick up that man's trail as soon as possible. You know Storme and Ben want to catch these rustlers.''

Anna nodded. ''We can go by his office. But, I need to . . . see Storme.'' Her breaths came raw and hurtful as her apprehension mounted over the frightful experience she had just endured. She needed to know that he was all right, that something hadn't happened to him when he had gone home to check about the stampede. She needed to tell him about the attack. A shudder rippled up her spine. She needed the strength and comfort of his arms around her, making her feel safe again. Please . . .'' She shifted her pleading stare between Elise and Wallace. ''Will you take me to him?''

Chapter Seventeen

Storme propped one stocking-clad foot against the front porch railing and leaned the chair back on two legs. A light breeze whispered across the night, the cooler air brushing against his bare chest in welcomed relief after the day's grueling heat. The half-moon hung high, shedding its dim light over the ranch yard. Beneath the blanket of stars shimmering like diamonds against the velvet sky, the crickets loudly chirped their songs throughout the valley. The faint sounds of cattle bawls drifted up from the far pastures south of the house.

Storme frowned as he sipped from the glass of whiskey in his hand and stared out at the peacefulness of the night that surrounded him. The plaguing sense that something was wrong had come upon him shortly before dark, and continued to choke out the usual contentment he found in nature's calming presence, in just being home again.

By the time he had returned to the ranch after Jasper rode to town to tell him about the stampede, the hands had most of the herd rounded up and were starting a count to see what the losses were this time. Cale and Tom had set about repairing the section of fence that had been cut, while Storme had ridden out with Winston and Ben in search of the rustlers' trail, losing their tracks in the rocky slopes that bordered the southwest section of the ranch.

There hadn't been a note left this time, no trail leading him to some gruesome discovery. Storme wondered then why the rustlers had started the stampede. He wondered now if this nagging sense was more a foreboding. Were the rustlers planning to attack the herd again tonight?

Or was he tracking the wrong path to his uneasiness altogether? Maybe he was just restless . . . and angry about the emergency that had interfered with his spending the evening with Anna. He would have much preferred listening to her sing and walking her home after the extravaganza practice, than running an elusive chase after these blasted rustlers.

Storme sighed, and lifted the glass to his lips, savoring the smooth warmth that slid down his throat. He smiled, pondering the idea of riding into town right now to see her, then quickly shoved the idea aside. *Don't be a fool.* It was well past Mrs. Harrington's nine-thirty curfew for visitors to come calling, and he wasn't about to risk getting Anna in trouble, or himself shot, by climbing the tree to her window. Besides, he had been over to see her twice already today . . . and if he didn't start exercising some control over his fondness for her, he knew his heart was going to break when the time came for them to part for good.

"You want a refill on that drink?" Ben sauntered out onto the porch, clean denims the only attire he had bothered to don after his bath. Dim shades of yellow lamplight filled the foyer and spilled out through the doorway, glistening in the dampness that still clung to his sandy hair.

Storme shook his head.

Ben filled the clear tumbler in his hand, then set the whiskey bottle down on the railing and leaned back against the tall, white column. "You're awful quiet tonight. Something on your mind?"

Storme shrugged. "The rustlers."

"Anything else?" There was a slight teasing in his low inquiry. "Miss Alexander perhaps?"

Anna was *always* there, hovering on the outskirts of his every thought. Storme downed the last bit of whiskey in his glass, then set the chair back on all fours and reached for the bottle. "I think I will have that refill."

"Hmm . . . don't want to talk about it, huh?" Ben arched his eyebrows in amusement and circled the amber liquid around in the glass. "I've noticed you've been spending a lot of time with her. You two getting serious?"

He was serious all right. Seriously in love with her . . . and there wasn't a damn thing he could do about it. A heaviness settled in Storme's chest. He sipped the whiskey. Whether or not he decided to stay at the ranch as Ben wanted, it didn't change the fact that Anna wouldn't be staying in town for long. He had decided against talking to her about sharing her trouble with the law with Ben. Storme didn't want to risk her safety, not after discreetly engaging his brother in a general conversation about the circuit judge, and learning that Judge Johnson couldn't be bribed, didn't make rulings without proof, and didn't interfere outside his jurisdiction. Storme wished like hell he could find a way to prove Anna's innocence. But even if he could, he knew she would still be leaving town . . . to chase her dreams of singing with a musical troupe.

"We're friends. We like spending time with each other. That's all."

"She seems like a nice woman. Why don't you get serious?"

Storme arched his brow. "You're a fine one to be giving advice. Why did you let Blaine walk off with Miss Crowley? And how did you get this reputation for being a scalawag, anyway?"

"It's not a crime that a man don't want to settle down." Ben scowled. "But we were talking about you."

"I've tired of that subject, little brother."

"Well, I'm not inclined to move on to this one." Ben pushed away from the column and went to stand at the top of the steps, sipping his drink as he stared out toward the moonlit yard.

Storme took a drink of whiskey and pondered his brother's aversion to the discussion. Since he had been home, the only woman he heard him talk much about was Elise, which only strengthened his concern that Ben's feelings for the woman went deeper than the friendship he claimed. Storme thought about how he would feel if Anna married someone else, and the sudden pain that slammed into his chest choked the breath right out of him, then twisted like a vise over his heart when he realized that she most likely *would* get married someday. Once she safely sailed away for Europe, she wouldn't have to worry about the law catching up with her and could start a new life. She was sweet and beautiful. Her lovely voice would draw the crowds wherever she sang. She would have men clambering all over each other vying to spend time with her and whichever one she chose to give her heart to would be the luckiest man alive. Jealousy burned a hole in his gut. He stared over at his brother's rigid back. Was Ben feeling the same pain? If so, Storme knew he might do well to pay attention to how his brother managed to live with it day after day.

Storme paused with the glass midway to his mouth as the groaning creak of wood and jangling harnesses signaled the approach of a wagon headed up the darkened road toward the house.

Ben's eyebrows shot upward in surprise. "Little late for a social call." The slight apprehension in his voice mirrored Storme's concern about the unexpected visit. "Hope nothing's wrong."

He did, too, but the troubling sense dug deeper at Storme's gut.

Ben glanced down at his half-clothed state. "I'm gonna go grab a shirt. You want one?"

Storme nodded, then rose and set his glass down on the railing, crossing over to stand at the top of the steps as Ben headed back inside. He peered hard into the shadows as the plodding hooves and the grinding strain of leather and metal rubbing together grew louder. Then the wagon emerged into the moonlight, and Storme's heart stopped at the sight Anna sitting on the bench seat with Elise and Wallace. Anxiety stabbed at his chest when he noticed that Lazaro and Corky were riding one on either side of the wagon.

Dammit! Something *was* wrong. He knew the cowhands wouldn't have left their watch at the boardinghouse, and Anna wouldn't be coming out this time of night, otherwise.

He took the steps two at a time and hurried across the grass, his gaze fixed on Anna's ashen face and widened stare. He reached the wagon as Wallace brought the horses to a stop and set the brake.

"Oh, Storme, am I glad to see you."

An icy sensation crawled up his spine at the quivering tone that strained Anna's voice. She stood up, and he circled his hands around her waist, then lifted her down. "What's wrong, Anna?"

She shook her head. "Hold me, Storme, please, just for a minute." She slid her arms around his neck and buried her face against his chest.

He could feel her hot tears against his skin, her body shaking in his arms. He pulled her close, frowning as he looked up at the wranglers' tightened jaws of concern, his alarm mounting when he saw the same grim expressions on Elise's and Wallace's faces.

"She's had a real bad fright," Elise quietly stated. "One of the rustlers attacked her at the Meeting Hall. He tried to kidnap her, Storme."

Shock cooled the flow through his veins. His muscles tensed.

Storme cursed himself for sitting here, doing nothing, when he had sensed something was wrong. He should have known Anna was in trouble. He should have been there.

Wallace shook his head. "I'm sorry, but he had a head start by the time I knew what had happened and went after him. Sheriff's out right now trying to pick up his trail. Anna insisted on coming out here to see you''—he nodded toward the cowhands—"so we brought your men along to ride guard."

Storme nodded his appreciation of Wallace's help and wisdom in not riding out alone. Gently, he pulled Anna's arms from around his neck and raked his stare over her bloodless face. He lightly touched the bruise at the corner of her trembling mouth, and anger surged through his blood. "How bad did he hurt you, Anna?" he whispered.

She swallowed. "Not much. I'm . . . all right." She bit her bottom lip.

Guilt squeezed his heart as he brushed the tears from her cheeks. He should have been there for her, taken care of her. A hollow pit formed in his stomach. He had failed her . . . but it wouldn't happen again. Storme took a deep breath, then reached down and scooped her up into his arms. She wrapped her hands tight around his neck and cradled her head in the crook of his shoulder. He glanced up at Wallace and Elise. "You're welcome to come inside. I'd like to talk to Anna alone right now, though."

"We understand." Elise offered a small smile.

Storme turned and headed toward the house, gaining the porch just as Ben came out, a white shirt hanging half-open on his frame and another held in his hand.

"What happened?" he questioned.

"One of the rustlers attacked her. That's all I know right now." Storme walked inside and carried Anna up the staircase, not stopping until he had entered his room and shoved the door closed with one foot. He didn't give a damn about propriety or reputations at the moment. He just wanted to be alone with her, comfort her, tell her how sorry he was . . . find out how the hell the rustler had gotten to her.

Moonlight spilled through the opened window, pale beams lighting his path across the room. He sat down on the edge of the bed, tightening his hold around her as he held her in his lap. He whispered soothing words into her ear and rained light kisses along the side of her face until he felt her trembles subside and her ragged breathing slow to normal.

She took a deep breath and released it on a shuddering sigh, then sat up. "I'm sorry. I didn't mean to fall apart. I was doing fine, until I saw you, and . . . I just needed you so bad, Storme. I needed to feel safe again."

He brushed a feather-light kiss against her lips, her words of needing him ripping at his soul. "I'm the one who's sorry, Anna. I should have been there. I promised I would protect you."

Anna shook her head, the anguish in his voice tearing at her heart. She cupped one hand against his strong jaw. "You have protected me, Storme, wonderfully. What happened was my fault. I went back alone, and I shouldn't have." She explained about forgetting her reticule, returning to the Meeting Hall, and Mrs. Harrington's concern about her going alone. "Since you had that trouble out here with the rustlers, I really didn't think there'd be a problem. But . . ." Cold shivers raced through her limbs as the memories of the rustler grabbing her rushed in. "He was waiting for me." She pressed closer to Storme, grateful for his solid, warm strength as she explained the details of the attack and of losing her gun to the man. "I did get a glimpse of him, Storme. Not a good one, though, he was wearing a bandanna over his face. But he's a white man, and he's got black hair and dark blue eyes."

Storme's eyebrows pulled together, forming a line along the ridge of his forehead. "Are you sure?"

Anna nodded, pondering the puzzlement that blazed in his narrowed brown stare. "Do you know who it might be?"

He hesitated, his mouth clenching in a tight line, then he shook his head. "But I'm getting closer to figuring it out. Right now, though, I'm more worried about you."

Her heart soared at his care for her, at the fire that blazed in his soft gaze. "I'm all right."

He ran one hand along her arm. "You're going to be. I intend to make sure of it." He reached up and cradled her head, pulling her closer, his voice ragged with concern as he whispered his apology for not being there and his promises he wouldn't let anything happen to her again.

Anna wrapped her arms tighter around his neck, finding the comfort she so desperately needed from his embrace. Oh, how she loved this man, loved the way he made her feel so safe . . . so special.

He held her for several minutes before tenderly setting her from his lap onto the bed, then he crossed the planking over to a tall oak dresser.

Anna heard the match strike, then candlelight softly flooded the large room, chasing away the shadows the moonlight hadn't reached. Storme opened the top drawer. She raked an appreciative gaze over the corded muscles of his bronze back, her fingers itching to follow the smooth, gliding path of her stare. The second she had seen him standing on the porch, an overwhelming relief had washed through her limbs, and a sense of security had settled in her soul. She knew she had nothing to worry about as long as he was near. Anna swallowed, wishing she could stay in the shelter of his protection, could be with him forever.

He pulled out a white shirt, then walked back and took hold of her hands, gently pulling her to her feet. His warm smile contrasted with the seriousness in his stare. "I hope you know that you're not going back to the boardinghouse."

She nodded, recalling the sparked flurry of concerns that had ignited after the attack. Mrs. Harrington had been distressed, and expressed strong regrets that she hadn't gone back with

Anna. Maryanne and Belle were shocked and upset. Katie and Patricia were as well, and had demanded to know why someone would try to kidnap her, leaving Anna little choice but to explain about the rustlers' threats. "Elise told Mrs. Harrington that she and Wallace could stay out here tonight, and bring me home in the morning." Anna was appreciative of Elise's generosity, and friendship, especially since it was the only reason Mrs. Harrington had finally agreed to let her come tonight, instead of waiting until tomorrow to see Storme and give him the attacker's description. "Blaine took Belle and his mother over to stay with Wallace's parents and was coming back to keep an eye on things at the boardinghouse. Mrs. Harrington said something about having the limb outside my window cut down tomorrow, just to be safe."

Storme nodded. "That's all good. But you're not going back in the morning, Anna."

A bubbly elation heated her veins at the thought of staying with him, then quickly cooled. "I have to, Storme. I have to think about my job. I need the money, and besides, there's another extravaganza prac—"

"Shhh . . ." He placed on finger against her lips. "We'll talk about this later. Right now, all I care about is making sure you're all right." He reached down and began to undo the buttons along her bodice.

Anna sighed, too drained to fight his stubbornness and more than willing to put off the inevitable disagreement as Storme slowly removed her clothes. Tears welled in her eyes at his tender ministrations, at the torment that showed in his every look. He kissed the bruises that had started to form on her ribs, each time vowing to kill the man that had put them there. He straightened and held his shirt out. Anna gave only a moment's thought to her nightgown packed in a bag down in the wagon, then slipped her arms inside. She breathed deep, welcoming his faint masculine scent that clung to the material and wrapped her in an added euphoria of contentment as he buttoned it closed.

Storme reached down and pulled the brown coverlet and top sheet back on the double bed. ''I want you to get some rest.''

Anna hesitated. She wanted to be with Storme, not sleep. But the inviting comfort of the thick mattress and fluffy pillows was hard to ignore. Her body ached in remembrance of her fight with the rustler, and her anxiety to see Storme on the long trip out here had taken more of a toll on her strength than she realized. Maybe she would rest . . . just for a short while. She glanced up at Storme. ''Please don't leave.''

Her heart pounded faster when he smiled and sat down, bracing his back against the tall, wooden headboard. She crawled onto the bed and into his open arms, pressing a soft kiss to his mouth before curling up against his warm chest and resting her head against his shoulder.

Storme held her for a long time, until he felt the weight of her relaxed slumber, and heard her even, shallow breathing. He carefully eased her from his lap, laying her head on the pillow, then pulled the sheet up over her. He placed a light kiss on her forehead, so thankful that she hadn't been hurt any worse, so glad and relieved to have her with him now. He walked over to the dresser and took another shirt out of the drawer and slipped it on, then leaned over and blew the candle out. He grabbed his boots as he headed toward the door. One hand braced on the brass knob, he paused and looked back, sighing. She looked so pretty with the soft moonlight glistening like gold in her hair and paling her smooth cheeks, so small and fragile in his bed . . . and too much like she belonged there— always.

He took a deep breath, then stepped into the hall and quietly closed the door. His jaw clenched as his anger came rushing in full force. *Damn these rustlers!* His rage was aimed just as much at himself for bringing this danger into Anna's life. But he planned to make sure she wasn't in danger anymore.

He pulled his boots on, then descended the stairs and headed toward the kitchen, where he heard the muted sounds of voices.

"How is she?" Elise asked as soon as he stepped through the doorway.

Storme forced a calm he was far from feeling. "She'll be fine. She's resting right now." He glanced at Ben's taut expression, then settled his stare on Wallace. "Thanks for being there for her and for bringing her out here."

Wallace frowned. "I'm just sorry I didn't do more. Anna was telling us about the rustlers' threats on the way out. If I'd known she was in danger, I never would have let her go in alone."

Storme nodded.

"You want some coffee?" Elise started to rise from the chair.

"No, thanks." Storme waved for her to stay put. "I'm going to step outside for a bit, and get some air." He walked out the back door and headed down the hill, his steps fueled by guilt and rage that settled as deep inside him as it had the day his father was killed. When he reached the barn, Storme entered the darkened confines and shoved his fist through the nearest wall, vowing to find this vengeful bastard who had hurt Anna, and kill him . . . if it was the last thing he ever did.

The moon had risen past the midnight hour by the time Storme made his way back to the house. The single candle burned low, casting a soft golden glow over the kitchen, and the lone figure sitting at the table.

Ben glanced up, a half-filled speckled tin of steaming coffee cupped between his hands. "I saw the holes punched in the wall when me and Wallace took his wagon down to unhitch the team. You all right?"

Storme nodded, flexing the soreness in his right hand. The walk he had taken after his bout of fury in the barn had helped cool his temper considerably, replacing it with an aching sadness at the decision he had reached. A decision that ripped his heart in two but would ensure Anna's safety.

He crossed the room and poured himself a cup of coffee from the blue-enamel pot on the stove, then made his way over and sat down across from his brother. "Wallace and Elise already retire for the night?"

"Yeah," Ben answered. "I let them have Pa's old room. Elise took some tea up and checked on Anna a little while ago. She was awake, and asking where you went."

Storme tensed, anxiety stabbing at his gut. "Is she all right?" He shoved the chair back and rose.

"She's fine. Just worried about you. And so am I." Ben motioned with one hand. "Sit back down. I want to talk to you."

Storme hesitated, jerking back in surprise as much at the unexpected command as at the harshness in Ben's tone. "There's nothing to talk about. I'm fine," he insisted, reclaiming his seat.

"Sure you are," Ben grated. "You look about as fine as you did the day Pa died. I won't say you've got no call to be mad about what happened tonight. But I know you, Storme, and I don't want to see you beating yourself up with guilt over this. You've done everything you can to protect her."

A dull, aching despair spread through Storme. "I was certainly doing a hell of a lot sitting here at the house while she was being attacked, wasn't I?"

"It's not your fault."

"You're wrong, little brother. I had a bad feeling all evening that something was up. I should have figured out that the stampede was nothing more than a diversion to get me away from town."

Ben sighed and shook his head. "And what does your gut tell you now, Storme?" He leaned forward, resting his arms on the table. "Does it tell you when they're going to strike next, and where . . . or just that they will? What if it's me they come after? You going to be able to figure out their plans ahead of time and prevent it?''

"I'm going to damn well try." Storme's irritation mounted at his brother's pointed questions. He gripped his hands around the warm coffee cup. "What's your point, little brother?''

Ben narrowed his eyes assessingly. "That you're not to blame for what happened tonight, any more than you are for what happened to Pa all those years ago, and you won't be responsible for whatever happens to me. And I don't want guilt over all this to drive your decision toward leaving this time''— his tone lost the hard edge—"like it did when Pa died.''

Storme took a long, deep breath and let his shoulders relax. He couldn't deny his brother's claim. Guilt *had* played a role in his choice to leave home. He wasn't sure it wouldn't come knocking again, either. But he knew how much Ben wanted him to stay, had seen his brother's growing interest every time he talked about possibly becoming a lawyer. "I'll do my best to make sure it doesn't. And as long as nothing happens to you, it won't be a problem.''

Ben arched one eyebrow. "What about Anna?''

Storme swallowed. "She'll be safe. Anna's planning to leave town soon." And he intended to make sure she did—on the first train out tomorrow. A hard lump lodged in his throat, choking his breath.

Ben slowly nodded. "That's why you keep saying you're just friends, I take it?''

No . . . that's why his heart was breaking. "Yeah.''

"Well, I'm sorry to hear that. I can see she means a great deal to you.''

Storme took a drink of the warm brew, forcing down the sadness that rose in his chest with engulfing intent. She meant everything to him. But Anna had dreams of singing and troubles of her own. Storme had nothing to offer her, except his love, and the prejudice that would always follow him. He couldn't protect her from the law, either. "It's for the best."

Ben eyed him doubtfully.

"She got a partial look at the rustler that attacked her," Storme said, hoping to block any further probing inquiries his brother thought to make. He wasn't in the mood to think about Anna leaving right now. Besides, he had something else on his mind he wanted to discuss with his brother.

Ben eased up straight and leaned back in the chair, the skepticism and questions fading from his brown stare. "Wallace told me how much she saw of the man. You got any idea who he might be?"

Storme had given a lot of thought to the man's description while he had been out walking, adding in all the other clues the rustlers had left, as well, and he didn't like the answer he kept circling back to. "You remember that army private who killed our father?"

Ben's jaw tightened. "Clyde Babcock. But he's dead. What does he have to do with this?"

"It's possible that man who attacked Anna is a relative out for revenge."

Ben furrowed his brow in thought. "All right, I give you the fact that the hair and eye coloring match up to that bastard, but I thought I was the only one who knew about you killing that private?"

Storme had debated all those years ago whether or not to tell Ben about the soldier's death. His brother had spent enough time with the Apache to learn the Indian ways of revenge, though, and had guessed the truth when the private came up missing, then confronted Storme with a demand for answers. But there had been no condemnation from his brother. Ben wanted that private dead just as much as Storme had. "That's what I thought, too, but look at what's happened so far. There's been too many subtle reminders of what I did to Clyde."

Ben cocked his head. "Shadow Canyon . . . the cattle left to

rot . . . the dead Mexican staked out,'' he whispered contempla-
tively, rubbing one hand over his chin. His stare widened with
a slow, dawning realization. ''You're right. That is too much
to ignore. So, what do we do now?''

Storme blew out a weighty sigh and shoved the cup of coffee
away. He shook his head in disgust. ''I wish I knew. But I still
don't have a clue about the rustlers' identity or how to find
them. Maybe the sheriff will pick up a trail on that man tonight.''

''Let's hope he does. If not, I guess we'll just have to wait
for them to make another move.''

Storme nodded, though sitting back was his least favorite
option, especially with the threats made against Ben's life. But
once he had Anna safely out of town, he could spend more
time watching out for his brother.

Ben pushed the chair back and rose. ''I'm going turn in
for the night. You can have my room. I'll sleep down in the
bunkhouse.''

Storme frowned. ''You don't need to do that. I can sleep on
the sofa in the office.''

Ben's stare drifted upward to the ceiling, where Storme knew
on the level right above was their father's old room. His worry
about Ben's feelings for Elise increased.

''Naw, I think I'll be more comfortable in the bunkhouse.''
He glanced down, a sly grin lifting one corner of his mouth.
''Besides, I figured you'd want to stay pretty close to Anna
tonight.''

Storme nodded. He would stay close to her every night if it
was possible. He carried both cups over to the sink as Ben
walked outside, closing the door behind him. Storme blew out
the candle and headed upstairs, passing by Ben's room and
stopping outside his own next door. He wanted to check on
Anna, wanted to make sure for himself that she was still all
right. He slowly eased the door open.

His heart pounded faster. Moonlight streamed through the
open window, casting a soft radiance on her long, gorgeous

hair spilled across his pillow. She was curled on her side, one pale, shapely leg resting on top of the sheet that covered her up to her waist. Not wanting to awaken her, he pulled his boots off, leaving them in the hall, then quietly closed the door and crossed over to the bed. She looked so peaceful, so pretty, he couldn't stop himself from running his finger along her smooth, creamy cheek. He lightly touched the bruise at the corner of her mouth, and a painful shudder rippled through him. *Damn.* Why hadn't he been there for her?

She stirred, her long, dark lashes fluttering. Storme pulled his hand back. A smile curved her mouth, and her eyes opened. "I've been waiting for you to come back."

Storme's heart tripped against his chest. He wished he could promise her that he would always come back, always be there for her. "How are you feeling?"

"Much better. I just needed a little rest." She sat up and scooted back against the headboard. The moonlight shimmered in her soft green eyes, lighting the flash of worry that sprang in their depths. "Elise told me that you left. Where did you go?"

He sat down on the edge of the bed. "Just out for a walk. I needed to do some thinking."

"About the rustlers?" She cocked her head and pulled her brows together. "You're not still blaming yourself for what happened tonight, are you? It wasn't your fault, Storme."

Hell yes, it's my fault. This revenge was against him, and she was in danger because he couldn't stay away from her. Storme brushed the hair back from her face, his fingers gliding through the silky, sleep-tousled strands. "I'm just glad that you're all right, Anna." He cupped his hand against her cheek, then leaned down, briefly pressing his lips to hers. "Go back to sleep."

"I *am* all right." She smiled, and circled her hand around his neck. "And I don't want to sleep." She pulled him down to her luscious mouth and kissed him with an urgency that made his heart soar, and his blood race to a pooling heat that throbbed in his loins.

Reluctantly, Storme tore his mouth away from hers and sat back before his desire could rage any hotter.

She ran her tongue along her bottom lip; a smoldering flame lit her hooded eyes. "Make love to me, Storme."

He took a deep breath, finding it far too easy to get lost in the sensuous way she looked at him. He shook his head. "You're hurt. I don't want to make it worse."

"You won't. You're always so gentle with me." She reached for his shirt, slowly undoing each button, igniting a rippling jolt of pleasure in him that strained his resistance.

Oh, how he wanted her, wanted to feel her beneath him, wanted to be inside her one last time before he put her on a train tomorrow and watched her ride out of his life, taking his heart with her forever. She pressed her warm palms against his bare chest, then slid her hands along his shoulders and down his arms as she pushed his shirt off, tossing the garment to the floor. Storme swallowed, hard, and captured her hands when she reached for the top button of his denims.

"Anna, you've had a rough night. You need to rest."

She shook her head. "I need you, Storme. I need to feel *you* touching me."

The plea in her voice ignited his regret, even as his passion for her grew stronger, drawing him closer to the smoldering flame in her stare. He closed his eyes and claimed her lips, his tongue hungrily exploring the recesses of her warm mouth. He worked the buttons loose and pushed the shirt aside. Gently, he trailed his fingers along her smooth skin, outlining one breast, a thrilled rush vibrating through him at the feel of the hardening bud. Storme pulled back, smiling as he stared into her softly flushed face. He eased the shirt from her shoulders, drinking his fill of her soft curves washed in the pale moonlight, hiding nothing of his fervor, his love for her as he met her stare. He stood to shed his pants, still holding her gaze with his own, then slipped between the sheets and took her into his arms. "I will make sure you have only good memories of tonight, little dove."

He captured her mouth in a slow, drugging kiss that sent Anna's heart soaring higher than his whispered promise had done. Oh, how she loved him. Needed him. His tender, kneading massage sent currents of desire raging through her. He slid his thigh on top of hers. Anna buried her hands in the thick, softness of his hair, then moved lower, caressing the hard contours of his back, his smooth, lean hips. She could feel his manhood pulsing against her hip, and heated need shot through her like liquid fire, pooling low.

He left her mouth, trailing kisses down her neck. She moaned in sweet ecstasy as his lips made a sensuous path along her breasts, capturing her taut nipple in a tantalizing kiss, firing her blood to a raging inferno that grew hotter as his hands stroked her stomach, her hips, down her thighs.

Storme took his time exploring every inch of her shapely curves. He worked his way back up, kissing her flat stomach, the bruises that ran along her ribs. Her thighs parted in welcoming response as his fingers touched the moist curls of her womanhood. He slipped inside to caress her velvety warmth, stroking deeper as she arched into his hand. He reached up, covering her mouth with his, swallowing her passionate cries, feeling the tremors that rippled through her limbs just before she exploded like warm honey against his touch.

Anna met his gaze as he moved to cover her with his hard, masculine body, reveling in his fervent stare. The moonlight caressed his skin in a golden hue. She ran her hands down his back, along his waist, arching upward as he slid inside her. His hands fired her flesh as he roved along her body, her heart pounding at the exquisite harmony of their joined bodies, moving in a sweet tempo that filled Anna with such desire, such love for this man and sent her soaring toward the peak of delight, then bursting in a white-hot release of ecstasy that shattered like a million stars behind her closed eyes.

A low growl issued from his throat as Storme followed her over the edge, lost in the rushing crescendo of heated ardor that hurtled him beyond the point of return and chased everything from his mind but his love, his need for this sweet, beautiful woman.

Storme stood on the front porch, watching the dawn crest on the horizon. He sipped his coffee, finding no joy in the birds' morning songs, or the sights and sounds of the ranch awakening to the new day as the hands moved about down at the barn. Instead, his heart beat with a heavy sadness. He had spent the early morning hours watching Anna sleep, enjoying the feel of her snuggled up against him, listening to her gentle breaths, her soft murmuring as she dreamed, hoping they were pleasant thoughts of him that brought the smile to her lips. He had never known such contentment as he had found having her in his home, his bed, nor a greater sorrow at knowing it couldn't last longer than one night.

He hadn't changed his mind about putting her on a train that day, but he wasn't looking forward to it, and wasn't at all certain that he would find the strength to go on with his own life once he did. The weight of his decision settled with crushing force in his soul. She would be safe, though, and that's all that mattered. He would have to tell her as soon as she awoke, so they could make the necessary arrangements.

He heard the soft footsteps crossing the foyer and glanced over his shoulder, a bittersweet smile curving his mouth as Anna walked out onto the porch. He turned, drinking in the sight of her as he raked an unabashed stare over the rose-flowered dress gently hugging her luscious curves.

"Good morning." Her smile spread wide, reaching her

lovely green eyes, and stealing his breath. She slipped her arms around his waist.

Storme set his cup down on the railing and pulled her into his embrace, careful not to hold her too tight as he recalled the bruises that rode across her ribs. Anger at the man who had dared to hurt her clawed at him, but Storme chased it away. He didn't want their last few hours together tainted with anything but sweet memories of what they had shared since meeting each other.

"How are you feeling?" He was glad she had left her hair down so he could run his hands through it one more time.

"Just fine," she whispered, her mouth curving in a mischievous smile. "Except you keep wandering off every time I go to sleep. I wish you'd stop that." She lifted up and kissed him, setting Storme aflame with her soft caress, her warm, eager exploration.

Anna frowned as Storme pulled back, puzzling at the sadness that hovered in his stare. But his warm smile heated her blood with distraction.

"Take a walk with me, Anna."

"All right." She eyed the blue-tin cup sitting on the railing. "Do you mind if I share your coffee?"

He smiled, reaching for the cup. "Not at all."

Anna took a welcome sip of the hot brew, then followed Storme down the steps. He took hold of her hand as they headed across the grass, leading the way around the side of the house and out toward the lush, sloping hills that graced the valley. The first rays of dawn tinged the sky in a brilliant blaze of pinks and pale blue. Anna glanced over her shoulder at the two-story structure, thinking how her mama had always wanted to have a big house near the mountains, then up at Storme. "You have a nice home."

"I'm glad you like it."

She nodded. Of course, she hadn't seen much of it, except his bedroom, but she didn't mind. She wouldn't trade the night she had spent in his arms for anything in the world. She only wished she could spend every night with him . . . but she knew that was a foolish dream. Nothing had changed for them. She would still have to leave town when she had the money.

Anna took another sip of coffee then handed the cup to him and shifted her gaze over the barn and numerous outbuildings spread out below. She could hear the faint sounds of cattle bawling, mingling with the birds that chirped their revelry as the morning skies slowly lightened, chasing away the remnants of the night. It was so peaceful. *No wonder Storme misses his home so much.* She sighed, wishing with all her heart that things could be different for him . . . for them.

They walked along for several minutes, sharing the cup of coffee, then Storme shifted course slightly and headed for a tall, lone oak, stopping beneath the wide branches. He tossed the empty cup to the ground and turned to face her, tightening his hold on her hand. A sudden uneasiness coursed through Anna's veins at the burning gravity that gleamed in his dark eyes.

"Anna, I've been doing a lot of thinking about what happened to you last night.

She placed her palm against his hardened jaw. "I'm fine, Storme. Really, I am. I realized that he must have been watching the building while we practiced, and I made a bad mistake going back alone. I won't make that mistake again."

"I'm not going to risk letting the rustler have that kind of chance again, either. Anna, I want you to leave town. Today."

Her heart stopped. She lowered her hand from his face and blinked back the tears that rose with flooding force as the pain ripped through her limbs. *No!* She didn't want to leave. She wasn't ready to give him up. Not yet. "I can't. I haven't saved enough money yet."

"I'll give you the money."

Her pride, as well as her reluctance to leave him, fueled her response, that and her growing panic at the thought of never seeing him again. *Please, God.* She wanted more time. "No, I won't take it."

"I want you out of harm's way." He rubbed his thumb in a slow circular motion along the top of her hand, his touch sending tingles along her skin.

"I told you I wouldn't go anywhere alone again."

"This isn't about believing you, darling. It's about you being safe. And you will be, as soon as you leave town."

She knew he was only trying to protect her, and his concern warmed her heart, even as he was breaking it with his insistence. "I have a job, Storme. And I promised Mrs. Harrington I would sing in the extravaganza. I'm still giving Belle lessons, too. I can't leave right now."

"None of that is more important than your safety," he argued. "Don't be stubborn about this."

"Then stop trying to get rid of me. I'll leave when I'm ready." She couldn't stop the tears that slid from her eyes. "Besides, I'm running from the law, and you said yourself that I'm safe here for now because *you* found the wanted poster. I refuse to run away just because you're having trouble with these rustlers. I'm not afraid, Storme. You've done so much for me. I want to help you now. I did get a look at him. I might recognize him if I saw him again."

"I don't want you close enough to get a look at him." He reached up and wiped the moisture from her cheeks. Damn! He hadn't meant to make her cry. He hadn't expected her to put up a fight about this, either. It only made him love her more that she didn't want to leave because of his troubles, that she was as willing to stand by him on this as she was against the townsfolk in defense of their relationship. But it didn't lessen his worry, though it did start him to seriously waffle over his decision. He sure as hell didn't want her to go. "And I appreciate that you want to help, but—"

"No." She pressed one finger against his mouth. "Please,

Storme, I don't want to argue about this. Besides, it's not your decision to make. It's mine. And I'm not leaving, not today.''

Storme was torn between elation and fear, but he couldn't argue with the fact that it *was* her decision. He had no hold on her, save the love he felt, and short of bodily putting her on the train, he knew he couldn't force her to go. ''Are you sure?''

She nodded.

Storme's pulse raced. ''All right, if that's your decision. But you're going to move out here. I'm not letting you stay at the boardinghouse.''

Anna cocked her head and eyed him skeptically. ''Now, you know Mrs. Harrington will never agree to that. And I can't afford to lose my job. You know that, too.''

Stubborn woman. Storme clenched his jaw. He was getting damn tired of this argument about her job. Why wouldn't she just take his money? ''Fine, then I'll move the whole damn boardinghouse out here, but you're not going back.''

Her smile sent heat coursing through his heart. She lifted up on her toes, bringing her mouth close to his. ''Now who's being stubborn?''

Chapter Eighteen

Storme led the horses from the barn, then backed the pair of bays up close to the buckboard and set about securing the harness. He glanced over where one of the wranglers finished hooking a team of horses to another wagon.

"Which straw did you draw, Lazaro?"

The *vaquero* looked up through hooded eyes. His grin lifted one corner of his black mustache. "The short one."

Storme smiled. "Good draw." And the favored choice among the wranglers when Winston had had the men draw straws earlier that morning to decide their time off for the Fourth of July Celebration. Long straws enjoyed the daytime festivities. Short straws would come in for the dancing and fireworks in the evening.

Lazaro pulled his mouth downward, forming a thin line. "Us being short-handed, this would be a good night for the rustlers to hit again."

Storme frowned, nodding his agreement. But since the attempt to kidnap Anna three nights earlier, there hadn't been any sign of the rustlers. He had a strong suspicion that this vengeance had moved to a new level, and they were done raiding cattle.

After fleeing the Meeting Hall, the rustler had headed through the mountains, and the sheriff had lost his trail. Storme hadn't had any better luck picking it up the next day, either, still leaving him with no more to go on than Anna's description and his gut sense that this revenge had to do with the private's death. Sheriff Hadley still hadn't heard anything from the sheriff in El Paso about that bank robbery, but Storme was hopeful news would arrive soon, and with any luck would bring him closer to identifying who was behind this vengeance.

The *vaquero* tilted his head back. "If you think they might strike, why do you let so many of us go to town at one time?"

Storme finished with the harness and rested his hand on the horse's back, staring across at the wrangler. He smiled. "Because my gut says even stronger that they won't, and you boys have worked hard. You deserve a break. Besides, a man needs to take a day off from his troubles every now and then." And that's exactly what Storme intended. He was going to enjoy this day with Anna and forget their troubles for a while.

"You are a good boss." Lazaro smiled, then pointed up the hill. "It looks like the girls are finally ready."

Storme turned around, his gaze falling on Anna. She stood on the front porch with the other girls from the boardinghouse. Storme chuckled as he watched Samantha sidestep Sebastian's gray paw swatting at her skirts, and recalled Miss Crowley's insistence that the 'mangy runt' be left behind in town . . . and Anna's just as adamant refusal. Anna came down the steps, smiling as she talked with the others.

She looked so happy, so pretty. She took his breath away. His smile grew wider as he raked his gaze over the green dress. He recalled her wearing it the night of Elise's wedding, and how the sunlight had shimmered on the gauzy lace, and glistened on her pale shoulders and arms. He couldn't wait for her to get closer. He hadn't had a glimpse of her lovely limbs in three days.

His gaze slid past the girls to Mrs. Harrington as she came out of the house, followed by Winston and three cowhands loaded down with valises and picnic baskets. Storme had been forced to follow through and move everyone out to the ranch in order to satisfy Mrs. Harrington and spare Anna's job and reputation. He frowned, recalling his plan to let Anna stay in his room and put the housemother down at the end of the hall in his father's old room. But Mrs. Harrington had insisted that Ben's room would be just fine, and with the woman's keen hearing, Storme hadn't dared to sneak in at night to be with Anna.

They had managed a few stolen moments for kissing, though, and Storme loved having her in his home. Maria had been glad for the company, too, and had expressed her appreciation of Anna's offer to help out with the chores while the housekeeper took care of her husband. Doc had ridden out just the day before, and, to Storme's relief, had said Garcia's leg was healing nicely.

The wranglers hadn't seemed to mind having the girls stay here, either, or escorting them to and from the restaurant every day. But for tonight, Mrs. Harrington had suggested it would be best to stay in town, since the fireworks wouldn't be over until late, and it was such a long trip back to the ranch. Storme had agreed, on the condition that he and Ben would stay in the parlor, and had already arranged for four of the hands to stand watch later outside the boardinghouse.

The group arrived at the wagons, their chatter and giggles filling the air as the hands loaded the bags and baskets in one wagon, then helped the girls climb into the back of the other. Caroline and Mrs. Harrington claimed the bench seat of the wagon Winston was driving.

Storme helped Anna climb up to the wagon seat of the other so she could ride beside him, whispering in her ear, "You look beautiful,'' and letting his hand glide down the length of her loose silky hair.

She smiled, a slight blush rising to her cheeks, and firing Storme's blood with renewed resolve that he would find a way to spend some time alone with her today.

Storme drove the wagon bearing all the girls, discouraging any private talk between him and Anna on the ride into town. They arrived as the late-morning sun hovered above, shedding its brilliance on the bustling crowd that filled the streets. Scalloped banners of red, white, and blue had been draped along the outside the various businesses, and several folks were lined up outside the mercantile to buy ice cream while they waited for the parade to begin.

Storme headed down the lane toward the boardinghouse, then pulled back on the reins, bringing the team to a stop. Winston guided the other wagon in beside them. Ben and the hands riding behind dismounted, tying their horses to the hitching post. Once the teams were unhitched and the valises carried inside, the group set out on foot toward town. Storme stayed to the back with Anna, slowing his steps until the others were a good way ahead, then he took hold of her hand and switched direction, heading for the stand of woods behind the train depot.

"What are you doing?" Anna questioned, arching one auburn eyebrow.

"I forgot something."

"Oh, and what is that, Mr. Warwick?" Her voice held a knowing tone of excitement.

"I forgot to tell you how lovely you look today."

"No, you didn't. You told me at the ranch," she lightly countered.

Storme glanced over, arching his brow and smiling. "No, I said you looked beautiful." He pulled her behind the sheltering privacy of the tall cottonwood and circled his arms around her back, gazing into her pretty green stare. "And you are." He leaned down and captured her warm, luscious mouth.

Anna's heart soared as she hungrily kissed him back. She slid her hands along the corded lines of his shoulders, her fingers tracing the beaded leather around his neck before circling around to the thick softness of his long hair. As much as she had enjoyed being out at the ranch with him, she had missed him terribly. Between Mrs. Harrington's ever-watchful eye and the girls' presence, they hadn't had a chance to be alone for more than a few minutes, and she had been giving considerable thought to how they could find a way to be together later that day.

Her blood tingled as he ran his hands along her back, then over her hips and up to cup her breasts. She pressed her palms against his shirtfront, loving the feel of his hard chest and the hard pounding of his heart beneath her touch. His thumbs brushed across her hardened nipples, sending jolts of desire coursing through her stomach and a liquid fire swirling lower. She tore her mouth from his, and gazed up into his dark, hooded stare. "Stop, you're going to muss me all up."

He smiled. "I definitely intend to do that, and more," he whispered.

"And I intend to let you." Anna grinned, then stepped back, smoothing her hands down the front of her skirt. "But not until after the extravaganza."

"If you're worried about your dress getting wrinkled, I have no problem with taking it off."

She chuckled, swatting at his hands as he reached behind her to the buttons. "I know you don't, but you're going to have to wait until after I sing."

He rested his hands on her shoulders, his face pulling into a mock frown. "You drive a hard bargain, Miss Alexander." He leaned down and brushed his lips to hers. "But I'm a patient man."

Anna knew he spoke the truth. He *was* patient, especially with the uproar of having so many females in his home. The girls were quite concerned for her when they were told about the rustlers' threats, but they were enjoying their stay at the ranch, and the attention of the wranglers—even Samantha, though she made sure to let the men know she was being courted by Blaine.

Storme trailed his fingers slowly down her arms, then took hold of her hands, lifting them up to place a kiss on the backs. "Are you nervous?"

Anna shrugged one shoulder. "A little." Then she drew her eyebrows together. "Storme, there's a lot of people here for the celebration. What if someone has seen my wanted poster and recognizes me?"

"They're all here to have fun, Anna. They won't be thinking about outlaws and wanted posters. It'll be fine," he assured her, hoping like hell he was right. The possibility of her being recognized had crossed his mind more than once over the last couple of days and prompted him to formulate several plans of escape if that happened. "I won't let anything happen to you. I promise."

She nodded her belief, then cocked her head, the corners of her mouth turning down. "Do you think of me as an outlaw, Storme?"

He shook his head. "That is a just a problem. It's not you. I think you're a smart, talented, beautiful woman"—he leaned down closer, smiling—"who doesn't kiss me near often enough."

Tears of happiness swelled behind Anna's closed eyes as he moved his mouth over hers in a tender exploration. The more time she spent with him, the deeper she fell in love, and the harder her sorrow seeped in when she forced herself to remember they couldn't be together forever. It was only a matter of time before he caught the rustlers, then she knew he would be leaving town . . . and before long, she would be gone, as well.

Storme pulled back, frowning as he wiped the tears that trickled from the corner of her eyes. "Why are you crying?"

She sighed, a small smile of enchantment touching her lips.

"Because you're so nice to me, and you worry about me . . . and you make me happy."

Storme's heart pounded faster. He released a slow sigh of contentment. "I'm glad, Anna. I know you have brought much happiness into my life."

She reached her arms around his neck. Storme circled her waist and held her tight, wishing they could stay like this forever. But he knew when the time came for them to part, that joyous light would be extinguished for the rest of the days he walked this earth. He shoved the sadness aside. He would have time for grief later. Today, he just wanted to enjoy being with her.

They watched the parade, and ate their picnic lunch in the grassy shade behind the mercantile with Winston and Caroline and Blaine and Samantha. Wallace and Elise came to join them later. Storme found as much enjoyment in watching Anna's excitement over the festivities and talking with her friends as he did in the attention she gave him. More than once, she had placed her hand through the crook of his arm while they were walking, or touched his shoulder as she whispered something in his ear, mindless of the stares from several folks . . . but Storme wasn't. He had seen the Garden Society ladies scowling at them, seen a few other looks of dislike aimed his way. There were plenty of other folks, though, who stopped to visit with them. When the horse racing started, Storme couldn't stop himself from chuckling out loud, along with Ben, as they stood watching Caroline and Anna jumping up and down like kids, cheering Winston on to victory.

But despite the fun he was having, Storme couldn't completely put the rustlers out of his mind. Every time he saw a black-haired stranger with blue eyes, he found himself searching his face for signs that he might be related to that private, and out for revenge. Always afterward, he would take hold of Anna's hand in reassurance to himself that she was safe, then search the crowd, looking for his brother, just to make sure nothing was amiss.

As the afternoon wore on, Anna asked him to bring her some iced tea to soothe her throat before the extravaganza started, and as they stood on the walkway in front of the mercantile while she drank the cool beverage, Storme shifted his glance over the people gathered along Main Street. He slid his stare past a stout, trail-dusty stranger, then jerked back. His pulse kicked up speed. Storme narrowed his eyes at the tanned, square-jawed face. Damn! He knew that man. They had chased the same bounty a time or two. Storme's stomach clenched into a hard knot.

He glanced down at Anna's pretty, flushed face, then back at Rafe Clever standing near the sheriff's office. He needed to find out what Rafe was doing here and if it involved Anna. In case it did, he knew he couldn't go strolling over there with her at his side, but he couldn't leave her alone.

To his relief, Storme saw Ben talking with Hal Hankins across the road. He caught his brother's eye and signaled for him to come over. Then he looked down at Anna, forcing a smile to his lips. "Is that helping your throat?"

"Yes, thanks."

Storme nodded. "Good. You stay and finish that. I'm going to have Ben stay with you while I run over to the sheriff's office for a minute."

She paused in mid-swallow, drawing her brows together. "Is something wrong?"

Storme didn't want to lie to her, but he didn't want to worry her right before she had to sing, either, especially if it turned out there wasn't any reason. Rafe could be here looking for anybody. "Nothing for you to worry about, darling," he answered low and even. "Just something I want to check out, all right?"

She hesitated, then nodded, her gaze gleaming with a bright

trust that nagged at Storme's conscience. He looked up as Ben climbed the mercantile steps. "I need you to stay with Anna."

"Sure, where you going?"

"Over to the sheriff's office." Storme smiled at Anna reassuringly, promising to be right back, then walked over and paused beside his brother, placing one hand on his shoulder. "Don't let anyone get close to her," he stated low enough so Anna couldn't hear above the noise of the crowd, and stared hard into his brother's eyes. "For any reason."

"All right," Ben whispered, nodding. "Is something wrong?"

"Just stay with her until I get back." Storme headed down the steps and across the road, his sight focused on the bounty hunter walking into the sheriff's office. Storme followed less than a minute later. He stopped just inside the room and shoved the door closed.

Rafe spun around, a grin slowly lifting his mouth. "Warwick? What a surprise. It's been a long time."

"Yeah, it has." He kept his tone casual and glanced around, grateful that Sheriff Hadley was nowhere in sight. He strode a little farther into the room, and shook the man's proffered hand. "What brings you to town?"

"A bounty, of course. What are you doing here?"

"I'm home visiting my brother, and looking for some cattle rustlers. Who are you chasing?"

"I'm after a woman."

Storme's heart hammered against his ribs, belying the calm, curious expression he forced. "Really? What she wanted for?"

Amusement flickered in Rafe's brown stare. His eyebrows arched high. "You've never struck me as being a stupid man, Storme. I'll lay odds that you're fully aware that woman you just bought iced tea for is wanted for murder."

Something is badly wrong. Anna clenched her hands into fists, her short nails digging into her palms. She bit her lip as she glanced at the stage where Katie and Patricia were singing, then out over the crowd gathered in the Meeting Hall. Women fanned themselves against the late-afternoon heat and sipped at iced drinks; most of the men had shed their coats and rolled back the sleeves on their shirts. Storme was nowhere in sight, and Anna was starting to panic.

The extravaganza was half over, and she hadn't seen him since he left the mercantile well over an hour ago. Throughout the day, she had seen him staring at any stranger who bore a resemblance to the rustler who had tried to kidnap her. Anna had glanced at every dark-haired man, as well, and the ones with blue eyes had all looked like possible suspects. Which made her realize she hadn't gotten as good a look at the rustler as she thought.

But had Storme seen someone he recognized? Is that what he needed to *'check out?'*

Anna frowned. If it had to do with the rustlers, why wouldn't Storme have said so? She blew out a weighty sigh. The longer he stayed gone, the more she feared it had something to do with her. Had her wanted poster turned up in town again? Had someone recognized her?

A large hand settled on her shoulder. Anna glanced back at Ben.

"He'll be back," he whispered.

She forced a weak smile, and nodded. She appreciated Ben's assurance, but it did nothing to settle her mounting worry. Ben didn't know about the trouble nipping at her heels. Belle came up to her side, drawing Anna's attention. She smiled at the girl and placed one arm around her slender shoulders, recalling with pride how well Belle had sung her song earlier.

Anna sighed, glancing back at the stage. She half watched the rest of the musical parody as she continued to fret over Storme's absence and kept glancing toward the opened front door, hoping he would come walking in soon. When the girls finished, and the applause died down, Sally Hankins made her way to the center of the stage to announce the next song.

"Good luck," Belle said, staring up with her violet eyes.

"Thanks." Anna glanced back briefly at Ben, seeing him shake his head in apology that Storme hadn't returned, then she made her way up the steps and out onto the stage. Anna forced herself to shift her gaze over the crowd as she sang, but her attention kept sliding toward the door. She was on the last verse when Storme appeared in the doorway, and the relief that washed through her at the warm smile on his face nearly made her forget the words. She didn't take her eyes from him until the song was done. He applauded along with the others in the hall. Anna saw him narrow his gaze and nod toward the side of the building. She smiled her understanding, then quickly hurried from the stage.

She hadn't seen anything in his expression to give her cause to worry, but why had he been gone so long? Anna desperately grasped at the relief that he had returned, and told herself everything was fine. Ben followed her as she wove a short path through the group of performers blocking the back door, then outside.

Anna ran ahead toward the side, then slowed her steps, sighing as Storme rounded the back corner of the building. "Why were you gone so long?"

He didn't say anything, but pulled her into his embrace.

"Is everything all right?" Ben questioned in a disquiet tone.

"Yes. Fine."

Anna's last thread of calm snapped at the sharp edge in Storme's voice and the way he tightened his arms around her. Everything wasn't fine. She could sense it in his tensed muscles. Anna moved back out of his embrace, frowning up at the hard set of his jaw.

"I just ran into a friend of mine. He needed a little help," Storme added in a calmer voice, as though he realized the cutting note that had come out before. "Thanks for staying with her, little brother."

Ben nodded, smiling. "No problem. By the way, Anna, you sounded great."

She smiled back. "Thanks."

Storme took hold of her hand. "Are you finished here?"

She swallowed. His tight grip shot worry through her veins, and reinforced her certainty that things weren't fine. She could hear the Holley twins singing the lively tune about the little dog, and knew the musical was drawing to a close. She nodded.

Storme shifted his gaze past her to his brother. "I'm going to take Anna for a walk. We'll see you later."

She said good-bye to Ben, then fell into step beside Storme as they headed down the road toward town.

"My brother's right," Storme said, his brown gaze burning bright with admiration. "You sounded wonderful. I'm sorry I missed most of your song, though."

"Storme, what's wrong? Why were gone so long?" She placed her hand on his arm. "Why are you so tense?"

He sighed. His shoulders slumped slightly, and his faced pulled into a hard frown. "Let's wait until we're alone."

Anna glanced around, seeing some of the menfolk who hadn't been interested in the musical standing around in conversation. "Where are we going?"

"Just over to the boardinghouse."

Anna nodded, shivering slightly at the prickling dread that crawled up her spine. *Oh God! What's happened?* Her mind whirled, seeking possibilities. Only one thought kept surfacing—someone had found out her real identity.

She walked beside him in silence as they crossed Main Street and continued in their quick, clipped stride down the narrow lane. He wove a path around the wagons parked out front, then stopped outside the gate and pulled her into his embrace. She rested her cheek against his chest, could feel his heart pounding. He placed his chin lightly atop her head. She wrapped her arms around his waist, her fear increasing at the way he clung to her, as though he might never have the chance to hold her again.

"Storme, tell me what happened."

He sighed, then pulled back, gripping her shoulders, a haunting pain shining in his intent gaze. "When we were at the mercantile, I spotted a man I recognized standing over by the sheriff's office. Another bounty hunter."

Anna tensed, her blood stilling. She swallowed, slowly. "He knows about me, doesn't he?" Storme nodded, and the bottom fell out of her stomach.

"Rafe got a lead from a station clerk in Kansas City. The man remembered an old woman with green eyes and who didn't look quite as old as she acted. The clerk also remembered that you had bought a ticket to Pleasant Grove. Rafe came looking for you. He saw us together earlier." Her eyes rounded in shock. Storme gently ran his hands along the top of her shoulders, feeling the tremors that shook her body. "But it's all right, Anna. He's gone."

She blinked her surprise. "How did you get him to leave?"

"I told him as much of the truth as I could—that I knew you weren't guilty, and I was trying to prove it. Then I offered him twice the reward on you if he'd agree to forget he ever saw you and leave town. I didn't want to ride out to the ranch to get the money, so I had to find Joe Montgomery and talk him into opening the bank for me. That's what took so long."

Doubts still singed the sparkle from her eyes. "And you trust this bounty hunter?"

"Yes." Storme knew some bounty hunters only cared about money, but most of them were willing to help each other out and could be trusted. "I've worked with Rafe before. He's always been a man of his word. And he also agreed that he if ran across anyone else looking for you, he'd tell them he had a lead that you're headed north."

She hesitated. "So . . . I'm safe?"

Storme nodded.

Anna's heart swelled with love, and warm comfort eased through her. Once again, Storme had been there when she needed him . . . like a guardian angel, always watching out for her, and deepening her trust, her soul-filled belief that she would always be safe with him.

"But only for right now," he cautioned, the dismay in his voice chasing her relief away. "Rafe came looking. Others will, too."

Anna swallowed as a cold knot of pain closed over her heart. She knew he was right. She shut her eyes, blocking out the expression on Storme's face. She also knew what he was going to say . . .

"Anna, you need to leave town."

But the words still ripped through her like flaming daggers, and the tears rose in stinging floods.

"I'm going to give you the money you need, and I want you on the first train out tomorrow," he continued. "As soon as you reach California, you get on the first boat you can."

An icy shiver raced through her blood. She knew she had no choice. If she had any hope for a future that didn't involve going to jail or swinging from a rope, she must leave while she had the chance. The pain sliced deeper. She reminded herself that she had known all along they would have to part sometime. Anguish clogged her throat. Oh God, she didn't want to go. She didn't want to leave him. She bit her lips as the sobs choked her.

He cupped her face in his hands, and brushed her tears away with his thumbs, but more fell to replace them, breaking his heart into even smaller pieces. She wasn't arguing with him this time, and he was fairly certain by the sad resignation in her eyes that she wasn't going to, but he wanted her promise. He had to know that she would do this for him, that she would be safe, and could have her dreams of singing. "Anna, you asked me to give you a chance at freedom for the life-debt I owed. Let me fulfill that promise. Tell me you'll take the money and leave town.''

Her shoulders slumped, and a small sigh escaped her lips. She nodded, slowly, then she slipped her arms around his neck. ''Hold me, Storme, please. Just for a minute.''

He wrapped his arms around her, pulling her close. He wished he could promise to hold her for a lifetime, wished like hell there was some way he could prove her innocence, some way he could keep her here. But the rustlers and their threats were breathing down his neck, and her troubles were about to catch up with her. Their time had run out, and the full realization sank in hard, striking his soul like hammerblows. Storme couldn't stop the moisture that filled his eyes. He was going to miss her so much.

He held her for a long time, until he felt her body stop shaking with her tears, and her sighs whispered through the thin cotton of his shirt; until the sun dipped lower in its descent toward evening, and the people had long since left the Meeting Hall and could be heard milling about Main Street as they waited for the dancing to start.

She pulled back slightly and gazed up at him with her sad, swollen eyes. Storme ran one finger gently along her cheek. ''We still have tonight, Anna,'' he whispered, grasping at the last thread of happiness before she boarded that train tomorrow, and left him to travel a lonely road of sadness for the rest of his life.

She nodded, a slow smile curving her beautiful mouth. The sparkle of desire flamed low in her green eyes, and sent his heart soaring, his blood heating with a need only she could fulfill.

Anna had been thinking about their last night together, as well. Her last chance to be in held in the comfort of his arms, to be with this man she loved with every fiber of her being, who would always hold her heart, no matter where she went. She wanted just a few more memories to take with her, knowing she would need them after she had left, and the grief of never seeing him again settled in to haunt the rest of her life. "Let's go to the mountains, Storme."

He smiled, even as he lifted one eyebrow in a questioning arc. "I would like nothing more. But what about the dancing, and the fireworks? You've talked about them all day. And I do owe you a dance."

Anna rested her palm against the strong line of his jaw. "I'll sing for you, and we can dance in the mountains. We'll build a fire by the stream to light the sky. I just want to be alone with you, Storme." She reached up, and pressed her mouth to his, parting her lips in an urgent quest that matched the velvet stroke of his tongue.

Storme broke off their kiss, the sensuous light in his dark, narrowed gaze making her heart trip in eager response and firing her blood even hotter. "We'll do all that, Anna, but there's another place I'd rather take you. There's a cave I know of in the mountains. We can be alone there and not have to worry about any of our troubles following us."

Anna nodded.

Before leaving town, they went to find Ben so Storme could tell him they were taking his horse, and so he could let the others know there wasn't any need to worry about them. Then they gathered blankets and food from the boardinghouse and headed out. In silent agreement, they didn't talk about her pending departure, or their troubles, as they rode high into the mountains, but shared stories of their childhood, each tucking away every detail like a cherished jewel of fond remembrances that they could pull out later when the sadness of being apart came to greet them. Storme brought up her dream about singing, but Anna couldn't find any enthusiasm in his compliments, or his assurances that any theater troupe would be lucky to have her in their show, only reminders of the reasons she had to leave, had to sail away where she would never see him again, and she had quickly changed the subject.

By the time twilight fell on the mountains, Anna had spread a makeshift pallet just inside the shallow cave, and Storme had built a small fire against the dropping temperature. She stood at the entrance, listening to the crickets chirp. She glanced around at the peaceful beauty of the tall spruce and fir trees, and the stars gathering overhead, then her gaze fell on Storme as he finished hobbling Ben's horse a few feet away on the narrow grassy mesa. He strode toward her, his smile warming her with contentment, even as it singed her blood with longing.

He removed his hat and tossed it to the ground, then did the same with his gun belt before he embraced her and captured her mouth, shattering her calm with a hunger that swelled her heart with deepening love and ignited a pool of liquid heat low in her stomach.

She ran her hands along his shoulders, then trailed her fingers down his chest. He covered her hands with his, stopping her when she reached for the buttons on his shirt. Anna tore her mouth away, glancing up.

He smiled. "Sing for me," he whispered. "I want to dance with you first."

She sang the song she had performed at Elise's wedding and melted in Storme's arms as he waltzed with her by the light of the fire, and when she finished, he asked her to sing another. But this time, she hummed more than she sang as their lips kept meeting, and their steps grew slower.

Then they slowly undressed each other. Anna drank in the sight of his bronze, muscled frame, brushed to a soft gold in the firelight, memorizing every inch of his handsome strength. He made slow, passionate love to her, whispering sweet affections as he stroked her with his gentle hands, his tender mouth, then melded his body with hers, taking her on a soaring journey that brought tears of ecstasy to her eyes as she cried out his name.

As they lay in the afterglow of their lovemaking, Storme braced himself on one elbow, staring down into Anna's face.

He lightly ran his finger along her cheek, then brushed through the gossamer strands of her hair. An owl hooted from a nearby tree. Storme paused, frowning at the knot that suddenly tightened his gut. He looked out over the grassy mesa, softly lit by the moon's full glow and the low fire beside them. He didn't follow many of the Apache ways anymore, but there were some beliefs he hadn't given up. An owl's hoot near a camp is a bad omen.

"Something wrong?" Anna placed her palm against his face.

He shook aside the uneasy feeling. Storme captured her hand and brought it to his lips. He looked into her worried gaze and shook his head as he kissed her hand. Tonight, he wasn't thinking of anything but her. He smiled. "I just need to kiss you again."

The night hours moved along, and Storme burned every soft moan and look she gave, every touch, every pale, luscious curve of her into his mind as they made love. When she dozed off in the early-morning hours, he watched her sleep, listened to her soft breathing, and as his heart broke with the coming of the dawn, wished there was some way he could safely keep her with him.

Anna stood on the station platform under the burning glare of the noonday sun, and hugged the housemother. "Good-bye, Mrs. Harrington."

"Bye, dear. I'm sure going to miss you." The housemother embraced her in a tight squeeze, then stepped back. She shoved the spectacles up the bridge of her nose. "But I understand. You take care of yourself."

Anna nodded, swallowing the sadness that clogged her throat. She would never forget this kind woman.

When she and Storme returned from the mountains early this morning, Anna was surprised that Mrs. Harrington hadn't offered them any reproach for staying out together. But when she spoke with the housemother alone, intending to offer a lie for her reasons in needing to leave town today, Anna had been further shocked to learn that Mrs. Harrington had suspected she was in some kind of trouble from the day she hired on. The housemother explained that she seen an old woman get off the train and head toward the mountains, and had later seen Anna coming back. Mrs. Harrington didn't ask for any details, and Anna didn't offer them. Then the housemother had thanked her for singing in the musical, and expressed her delight that the investor had decided to build an opera house in town. The investor had also been impressed with Anna's performance and had wanted to talk to her about coming to Denver to sing in his show there. He had left his card with the housemother, and though Anna knew she couldn't go, she had tucked it away in her bag when she packed, anyway.

"All aboard!" the conductor called out, as people filed out from the restaurant after the brief stop for lunch.

Anna waved a final farewell to the girls—her friends—as they gathered outside. She had said her tearful good-byes at the boardinghouse, offering them the partial truth of her reasons for leaving town—that Storme thought it would be safer because of the rustlers and that she was giving thought to joining a small theater troupe somewhere. But there had been no half-truths in her heartfelt assurances that she was going to miss them all.

She turned away as her tears rose fresh and made her way with heavy steps toward the train, where Storme stood waiting, holding her valise and the ticket that would take her to California. They had said good-bye on the mountain, and Anna had wanted so badly to tell him how much she loved him. She had hoped Storme would say the same, would beg her to stay, promise her they would find a way to be together . . . but he hadn't. And she had kept her silence.

She didn't blame him. He couldn't fix her problem, and she was the one who had made the decision to run. It would have to be enough knowing that he cared about her, and had done so much to help her. She didn't want to burden him with any more by asking him to live with the knowledge that he would own her heart and soul forever.

"You have everything you need?" he softly questioned.

Anna's heart crumbled, and her tears came harder. *No, I don't have you any longer.* She blinked and nodded, knowing he meant the money she had safely tucked in her reticule. "Thank you, Storme. For everything." She lifted her palm to his cheek. "I . . ." She swallowed the words of love that rose. "I'll miss you, Storme. And I'll never forget you."

She watched the rise and fall of his chest as he took a deep breath and slowly released it. "I'll miss you, too, Anna. And you will be in my thoughts, always," he whispered the last.

The train whistle shrilled its final call, and billows of smoke drifted from under the cars to filter along the platform.

"You need to get on board, ma'am," the conductor said as he climbed the steps up to the passenger car.

Anna lowered her hand, and glanced over her shoulder, nodding to the portly man. She reached for her valise, but Storme leaned over and set the bag on the metal platform at the top of the steps, then handed her the ticket.

"Good-bye," she choked out on a sob, then bit her bottom lip as she reached up to give him a hug.

Storme wrapped his arms around her. Anna didn't care who watched. She pressed her lips to his and kissed him with all the love that swelled in her heart.

He lifted his head, and gazed into her eyes. "Good-bye, Anna." Then he leaned down and kissed her briefly again, and stepped back.

Anna grabbed the rail and climbed up on the bottom step as the train started to pull out. She turned, and stood there, gazing one last time at his handsome face, her heart weeping with sadness that her future couldn't be with him.

She saw Storme pass his hand over one eye, then he waved.

She waved back at him, then at the girls as the train pulled by, leaving the station. With every rackety-clack turn of the iron wheels, Storme drifted father from her view, and even when the train drew far enough ahead that she couldn't see him any longer, still Anna stood there on the step, watching as the town became only a small dot on the horizon, wishing there was some way she could stay.

The train picked up speed as it headed westward toward the mountains. Anna turned and climbed up to the platform between the two passenger cars. She bent down to retrieve her valise and reached for the brass knob on the door. Her fingers barely brushed the warm metal when the barrier was opened from the inside, and a tall man blocked her path.

"We meet again," he said, forcing her to move back as he stepped outside the car and closed the door.

Anna frowned at the vaguely familiar gravely voice, and peered hard at his sly grin and the deep scars that crisscrossed both of the stranger's cheeks. She lifted her gaze higher. "I'm afraid you're mistaken. I don't know you—" Shocked, she stared into his dark blue eyes and saw the tufts of black hair peeking out beneath his wide-brimmed hat. Her heart stopped as the memories of that night in the Meeting Hall came rushing in.

"I see you do remember me, pretty lady."

A sickening wave of terror rose in Anna's stomach. She backed up against the opposite car and opened her mouth to scream, barely issuing a squeak above the train's chugging clatter before he clamped his hand over her mouth. Anna swung her valise into his side.

He didn't even flinch, but glared at her through hooded eyes. "Don't fight me, or you'll regret it. And don't bite me again, either, or I'll make you *and* your Injun friend both suffer for it."

Anna froze, not doubting the seriousness in his tone. Fear for Storme constricted her throat. The dirty sweat from the rustler's hand assailed her nose in gagging threat. Her pulse racing with increased worry that he intended to use her to get to Storme, Anna bit into his palm and swung her bag at her assailant again.

"You bitch," he growled.

To Anna's dismay he didn't pull his hand away, but instead circled his free arm around her waist, jerking her against his chest, and lifting her off her feet. Then he carried her down to the bottom step and jumped off the train.

Chapter Nineteen

Storme lifted the whiskey bottle to his mouth, welcoming the warm liquid that slid down his throat, wishing it would hurry up and dull this ache inside him. He took another swallow, then rested the bottle against one denim-clad thigh. The vast array of stars twinkled overhead. The half-moon glowed bright against the velvet sky, and slowly crept higher toward the midnight hour, long past the time he knew the train would have stopped in Albuquerque for the night.

Was Anna asleep in her hotel room, he wondered. Or was she staring out the window, gazing up at this same sky . . . and thinking of him? His blood hummed at the latter thought. A small smile dared to rise over his sadness. He closed his eyes, relishing the sense of her spirit that sang through his soul. *Yes, she's thinking of me.* He could feel it.

Storme pictured her pretty face, recalled the vivid images of her soft, pale skin gleaming in the firelight at the cave last night . . . her tears as she had kissed him good-bye at the station this afternoon. He took a deep breath, only to have it lodge in his throat. Damn, he missed her. Storme blinked back the moisture that stung his eyes, and took another drink of whiskey. The humming dimmed in his veins. The memory of the owl's hoot slammed into his thoughts. He frowned at the sudden apprehension that clenched his gut.

No, Anna is safe. He had seen to that himself, had watched the train leave, taking her away from him for good. He didn't doubt the owl's bad omen, but he was certain it had been meant for him—a foreboding of this stark, gripping pain that he would somehow have to learn to endure. He had let his heart, his soul, love her more than he knew was wise, and now he would pay the price with loneliness . . . for the rest of his life.

He propped his booted foot against the front porch rail, leaned the chair back on two legs, and lifted the bottle, pounding down a long swallow. He stared out at the ranch shrouded in the hazy moonlight. The bunkhouses sat dark and quiet, but he knew the hands would be rising soon to head out and relieve the wranglers riding guard over the herd. The crickets chirped their songs into the night, and the occasional sounds of bawling cattle drifted up from the south pastures.

He sighed, and swallowed down the grief with another splash of the amber whiskey. He had thought more than once about getting on that train with her, and traveling wherever she wanted to go, wherever they had to go to keep her safe. But he couldn't leave right now. He had to deal with the rustlers, and he hadn't forgotten Ben's request that he stay at the ranch, either. Besides, Anna hadn't asked him to come along. She cared about him, Storme didn't question that, but she had never said she loved him, had never led him to believe she wanted anything more from him than what little time they had together.

In spite of that, though, he had come damn close several times to asking her to stay, of professing his love and making rash promises to protect her from the law. But he knew she wasn't safe here. He couldn't be sure that another bounty hunter or lawman wouldn't show up in town tomorrow, or the next day, or next week, and not be so inclined to look the other way as Rafe had done. Storme wasn't letting Anna go to jail—and certainly not hang. She deserved a future. She deserved to have her dream of singing onstage. Her happiness, her freedom, was worth whatever anguish he had to bear.

Storme lifted the bottle. The whiskey slid hard passed his choking sorrow. And what about the townsfolk? He was giving strong consideration to settling down at the ranch again. But how well would the folks around here tolerate that decision? How long before more adversity came riding in to taunt him? Storme tilted the bottle up. The whiskey burned a path down his throat, and settled like a rock in the pit of his stomach. His relationship with Anna had served to bring threats to her life by the rustlers and caused her to be shunned by several of the ladies. Even if she had wanted to stay, wanted to be with him, she had enough disturbance in her life without adding to it by taking on his troubles.

He wasn't sure he would be doing Ben any favors, either, if he stayed. His brother was well liked and respected in Pleasant Grove. Storme didn't want to do anything to change that for him. He sure as hell didn't want to see his brother meet the same fate their father had. Storme stared up at the moon again, a little surprised his brother hadn't come home yet. He had appreciated his brother being at the train station when Anna left. He had appreciated it just as much when Ben opted to stay behind in town for a while and give Storme some time alone.

A round of gunfire suddenly resounded from the north, echoing through the sky.

Storme paused with the bottle midway to his mouth, gauging the shot to be about a mile up the road. His gut tightened, and alarm raged full force through him. *Dammit! Where's Ben?*

Another blast sounded.

Storme dropped the chair back on all fours and stood, setting the whiskey bottle on top of the porch railing. He grabbed his gun belt and was strapping it on as he headed down the steps. A third shot resonated on the air. Halfway down the hill he saw a light shine through the windows of one of the bunkhouses, then Winston, Cale, and Lazaro came running outside and headed toward the barn, arriving at the same time Storme did.

"Reckon we got us some more trouble?" Winston raked a hand through his tousled red hair, then shoved his hat on his head.

Storme didn't want to think the worst just yet, but it was hard not to, especially since Ben wasn't home. "Either that, or someone's just trying to get our attention. Saddle up, and let's go find out." Storme turned to Cale and Lazaro. "You boys ride out and check the outskirts of the ranch, make sure no one's lurking around." Several more cowhands came running from the bunkhouse, shrugging into boots and gun belts along the way. Storme had some of the men ride out to check on things with the herd, and ordered the rest to stand guard here.

Several minutes later, the horses were saddled and Storme was riding fast along the ranch-yard road with Winston at his side. He reined the gelding back to a walk as the high iron arch loomed ahead, and pale moonbeams illuminated the arrow centered in the pathway underneath. A light breeze rustled the feathers on the long, narrow shaft.

"Damn, that looks like the rustlers' calling card." Winston issued a disgusted grunt, then turned his head to the side and spit a stream of tobacco juice into the dirt.

A cold knot fisted in Storme's gut as he stared at the white paper tacked to the dirt, surprised to see it was an envelope this time. He reined his mount to a halt and dismounted. Winston followed, wrapped a gloved hand around the top of the arrow, and yanked it up from the ground.

Storme leaned down and grabbed the envelope, frowning at the feel of the bulky contents inside. A hollow pit formed in his stomach as he ran one finger over the object, tracing out a small heart shape. Storme swallowed, hard, then turned the envelope over and tore the flap open. He reached inside, and his heart stopped when he felt the thin chain. Jolting pain stabbed at his chest as he pulled the pendant out.

No! It can't be Anna's necklace! Blood roared in his ears. He remembered seeing it around her neck at the train station. *How could the rustlers have gotten it?* Anna was gone. He stared at the broken chain, at the engraved *A*. The owl's bad omen rushed into his thoughts.

Winston pulled his eyebrows together in a furrowed line. "Is that . . . Miss Alexander's necklace?"

Storme clenched his jaw, and nodded. He reached into the envelope again and pulled out a slip of paper, then angled the note under the moonlight.

> *Your pretty lady didn't get far on that train.*
> *If you want to see her alive, meet me at Hoehne*
> *Pass at dawn. Come alone, or you'll find her dead.*
> *C. B.*

Fear for Anna pulsed through Storme in hammering waves and warred for space with his mounting anger. Hoehne Pass. The same place his father had been killed. Storme stared at the initials, wondering if they were just another reminder of Clyde Babcock, or if they belonged to a relative? He still didn't know who these rustlers were, but he didn't have any more doubts what this revenge was about.

"What's it say? You look madder than a peeled rattlesnake."

"The rustlers have Anna," he grated.

Winston issued a sharp whistle, then spit a stream of tobacco juice to the ground. "We'll get her back, Storme, don't worry."

"Damn right, I'll get her back." He stared off toward the

mountains, silhouetted like a dark rock rising in the distant north. Guilt settled deep in his soul. She was in terrible danger. He could strongly sense it, now that he wasn't wallowing in his sorrow at her departure. How could he have let her down? He had promised to protect her. All this time he had thought she was safely headed west on the train, and instead she was in trouble. She had needed him.

Storme's mind raced with a plan.

"We're gonna need some help, boss, I'll go round up the men—"

"No." Storme shoved the note and envelope in his front pants pocket and clutched the necklace tightly in his hand. "This trouble came calling because of me. This is my fight. I'm going alone."

"What about Ben? He's gonna wanna know about this, and ride along."

Storme knew Winston was right, but he wasn't taking any chances with his brother's life. He had enough to worry about just finding Anna and bringing her back safe. "When he gets home, tell him what happened. Tell him this revenge *does* have to do with the man who killed our father."

"You sure 'bout that now?"

Storme nodded. The day after Anna was attacked at the Meeting Hall, he had confided his suspicion to the foreman, though not the details of what he had done to the private, and purposely withheld the confirming information about Hoehne Pass now so Ben and Winston wouldn't follow. "Then I want you to make sure Ben stays put here at the ranch."

Winston arched his red eyebrows, his face registering a strong aversion to the order. "Well, that'll load him to the muzzle with anger. He'll take a big chunk outta my ass if I try to stop him from goin' after you."

Storme gathered up the reins and climbed into his saddle, then glanced down at the foreman. "I'll pay you extra for the damage. Just keep him here."

* * *

Darkness hovered in the predawn hour as Storme crawled on his belly through the grass, stopping behind the short scrubs. A horse's neigh sounded on the crisp cool air, and brought a surge of satisfaction pumping through Storme's blood that his hunch had paid off. Since the note said he would find Anna dead if he didn't come alone, Storme suspected that the rustlers planned to keep a close watch on Hoehne Pass, and wouldn't be camped too far away. He thought they would hide out in the mountains, though, and had started his search there, then worked his way around in a wide half-circle that had finally brought him to this narrow tributary of the east fork of the Pecos River, just north of where it started its slow flow through Lazy W land. He drew the Colt from his holster and eased the hammer back, locking it in place. With his free hand, he parted the leafy scrubs. Moonbeams shimmered like pale milk-glass on the shallow stream, and barely thirty yards away on the opposite bank a low burning fire illuminated the camp situated in a sparse group of cottonwoods and pines.

Storme's breath caught at the sight of Anna sitting on the ground near the campfire, her hands bound behind her back. The flame's soft glow spun gold in the loose strands of hair hanging in disarray about her shoulders. Light danced across her bloodless face, her widened stare, revealing her taut fear. One sleeve of her flowered dress had been ripped, exposing the creamy flesh of her upper arm. It tore at his soul to see her tied up and afraid. It grated at his thoughts, as it had throughout his search, wondering what she had been forced to endure since being kidnapped.

Storme glared at the black-haired Mexican who knelt on the ground beside her, strapping two sets of bulging saddlebags closed. A few yards off to one side, a broad-shouldered man had his head dipped down, his wide-brimmed hat concealing his face as he tied the leather rifle case to the large saddled bay standing near two other waiting mounts. The desire to avenge Anna's suffering raged strong through Storme. But given the number of horses, and his lack of knowledge as to how many were riding with this gang seeking revenge, he forced down the desire to shoot both men right now, not willing to risk Anna's exposed position by giving away his presence too soon.

The Mexican tossed the saddlebags up on one shoulder, then reached over and ran his fingers along Anna's cheek.

"Get away from me!" she snapped, as she jerked her head to one side.

"Leave her alone, Chavez. I told you I don't want your filthy hands on her until *after* I have my turn with her."

Storme's heart stopped mid-beat, as much at the unexpected familiar gravelly voice as at the threatened intent to Anna. He swung his attention to the man now glaring over the bay's back. *Clyde Babcock?*

Shock rippled through Storme's veins. *No, it can't be.* He stared at the man's long, thin face, at the shadowy crevices that marred his cheeks.

"Load those saddlebags up. I want to be at Hoehne Pass in plenty of time to greet that Injun right."

Storme swallowed his surprise; anger pulsed through him. He would never forget that voice, those beady eyes, that face he had cut so the ants could feast on his blood while the private slowly died beneath the broiling sun. All the clues clicked into place; all his questions of who could have known what he had done seven years ago were stunningly answered.

It is Clyde!

Storme shook his head. But how the hell had the private survived? And where had he been all these years? Storme glanced over at Anna's worn, frightened appearance, guilt tightening his gut, Clyde's vow to take away everything he cared about burning through his thoughts. The private had taken his father's life, threatened to do the same to his brother, and now kidnapped Anna. Storme's wrath rose like dark clouds swiftly building on the horizon. However Clyde had managed to escape death in Shadow Canyon, the man wouldn't be breathing for much longer.

"Hurry it up, Chavez." Clyde came around the front of the horse and sauntered over to the campfire. "Then go find out what's taking Rafael so damn long to take a piss."

Storme quickly scanned the darkness surrounding the outskirts of the camp, pleased at the confirming information about a third man. His thoughts raced as he calculated how fast he could get across and sneak through the shadows. If his luck was holding, he could surprise Chavez and Rafael before they had a chance to return to camp. Then he would deal with Clyde.

The Mexican rose to his feet, his pudgy, brown face registering dislike at being ordered around as he stared eye-to-eye with the private.

"Get your hands up! Now!" The harsh male voice rang out from the cover of the darkness.

What the— Confusion pounded in Storme's chest.

Anna jumped and shifted her body to look behind. Clyde and Chavez both made a reach for the guns strapped around their hips, then froze, and slowly lifted their hands above their heads.

Eyes narrowed in aggravated disbelief, Storme stared past the two men's backs to the tall white man emerging from the shadows at the west edge of the camp. The stranger held a long-barreled six-shooter in one hand, and had his other arm wrapped around the throat of a Mexican man whose hands were bound, his mouth gagged, and his short, thin body positioned in front as a human shield. Storme assumed the wide-eyed captive was Rafael. *But who the hell is that stranger?* Whoever he was, he would be a dead man if he brought any harm to Anna.

Storme watched her awkwardly rise to her knees, saw her foot catch on her hem, adding to her struggle to stand. His heart ached for her at this unwelcome development; his pulse hammered with added caution as to how to get her out of that camp.

"You!" The stranger waved his gun at Chavez. "Reach for that weapon real slow like, and toss it over here. Then I want the saddlebags to follow."

Chavez eased his right arm down, lifted the gun from his leather holster with two fingers, and tossed it onto the grass in the stranger's direction. Then he pulled the saddlebags off his shoulder. The leather pouches landed in a heap near the surrendered weapon.

With slow, cautious steps, the stranger moved himself and his human shield a little farther inside the camp, stopping several yards from the thrown objects. Yellow firelight shimmered over the man's tanned face. Straight blond hair hung long and loose beneath his black hat. "Your turn, Babcock."

"Who the hell are you?" Clyde demanded, making no move to comply.

"U.S. Marshal Jared Bray. You boys are under arrest for that bank robbery in El Paso." The lawman glanced over at Anna. "And it just so happens that I recognize you from your wanted poster, Miss Olsson. For whatever reason you ended up here with these fellas, looks like you'll be heading back to Missouri now."

Damn! Storme saw Anna stiffen, could sense her elevated alarm. Clyde and Chavez both straightened with a slight start, and whipped brief stares in her direction. She looked around as though deciding which way to dart off, and Storme's heart leapt into his throat. *No, darling, don't run.* He held his gun steady. He didn't want to kill a U.S. Marshal, but he would without a moment's hesitation if she did take off and the man tried to stop her. She stayed put, and Storme released the breath he had been holding, but there was no ease to his concern for her.

The marshal motioned with his gun. "Toss that Colt over here, Babcock. Now!"

Clyde kept his hands above his head. "You're making a mistake, marshal. My name's not Babcock. And we didn't rob any bank. We're bounty hunters. We've been tracking this lady's trail."

Storme's blood boiled at the lie. He could see annoyance furrowing Anna's brow when she looked over at Clyde, saw her mouth open as though to offer a protest, but she didn't get the chance.

" 'Fraid you're gonna have to sell that lie somewhere else." Marshal Bray said, shaking his head. "The Mexican officials were real descriptive about the five men they've been combing the border for—especially you, 'scar-face.' And the bank clerk in El Paso got a good gander at Rafael here." He nodded toward the wide-eyed Mexican he held by the throat. "I also had a real interesting conversation with the local sheriff, and a man named Ben Warwick, last night."

Storme arched one eyebrow, feeling certain Ben had learned that Clyde was still alive, and glad he hadn't told Winston anything about Hoehne Pass. He knew his brother would be chomping at the bit to find Storme and relay the information. Storme was also certain that Sheriff Hadley's wire to El Paso had brought Marshal Bray here. He hoped the lawman hadn't said anything about Anna's poster to the sheriff and Ben, and wished like hell that the marshal hadn't recognized her. It was an added complication Storme wasn't quite sure how he was going to handle.

"I know all about the rustling trouble you've been causing, and that Dewey Cartwright and Miguel Ramos turned up dead not too long ago." A wry smile curved Marshal Bray's mouth.

"You boys are gonna wish you had, too . . . cuz when we get done with you in Texas, you're going down south again, so they can throw your sorry escaped asses back in prison. Now, this is the last time I'm gonna tell you." Impatience thickened the marshal's deep tone. "Throw that weapon over here!"

Clyde barely turned his head, just enough for Storme to catch a partial glimpse of the side of his face as he cut a quick glance at Chavez. Storme tensed, tightening his hand around his six-shooter, not trusting the private in the least, and wishing that Anna was standing farther than just an arm's length away from the man.

Clyde slowly reached one hand down and gripped the wooden handle in the two-finger method of surrender. He eased the weapon from his holster.

And all hell broke loose.

Chavez issued a harsh growl and lunged forward, diving for his tossed gun. Marshal Bray fired, hitting the Mexican in the neck and stopping him cold. In that same split instant, Clyde jumped sideways, grabbing Anna's arm with one hand as he jerked his gun up into the other, and shot the marshal's pistol from his grip. Storme fired at Clyde in the same second that the private moved, and his missed aim slammed into the bound Mexican's chest instead, the impact causing the marshal to stagger back a couple of steps.

Anna stood between Storme's aim and Clyde, frantically trying to kick and twist her way free of the private's hold, and preventing Storme from risking another shot at the man. The marshal dropped his dead shield, and bolted to the side where his gun had gone flying. Clyde fired twice more and hit the lawman in the right hip and shoulder, sending him sprawling backward to the ground.

Storme held his aim steady, waiting, hoping Anna could break free long enough for him to get a clear shot at the private.

But her struggles were no match for Clyde's strength as he dragged her with him, weaving his way around the two dead Mexicans and stopping near the lawman's feet.

A crimson pattern slowly stained Marshal Bray's white shirt. The lawman looked toward his gun, still lying several feet from his outstretched hand, then back at the six-shooter Clyde aimed at his head.

"Sorry, marshal," Clyde grated. "I'm not spending another minute in that Mexican hellhole."

Anxiety tightened Storme's gut into a hard knot. *Move, Anna!*

She took a short step away from Clyde, giving Storme the opening he needed. He eased back on the trigger, then his heart stopped. He jerked the gun up, barely stopping himself from firing as Anna suddenly threw herself against the private's side, knocking him off balance and sending his fired shot at the marshal sailing harmlessly into the shadows instead.

"You bitch," Clyde snarled, quickly gaining his footing. Storme jumped to his feet, anger fueling his adrenaline when Clyde removed his hand from Anna's arm and wrapped his fingers around her neck, bringing her face up close to his. "I warned you when you tried to escape last night not to give me any more trouble, or I wouldn't wait for that Injun to watch what I'm gonna do to you. I don't make idle threats, pretty lady." He shoved her backward.

Storme winced at the sound of Anna's frightened scream as she hit the ground. "Babcock!" he roared, drawing the man's attention, firelight revealing the surprise in the private's widened eyes.

Clyde swung his gun up and around.

Storme fired without hesitation, and watched his bullet drill a hole through the private's forehead. The man's body jerked upward slightly; the gun slipped from his fingers. "Annaaaa!" Storme was over the scrubs and running down the short incline of the dry, sandy river bed before Clyde's body fully hit the ground.

"Storme!"

His heart pounded painfully hard at the frantic need in her voice, at the sight of her struggling to sit up. He crashed his way through the knee-high water, then up the bank, quickening his pace as he raced toward her. His hat flew off when he dropped to his knees and slid the last few inches to her side. "Anna," he whispered hoarsely. The tears slipping from her eyes tore at his soul. He wrapped his arms around her, crushing her against his chest, then he pulled back, gently gripping her shoulders, moving his hands up to cup her face. "I've been so worried about you. Are you all right, little dove?"

"Yes." A sigh of relief broke through her trembling lips. "Especially now that you're here." She raked her gaze over his handsome face, relishing the sight of him, the euphoric comfort of his presence. "He told me he left my necklace for you." Anna smiled. "I knew you'd find me, Storme."

Trust shimmered in her green gaze. He should have taken better care of her, should never have let her out of his sight and allowed Clyde the chance to take her. Storme yanked his knife out and quickly cut the ropes from her wrists, then replaced it back in the sheath attached to his gunbelt. He rubbed his thumbs against her cheeks, brushing away the drops that moistened her smooth skin.

"Hold me, Storme." She slipped her arms around his waist.

He pulled her up to her knees, closing his eyes as he drew her into his embrace. "I'm so sorry I put you in this danger," he whispered against her hair.

"It's not your fault."

Storme kissed the side of her brow, ran his hands through her hair, along her back, pulled her closer, wanting to chase away the tremors that shook her body. Through slitted eyes, he glanced over at Clyde's inert form lying face down in the grass. *Every bit of this is my fault.* He shouldn't have walked away. He should have waited, and made sure that private was dead all those years ago.

"You didn't know Clyde was on the train. You didn't even know he was alive. He told me that you thought he died in Shadow Canyon."

Every muscle in Storme's body tensed. He recalled not telling Anna what he had done to the private . . . because he hadn't wanted her to think he truly was a savage. It would kill him faster than a bullet to the heart if that had happened. He drew back slightly, keeping his arms around her as he stared down at her. "What else did Clyde tell you?"

Anna touched one hand to his face, lightly stroking the faint coating of stubble that roughened his bronze skin, hating the apprehension that darkened his brown eyes. "Everything," she whispered, shivers racing through her at the memory of Clyde's ranting hatred and accusations, and his plans to kill Storme. She didn't doubt the things Clyde had said about what happened in Shadow Canyon, and she didn't judge Storme for wanting that private dead. During the long hours of captivity, she had found out just what a hate-filled man Clyde really was, and not once had her faith in Storme's honor wavered. "And not a single thing made me change the way I feel about you."

Her words sent Storme's heart soaring. He sighed, and smiled. "I am *real* glad to hear that, darling." He leaned down intending to kiss her, needing to touch her warmth, to feel the life-pulsing promise of her well-being, to taste her loving sweetness, but a movement caught the corner of his eye and made him pause. He glanced past her shoulder, and met the marshal's watchful blue stare.

The lawman inched his way a little closer to the dropped gun. Storme tightened his hold around Anna, feeling her tremors, seeing the reminder of her trouble flash across her eyes as she followed his gaze. "I'm not going to let anything happen to you,'' he assured, brushing the back of one hand against her cheek.

She nodded, her heart pounding as she clung to him, needing his comfort, his strength. She didn't doubt the promise in his words, his tone. She trusted Storme, knew he wouldn't let anything happen to her, but she couldn't help wondering how he planned to make good on his word.

Storme stood, and helped her up. He took hold of her hand and crossed the short distance to the marshal's side. Intense pain mingled with uncertainty in the marshal's pinched expression as he glanced between them. Storme placed his arm around Anna's waist in a protective, possessive hold.

Marshal Bray's Adam's apple rippled along his throat as he swallowed. "I'm a . . . dead man . . . aren't I?"

Storme stared at the blood that soaked the marshal's shoulder. The wound was high, just barely more than a deep graze, and not life-threatening. He shifted his gaze lower to where the man gripped his right hip with his left hand, unable to say the same about the steady flow that seeped between his fingers and spread over the grass in an ever-widening pool. But he knew Marshal Bray wasn't talking about his wounds killing him. Storme's stomach contracted into a tight fist. He wasn't going to kill the man. If he had to, though, he would leave the marshal here, and not send help back until *after* Anna was safely headed out of the territory—which Storme knew could well be too late for the man. "Depends on how smart you are, marshal."

"Storme, those wounds look bad. We need to help him." Anna bit her bottom lip.

Storme tightened his hold on her waist, preventing her from moving closer to the man's side.

"Smart enough," the marshall said, "to know I owe her . . . for saving my life."

Good. "Let's talk about how you can repay this debt then."

The marshal pulled his pale eyebrows together. "I'm willing . . . to look the other way . . . and forget I saw her here."

Storme shook his head. "Not good enough, marshal. She's not a murderer. That's why she didn't just stand by and let Clyde shoot you. Even now, she's wanting to help you." He lowered his tone to a deep, determined level. "But make no mistake, *I* will walk away from helping you, and take her with me."

From the corner of his gaze, Storme saw Anna's eyes round in shock, and gently squeezed her waist in reassurance. He knew what a kind heart she had, admired her brave spirit, and knew she wouldn't feel right about leaving the marshal, even to save herself. Storme wasn't as inclined, though. He loved her too much to take any risks with her life, her future. But he hoped they wouldn't have to walk away.

The marshal hesitated, glancing between them, then his chest flattened as his breath rushed out on a heavy sigh. "What do you want?"

Storme's body vibrated with confidence at the marshal's acquiescence. U. S. Marshals were appointed by the President and not bound by jurisdictions. This lawman had the power to make things right for Anna. "I want you to listen to Anna's side of what happened in Missouri, and why she's wanted for murder. Then I want you to give her what she deserves." He paused, glancing over at Anna, hiding nothing of his deep love for her. "Her freedom back." He pinned a hard stare on the marshal. "You promise to get that murder charge dropped, I'll make sure you live."

The marshal nodded. "You have my word on it, Mr—"

"Storme Warwick."

Marshal Bray's brow furrowed in narrow lines. "Ben's . . . brother?"

Storme nodded, lowering his hand from Anna's waist. "That's right." He pulled the knife from his sheath, rounded to the man's wounded side and squatted. "And your word had better be good, marshal."

"It is," the man assured, shifting his stare to include Anna as she knelt beside Storme.

"I appreciate your help, marshal." Anna smiled, and turned to Storme, placing her hand on his shoulder. She swallowed back the rush of overwhelming affection that clogged her throat. "Thank you," she whispered, wanting to say more, wishing they were alone so she could tell him how much she adored him, how much his kindness and caring meant to her . . . how much she wanted to be with him, always.

"Anytime, darling." The love shining in her eyes melted Storme's heart and tugged at his longing to find a way to keep her in his life. But he had Ben's request to think about, and the ranch . . . and Anna's dream of singing. He couldn't change who he was, either, or promise that someone else wouldn't hurt her trying to take revenge against him. But he sure didn't want to stand at the train station and watch her ride out of his life again . . . this time for good. He looked down at the marshal's wound, and started to cut away a section of the bloodied shirt near his hip.

"Where is Ben?" the marshal asked. "We heard gunfire on our way to your ranch. He was supposed to go get you and meet up with me."

Storme arched his brow, imagining the protestations he would suffer hearing from Ben about not needing his big brother's protection . . . and the hefty bonus he owed Winston for keeping Ben at the ranch. He lifted one corner of his mouth in a small smile. "Haven't seen him. I guess he must've got tied up with something else."

Anna noticed how quiet the house was now after the whirlwind of activity that had ensued when she and Storme arrived at the ranch early this morning, bearing the wounded marshal on a travois. Storme had kept her close to his side as he ordered several wranglers to carry the marshal inside and settle him in his father's old room, then he explained to Ben and the other men what had happened with the rustlers. Ben had displayed a great deal of annoyed anger that he hadn't been there at the camp to help. Winston sported a black eye that Anna still wasn't sure how the foreman had gotten. Cale had ridden to town to fetch Doc Garrick and the sheriff, and the explanations of the long night had been repeated when the two men showed up at the ranch mid-morning. Nothing was said about Anna's troubles, though, or the bargain with the marshal. Storme had made the lawman promise their agreement would stay just between them. Later Storme had ridden back out to the campsite with the sheriff, Ben, and Winston to take care of the dead rustlers. Storme had insisted that Anna stay behind to rest, and she hadn't argued, grateful for the bath Maria had drawn for her, and the blue cotton skirt and white peasant blouse the housekeeper had lent her, since Anna's valise had disappeared somewhere beside the railroad tracks when Clyde forced her off the train. She had soaked away the memories of the horrible night, thankful that Clyde had been so bent on his revenge against Storme that he hadn't done more than bruise her some and batter her with words of what he intended, and hadn't let his cohorts touch her. She had filled her mind with pleasant thoughts, all centering around Storme. Her dreams as she had napped were sweet images of his bravery, his stalwart determination to find her and save her from the deadly destruction the rustlers had planned, and the love she had seen burning in his eyes when he had come running to her side, the peace and comfort of being held in his strong embrace.

She had seen him when he returned from the camp early this afternoon, but only for a brief moment before he had headed back out to ride to town and send a wire for the marshal that would start the proceedings to seek Anna's freedom. Maria had awakened her just a short while ago—before the housekeeper had left to tend to Garcia, still bedridden with his broken leg—and let her know that Storme had returned.

Anna had missed him a great deal, even though it had only been a few hours. She had been giving a great deal of thought to her future now, and to the depth of her love for Storme. She was anxious to see him, talk to him, tell him what was in her heart.

Anna stepped outside onto the front porch, taking a deep breath as the distant mountains filled her sight, their majestic, ragged peaks towering up to the heavens. So beautiful. So peaceful. *The mountains are nature's greatest gift, my little Annika.* Anna smiled, hoping her mama was looking down right now, seeing this same view.

Dark pink and purple streaks coated the edges of the early twilight sky. The sounds of the birds' gentle chirping and the faint lowing of cattle drifting up from the south pastures filled the still air that hovered over the valley. A warm contentment— a sweet sense of peace and freedom that she had never thought to feel again—settled in Anna's soul. Joy sang through her veins. No more running, hiding. No more worries. No more lies. Freedom. She could go or stay, the choice was hers now . . . and she so badly wanted to stay.

But what if Storme didn't want her to stay? What if he didn't love her the way she believed he did? What if the marshal couldn't clear her of the murder charge?

After they had tended to the marshal's wounds as best they could, Storme had rounded up the horses and made the travois, while Anna had told Marshal Bray every detail of what happened in Missouri. The marshal said it would take some time to get her cleared, and that she might have to travel with him to Marshal Headquarters in Fort Smith before they would grant his request to pardon her. What if something went wrong?

Anna bit her bottom lip. No, it would be fine. The marshal assured her it was all just a matter of paperwork. He believed her story of self-defense, as well as being extremely grateful to her for saving his life. Besides, Storme had promised he would go with her, would stay by her side every second. He was such a kind man, so protective, so giving. Storme cared about her deeply, she knew he did . . . and oh, how she loved him.

She glanced down the hill, searching for Storme among the wranglers who stood outside the barn unsaddling their horses. She spotted him, off alone talking with his brother near one of the corrals across the way. He stood with his back to her, one boot propped on the bottom fence rail, elbows braced on the top, his hair hanging loose beneath his hat and brushing across his broad shoulders.

Her heart pounded faster. Now that she didn't have the noose of her crime choking her, she didn't feel forced to hold back her feelings for him. She wanted Storme to know how much she loved him, needed him, wanted him in her life. She knew Storme was thinking about staying at the ranch. He had told her on the way back this morning that Ben was giving thought to becoming a lawyer. Anna would love nothing more than to see Storme stay here where he belonged. She knew how much this ranch meant to him, how much he had missed his home ever since he took up bounty hunting. She also knew that he would be concerned about the townsfolk. But Storme had made a lot of friends since he came home. Mrs. Harrington, and the girls. The Sandersons, the councilmen, and a good number of other folks who were grateful to him for helping to stop Dodding's dam. The Garden Society ladies would always be snooty toward him, though. Anna chuckled slightly. But who really cared what those guinea hens thought? They didn't know Storme. Not like she did.

He pushed away from the fence and turned. Anna swallowed back a rush of emotion as she watched him embrace his brother in a brief hug, then the two men parted and headed toward the barn. Storme spoke to a couple of the cow hands, then glanced up toward the house, and Anna smiled when he saw her and waved. She waved back, her pulse racing as Storme briefly turned to say something to the men, then sauntered away and started up the hill.

Storme thought his heart was going to pound right through his chest at the sight of her. He quickened his pace along the grassy yard. He was anxious to hold her, talk to her. He had made a lot of decisions today, decisions that would make him the happiest man alive if Anna agreed with them. Ben had agreed, reluctantly at first, but his brother understood how much Storme loved Anna, wanted to be with her, and that he didn't want to ask her to give up her dream of singing. Storme didn't want his brother to forget about becoming a lawyer, either, and had encouraged Ben to pursue that career. He had promised that he would spend as much time at the ranch as he could, depending on Anna's travels, and handle as many of the affairs as possible. He had also suggested that they let Winston take charge when neither of them could be here to oversee things. Ben had agreed that the foreman could be trusted, and was certainly capable of handling the men and the ranch, then decided that Storme was right, it was time for him to make a change in his life, too.

Storme took the porch steps two at a time, and tossed his hat onto the chair. The sparkle in Anna's eyes, the smile that widened her full lips sent pleasure coursing through his veins. He was so thankful that she was all right. So glad that she was here, safe. He had thought of little else all day but how much he needed her. "Did you rest well, little dove?"

"Yes, but I'm glad you're back. I've been wanting to talk to you."

Storme brushed his hand against her smooth cheek. "What's on your mind, darling?"

"You."

She stepped closer, and pressed her palms against his chest, her warmth seeping through his shirt, tingling his flesh. Her throat rippled as she swallowed, drawing Storme to want to lean down and press his lips along the same path. Then she slowly moved her hands up to his shoulders, igniting a fiery trail with her touch. "I have waited all day to tell you something." He felt one soft finger lightly tracing the beaded leather around his neck. She gazed up at him; a soft sigh whispered through her parted lips. "I love you. I don't want to be without you."

Storme's pulse raced with heated excitement. Oh how he liked the way she wasn't afraid to speak her mind.

"Well, it just so happens that I've been waiting all day to tell you the same thing." He circled his arms around her waist, pulling her close. "I love you, my little dove. I have loved you from the moment I met you. And I want you in my life, always." He pressed his lips to hers, his heart soaring at her eager response, his soul singing at the sweetness of her touch.

He pulled back, and placed his forehead gently against hers. "Anna, I can't promise you that trouble won't follow me because of who I am, but I give you my word that I will do everything in my power to protect you. I love you so much. And I want you to have your dreams. I want you to sing. We'll go wherever you want to go. All that matters to me is that you're happy."

Tears slipped from her eyes. Storme frowned, and straightened. "Anna, what's wrong?"

She smiled. "You make me so happy, Storme. I don't want to be anywhere but right by your side. I don't need guarantees. I know you'll always protect me." She placed her warm palms against his cheeks, her eyes gleaming bright, her pretty face glowing with radiant happiness. "And I don't want to sing. It was a dream I had as a child. It was the only salvation I had when I thought that I would always be hiding from the law. I enjoyed singing at Elise's wedding. I enjoyed performing in the extravaganza. And I wouldn't mind doing something like that every now and then, maybe even giving lessons again. But you're my dream, now, Storme, and this is your home. This is where you belong . . . and with you is where I want to be."

A warm glow spread through Storme's soul.

"You know, darling, we can travel to all those places you wanted to see."

She arched her brow. "Really?"

Storme nodded. "Anywhere you want to go." He leaned down brushing his lips lightly against hers. "And whenever you're ready, we can always come back home."

Put a Little Romance in Your Life With
Constance O'Day-Flannery

__Bewitched 0-8217-6126-9	$5.99US/$7.50CAN
__The Gift 0-8217-5916-7	$5.99US/$7.50CAN
__Once in a Lifetime 0-8217-5918-3	$5.99US/$7.50CAN
__Second Chances 0-8217-5917-5	$5.99US/$7.50CAN
—This Time Forever 0-8217-5964-7	$5.99US/$7.50CAN
__Time-Kept Promises 0-8217-5963-9	$5.99US/$7.50CAN
__Time-Kissed Destiny 0-8217-5962-0	$5.99US/$7.50CAN
__Timeless Passion 0-8217-5959-0	$5.99US/$7.50CAN

Celebrate Romance With Two of Today's Hottest Authors

Meagan McKinney

__In the Dark	$6.99US/$8.99CAN	0-8217-6341-5
__The Fortune Hunter	$6.50US/$8.00CAN	0-8217-6037-8
__Gentle from the Night	$5.99US/$7.50CAN	0-8217-5803-9
__A Man to Slay Dragons	$5.99US/$6.99CAN	0-8217-5345-2
__My Wicked Enchantress	$5.99US/$7.50CAN	0-8217-5661-3
__No Choice But Surrender	$5.99US/$7.50CAN	0-8217-5859-4

Meryl Sawyer

__Thunder Island	$6.99US/$8.99CAN	0-8217-6378-4
__Half Moon Bay	$6.50US/$8.00CAN	0-8217-6144-7
__The Hideaway	$5.99US/$7.50CAN	0-8217-5780-6
__Tempting Fate	$6.50US/$8.00CAN	0-8217-5858-6
__Unforgettable	$6.50US/$8.00CAN	0-8217-5564-1

Call toll free **1-888-345-BOOK** to order by phone, use this coupon to order by mail, or order online at **www.kensingtonbooks.com**.

Name _____

Address _____

City _____ State _____ Zip _____

Please send me the books I have checked above.

I am enclosing	$_____
Plus postage and handling*	$_____
Sales tax (in New York and Tennessee only)	$_____
Total amount enclosed	$_____

*Add $2.50 for the first book and $.50 for each additional book.

Send check or money order (no cash or CODs) to:

Kensington Publishing Corp., Dept. C.O., 850 Third Avenue, New York, NY 10022

Prices and numbers subject to change without notice.

All orders subject to availability.

Visit our website at **www.kensingtonbooks.com**.